CENTURION

CENTURION

SIMON SCARROW

headline

First published in 2007
by HEADLINE PUBLISHING GROUP

4

Cataloguing in Publication Data is available from the British Library

Hardback 978 0 7553 2776 8
Trade paperback 978 0 7553 3410 0

Typeset in Bembo by Avon DataSet Ltd,
Bidford-on-Avon, Warwickshire

Printed and bound in UK by
CPI Mackays, Chatham ME5 8TD

Headline's policy is to use papers that are natural, renewable and recyclable
products and made from wood grown in sustainable forests. The logging and
manufacturing processes are expected to conform to the environmental
regulations of the country of origin.

HEADLINE PUBLISHING GROUP
An Hachette Livre UK Company
338 Euston Road
London NW1 3BH

www.headline.co.uk

This book is dedicated to all my former students, whom I felt privileged to teach. And thanks for all that you taught me in return!

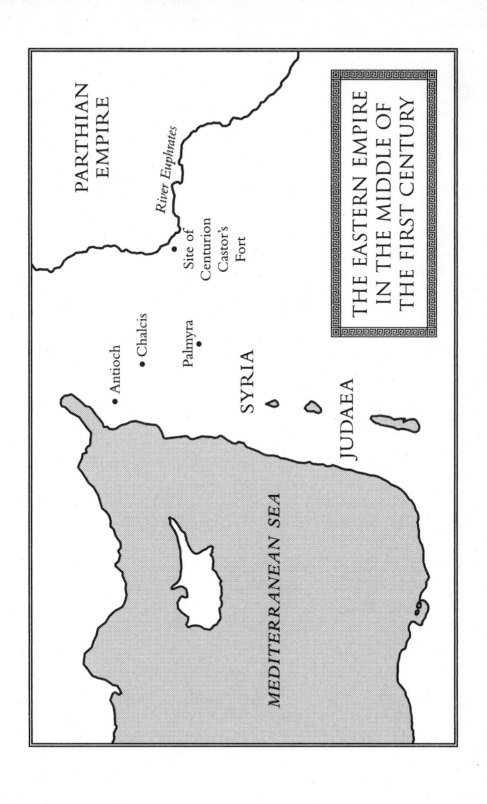

PARTHIAN EMPIRE

River Euphrates

Site of Centurion Castor's Fort

Antioch

• Chalcis

Palmyra

SYRIA

JUDAEA

MEDITERRANEAN SEA

THE EASTERN EMPIRE
IN THE MIDDLE OF
THE FIRST CENTURY

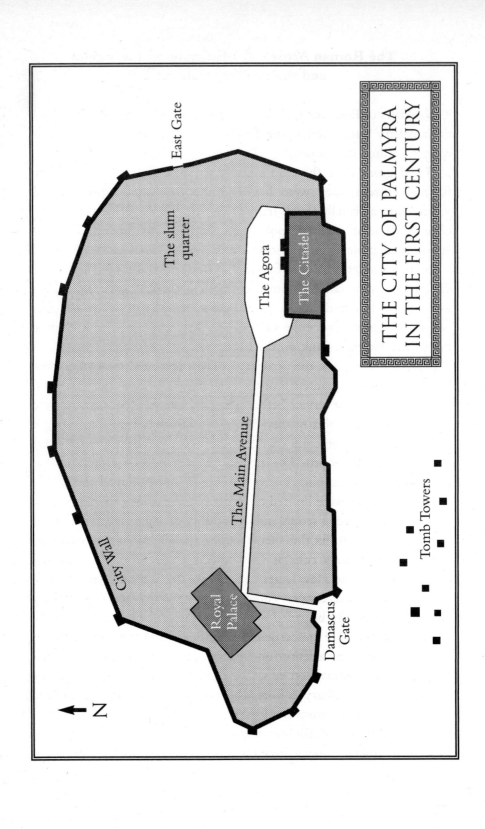

THE CITY OF PALMYRA
IN THE FIRST CENTURY

East Gate

The slum
quarter

The Agora

The Citadel

The Main Avenue

City Wall

Royal
Palace

Damascus
Gate

Tomb Towers

N

The Roman Army – A brief note on the legions and the auxiliary cohorts

The soldiers of Emperor Claudius served in two bodies, the legions and the auxiliary units, such as the Tenth Legion and the Second Illyrian cohort featured in this novel.

The legions were the elite units of the Roman army. Manned by Roman citizens, they were heavily armed and well equipped and subjected to a brutally tough training regime. Besides being the cutting edge of Roman military policy, the legions also undertook great engineering projects such as road and bridge building. Each legion had a nominal strength of some five and a half thousand men. These were divided into nine cohorts composed of six centuries containing eighty men (not a hundred, as one might assume) and one more, the first cohort, which was twice the size of the others and tasked with holding the vulnerable right flank on the battle line.

Unlike the legions, the auxiliary cohorts recruited their men from the provinces and granted Roman citizenship on those who survived over twenty years of service before being discharged. The Romans were not able to field good quality cavalry or missile troops, but being a practical race they subcontracted many of these specialisms to the non-citizen auxiliary cohorts. The auxiliaries were equally professional in their approach to training, but were more lightly equipped and lightly paid. Their duties were limited to garrison and policing roles in peacetime and they acted as scouts and light troops on campaign, where their primary role was to fix the enemy in place while the legions closed in for the kill. Auxiliary cohorts were usually made up of six centuries, although there were a few larger cohorts, like the Second Illyrian, which also had an added cavalry component. On active service auxiliary cohorts were usually brigaded with the legions.

As far as ranks are concerned, the legionary and auxiliary centuries were commanded by a centurion with an optio as second-in-command. Cohorts were commanded by senior centurions in the legions, and by a prefect in an auxiliary cohort who was usually a very experienced centurion promoted from the legions. Legions were commanded by a legate with a staff of tribunes, young aristocratic officers undergoing their first military experience. When an army was gathered the commander was usually an individual of proven military competence chosen by the Emperor. This man often held other posts, such as a regional governorship as was the case with Cassius Longinus who appears in this book.

CHAPTER ONE

As dusk settled over the camp the cohort's commander peered down the cliff towards the river. A faint mist covered the Euphrates and spilled over the banks on either side, rising even above the trees that grew along the river, so that it seemed like the smooth belly of a snake, gently undulating across the landscape. The thought made the hairs rise on the back of Centurion Castor's neck. He pulled his cloak tightly about his chest, narrowed his eyes and stared towards the land spreading away on the far side of the Euphrates: Parthian territory.

It was over a hundred years since the might of Rome had first come into contact with the Parthians and, ever since, both empires had been playing a deadly game for control of Palmyra, the lands to the east of the Roman province of Syria. Now that Rome was negotiating a closer treaty with Palmyra her influence had spread to the banks of the Euphrates, right on the frontier with her old foe. There was no longer any buffer state between Rome and Parthia and few men had any doubt that the simmering hostility would flare up into a new conflict before long. The legions back in Syria had already been preparing for a campaign when the centurion and his men had marched out of the gates of Damascus.

The thought made Centurion Castor bitterly resent, once again, the orders he had received from Rome to lead a cohort of auxiliaries across the desert, far beyond even Palmyra, to establish a fort here on the cliffs above the Euphrates. Palmyra was eight days' march away to the west and the nearest Roman soldiers were based at Emesa, six days beyond Palmyra. Castor had never felt so isolated in his life. He, and his four hundred men, were at the very end of the Empire, posted on this cliff to watch for any sign of an attack by Parthia across the Euphrates.

After an exhausting march across the barren, rocky desert they had set up camp near the cliff and begun work on the fort they would garrison until some official back in Rome eventually decided to relieve them. During the march the cohort had baked under the sun during the day, and huddled in their cloaks each night as the temperature had dropped like a stone. Water had been strictly rationed, and when they had finally reached the great river that cut across the desert and watered the fertile crescent that lined the banks his men had rushed down into the shallows to slake their thirst, deliriously scooping water to their cracked lips, before their officers could restrain them.

Having served for three years in the Tenth Legion's garrison at Cyrrhus, with its fine well-watered gardens and all the pleasures of the flesh that a man could want, Castor regarded his temporary posting with growing dread. The cohort faced the prospect of spending months, perhaps years, in this far-flung corner of the world. If boredom didn't kill them first, then the Parthians surely would. That was why the centurion had driven his men to work on the fort as soon as they found a spot on this cliff that afforded fine views over the ford below, and the rolling plains of Parthia beyond. Castor knew that word of the Roman presence would reach the ears of the Parthian king within days and it was vital that the cohort threw up strong defences before the Parthians decided to take any action against them. For several days the auxiliaries had toiled to level the ground and prepare foundations for the walls and towers of the new fort. Then the masons had hurriedly dressed the slabs of rock that had been hauled by wagon from the surrounding outcrops on to the site. The retaining walls were already at waist height and the gap between them filled with rubble and spoil, and as he glanced over the site in the dying light Centurion Castor nodded with satisfaction. In five more days, the defences would have risen high enough for him to move the camp inside the walls of the new fort. Then they could afford to feel more secure from the Parthians. Until then the men would labour every hour that daylight allowed.

The sun had set a while ago and only a faint band of russet light still gleamed along the horizon. Castor turned to his second-in-command, Centurion Septimus. 'Time to finish for the day.'

Septimus nodded, drew a lungful of air and cupped a hand to his mouth as he bellowed the order across the construction site.

'Cohort! Down tools, and return to camp!'

Across the site Castor could see the dim shapes of men wearily stacking their picks, shovels and wicker baskets before taking up their shields and spears and shuffling into the lines forming outside the gap where the main gate would be. As the last of them moved into position the wind began to rise, out of the desert, and squinting towards the west Castor saw a dense mass rolling steadily towards them.

'Dust storm coming this way,' he grumbled to Septimus. 'Better get down to the camp before it hits.'

The other man nodded. Septimus had served on the eastern frontier for most of his career and well knew how quickly men could lose their sense of direction once they were engulfed in the choking, abrasive sand whipped up by the winds that swept these lands.

'Those lucky bastards down in the camp are well out of it.'

Castor smiled briefly. A half-century had been left to guard the camp while their comrades toiled away up on the cliff. He could imagine them already retreating into the shelter of the sentry turrets, out of biting wind and sand. 'Well then, let's get the men moving.'

He gave the order to advance and the men trudged forward, down the winding track that led to the camp, just over a mile from the site of the fort. The wind picked up as the gloom thickened over the landscape and the soldiers' capes fluttered and whipped about them as they descended the rock-strewn route from the cliff.

'Shan't be sorry to leave this place, sir,' Septimus growled. 'Any idea how long before we're replaced? There's a warm billet waiting for me and the lads at Emesa.'

Castor shook his head. 'No idea. I'm as keen to get out of here as you are. All depends on the situation in Palmyra, and what our Parthian friends decide to do about it.'

'Fucking Parthians,' Septimus spat. 'Bastards are always stirring it up. It was them that was behind that business down in Judaea last year, wasn't it?'

Castor nodded as he recalled the uprising that had flared up east of the Jordan river. The Parthians had supplied the rebels with arms and a small force of horse-archers. It was only thanks to the gallant efforts of the garrison at Fort Bushir that the rebels and their Parthian allies had been prevented from inciting the whole of Judaea to rise up against Rome. Now, the Parthians had turned their attention to the oasis city of Palmyra – a vital link in the trade routes to the east and a buffer between the Roman Empire and Parthia. Palmyra enjoyed considerable independence and was more of a protectorate than a subject state. But the king of Palmyra was growing old and the rival members of his household were jockeying for position to become his successor. One of the most powerful of the Palmyran princes had made little secret of his desire to throw in his lot with Parthia, if he became the new ruler.

Castor cleared his throat. 'It's down to the governor of Syria to convince the Parthians to keep their hands off Palmyra.'

Centurion Septimus cocked an eyebrow. 'Cassius Longinus? Think he's up to it?'

Castor was silent for a moment as he considered his reply. 'Longinus can handle it. He's no imperial lackey; he's earned his promotions. If he can't win the diplomatic battle then I'm sure he'll take them apart in a fight. If it comes to that.'

'Wish I shared your confidence, sir.' Septimus shook his head. 'From what I heard, Longinus took to his heels pretty quickly last time he was in trouble.'

'Who told you that?' Castor snapped.

'I got it from some officer in the garrison at Bushir, sir. Seems that Longinus was at the fort when the rebels turned up. The governor was in his saddle and out of there quicker than a Subura whore goes through your purse.'

Castor shrugged. 'I'm sure he had his reasons.'

'I'm sure he did.'

Castor turned to his subordinate with a frown. 'Look, we've no business debating the governor's finer points. Especially not in earshot of the men. So keep it to yourself, understand?'

Centurion Septimus pursed his lips for a moment and then nodded. 'As you wish, sir.'

The column continued down the slope, and as the wind strengthened the first swirl of dust swept across the track. Within moments all sign of the surrounding landscape had vanished and Castor slowed his pace to make certain that he was still leading his men along the track to the camp. They edged forward, shoulders hunched as they did their best to shelter behind their shields from the blasts of sand. At length the track levelled out as they reached the foot of the slope. Even though the fort was only a short distance ahead, the sand and gathering darkness hid it from view.

'Not far now,' Castor muttered to himself.

Septimus overheard him. 'Good. First thing I do when I reach my tent is clear my throat with a drop of wine.'

'Good idea. Mind if I join you?'

Septimus gritted his teeth at the unexpected request, and moodily resigned himself to sharing the last flask of the wine he had brought across the desert from Palmyra. He cleared his throat and nodded. 'It'd be a pleasure, sir.'

Castor laughed and slapped him on the shoulder. 'Good man! When we get back to Palmyra, the first drink's on me.'

'Yes, sir. Thank—' Septimus suddenly drew up sharply and strained his eyes along the track ahead of them. Then he thrust up his hand to signal the column to halt.

'What's the matter?' Castor said quietly as he stood close to the side of his subordinate. 'What is it?'

Septimus nodded towards the fort. 'I saw something, just ahead of us. A horseman.'

Both officers stared into the swirling sand before them, straining their ears and eyes, but there was no sign of anyone, mounted or on foot. Just the smudges of stunted shrubs that grew either side of the track. Castor swallowed, and forced his tensed muscles to relax.

'What exactly did you see?'

Septimus glanced at him with an angry expression, sensing his superior's doubt. 'As I said, a horseman. About fifty paces ahead. The sand cleared for a moment and I saw him, just for an instant.'

Castor nodded. 'Sure it wasn't just a trick of the light? Could easily have been one of those bushes moving.'

'I'm telling you, sir. It was a horse. Plain as anything. I swear it by all the gods. Up there ahead of us.'

Castor was about to reply when both men heard a faint metallic ringing above the moan of the wind. The sound was unmistakable to any soldier: the clash of sword against sword. An instant later there was a muffled shout, and then nothing apart from the wind. Castor felt his blood chill in his veins as he turned to Septimus and spoke quietly.

'Pass the word to the other officers. Have the men formed up in close order across the track. Do it quietly.'

'Yes, sir.' Centurion Septimus saluted and dropped back to pass the word down the line. While the men fanned out on either side of the track Castor took a few strides closer to the camp. A freak shift in the wind gave him a faint glimpse of the gatehouse and a body slumped against the timber frame, which was studded with several arrows. Then a veil of dust hid the camp from view again. Castor backed away towards his men. The auxiliaries stood in a line four deep across the track, shields held high and spears angled forward as they gazed anxiously towards the camp. Septimus was waiting for his commander at the head of the century on the right flank. Beside them the slope rose up into a tangle of rocks and undergrowth.

'Did you see anything, sir?'

Castor nodded and waited until he stood beside the other officer before he spoke in a low voice. 'The camp's been attacked.'

'Attacked?' Septimus raised his eyebrows. 'Who is it? The Parthians?'

'Who else?'

Septimus nodded and his hand slid down and grasped the handle of his sword. 'What are your orders, sir?'

'They're still close. In this sandstorm they could be anywhere. We have to try to get back inside the camp, clear them out and get the gate closed. That's our best chance.'

Septimus smiled grimly. 'Our only chance, you mean, sir.'

Castor did not reply, but flicked the folds of his cape back over his shoulders and drew his sword. He raised it high and glanced along the line to make sure that the other officers were following his example and passing the signal on. Castor had no idea how many enemies they faced. If they were bold enough to storm and take the camp, then they must have attacked in some strength. The mist over the river and the rising sandstorm would have covered their approach. Castor drew small comfort from the fact that the same sandstorm would now provide some cover for the rest of the cohort as they approached the fort. With luck, the auxiliaries might even surprise the enemy in turn. He slowly lowered his sword arm, the tip arcing down towards the fort. The signal was repeated down the line and on to those men to his left who were hidden in the gloom and dust.

Castor drew his sword in until the side of the blade rested against the rim of his shield and then he stepped forward. The line rippled after him as the auxiliaries trod steadily over the broken ground towards the camp. The officers kept the pace slow enough to be able to dress the line as it advanced. To the right the slope gave way to open ground as the flanking century moved away from the cliff. Castor stared ahead with narrowed eyes, looking for any sign of the enemy, or the fortifications of the camp. Then he saw it, the bulk of the main gate emerging from the sweep of dust and sand. The outline of the raised palisade on either side resolved itself into sharp detail as the auxiliaries closed on the camp. Apart from the body resting against the gate post there was no sign of anyone else, living or dead.

The sound of hooves thrummed across the ground to his right and Castor turned to look just as one of his men on the end of the line cried out and snatched at the shaft of an arrow that had pierced his chest. Dim shapes burst through the veil of the sandstorm as several Parthian horse-archers galloped up to the auxiliaries and loosed their arrows into the unprotected right sides of the Roman soldiers. Four more men were hit and tumbled to the ground while another doubled over, but tried to stay on his feet as he wrestled with an arrow that had passed through his thigh and pinned it to the other leg. The Parthians wheeled their mounts to one side and raced back out of sight, leaving the auxiliaries staring after them in surprise and terror.

Almost at once there was a cry from the left as the enemy made another attack.

'Keep moving!' Castor cried out in desperation as he heard yet more horses passing behind the cohort. 'Run, boys!'

The ordered lines of the cohort dissolved into a mass of men running towards the main gate, Castor amongst them. Then he saw the gates closing and at once scores of faces appeared above the palisade. Bows were raised and again the sound of arrows hissed through the air and more of the auxiliaries were struck down as they drew up helplessly in front of the camp. There was no let-up in the rain of arrows that clattered off shields, or pierced flesh with a wet thud. Voices were crying out on all sides and with a sick feeling in the pit of his stomach Castor realised that his men were as good as dead, unless he did something.

'On me!' Castor roared out. 'Close up on me!'

A handful of men heeded the order and raised their shields round Castor and the cohort's standard. More men joined them, roughly jostled into position by Septimus as he made for his commander. Once there were perhaps fifty men formed into a tight circle, with shields raised, Castor shouted the order to retreat along the track towards the cliff. They fell back slowly into the dusk, leaving their wounded comrades pleading desperately not to be abandoned to the Parthians. Castor steeled his heart. There was nothing he could do for the injured. The only shelter left to the survivors of the cohort was the partially built fort on the cliff. If they could reach that then there was a better chance of making a final stand. The cohort was doomed, but they would take as many of the Parthians with them as possible.

The small band of auxiliaries reached the foot of the cliff before the enemy realised their intention and came after them in earnest. Horsemen rode out of the darkness to loose their shafts and then reined in and steadily notched and aimed more arrows once they realised there was no further need for hit and run tactics. As the cohort edged up the track they presented a narrow target to the enemy, and a solid wall of shields protected the rear of the small band of survivors as they climbed back up to the construction site. The Parthians followed them, as closely as they dared, shooting arrows the moment a gap opened in the shields. As they realised the futility of trying to shoot through the shields they switched their aim to the unprotected legs of their quarry, forcing them to crouch low and slowing them down as they toiled up the track. Even so, five more men were injured before the track evened out and the small column of auxiliaries reached the perimeter of the site. Up on the cliff the wind was still keen, but they were at least free of the clouds of dust and could see clearly over the billowing sand that blotted out the surrounding landscape.

Leaving Septimus to command the rearguard, Castor led the rest in through the foundations of the main gate. The walls were too low to keep the Parthians out of the fort, and the only place the auxiliaries could make a stand was at the nearly completed watchtower in the far corner of the fort, on the very edge of the cliff.

'This way!' Castor bellowed. 'Follow me!'

They hurried across the maze of straight lines of rocks that marked the locations for the buildings and thoroughfares planned for the fort.

Up ahead the bulk of the watchtower loomed against the star-scattered night sky. As soon as they reached the timber-framed structure Castor stood by the entrance and waved his men inside. There were barely more than twenty with him and he knew that they would be lucky if they survived to see the next dawn. Ducking inside, Castor gave orders for the men to man the platform above the tower and the window slots on the floor above the entrance. He kept four soldiers with him to defend the entrance as they waited for Septimus and the rearguard to catch up with them. There was only a brief delay before several dim figures burst through the uncompleted gatehouse and raced towards the watchtower. Moments later a wave of enemy warriors appeared and chased after them with cries of triumph.

Castor cupped a hand to his mouth and shouted. 'They're right on you! Run!'

The men of the rearguard were weighed down by their armour and already exhausted from the day's labour, and they stumbled across the site. One tripped on a loose rock and tumbled to the ground with a shrill cry, but not one of his comrades even paused to look back, and moments later he was engulfed by the wave of Parthians surging towards the watchtower. They swarmed over the fallen auxiliary for a moment, hacking and slashing at him with their curved blades. His death brought his comrades just enough time to reach the watchtower and they piled inside, lowering their shields as they gasped for breath. Septimus licked his lips as he forced himself to straighten up and report, chest heaving.

'Lost two men, sir . . . One back on the track, and the other just then.'

'I saw.' Castor nodded.

'What now?'

'We hold them off for as long as we can.'

'And then?'

Castor laughed. 'Then we die. But not before we send at least forty of them ahead of us to line our path to Hades.'

Septimus forced himself to grin, for the sake of the men watching the exchange. Then he glanced over Castor's shoulders and his expression hardened. 'Here they come, sir.'

Castor turned round and raised his shield. 'We have to hold them here! Form up!'

Septimus stood at his side and the four men raised their spears ready to thrust over the heads of the two officers. Beyond the entrance the dark mass of the Parthians charged across the rubble-strewn ground and hurled themselves at the shields blocking the door. Castor braced himself an instant before the inside of his shield lurched towards him under the impact. Then he dug his iron-shod boots in and thrust back, punching his weight behind the shield boss. There was an explosive gasp as the blow struck home. Over his shoulder the sharp point and shaft of one of the auxiliaries stabbed out and there was a cry of agony from outside the watchtower. As the spear was drawn back a flicker of warm droplets spattered across Castor's eyes. He blinked them away as a sword blow hacked against the outside of his shield. Beside him, Centurion Septimus pressed his shield forward into the mass of the enemy crowding the entrance and thrust his sword at any exposed flesh he could see between the rim of his shield and the door frame.

As long as the two officers stood their ground and were supported by the men behind, ready to stab out with their spears, the enemy could not get in through the entrance. For a moment Castor felt his spirits rise as the fight began to go their way for the first time.

Too late he sensed the flicker of movement low to the ground just outside the entrance as one of the Parthians crouched low and swept his blade beneath the rim of Castor's shield. The edge of the blade cut deep into his ankle, severing leather, flesh and muscle before it fetched up against bone. The pain was instantaneous, like a red-hot bar thrust into the joint. Castor staggered backwards with an explosive cry of pain and rage.

Septimus glanced back quickly, seeing his commander slump to one side of the entrance. 'Next man! Into line!'

The nearest auxiliary, crouching low to protect his legs, pressed himself forward, alongside Septimus, as his comrades thrust their spear tips at the enemy in a flurry of attacks to drive them back from the entrance. Then all at once there was a shout of alarm from the darkness and the crash of heavy masonry outside the watchtower. As Castor leaned round the frame to look he saw a piece of dressed stone smash down on to the Parthians, crushing a man's head as it drove his body to the ground. More rocks and stones fell on the attackers, killing and maiming several before they could scramble back across the site to a safe distance.

'Bloody marvellous,' Septimus growled with pleasure at the sight. 'See how they like being hit without a chance to fight back. Bastards.'

As the enemy moved out of range the barrage of stones tailed off and the sounds of combat gave way to the jeers and whistles of the auxiliaries in the watchtower, and the moans and cries of the injured men in front of the entrance. Septimus took a last glance outside before he motioned one of the men to take his place. Leaning his shield against the wall he knelt down to examine Castor's wound, straining his eyes to make it out by the wan glow from the starry heavens shining through the entrance. His hands gently probed the injury and felt the shards of bone amid the mangled flesh. Castor sucked in a deep breath and clenched his teeth as he fought back the impulse to cry out in agony.

Septimus glanced up at him. 'I'm sorry to say your fighting days are over.'

'Tell me something I don't know,' Castor hissed.

Septimus smiled briefly. 'I have to stop this bleeding. Give me your scarf, sir.'

Castor loosened the cloth, unwound it and passed it down. Septimus held one end behind the calf and then glanced up. 'This is going to hurt. Ready?'

'Just get on with it.'

Septimus wound the cloth round the leg, over the wound, and then bound it tightly over the ankle and tied it off. The searing pain was like nothing Castor had ever endured before and despite the cold of the night he was sweating freely by the time Septimus finished the knot and rose to his feet.

'You'll have to prop me up on the stairs when the time comes to make our last stand.'

Septimus nodded. 'I'll see to it, sir.'

The officers stared at each other for a moment as they considered the full import of their last exchange. Now that they had accepted the inevitable Castor felt that the burden of anxiety over the fate of his command had lifted. Despite the torment of his wound, there was a calm sense of resignation in his heart, and a determination to go down

11

fighting. Septimus glanced away, through the door, and saw the enemy standing in clusters about the site, out of range of the rocks and stones that the auxiliaries had thrown from the watchtower.

'Wonder what they'll do next?' he mused. 'Starve us out?'

Castor shook his head. He had served in the region long enough in the east to know the nature of Rome's old enemy. 'They'll not wait for that. There's no honour in it.'

'What then?'

Castor shrugged. 'We'll know soon enough.'

There was a moment's silence before Septimus turned away from the entrance. 'So what is this? A raid? The opening of a new campaign against Rome?'

'Does it matter?'

'I want to know the reason for my death.'

Castor pursed his lips and considered the situation. 'It could be a raid. Maybe they saw the construction of this fort as an act of provocation. But it's equally possible they want to clear a path across the Euphrates for their army to cross. It could be the first move towards taking control of Palmyra.'

Castor's thoughts were interrupted by a shout from outside.

'Romans! Hear me!' a voice called out in Greek. 'Parthia calls on you to lay down your arms and surrender!'

'Bollocks!' Septimus snorted.

The man outside in the dark did not respond to the taunt and continued in an even tone. 'My commander calls on you to surrender. If you lay down your weapons, you will be spared. He gives his word.'

'Spared?' Castor repeated softly before he shouted out his reply. 'You will spare us and permit us to return to Palmyra?'

There was a short pause before the voice continued. 'Your lives will be spared, but you will be taken prisoner.'

'Slaves is what we'll be,' Septimus growled and spat on the floor. 'I'll not die a fucking slave.' He turned to Castor. 'Sir? What should we do?'

'Tell him to go to Hades.'

Septimus smiled thinly, his teeth luminous in the moonlight. He turned to the entrance and shouted his reply. 'If you want our weapons, come and get them!'

Castor chuckled. 'Hardly original, but a nice touch.'

The officers exchanged a grin and the other men smiled nervously, until the voice called to them one last time.

'So be it. Then this place will be your grave. Or rather . . . your pyre.'

A faint glow had appeared on the far side of the construction site and as Septimus watched a small flame flared up, silhouetting the warrior crouched over his tinder box. The flame was efficiently fed so that it quickly flared up into a small blaze as men gathered round to light torches hastily gathered from the surrounding scrub. Then they approached the watchtower and as Septimus watched the first of the fire arrows was offered to a torch until the oiled rags caught alight. At once the archer drew his bow and shot at the watchtower. The arrow blazed through the darkness and thudded into the scaffolding, scattering a small shower of sparks. Immediately, other arrows flamed towards the structure, embedding themselves in the wood with splintering cracks and burning as they lodged there.

'Shit!' Septimus clenched his fist round the handle of his sword. 'They mean to burn us out.'

Castor knew there was no water in the tower and he shook his head. 'There's nothing we can do about it. Call the men down from the watchtower.'

'Yes, sir.'

A short while later, as the last of the survivors crowded into the small guard room at the foot of the tower, Castor hauled himself up and leaned against the wall so that he could address them.

'It's all over for us, lads. We stay here and burn, or go out there and take some of those bastards with us. That's it. So when I give the order, you follow Centurion Septimus out of the tower. Stay close to each other and run hard at them. Understand?'

A handful of them nodded and some managed a few words of acknowledgement. Septimus cleared his throat. 'What about you, sir? You can't come with us.'

'I know. I'll stay here and deal with the standard. They can't be allowed to take that.' Castor held his hand out to the cohort's signifer. 'Here, let me have it.'

The standard-bearer hesitated a moment, and then stepped forward and handed the shaft over to his commander. 'Take care of it, sir.'

Castor nodded as he grasped the standard firmly and used it to support the weight on his injured leg. Around them the crackle and soft roar of flames filled the warm air and a lurid orange glow lit up the ground around the watchtower. Castor staggered towards the narrow wooden staircase in the corner. 'When I get to the roof, I'll give the order to charge. Make every thrust of your spears and every blow of your swords count, lads.'

'We will, sir,' Septimus replied softly.

Castor nodded and clasped the centurion's arm briefly, and then, gritting his teeth, he made for the roof, painfully working his way up the wooden stairs as the air grew heated around him and wisps of smoke curled into the orange light seeping through the windows and arrow slits. By the time he reached the roof, the side of the watchtower closest to the enemy was ablaze. Castor could see scores of Parthians waiting in the bright glare of the flames and he drew a deep breath.

'Centurion Septimus! Now! Charge!'

There was a thin chorus of war cries from the base of the tower and Castor saw the Parthians raise their bows, concentrating their aim, and then the air was filled with the flitting dark splinters of their arrows. Over the parapet he saw the small compact body of his men charging out across the site. Their shoulders were hunched down behind their shields as they ran straight at the enemy, following Septimus as he bellowed insults at the Parthians. The archers stood their ground and shot their arrows as fast as they could at the moving target. Those who still had fire arrows to hand loosed those and brilliant flaring paths cut through the air towards the auxiliaries. Several lodged in shields and burned there as their owners ran on. Then Castor saw Septimus suddenly draw up and stand still, his sword dropping from his hand as he clutched at the point of an arrow that had passed through his neck as the last of his cries still echoed over the site. Then he slumped to his knees and toppled forward on to the ground, writhing feebly as he bled to death.

The auxiliaries closed round his body and raised their shields. Castor watched them in bitter frustration. The impetus of the charge had died with Septimus and now they were picked off one by one as Parthian arrows found their way in between the shields and pierced the flesh of the men behind. Castor did not wait to see the end. Leaning heavily on the standard he crossed to the far side of the platform and looked down the cliff towards the river. Far below the mist had cleared and moonlight rippled off the swirling current as it flowed over some rocks. Castor tipped his head back and looked into the serene depths of the heavens and breathed the night air deep into his lungs.

A sudden crash of timber from the far side of the tower made him glance round and he knew that there was no time left if he was to make sure the standard did not fall into enemy hands. Through the wavering curtain of the flames and smoke he could see the shimmering ranks of the Parthians and he knew that this was only the beginning. Soon a tide of fire and destruction would spill across the desert and threaten to engulf the eastern provinces of the Roman Empire. Castor grasped the shaft of the standard firmly in both hands and limped to the very edge of the platform. He took one last deep breath and gritted his teeth and then hurled himself into the void.

CHAPTER TWO

'This is as good as life gets.' Macro smiled as he leaned back against the wall of the Bountiful Amphora, his usual drinking hole, and stretched his legs out in front of him. 'Finally, I got my posting to Syria. You know what, Cato?'

'What?' His companion stirred and blinked his eyes open.

'It's every bit as good as I hoped it would be.' Macro shut his eyes and relished the warmth of the sun on his weathered face. 'Good wines, fairly priced women who know a trick or two and fine dry weather. There's even a decent library.'

'I'd never have thought you'd take an interest in books,' said Cato. In recent months Macro had nearly sated his epicurean desires and had taken to reading. Admittedly his preference was for bawdy comedies and erotica, but, Cato reasoned, at least he was reading something and there was a chance that it might lead to more challenging material.

Macro smiled. 'This is a good enough spot for now. A warm climate and warm women. I tell you, after that campaign in Britain I never want to see another Celt as long as I live.'

'Too right,' Centurion Cato murmured with feeling as he recalled the cold, the damp and the mist-wreathed marshes through which he and Macro, and the men of the Second Legion, had fought their way across the Empire's most recent acquisition. 'Still, it wasn't so bad in the summer.'

'Summer?' Macro frowned. 'Ah, you must mean that handful of days we had between winter and autumn.'

'You wait. A few months on campaign in the desert and you'll look back on those times in Britain as if it was Elysium.'

'That may be,' Macro mused as he recalled their previous posting on the frontier of Judaea, in the middle of a wasteland. He shook off the memory. 'But for now, I have a cohort to command, a prefect's pay and the prospect of a decent rest before we have to risk life and limb for the Emperor, the Senate and People of Rome' – he intoned the official slogan wryly – 'by which I mean that sly, conniving bastard, Narcissus.'

'Narcissus . . .' Repeating the name of Emperor Claudius' private secretary, Cato sat up and turned to his friend. He lowered his voice. 'Still no reply from him. He must have read our report by now.'

'Yes.' Macro shrugged. 'So?'

'So, what do you think he will do about the governor?'

'Cassius Longinus? Oh, he'll be all right. Longinus has covered his tracks well enough. There's no firm evidence to link him to any treachery and you can be sure that he'll do his level best to be the Emperor's most loyal servant now that he knows he's being watched.'

Cato glanced round the customers sitting at the nearest table and leaned closer to Macro. 'Given that we are the men Narcissus sent to watch Longinus, I doubt that the governor would shed any tears over our deaths. We have to be careful.'

'He can hardly have us killed.' Macro sniffed. 'That would look too suspicious. Relax, Cato, we're doing just fine.' He stretched out his arms, cracked his shoulder and then tucked his hands behind his head with a contented yawn.

Cato regarded him for a moment, wishing that Macro would not dismiss the danger posed by Cassius Longinus so easily. A few months earlier the governor of Syria had requested that another three legions be transferred to his command to counter the growing threat of a revolt in Judaea. With a force that size at his back Longinus would have posed a serious threat to the Emperor. It was Cato's conviction that Longinus had been preparing to make a play for the imperial throne. Thanks to Macro and Cato the revolt had been crushed before it could spread across the province, and Longinus had been deprived of the need for his extra legions. No man as powerful as Longinus would easily forgive those who had frustrated his ambitions and Cato had been living in wary anticipation of revenge for several months. But now the governor faced a real threat from the growing menace of Parthia, with only the Third, Sixth and Tenth Legions and their attached auxiliary cohorts to confront the enemy. If war came to the eastern provinces then every available man would be needed to face the Parthians. Cato sighed. It was ironic that the threat from Parthia was welcome. That should divert the governor's mind from thoughts of revenge for a while at least. Cato drained his cup and leaned back against the wall, staring out across the city.

The sun was close to the horizon and the roof tiles and domes of Antioch were gleaming in the brilliant hue of the fading light. The centre of the city, like most of those that had fallen under Roman control, and before that to the Greek heirs of Alexander the Great's conquests, was filled with the kind of public buildings that were to be found right across the Empire. Beyond the lofty columns of the temples and porticoes, the city gave way to a jumble of fine townhouses and sprawling slums of grimy flat-roofed buildings. In those streets the air was ripe with the smells of densely packed humanity. That was where most of the off-duty soldiers spent their time. But Cato and Macro preferred the relative comfort of the Bountiful Amphora where its slightly elevated position took advantage of any breeze that wafted over the city.

They had been drinking for most of the afternoon and Cato began to doze off into the warm embrace of weary contentment. For the last month they had been relentlessly drilling their auxiliary cohort, the Second Illyrian, in the huge army camp outside the walls of Antioch. The cohort was Macro's first command as prefect and he was determined that his men would turn out smartly and march faster and fight harder than any other cohort in the army of the eastern Empire. Macro's task had been made more difficult by the fact that nearly a third of the men were raw recruits – replacements for those lost in the fight at Fort Bushir. As the army had been placed on a war footing every cohort commander had been scouring the region for men to bring their units up to full strength.

While Cato had taken charge of the cohort's training and set about ordering the necessary equipment and supplies, Macro had tramped up and down the coast from Pieria to Caesarea in search of recruits. He took ten of the toughest soldiers with him, and the cohort's standard. In each town and port Macro had set up a stall in the forum and delivered his pitch to an audience of the idle and restless men who were to be found in every town square across the Empire. In a booming parade-ground voice he promised them an enlistment bounty, decent pay, regular meals, a life of adventure and, if they should live to see it, the award of Roman citizenship when they were demobbed after the small formality of twenty-five years' service. With a bit of training they would look every bit as impressive and manly as the soldiers standing behind Macro. When he had finished a motley crowd of hopefuls would approach the stall and Macro took the healthiest specimens and turned away all those who were unfit or witless or too old. In the first few towns he was able to pick and choose, but as the recruitment tour wore on he found that other officers had been before him and had already taken the best men. Even so, by the time he returned to the cohort, he had enough men to bring it up to full strength, and sufficient time to train them before any campaign could begin.

Macro spent the long winter months drilling the new recruits while Cato put the rest of the men through gruelling route marches and weapons practice. As the Second Illyrian trained, a steady stream of other units arrived at Antioch and joined the growing camp outside the fortress of the Tenth Legion. With them came throngs of camp-followers and the avenues and markets of Antioch resounded with the cries of street vendors. Every inn was filled with soldiers and queues of men waited outside the brightly painted brothels which reeked of cheap incense and sweat.

As the sun set over the city, Cato's gaze took all this in without any sense of judgement. Although he was barely in his twenties he had already served four and half years in the army and had grown used to the ways of soldiers and the effect they had on the towns they passed through. Despite an unpromising start Cato had turned out to be a good soldier, as even he was prepared to admit. Quick wits and courage had played their part in transforming him from a pampered product of the imperial household into a commander of men. Luck had played its part too. He had been fortunate to find himself appointed to Macro's century when he had joined the Second Legion, he reflected. If Centurion Macro had not recognised some potential in the thin, nervous-looking recruit from Rome, and taken him under his wing, then Cato had little doubt that he would not have survived for long on the German frontier, and the campaign that followed in Britain. Since then the two of them had left the Second Legion and had served briefly in the navy before being sent east to join Macro's present command. In the coming campaign they would be fighting as part of an army again and Cato felt some small relief that the burdens of independent command would be lifted from their shoulders: relief tempered by instinctive concerns about the realities of entering a new campaign.

Far better soldiers than Cato had been struck down by an arrow, slingshot or sword thrust they had not seen coming. So far he had been spared, and he hoped that his good luck would continue if there was a war against Parthia. He had fought the Parthians briefly the year before and well knew their accuracy with a bow, and the speed with which they could mount a sudden attack and then melt away before the Romans could respond. It was a style of fighting that would sorely test the men of the legions, let alone those of the Second Illyrian cohort.

Or perhaps that was not fair, Cato reflected. The men of his cohort actually had a better chance against the Parthians than the legionaries. They wore lighter armour and a quarter of them were mounted, so that the Parthians would have to be far more wary in attacking the cohort than in any assault they mounted on the slow-marching heavy infantry of the legions. Cassius Longinus would have to proceed cautiously against the Parthians if he were to avoid the fate of Marcus Crassus and his six legions nearly a hundred years earlier. Crassus had blundered into the desert and after several days of harassing attacks under the pitiless glare of the sun his army had been cut to pieces, along with its general.

As the sun finally sank below the horizon there was a distant blare of bucinas from the army camp announcing the first watch of the night. Macro stirred and eased himself away from the rough plaster of the wall.

'Better get back to the camp. I'm taking the new boys out into the desert tomorrow. Their first time. It'll be interesting to see how they cope.'

'Best to go easy on them,' Cato suggested. 'We can't afford to lose any before the campaign begins.'

'Go easy on 'em?' Macro frowned. 'Will I fuck. If they can't hack it now, then they never will when the real fighting starts.'

Cato shrugged. 'I thought we needed every man.'

'Every man, yes. But not one makeweight.'

Cato was silent for a moment. 'This is not the Second Legion, Macro. We can't expect too much from the men of an auxiliary cohort.'

'Really?' Macro's expression hardened. 'The Second Illyrian ain't just any cohort. It's my cohort. And if I want the men to march, fight and die as hard as the men of the legions, then they will do it. Understand?'

Cato nodded.

'And you will do your part in making that happen.'

Cato's back stiffened. 'Of course I will, sir. Have I ever let you down?'

They stared at each other for a moment before Macro suddenly laughed and clapped his friend on the shoulder. 'Not yet! You've got balls of solid iron, boy. I just hope the rest of the men can match you.'

'So do I,' Cato replied evenly.

Macro rose to his feet and rubbed his buttocks, which had lost a little feeling after some hours on the hard wooden bench of the inn. He picked up his centurion's vine stick. 'Let's go.'

They set off through the forum, already filling with brothel touts and sellers of trinkets and the first of the off-duty soldiers from the camp. Fresh-faced recruits hung together in loud packs as they made for the nearest bars, where they would be fleeced by experienced conmen and swindlers who knew them for what they were and had all manner of petty rackets at their fingertips. Cato felt a twinge of pity for the recruits but knew that only experience would teach them what they needed to know. A few sore heads and the loss of their purses would ensure they kept their wits about them in the future, if they lived long enough.

As ever, there was a strict division between the men of the legions and those of the auxiliary cohorts. The legionaries were paid far more and tended to regard the non-citizen soldiers of the Empire with a degree of professional disdain – a sentiment which Cato could under-stand, and Macro wholly agreed with. The feeling extended beyond the camp and into the streets of Antioch where the men from the cohorts generally kept a respectful distance from the legionaries. But not all of them, it seemed. As Cato and Macro turned on to one of the streets leading from the forum they heard an angry exchange of shouts a short distance ahead. Beneath the glow of a large copper lamp hanging over the entrance to a bar a small crowd had gathered round two men who had tumbled out into the street and now rolled in the gutter in a mad flurry of blows.

'There's trouble,' Macro grumbled.

'Want to give it a miss?'

Macro watched the fight for a moment as they approached and then shrugged. 'Don't see why we should get involved. Let 'em sort it out amongst themselves.'

Just then there was a brief fiery glimmer in the hand of one of the fighting men and someone cried out, 'He's got a knife!'

'Shit,' Macro growled. 'Now we're involved. Come on!'

He increased his pace, and thrust aside some of the other men who had come out of the bar to investigate the commotion.

'Oi!' A burly man in a red tunic turned on Macro. 'Watch where you're going there!'

'Hold your tongue!' Macro raised his vine stick so that the man, and all the others, could see it, and pushed his way through to the men fighting in the gutter. 'Break it up, you two! That's an order.'

There was one final scuffle and a deep explosive grunt and then the men rolled apart. One, a thin wiry man in a legionary tunic, moved like a cat on to his feet and rose in a crouch, ready to continue the fight in an instant. Macro rounded on him, brandishing his vine stick.

'It's over, I said.'

Then Cato saw the small blade in the man's hand. It no longer glittered, but was obscured by a dark film that dripped from the point. On the ground the second man had risen up on his elbow while his other hand clutched at his side. He gasped for breath and winced in agony.

'Fuck . . . Oh, shit it hurts . . . Bastard's stuck me.'

He glared at the legionary for an instant, then groaned in pain and slumped back on the ground in the wan glow of the lamp overhead.

'I know him,' Cato said softly. 'He's one of ours. Caius Menathus, from one of the cavalry squadrons.' He knelt down beside the man and felt for the wound. The auxiliary's tunic was sodden with the warm gush of blood when the knife had been withdrawn and Cato glanced up at the men clustered round.

'Get back!' he ordered. 'Give me some room!'

Cato had left his vine cane at the camp, and his youth caused some of the veterans to hesitate to obey his command. But the men from the Second Illyrian, Menathus' companions, recognised their officer and drew back at once. After a brief moment the others followed suit and

Cato turned again to the injured man. The tear in the cloth was small but the blood was flowing freely, and Cato quickly pulled the tunic up to expose the red-smeared flesh of the man's torso. A faintly puckered wound, like a small mouth, glistened in the glow of the lamp and disgorged a steady pulse of blood. Cato clamped his hand over the wound and pressed hard as he glanced up at the nearest men.

'Get a board of wood, something to carry him on, now! And you, run back to the camp and get hold of a surgeon and send him to the hospital. He's to be ready for us the moment this man arrives. Tell him Menathus has been stabbed.'

'Yes, sir!' The auxiliary saluted and turned away, running down the street towards the town gates.

As Cato turned back to Menathus, Macro stepped cautiously towards the legionary holding the knife. The man had backed away from the crowd towards the opposite side of the street and was still in a crouch, eyes staring wildly as Macro approached him.

Macro smiled and held out his hand. 'That's enough trouble for tonight, son. Give me the knife, before you do any more damage.'

The legionary shook his head. 'Bastard had it coming to him.'

'I'm sure he did. We'll sort it all out later. Now give me the knife.'

'No. You'll have me arrested.' The man's voice was slurred with drink.

'Arrested?' Macro snorted. 'That's the least of your troubles. Drop the knife before you make it worse for yourself.'

'You don't understand.' The legionary waved the knife towards the man on the ground. 'He cheated me. In a game of dice.'

'Bollocks!' a voice cried out. 'He won fair and square.'

There was a chorus of angry agreement, matched a moment later by furious denials.

'SILENCE!' Macro roared.

At once the men stilled their tongues. Macro glared round at them and then returned his attention to the man with the knife. 'What's your name, rank and unit, legionary?'

'Marcus Metellus Crispus, optio, fourth century, second cohort, Tenth Legion, sir!' the man rattled out automatically. He even attempted to stiffen to attention as he said it, but staggered drunkenly to one side after a moment.

'Optio, give me the knife. That's an order.'

Crispus shook his head. 'I ain't going in the guardhouse for that cheating bastard.'

Macro pursed his lips thoughtfully and then nodded. 'Very well then, but we'll have to deal with this matter first thing in the morning. I shall have to speak to your centurion.'

He started to turn away, and Crispus relaxed a moment and let his guard down for the first time. Then there was a blur. Macro's cane swept up and out and arced round viciously as he swirled back towards Crispus. There was a sharp crack as the blow connected with the man's head and Crispus collapsed. His knife clattered on to the street a short distance away. Macro stood over him, arm raised, but there was no movement – the man was out cold. Macro nodded with satisfaction and lowered his cane.

'You four.' He gestured to some men from the Second Illyrian. 'Scrape this piece of shit up and take him back to our guardhouse. He can stew there while I sort this out with his commander.'

'Wait.' A man stepped from the crowd and loomed over Macro. He was a head taller and broad to match and in the orange light of the lamp his face looked hard and weathered. 'I'll take this man back to the Tenth. We'll deal with it.'

Macro stood his ground and sized the man up. 'I've given my orders. I'm placing this man under arrest.'

'No, he'll go with me.'

Macro smiled faintly. 'And who might you be?'

'The centurion from the Tenth Legion who's telling you what's going to happen,' the man smiled back. 'Not a pissing little centurion from an auxiliary cohort. Now, if you auxiliary boys wouldn't mind moving along . . .'

'Small world,' Macro replied. 'I'm not a centurion from an auxiliary cohort either. I'm the prefect of the Second Illyrian, as it happens. I keep my vine cane for old times' sake. From my days as a centurion of the Second Legion.'

The other officer stared at Macro for a moment before stiffening and saluting.

'That's better.' Macro nodded. 'And who the fuck are you?'

'Centurion Porcius Cimber, sir. Second century, third cohort.'

'Right then, Cimber. This man's in my custody. You find your legate

24

and explain the situation to him. His man will be disciplined for taking a knife to one of mine.'

Macro was interrupted by a deep groan from the ground as Menathus suddenly writhed, breaking free of Cato's hold. The blood pumped out at once.

'Where the hell's that carrying board?' Cato yelled, then pressed his hands on the wound again and leaned over Menathus. 'Keep still!'

'Shit . . . I'm cold,' Menathus muttered and his eyes rolled aimlessly as the lids flickered. 'Oh . . . shit, shit . . . it hurts.'

'Hold on, Menathus,' Cato said firmly. 'We'll get the wound seen to. You'll be all right.'

The crowd of soldiers, and the handful of townspeople who had joined them, stood and gazed on the scene in silence as Menathus groaned, his breath coming in sharp ragged hisses. Then he started trembling violently and his body spasmed, every fibre tense as rock for an instant, before he slumped back on to the street, his breath escaping from his lips in a long last sigh. Cato pressed his ear to the man's bloodied chest for a while and then drew back, withdrawing his hand from the knife wound.

'He's gone.'

For a moment the crowd was still. Then one of the auxiliaries growled, 'Bastard murdered him. He's going to die.'

There was an angry chorus of agreement and at once the crowd shuffled into two groups, as auxiliaries and legionaries confronted each other. Cato saw hands bunch into fists, men crouching slightly as they braced their legs to charge, and then Macro strode between them and raised his arms into the air.

'That will do! Enough! Keep your distance there!' His expression was furious and he stared from side to side, daring the men to defy him. Then he nodded to Centurion Cimber. 'Take your men back to the camp. Now.'

'Yes, sir!' Cimber saluted and thrust the nearest of them down the street towards the gate. 'Move, you bastards! Show's over.'

He continued to push and shove the angry legionaries away from the bar and the body lying in the street. One of the auxiliaries called after them. 'You ain't seen the last of us! There's a score to settle for Menathus!'

'Silence!' Macro bellowed. 'Shut your mouths! Centurion Cato?'

'Yes, sir?' Cato stood up, wiping his bloodied hands on the sides of his tunic.

'Give Cimber a head start and then get our men back to camp. Make sure that the prisoner doesn't come to any harm.'

'What about Menathus?'

'Take him as well. Get the hospital orderlies to prepare the body for a funeral.'

As they waited for the legionaries to reach a safe distance Cato edged closer to his commander and spoke softly. 'Not a good situation. Last thing we need is for the men to enter a campaign with bad blood between them and the boys from the Tenth.'

'Too right,' Macro grumbled. 'And now that our man's dead, there's no future for Crispus either.'

'What'll happen to him?'

'Knifing a fellow soldier?' Macro shook his head wearily. 'No doubt about it. He'll be condemned to death. And I doubt that Crispus' execution will be the end of it.'

'Oh?'

'You know what soldiers are like for bearing a grudge. It's bad enough when the men belong to the same unit. But this will lead to a feud between the Second Illyrian and the Tenth, mark my words.' Macro gave a deep sigh. 'And now I'll have to write up a bloody report for the governor and see him first thing in the morning. I'd better be off. Give me a moment, then get our lads moving.'

'Yes, sir.'

'I'll see you later, Cato.'

As Macro strode off down the street Cato stared at the body at his feet. The campaign had not even begun and already they'd lost two men. Worse, if Macro was right, the damage done by a single drunken brawl would fester in the hearts of the men. Just when they needed every ounce of their wits about them if they were to defeat the Parthians.

CHAPTER THREE

The body of the auxiliary had been placed on a bier and carried to the pyre by his comrades just before dawn. The pyre had been constructed a short distance from the camp gates. The dead soldier's century had mounted the honour guard, but almost every man of the cohort had been there to bear witness. Macro had noted their sullen, vengeful mood while he gave a brief oration for Menathus and then lit the pyre. The men watched the flames catch the oil-drenched wood and then crackle into life, sending up a swirling vortex of smoke and sparks into the clear sky. Then, as the pyre began to collapse in on itself, Macro nodded to Cato to give the order to return to camp and the men turned away quietly and marched off.

'Not in the happiest of moods, I think,' Cato muttered.

'No. You'd better find them something to do. Keep 'em occupied while I see Longinus.'

'How?'

'I don't know,' Macro said tersely. 'You're the smart one. You decide.'

Cato glanced at his companion in surprise but kept his mouth shut. He knew that Macro had spent the whole night dealing with the report and the preparations for the funeral, on top of the previous day's drinking, and his black mood was inevitable. So Cato simply nodded.

'Weapons drill. With training weapons. That should wear them out.'

A few hours with the double-weighted swords and wicker shields would exhaust even the strongest of men and a thin smile flickered across Macro's expression.

'See to it.'

Cato saluted and turned to follow the men heading in through the main gate. Macro watched him for a moment, wondering when Cato would fully master the drill technique that Macro had taken so many years to become familiar with. Where Macro could shout instructions, and not a little invective, loud enough to be heard across the parade ground for hours at a stretch, Cato had not yet developed his lungs to the same degree and tended to come across as more of a schoolteacher than the front-line centurion he had proved himself to be. A few more years under his belt, Macro reflected, and the young man would carry it off as naturally as any other officer. Until then? Macro sighed. Until then, Cato would just have to keep proving himself worthy of the rank that so few men of his age had ever risen to. Macro turned towards the gates of Antioch. The governor had commandeered one of the finest houses in the city as his headquarters. No rudely constructed praetorium for Cassius Longinus, then. Nor the relative discomfort of a suite of well-appointed marching tents. Macro smiled grimly. If one thing was for certain in the coming campaign, it was that the army's general would travel in the kind of luxury that most of his men could only ever dream about as they tramped in full armour under the burden of their heavily loaded equipment yokes.

'I do love a man who leads by example,' he said softly to himself as he trudged off to his appointment with Longinus.

The governor of Syria looked up from the report and leaned back in his chair. On the other side of the desk sat Macro and Legate Amatius, commander of the Tenth Legion. Longinus regarded them silently for a moment, and then raised his eyebrows.

'I can't say I'm terribly happy about the situation, gentlemen. One man dead, and another man facing punishment. I imagine this will cause a lot of bad feeling between your two commands. As if preparing the army for war wasn't demanding enough, I now have to deal with this.'

Macro felt his anger rise at the accusing tone of his superior. It was hardly his fault that Menathus was dead. If he and Cato hadn't stepped in to prevent the situation from escalating out of control, then there'd have been far more funeral pyres casting their pall across the sky outside the camp that morning. It was hardly likely that Crispus was the only legionary carrying a blade in the crowd outside the bar last night. Or that none of Macro's men was similarly armed. In an atmosphere of drunken dissent the brawl could easily have become more widespread and far more ugly. Macro bit back on his irritation as he replied.

'It is unfortunate, sir, but it could have been worse. We have to make

28

sure that the lads settle down and forget the business as soon as possible. My lads, and those of the Tenth, sir.'

'He's right.' Legate Amatius nodded. 'The, er, matter has to be resolved as swiftly as possible, sir. My man has to be tried and punished.'

'Punished . . .' Longinus stroked his chin. 'And what punishment would be suitable for this man Crispus, I wonder? Clearly an example has to be made, if we are to discourage any more incidents like last night's.'

Amatius nodded. 'Of course, sir. Nothing short of beating will do. That and breaking the man back to the ranks. My men won't forget that in a hurry.'

'No.' Macro shook his head firmly. 'That won't do. A man has died, needlessly, as a result of Crispus' pulling a knife. He could have fought it out fairly, and he didn't. Now he must face the full consequences of his actions. The regulations are clear enough. It was in your standing orders, sir. Any man off duty within the walls of the city was forbidden to carry weapons, I imagine with just such an incident as happened last night in mind. Isn't that so, sir?'

'Yes, I suppose.' Longinus opened his hand towards Macro. 'And how do you think he should be punished?'

Macro steeled his heart. He derived no satisfaction from the thought of sending Crispus to his death, but he knew that the consequences of not doing so would cause a great deal of harm to the army's discipline. He met the governor's gaze directly. 'Execution, to be carried out by the men of his century, before the rest of his cohort.'

'Who's his cohort commander, by the way?'

'Centurion Cato, as it happens,' Amatius said sharply. He looked at the governor. 'In his absence, I can tell you that the men would not stand for the punishment Prefect Macro suggests. And why should they? After all, the man he killed was a bloody auxiliary. I regret the death every bit as much as Prefect Macro, but the loss of that man's life hardly compares to the loss of a legionary, and a Roman citizen. Especially since this was simply the result of some drunken fight in the street.' He turned to Macro. 'I know what happened, Macro. I've made my own enquiries. It seems that your man cheated the legionary during a game of dice.'

'That's not what my men say, sir.'

'Well, they wouldn't, would they? They want the hide off my man. They'd say anything to have that.'

'Just as your men would say anything to save his skin,' Macro replied icily. 'I think we have to accept that the men's accounts will be biased. But I was there. I saw what happened. With respect, sir, you didn't. Crispus is guilty. He has to be punished according to military law.'

Amatius frowned for a moment before he replied with forced cordiality. 'Look, Prefect, I understand your feelings on this. It's only natural that you'd share your men's desire for revenge.'

'Not revenge, sir. Justice.'

'Call it what you will. But hear me out. If your man had pulled the knife, you'd want him spared, wouldn't you?'

'What I want is irrelevant, sir,' Macro responded firmly. 'The punishment for such a crime is clear enough.'

'Look here,' Amatius persisted. 'Macro, you were once a legionary, weren't you?'

'Yes, sir. So?'

'So you must have some loyalty to your comrades in the legions. You would not want a comrade to be executed over the death of some mere provincial levy, surely?'

Macro felt his blood pound through his veins as his rage swelled at this description of his men as provincial levies. They were the Second Illyrian. The men who had fought off a rebel army, backed by Parthia, and crushed the uprising in Judaea the previous year. The men were tough and had guts, and they had proved themselves where it counted, in battle. Macro was proud of them. Proud enough to place his loyalty to them above anything he owed to the brotherhood of the legions. That thought came to him in a rush and took him by surprise. Then he realised it was true. He had taken to his new command more than he had thought. Macro felt a strong sense of responsibility and duty to his men and he was damned if he was going to let a pampered aristocrat like Amatius try to drive a wedge between him and the men of the Second Illyrian.

Macro took a deep breath to calm himself before replying. 'No legionary I know of would stoop low enough to make that kind of appeal . . . sir.'

There was a sharp intake of breath as Amatius sat bolt upright and glared at Macro. 'That's gross insubordination, Prefect. If you were in my legion I'd break you for that.'

Longinus cleared his throat. 'But he's not in your legion, Gallus Amatius, so he's not under your jurisdiction. However,' Longinus smiled, 'he is under my command and I will not tolerate such dissension between my officers. So, Prefect, I will ask you to withdraw that last remark and apologise.'

Macro shook his head. 'Go to Hell, sir.'

'I'm sure I will. But not on your say-so. Now you will apologise, or I shall have to find someone else to command the Second Illyrian.'

'I'm sure one of my officers would relish the chance to whip those auxiliaries into shape,' Amatius added with relish. 'One of my tribunes perhaps.'

Macro clenched his jaw. This was unbearable. The two aristocrats were using him for their sport, but much as he would like to openly reveal his contempt for them and their kind – politicians playing at soldiers – he dared not let his pride come before the best interests of his men. Some smart-arsed tribune from the Tenth Legion with a taste for glory was the last thing the cohort needed when it went up against the Parthians. Macro swallowed hard and turned to Amatius with a frigid expression.

'My apologies, sir.'

Amatius smiled. 'That's better. A man should know his place.'

'Indeed,' Longinus added. 'But there, that's settled. We still have to decide what to do about this legionary of yours.'

'Yes, sir.' Amatius composed his face. 'A punishment along the lines I suggested is sufficient, given the circumstances. While I can understand the prefect's feelings on the matter, we are talking about the life of a Roman citizen after all.'

Macro decided to make one last attempt to reason with the governor and leaned towards him as he spoke. 'Sir, you cannot allow this man to escape the punishment he is due. You have to think about how it will be seen by the entire army. Unless you make it clear to the men what the consequences will be if they break regulations and carry knives off duty, then they'll continue doing it, and with things the way they are this won't be the last death on the streets of Antioch. Believe me, sir, it

31

gives me no pleasure to ask for the man's death, but you must consider how much damage will be done by sparing him.'

Longinus frowned, then abruptly stood up and strode across the room to the balcony that overlooked the garden courtyard of the house. Beyond the tiled roof of the slave quarters that backed on to the garden he stared out across the city, over the walls to the long palisade that enclosed the army's camp on rising ground a short distance beyond. A faint cloud of dust to one side of the camp indicated some activity: a patrol, or one of the units training on the expanse of ground that had been cleared and flattened for exercises and the occasional parades. He stared for a moment longer and then turned back to the two officers still seated in front of his desk.

'Very well, I've made my decision.'

Cato slowly made his way down the line of posts set to one side of the huge exercise ground. The infantry contingent of the Second Illyrian stood in lines in front of each post, every man armed with a wooden training sword with a heavy lead weight in the pommel, and another just ahead of the wide rim of the guard. In their left hands they clutched the handles of their wicker shields, also designed to be heavier than their battlefield equivalent. If a man could learn to wield such equipment with ease while training then he would fight with greater strength and confidence against an actual enemy. But for now, the auxiliaries just charged at their practice posts with a roar and set about them with a savage flurry of blows until Cato blew his whistle, and then each man would recover, and retire to the end of the line while the next man charged the post.

They were going at it with a will, Cato noticed, and he could imagine that each one of them had mentally imposed Crispus over each of the stakes. Be that as it may, they had been drilling for the best part of the morning under a hot sun without complaint. He decided to keep them at it until noon before sending them back to their tents to rest. The afternoon would be spent with the mounted contingent, practising attacks against the same stakes while riding at speed in and around them, an altogether trickier proposition for mounted men. Thanks to the relentless training Cato was confident that the Second Illyrian would give a good account of themselves when they marched to war against

Parthia. He smiled to himself. He was already taking it for granted that there would be a war.

The coming campaign was never far from his thoughts, and despite his confidence in his men Cato was anxious about fighting the Parthians. He realised well enough the difficulties the Roman soldiers would face in dealing with Parthian tactics. The enemy had developed their skills in mounted warfare over hundreds of years and now fielded one of the most formidable armies in the known world. Their method was simple, and unvarying. The first attack would be made by horse-archers who would pepper their foes with arrows, attempting to break their formation up, and then the small corps of heavily armoured cataphracts would charge home with their lances and shatter their opponents. The tactics had worked well against most of their enemies, and had resulted in the destruction of the army of Crassus several decades earlier. Now a new Roman army was preparing to face the might of the Parthians, and with not a little trepidation.

'Sir!' One of the optios assisting Cato with the training called out to him, and thrust his staff towards the hills to the east. Cato turned and scanned the near horizon of rocky slopes studded with clusters of cedar trees. Then something flashed in a shallow ravine leading down towards Antioch. He squinted and raised a hand to shade his eyes as he tried to make out more detail. A column of tiny figures on horseback was emerging from the mouth of the ravine. The optio strode over to join him and both men stared into the distance as the relentless dull thuds of the training continued behind them.

'Who the hell are they?' the optio muttered.

Cato shook his head. 'No way of telling just yet. Could be a caravan from Chalcis, Beroea, or perhaps even Palmyra.'

'Caravan? I don't think so, sir. I can't make out any camels.'

'That's true.' Cato stared as the distant party of horsemen continued to emerge from the ravine until at least a hundred men had appeared. As sunlight glittered off weapons and armour he felt the first icy trace of fear tingle down the back of his neck. Lowering his hand, he quietly gave his orders to the optio. 'Get the men back into the camp and call out our cavalry. I want them out here ready for action. Send word to the general that we've sighted a column of horsemen to the east.'

'Who shall I say they are?'

Cato shrugged. 'No way to be sure just yet. But there's no point in taking any chances. Now go.'

The optio saluted and then turned away, bellowing orders to the auxiliaries to cease their weapons drill and form up. The men wearily tramped into position and when all was ready the small column marched across the parade ground towards the camp gate, leaving Cato to watch the distant horsemen. By the time the last rider had emerged from the ravine he estimated that there must be at least two hundred of them. And at their head the thin red and gold strip of a banner flickered lazily in the shimmering air. The horsemen continued their measured approach towards Antioch, and the army camp sprawled across the landscape before the city's walls. This was no attempt to surprise any unwary Roman patrols, Cato reasoned. The horsemen fully intended to be seen.

From inside the camp there was the shrill blast of notes from a bucina and a short while later the first of the Second Illyrian's mounted squadrons trotted out of the gate and formed up in two lines at the edge of the parade ground, waiting for the men of the other three squadrons to take up position on their right. As the last of the cavalrymen edged his beast into line and the cohort's mounted contingent tightened their grasp of their spears as they scrutinised the distant horsemen, a small party of staff officers emerged from the gates of the city and galloped along the track towards Cato and his men. Cato instantly identified the flamboyant red crest of the leading figure and felt some small comfort that the governor of Syria would take charge of the situation. The party of officers drew up in a flurry of dust and small stones and Cato saw that Macro and the legate of the Tenth were riding with the governor and his staff. Longinus thrust his arm out towards Cato.

'Centurion! Report.'

'It's as you can see, sir.' Cato nodded towards the approaching column. 'They're armed, but they've made no hostile moves yet.'

Longinus stared at the riders for a moment. The distant column had halted and formed a line across the track leading back into the ravine, and now a small party of horsemen, surrounding the standard Cato had seen earlier, detached themselves from the main body and galloped across the flat expanse of land between the hills and the camp. As they drew closer the dull, flat blasts of a horn carried across to the Romans.

Longinus turned to Legate Amatius on the horse beside him. 'Seems someone wants a truce.'

'Truce?' Amatius shook his head in wonder. 'But who the hell are they?'

Cato stared at the approaching riders, no more than half a mile away now. The dust kicked up by their mounts formed a backdrop that made it easier to pick out the details of their conical helmets and flowing robes, and the bow cases slung from their saddles. He lowered his hand and turned back to his commander.

'They're Parthians, sir.'

'Parthians?' Longinus' hand slipped on to the hilt of his sword. 'Parthians . . . What the hell are they doing here? Right under our bloody noses.'

The horsemen reined in no more than a hundred paces from Cato and the other officers, and after a moment's pause one of them edged his horse forward and walked it warily towards the Romans.

'Shall I order our men forward, sir?' Macro asked, gesturing to the squadrons from the Second Illyrian.

'No. Not yet,' Longinus replied quietly, his gaze fixed on the approaching rider.

'Parthians.' Amatius scratched his chin nervously. 'What do they want?'

Longinus tightened his grip round the handle of his sword and muttered, 'We'll know soon enough.'

CHAPTER FOUR

The Parthian stopped a short distance from the Roman officers and bowed his head. He pulled the silk scarf from about his face to reveal dark features. Cato saw that he wore smears of kohl round his eyes and had a neatly trimmed moustache and beard. He smiled slightly before speaking in faintly accented Latin.

'My master, Prince Metaxas, sends his greetings, and would speak with the governor of the province of Syria.' He glanced over the Roman officers. 'I assume that one of you finely dressed officers can send word to the man I seek.'

Longinus puffed his chest out irritably. 'I am Cassius Longinus, governor of Syria and commander of the army of the eastern Empire. What does your master want?'

'Prince Metaxas has been sent by our king to discuss certain disputes between Parthia and Rome, in the hope that the two powers might resolve these disputes without recourse to force. Our king does not wish to cause any unnecessary loss of life amongst the ranks of your fine legions.'

'Oh, is that right?' Legate Amatius bristled. 'Well, let's just see how well his dandy little horsemen do when they come up against the Tenth.'

'Quiet!' Longinus snapped at his subordinate. He glared at Amatius and then turned back to the Parthian emissary. 'I will speak to your master. Bring him here.'

The Parthian flashed a smile. 'Alas, my master has heard that some Romans have not always honoured the traditions of the truce.'

Longinus' expression darkened as he replied coldly, 'You dare to accuse me of such infamy?'

'Of course not, my lord. Not you, as such.'

'Then bring your master here to talk to me. If he has the stomach for it.'

'The stomach?' The Parthian was puzzled. 'Forgive me, my lord, I am uncertain of this idiom.'

'Tell your master that I will not speak with his slave. Tell him that I will speak to him here and now, if he has the courage to venture from behind his escort.'

'I would gladly tell him this, but I would anticipate that he might respond to your offer in kind.' The Parthian gestured at the other officers and the cavalry of Macro's cohort. 'I am sure that so great a general as yourself would be brave enough to venture beyond the protection of such a formidable-looking bodyguard. But, in deference to your understandable anxieties, my master has permitted me to suggest that you and he meet between our forces.'

Longinus glanced briefly at the open ground between the camp and the richly robed horsemen. 'Alone, you say?'

'Yes, my lord.'

'Don't do it, sir,' Amatius muttered. 'Bound to be some sort of barbarian trick. You've no idea what treachery that kind are capable of.'

Macro cleared his throat. 'I don't know. I doubt there's much harm this Prince Metaxas could do by himself.'

Amatius rounded on Macro. 'What the hell do you know, Prefect? The Parthians could shoot the governor down well before he even reached the spot.'

Macro shrugged. 'That's possible, sir. But they'd risk hitting their own man too. Besides, there's the question of losing face. If the governor backed down . . . Well, I'm sure that at least the people back in Rome would understand.'

'My lords!' The Parthian raised a hand. 'I beg your pardon for intervening in your dispute, but if you deem such a meeting to present too much of a danger then might I suggest that both supporting forces retreat to well beyond bowshot, and that my prince and the governor meet with, say, three companions each? Would that not assuage your suspicions and fears?'

'Fears?' Longinus bristled. 'I'm not afraid, Parthian. Romans fear no one, least of all the barbarians of the east.'

'I am delighted to hear that, my lord. In which case, may I inform my master that you and your companions will meet with him?'

Cato tried to hide his amusement that the governor had been so

37

easily manoeuvred into consenting to the Parthian's offer. Longinus, however, was furious and took a while to recover control of himself. As he glared round he caught sight of Cato's expression and he thrust out his finger. 'Centurion Cato, you will accompany me, since you seem to be in such good humour. You, your friend Macro and Legate Amatius. The rest of you, join those mounted men. You will remain here. If I give the signal, you come to our aid as swiftly as possible. Go!'

He turned back to the Parthian and growled. 'Tell your master we will meet – once the rest of his men have retired to a safe distance.'

'Very well, my lord.' The Parthian bowed his head, and at once turned his mount round and galloped back towards his companions, before there was any chance for the governor to change the conditions of the meeting. As they watched him go Macro turned to Cato and spoke quietly.

'Thank you so very much for involving me.'

'Sorry, sir.' Cato gestured towards the mounted squadron. 'I'd, er, better find myself a horse.'

'Fine. You do that. Before you cause any more trouble.'

While Cato trotted off in the wake of the other officers, Amatius, Macro and the governor watched as the Parthians wheeled their horses round and walked them away, leaving behind the emissary, the standard-bearer and two others. Macro puffed his cheeks out.

'Any idea what they might want, sir?'

'No. Not a clue.' Longinus was silent for a moment before he continued. 'I don't understand how they got so close to the army without being spotted. Our patrols and frontier posts must be blind. Someone's going to pay for this,' he concluded sourly.

At the sound of an approaching horse the three officers glanced round as Cato rode up to them and reined in. Longinus glanced at his companions. 'Keep your eyes open. At the first sign of danger, you shout a warning and lay into the bastards. But remember, this is a truce. We only make a move if they act first. So keep your hands clear of your weapons and in full view.'

Amatius sniffed. 'Let's hope their prince tells his people to do the same.'

'Quite.' Longinus nodded, then drew a deep breath to calm his nerves. 'Better get on with it then. Let's go.'

He gently dug the heels of his calfskin boots into the flanks of his horse and urged it forward. The others followed suit and the small party of Romans warily picked their way across the open ground towards the Parthians. As he rode a short distance behind and to one side of his commander Cato had to contain the impulse to rest his hand on the pommel of his sword. Instead he gripped the reins in both hands and stiffened his back so that he might appear haughty and fearless to the Parthians. But inside his stomach was a tight knot of fear and his heart pounded in his chest. He felt contempt for himself even as he struggled to maintain his brave façade. A glance to his side revealed Macro staring intently at the Parthians, his expression curious and appraising rather than tense and fearful. Cato snatched at the crumb of comfort that his fearless friend would be more than a match for any Parthian warrior that ever lived if the enemy had planned any treachery.

The two parties of horsemen drew closer to each other, the silence and stillness of the midday broken only by the sound of horses' hooves scraping and thumping the uneven ground. Cato saw the elaborate decoration on the Parthians' bow cases and the fine quality of their robes. Their mounts were smaller than the Roman horses, and seemed to be well cared for, muscular and moving with a fluid grace. There was little to distinguish the Parthians in their accoutrements, except that the man carrying the standard had a large wicker basket hanging from his saddle. By mutual consent the two sides drew up two spears' length apart and for a moment exchanged searching stares. Then the tallest of the Parthians suddenly pulled aside his face cloth and began to speak.

The emissary listened intently and then bowed his head before turning to the Romans.

'The prince wishes you eternal good health and prosperity. For you, your emperor and all your people. He also wishes to commend you on the fine lands you have acquired on behalf of Rome. He says that he was most impressed by your lines of watchtowers and forward outposts that guard the approaches to Antioch. They presented something of a challenge for us to approach and pass through unseen.'

Longinus' lips pressed together in a thin line as he heard the last words and his free hand momentarily clenched. Then he raised it suddenly.

'That's enough of the courtesies. I take it we're not here to discuss the details of your sightseeing. Get to the point. What does the prince want?'

There was a brief exchange between the emissary and the prince before the former spoke again. 'Parthia demands that Rome desists from any attempt to spread its influence any further towards the Euphrates.'

'Rome has every right to protect her frontiers,' Longinus responded firmly.

'Ah, but your frontiers seem to have a habit of creeping forward, like thieves towards the homes of fresh victims.'

'What do you mean? We still honour the existing treaty.'

'Between Parthia and Rome, yes,' the emissary conceded. 'But what of your arrangement with Palmyra? You use her lands as your own and your soldiers march up to the very borders of Parthia.'

'King Vabathus has signed a treaty with Rome,' Longinus said evenly. The prince snorted as the words were translated for him. Then he launched into a long outburst whose ill-humour was apparent to the Romans even before the emissary attempted to speak for his master. Macro glanced at Cato and raised his eyes wearily. Cato did not respond. His friend was a professional soldier to the core, but he hated any aspect of politics or diplomacy and it was clear to Cato that Macro's presence at this tense encounter was something of a liability for the Roman side. Cato widened his eyes and did his best to shoot a warning look at his friend. Macro briefly raised a questioning eyebrow and then shrugged slightly as the emissary spoke for his master.

'Prince Metaxas says that the true intent of your treaty is a poorly kept secret. Everyone knows that it is merely a move towards annexation of Palmyra.'

'King Vabathus entered into the treaty freely enough.'

'And if the king, or a successor, was to decide that the treaty should be ended? What then?'

Longinus had already taken the bait once, and paused a moment to consider a suitable response. 'But there is no question of that happening. Palmyra and Rome are partners.'

The Parthian prince laughed harshly and stabbed his finger towards the Roman governor as he made his response.

'Partners?' the emissary translated. 'The only partners you have are

Vabathus and his cronies. The great houses of Palmyran aristocracy denounce the treaty openly. There are even those in the royal palace who think the king little more than a traitor. Your treaty is a sham, and soon the king will be forced to renounce it. And if he fails to do that you can be sure that his successor will cut the chains that bind Palmyra to Rome. If Rome attempts to intervene in Palmyran affairs by force, then Parthia will do all it can to protect its neighbour from Roman aggression.'

Now it was Longinus' turn to laugh. 'Parthia the protector? That's a new one! Your desire to seize Palmyra is transparent. What makes you think the people of Palmyra will welcome Parthian intervention?'

'We have our reasons to believe they will. And we have made it known that we will protect their independence. From Rome and any other interlopers.'

'And you think they believe that? Why should they have any more faith in your good intentions than ours?'

'Because we have not sent soldiers into their lands to build fortifications that will slowly but surely become the bars of their cage. Already you have attempted to build a fort on the very banks of the Euphrates, and before long the camps of Roman armies will sprout along the banks of the river, like knives aimed at the throat of Parthia.'

Macro leaned towards Cato and whispered, 'These Parthian buggers are partial to a poetic turn of phrase, aren't they?'

'Shh!' Cato hissed as loudly as he dared. There was a pause as the Parthian emissary, Longinus and the legate of the Tenth turned to look at Macro and Cato before the emissary resumed his master's diatribe.

'Parthia will not tolerate such naked aggression. The fort was a clear sign of Roman intentions and you are warned not to attempt any such incursions again.'

'Was?' Longinus interrupted. 'What has happened to the fort?'

'It has been razed.'

'And the auxiliary cohort sent to construct it. What of them?'

'They were destroyed.'

'Destroyed?' Longinus was startled. 'What of the prisoners? Where are they?'

'Regrettably, there are no prisoners.'

'Bastards,' Legate Amatius grumbled. 'Murdering swine.'

41

The emissary shrugged. 'They did not surrender. Our men had no choice but to wipe them out.'

Longinus was silent for a moment before he responded. 'Five hundred men, and one of the best field officers in the army. Centurion Castor . . .' He glared at the Parthian prince. 'Tell your master that this is an act of war.'

Metaxas smiled as his emissary translated his reply. 'Which? The destruction of your cohort, or the threat it posed to our sovereignty?'

'Don't try to confuse the issue!' Longinus snapped. 'He knows what I mean. When word of this reaches the ears of the Emperor I doubt there is any power in this world that will prevent him from wreaking a terrible revenge on Parthia. And it will be a fate you have drawn down on yourselves.'

'We have no wish to provoke war, my general.'

'Bollocks!' Amatius snorted. 'You wipe out one of our cohorts and you say you don't wish to provoke a war!' The legate's hand slipped towards the handle of his sword and the gesture was noticed at once by the Parthians. With a sudden rasp one of the prince's escorts drew his sword and the curved blade glinted in the sunlight. Prince Metaxas snapped an order at the man and with a brief show of reluctance he returned the blade to its scabbard.

'Sir.' Cato spoke softly to the legate. 'I'd take your hand off your sword.'

Amatius' nostrils flared as his eyes fixed on Cato. Then he blinked and nodded and released his grip. 'All right then. But there will be a reckoning for Centurion Castor and the men of that cohort. One day.'

The emissary was unimpressed. 'Perhaps, but not in this life. Not if Rome truly values peace on its eastern frontier. My master says that you are to remove your forces from the lands of Palmyra. Furthermore, you are not to intervene in its internal politics. Breach of either condition will force Parthia to take military action. Much as the prince, and his father, King Gotarzes, desire peace, they will be forced to wage war on Rome. Such a war would cost Rome dearly. Many more of your countrymen would share the fate of Crassus and his legions. Those are the words of my master,' the emissary concluded. 'You have heard our warning, my lord, and there is no more to be said.'

The Parthian prince made one last comment to his emissary and then gestured to his companion carrying the wicker basket on his saddle. The man unlooped the handles from his saddle horn and let the basket drop heavily to the ground beside his horse. Then the Parthians wheeled their horses round and the emissary spoke to the Romans one last time.

'My master bids you accept a gift. A gift plucked from the banks of the Euphrates. Consider it a token of the future should you choose to defy the kingdom of Parthia.'

The Parthians spurred their horses into a gallop and pounded back towards the distant line of their comrades who were already breaking formation to turn away from Antioch and disappear back into the ravine. For a moment the Romans watched them depart through the dust kicked up by their horses. Then Longinus turned his gaze to the wicker basket lying on the rocky soil. He gestured towards it.

'Centurion Cato.'

'Sir?'

'See what's in there.'

'Yes, sir.' Cato slipped his leg over the saddle horns and dropped to the ground. He approached the basket cautiously, as if it might be filled with snakes or scorpions. Swallowing, he reached down and pulled the handles apart. Inside there was a plain earthen jar, the size of a large watermelon. The bottom had cracked when the basket hit the ground and the odour of olive oil reached Cato's nose as it slowly drained through the fibres of the basket. A dark tangled mass glistened in the top of the jar, and as the oil continued to drain it settled and gleamed on the domed surface beneath.

'What is it?' Amatius snapped. 'Show us, man!'

Cato felt the bile rising in his throat as he leaned forward and grasped the oily dark tendrils. With gritted teeth he drew the heavy burden from the jar and raised it aloft. Oil ran down the ashen skin of the severed head and dripped from its parted lips on to the parched soil below.

Legate Amatius grimaced as he stared at the grisly spectacle. 'Centurion Castor.'

CHAPTER FIVE

'Gentlemen.' Cassius Longinus stared solemnly round the banqueting hall of his headquarters. He stood on a podium and surveyed the expressions of the centurions, tribunes and legates assembled before him. 'War with Parthia has come.'

The officers exchanged glances and an excited murmur rippled across the hall before it died away and every face turned to the governor of Syria with an eager expression. News of the party of Parthian horsemen that had appeared before the very walls of Antioch the previous day had swept through the camp and the streets of the city. The rumour-mongers had been tirelessly at work, until the event portended everything from an historic alliance between Rome and Parthia to the mortal terror of the prospect of a vast Parthian army no more than a day's march away intent on the slaughter of every man, woman and child in Antioch. Longinus' first words had eliminated some of the more fanciful notions and now his officers listened in tense anticipation for more detail. The governor waited until there was complete silence before he continued.

'Some days ago, the Parthians surprised one of our outposts and slaughtered the garrison. Our visitors presented us with the head of its commander, Centurion Castor of the Tenth Legion.'

The men standing around Cato and Macro grumbled angrily and Macro nudged his companion and muttered, 'Pity the Parthians that come up against our lot. This has the makings of some good fighting.'

'Good fighting?' Cato frowned. 'I'm not sure I share your enthusiasm for this particular campaign. The Parthians are not going to die easily.'

'Oh, come on! We've faced worse.'

'Really? Do enlighten me.'

Macro stared at his friend for a moment and then pursed his lips. 'Fair point. The Parthians are hard bastards,' he conceded and then rubbed his hands together. 'It'll be a tough nut to crack.'

Cato stared at Macro for a moment and then shook his head. 'Sometimes I swear that you think this is all some kind of game.'

'Game?' Macro looked surprised. 'No. It's better than that. It's a calling. It's what real soldiers live for. But of course you wouldn't understand. Being a philosopher and all that.'

Cato sighed. As far as Macro was concerned the extensive education that Cato had enjoyed before joining the legions was more of a curse than a benefit, as he never tired of making clear. For his part, Cato felt that the army was now his family and as long as he performed his duties as professionally as possible the cultural baggage he carried with him was irrelevant, except on those rare occasions when his esoteric knowledge might actually find some practical application. And then even Macro grudgingly relented, although he tried to conceal any flicker of admiration he might feel for Cato's learning.

Longinus held up his hands to still the angry tongues of his officers. 'Gentlemen! I know how you feel about this news. I share your grief and rage and I swear, by almighty Jupiter, that we will avenge Centurion Castor and his men. We will bring fire and the sword to the Parthians such that they never again dare to disturb the peace of our lands, and those of our allies. Our goal is nothing less than the elimination of Parthia as a military power, and we will not rest until their king kneels before the Emperor and begs for his mercy!'

The officers stamped their feet in approval and Macro nudged Cato. 'That's more like it. Longinus is my kind of general!'

Cato frowned. 'Have you forgotten why we were sent east in the first place?' He lowered his voice. 'The man was plotting against the Emperor.'

'We never proved that.'

'No,' Cato admitted. 'There is no conclusive proof, that is true. But we know what he was planning. We know the nature of the man, Macro. I don't trust him. Nor should you.'

Macro considered this for a moment and then scratched his chin with scarred knuckles. 'Maybe this is his chance to redeem himself.'

'Or maybe he is still trying to win a reputation, and a following, and make himself powerful enough to challenge the Emperor. Either way we should be wary of him. If he goes into this war recklessly, then we're in great danger.' Cato tipped his head towards the other officers in the hall. 'All of us. We need a soldier's general to lead us against the Parthians, not an ambitious politician. Besides, this campaign will present him with ample opportunity to get rid of us. Mark my words. We must be careful.'

Macro nodded thoughtfully. 'Fair enough.'

On the podium, Longinus signalled for quiet again. 'I have sent orders to the legates of the Third and Sixth Legions to join us here. As soon as the army is assembled we will march east and crush the Parthians. Until then, my comrades, we must ready our men for war. Every officer will prepare a full inventory of his equipment, recall any soldiers on detached duty and make all necessary requisitions. It is my intention that the army break camp the moment we are ready. You will receive your full orders for the coming campaign within days. I end with this thought . . . In the years to come, when we are all old men, people will look on us in wonder and say, there go the men who crushed Rome's oldest and deadliest enemy. If we triumph – no, when we triumph, as we certainly will, then we shall have won more than a victory. Our deeds will win us all a share of immortality, and no true Roman can wish for more than that.' Longinus drew his sword and stabbed the point into the air over his head. 'For Rome and victory!'

All around Cato and Macro the officers punched their fists into the air and echoed the cry. After a quick glance at Cato Macro followed suit and joined in the cheering with a lusty roar. Cato sighed and shook his head before joining in half-heartedly. Not for the first time, despite his hard-won sense of himself as a soldier, he felt detached from the hardy professionalism of the other officers. Up on the podium Cassius Longinus was milking the martial mood for all he was worth, turning to one section of the audience at a time and thrusting his sword up in the air. At length he sheathed the weapon and stood back from the podium as the senior centurion of the Tenth Legion stepped forward and slammed his vine cane down on the flagstone and bellowed, 'Dismissed!'

The officers turned and began to shuffle towards the doors, talking animatedly about the prospect of a new campaign. It would be the first action that many had seen since their posting to the province of Syria.

The wary balance of power that had existed between Parthia and Rome since the days of the first emperor, Augustus, had finally crumbled. The long game of diplomacy and subterfuge that had been played out between the agents of the two empires was over and now the clash of great armies would decide the conflict.

'Prefect Macro! Centurion Cato!'

Cato started at the shout echoing off the walls and with Macro he turned to see the senior centurion staring at them. 'Remain behind!'

'Shit,' Macro muttered as the nearest officers briefly shot them curious looks. 'What now?'

Cato shrugged his shoulders and began to ease his way through the crowd leaving the hall as he led the way towards the podium. Cato saw that Longinus and Legate Amatius were watching as he and Macro strode towards them. They stood before the podium as the last of the officers left the hall. Longinus nodded to the senior centurion.

'That's all. You may leave.'

'Yes, sir!' The centurion saluted smartly and turned to march after his comrades, nailed boots echoing across the flagstones. He left the hall, pulling the doors closed behind him, and then Longinus turned to Macro and Cato.

'There's one other matter to be resolved before my army goes to war. I have decided the fate of Legionary Crispus.'

All three subordinates stared intently at their commander as Longinus continued. 'In view of the gravity of the offence, and the utmost need to preserve discipline given the present circumstances, I have decided that Crispus must be put to death.'

'No!' Amatius shook his head. 'Sir, I protest. You gave me to believe that he would be spared.'

'I said no such thing,' Longinus snapped. 'Did I?'

Amatius sucked in a breath through clenched teeth. 'No, sir. But you implied it.'

'Implication is not proof.' Longinus glanced meaningfully at Macro and Cato before he continued. 'Crispus will be broken by the men of his century, before the assembled ranks of the Second Illyrian. At dawn tomorrow. You will communicate the news to the prisoner, Legate, and see that he is held securely until the execution is carried out. I have heard of incidents when condemned men have escaped in the past. If

47

Crispus is permitted to abscond, then the men assigned to guard him will take his place. Make sure that they understand that. Clear?'

Amatius swallowed his anger and turned to Macro with a bitter expression. 'I imagine you're delighted by the news.'

Macro stared back for a moment before he replied, 'If you imagine that, sir, then I fear that you will never understand the soldiers that you command.'

Amatius glared at Macro for an instant, then turned back to Longinus and stiffened his back. 'Is that all, sir?'

'That's all. Have Crispus' comrades report to the parade ground outside the camp at first light. They are to wear tunics only and be issued with cudgels.'

'Yes, sir.'

Amatius' tone was subdued and Cato could well understand why. The haughty legionaries would be humiliated by appearing before the auxiliaries of the Second Illyrian without their armour and weapons. That was quite deliberate. Army discipline demanded that the comrades of a condemned man shared his shame so that they would be sure to punish him for humbling them. In future, they might be more careful about letting another man commit an offence that would rebound on them. Since Amatius would be obliged to lead the party from the Tenth and bear witness to the execution, he too would take some small share of the shame, hence the smouldering hatred in his eyes as he glared at Macro and Cato briefly before striding from the hall, and slamming the door behind him with a crashing boom.

For a moment nothing was said, then Macro dipped his head in acknowledgement to Cassius Longinus.

'Thank you, sir. It was the right decision.'

'I don't need you to tell me that,' Longinus snapped.

'Very well, sir. But thank you anyway.' Macro paused. 'Is there anything else?'

'No. Just make sure this doesn't happen again. I've had enough of the pair of you interfering in my business in Syria. If it hadn't been for the Parthians I'd have got rid of you. By now you'd be well on your way back to Rome to report in person to that snake, Narcissus. As it is . . . I need every man I can scrape together to face the Parthians. There's no question that I would defeat them if I had the reinforcements I asked for. But there's only the three legions and a handful of auxiliary units available to take them on. The odds are not good.' Longinus smiled coldly. 'So if I succeed then the glory is greater. But if I fail, then I shall draw some small comfort from the knowledge that you two will be dying alongside me.'

Cato wondered at the change in Longinus' mood from the triumphalism of his address to his assembled officers. Then he realised that this was what Roman aristocrats trained so many years for: the perfectly pitched performance to win over their public, despite any personal misgivings over the cause that they were promoting. And Longinus had been persuasive enough, Cato reflected. It seemed that Cato alone had not been swept along on the wave of his rhetoric. Even Macro, who knew of the governor's dubious political manoeuvres, had been momentarily carried away by the prospect of action and glory.

'Leave me,' Longinus ordered. 'Go and make your preparations for the execution.'

He gestured casually towards the door. Macro and Cato stood to attention, saluted, and turned away, marching in step as they left the Roman governor of Syria alone in his makeshift audience chamber.

In the thin light of pre-dawn the men of the Second Illyrian were stirred from their tents by the harsh cries of their optios and centurions as the officers strode down the tent lines, yanking back the tent flaps and bellowing at the rudely awakened men inside. Hurriedly pulling on their rough woollen tunics, boots and chain-mail corselets, they emerged into the cool air before cramming on their skullcaps and helmets and tying the chin straps. Lastly, they gathered shields and javelins and took up their positions in the centuries forming in front of the tents. The cavalry squadrons, with their longer blades and thrusting spears, formed up on the flanks. Their mounts would not be needed for the assembly to bear witness to the execution, and they remained tethered in the horse lines, chewing contentedly on the barley in the feed bags that had been brought to them as soon as their riders had risen from their tents.

Macro, with Cato at his shoulder, paced down the lines inspecting his men. The execution of Crispus would be a formal affair. Even though the legionary was a condemned murderer he was still a soldier and would be accorded appropriate respect even as he died. Though the man he had killed was one of their comrades the men of the Second Illyrian would pay Crispus the honours due to a fellow soldier passing from this world into the shades. Every man had turned out neatly and had made sure that his helmet had been polished the night before, along with the trim and boss of his shield and every clasp and decorated facing of his scabbard. Macro regarded them with pride. He could ask for no better body of men to command, even in the legions, he admitted grudgingly, though he would never own up to such an opinion in public. The blood he had shed in the Second Legion and the comrades he had lost over the years had left him with an engrained love of the Eagles he had known for so long.

As he strode past the last of his men, Macro glanced round at Cato, who was the officer immediately responsible for the turnout of men on parade, as well as the numerous details of camp administration.

'A fine body of soldiers, Centurion Cato!' Macro's best parade-ground voice carried to the farthest men in the cohort. 'The Praetorian Guard itself couldn't have made a better showing!'

It was the kind of easy rhetoric calculated to lift the men's spirits and Macro winked at Cato as he bellowed his praise. Both men knew that, easy as the words were, they worked, and the men would carry themselves with a little more pride for the rest of the day. Or at least until they had witnessed the execution, Cato mused unhappily. He understood the reasoning behind the punishment well enough but still some part of him recoiled at the thought of brutally putting a man to death. Unlike Macro, he drew little pleasure from the games that ambitious politicians put on in every town and city of the Empire. If a man had to die then it was best that he die in pursuit of a purpose. Let Crispus be placed in the front rank of the army when they faced the Parthians. There at least he could die facing his enemy with a sword in his hand, for the honour of Rome, and his own personal redemption in the eyes of his comrades.

Cato drew a deep breath as he acknowledged Macro's comment. 'Yes, sir! No one can doubt that the Second Illyrian is the best cohort in the service of the Emperor!'

He turned towards the men and shouted. 'Let's hear it!'

The men let out a deafening roar and pounded their spears against their shields for a moment, and then grounded them as one. The abrupt silence made Macro chuckle with pleasure.

'As mean as they come, Centurion Cato. The Gods know what they'll do to the Parthians, but they scare the shite out of me!'

Cato, and many of the men, could not help grinning. Then Macro raised his vine cane to attract their attention once again.

'Move them out, Centurion.'

'Yes, sir.' Cato sucked in another breath. 'Second Illyrian, right face!'

The ten centuries of infantry and four squadrons of cavalrymen shouldered their spears and then turned on the spot.

Macro and Cato strode to the head of the column, and took up their places just ahead of the cohort's standard and the two bucinators carrying their curved brass instruments. Macro paused for an instant, then gave the order. 'Advance!'

With a rhythmic crunch of nailed boots the cohort marched towards the camp gate and out on to the parade ground. On the far side was the area assigned for the execution, where two rows of stakes ran six feet apart. Macro led the Second Illyrian across the dusty expanse and then halted the column.

'Cato, have them form up on three sides of the run.'

'Yes, sir.' Cato saluted and turned away to carry out his orders. Macro took his place at the head of the lines of stakes, on the side left open by the cohort. As the last of his men completed the open-sided box around the run Macro saw a small column of soldiers in red tunics leave the camp and march towards them. A figure, piniored between two men, half walked and was half dragged along in the middle of the column. Every one of his comrades carried a stout wooden stave: pick handles drawn from stores. At the rear of the column rode the governor and the legate of the Tenth. Macro called his men to attention at their approach and the cohort presented their arms as Longinus reined in. Amatius attended to his legionaries and assigned one man to each of the posts while Crispus was steered towards the end of the run. When every man was in place a hush hung over the scene, until Longinus raised his hand.

'By the power vested in me by the Emperor, the Senate and the People of Rome I hereby confirm the death sentence passed on Titus Crispus. Has the prisoner any last words before the sentence is carried out?' He turned to Crispus, but the legionary was breathing hoarsely and trembling as he stared at the two rows of his comrades in abject terror. Then the sense of the governor's words filtered through his fear and he glanced up at Longinus beseechingly.

'Sir, I beg you! Spare me. It was an accident! I swear it!' His legs collapsed and he slumped into the dust. 'Let me live!'

Longinus ignored the pleas and nodded to Amatius. 'Get on with it.'

The legate strode over to Crispus and growled, 'Stand up!'

Crispus tore his gaze away from the governor and threw himself across the ground at the feet of his legate.

'Sir, for pity's sake, I'm a good soldier! You know my record. Spare me! You can't do this.'

'Stand up!' Amatius shouted. 'Have you no shame? Is this how a legionary of the Tenth faces death? Get up.' He swung his boot at Crispus and it thudded into the prisoner's ribs.

'Ahhh!' Crispus gasped painfully as he clutched his side. Amatius grabbed his arm and roughly hauled Crispus to his feet, thrusting him towards the end of the run where his comrades waited, staves grasped firmly in both hands. For a moment there was silence across the parade ground, broken only by a faint keening whimper from Crispus. Then Longinus cleared his throat.

'Carry out the sentence!'

Amatius drew his sword as he pushed Crispus forward. The legionary dug his heels in and scrabbled backwards until the legate delivered a sharp jab into his back. Crispus screamed as the two lines of his comrades began to swing their clubs.

Cato had felt a growing sick sensation gnawing at his guts as he had watched the preparations and he whispered to Macro, 'Is there any chance of him making it to the far end?'

'There's always a chance,' Macro responded flatly.

'Have you ever seen a man survive the run?'

'No.'

Amatius drew his sword back for another thrust and Crispus cried out as he glanced over his shoulder.

'Go, man!' Amatius shouted angrily. 'Before you shame us all.'

Some spirit of defiance and courage must have gripped Crispus at the end, for he suddenly darted forward, into the run. He moved swiftly and ducked his head down low as he sprinted, so that the first two pairs had no chance to hit him with their clubs. But one of the third pair had just enough time to swing his club and strike home; a glancing blow off Crispus' shoulder. He staggered to one side, straight into the club of the next man who smashed him on the hip. Crispus cried out, but lurched on towards the next pair. The first man caught him on the upper arm, while the other struck him hard on the ribs, causing an explosive gasp of pain to rip from Crispus' lips. He stumbled on, under a rain of blows, until he was a quarter of the way down the run. Then a blow, swung low, smashed his shin and he crumpled to the ground with a scream. The nearest legionary stepped forward and swung his club at Crispus, cracking his jaw. Blood and teeth flew across the sand and Crispus rolled into a ball on his side, drawing his arms over his battered head. The nearest legionaries stared at him and then glanced towards their legate.

'Finish him!' Amatius thrust his finger at the figure on the ground. 'Finish him!'

The legionaries closed in around Crispus and Cato saw their clubs rise and fall in a frenzy of blows. The wooden shafts flicked blood into the air and their ends were stained with blood as they pounded Crispus mercilessly. Fortunately, there was no sound from the prisoner after the first few seconds. Amatius let his men continue for what seemed like an age to Cato, and all the time the rest of the witnesses stood and watched impassively.

At length Amatius called a halt to the beating, and the blood-spattered legionaries drew back, panting. On the ground, surrounded by splashes of blood soaking into the sand, lay the barely recognisable shape of a man. They had broken most of his limbs and his skull had been smashed to a pulp so that bone and brains spilled on to the sand in a mess of wine-red and grey porridge. Cato swallowed his bile and tore his gaze away from the sight, glancing up and across the parade ground. A distant movement caught his eye and then he squinted and saw a man on horseback racing round the corner of the fortress and making across the parade ground towards the execution party and the Second Illyrian. At the sound of drumming hooves, officers and men began to turn their attention towards the horseman.

'There's trouble,' Macro muttered as he saw the grimy bandage round the head of the approaching rider. At the last moment the rider reined in savagely, scattering dirt and gravel. He saluted and immediately reached inside his tunic, groping for something.

'Who the hell are you?' Longinus demanded.

The man licked his dried lips before he replied, 'Tribune Gaius Carinius, on detached duty from the Sixth Legion, sir. I've come from Palmyra.' He found what he was looking for and wrenched a waxed tablet from inside his tunic and thrust it towards the governor. 'A dispatch from the ambassador, Lucius Sempronius, at Palmyra, sir.'

Longinus took the tablet. He glanced at the rider. 'What's happened?'

The man swallowed hard, struggling for breath. 'There's been a revolt in Palmyra, sir. Parthian sympathisers. They mean to depose the king and tear up his treaty with Rome.'

CHAPTER SIX

Cato watched as the tribune eased himself on to one of the chairs that had been set in an arc in the governor's study. He glanced round at the other officers who had been summoned there by Cassius Longinus. In addition to Amatius and the commanders of the other auxiliary cohorts in the camp, there was Macro and himself. Cato wondered why he had been included.

Longinus gestured towards the tribune, who still bore the grime of his hard ride. He had only had a brief chance to take refreshments while the officers had been hurriedly assembled in the governor's house. 'Carinius, if you please. Tell them what you told me while we were waiting.'

Carinius nodded, and cleared his throat. 'Five days ago the youngest son of King Vabathus, Prince Artaxes, announced to the Palmyran court that he would succeed his father.' Tribune Carinius paused to smile briefly. 'The trouble is that Artaxes is the youngest of the three sons, and so not immediately in line to inherit the throne. However, the oldest son, Amethus, is not politically astute and the second son, Balthus, spends all his days hunting, drinking and womanising. Artaxes is definitely the brains of the family, as well as the biggest threat to Rome. He was sent east as a child to be educated at the Parthian court. It seems that somewhere in his education he learned to hate Rome with a passion, and he has managed to persuade many of the Palmyran nobles to share his views.'

'I see.' Amatius nodded. 'But surely the king would not tolerate such a challenge to his authority?'

Longinus tapped the waxed tablet sent by the Roman quaestor who served as Rome's ambassador at the court of King Vabathus. 'The king is old. And Artaxes is his favourite son. The only thing to divide his affections is his loyalty to Rome. But who knows how far that loyalty will stretch in the current situation? Sempronius says that Thermon, the king's chamberlain, acts in his name. He, at least, is dependable. So he should be given the amount we pay him on the quiet. According to the ambassador, Artaxes demanded the crown at once. The chamberlain refused and fighting broke out amongst their supporters. Artaxes had managed to win over one of the king's generals and has nearly a thousand men under his control. Thermon could only count on the king's bodyguard and the households of those nobles who remained loyal to the king. And Sempronius and his retinue, of course. They have retreated into the citadel, together with the king and his oldest son.'

'What of the other son, the hunter?' asked Cato. 'What's happened to him?'

Longinus turned to the tribune. 'Well?'

'Balthus was hunting in the hills to the north when Artaxes made his move. There was still no word of him when the quaestor sent me to find you, sir.'

'Too bad,' Macro commented. 'We could use him on our side right now.'

'I wouldn't be too sure of that,' said the tribune. 'Balthus is no great lover of Rome. We're just fortunate he hates the Parthians, and only dislikes us.'

Macro cocked his head to one side. 'Well, my enemy's enemy and all that. He could still prove useful to us.'

'Perhaps,' Longinus considered. 'But we'll use him only if we really have to. The last thing Rome needs is to remove one threat only to have another put in its place. In any case, as far as we know the king and his allies are trapped in the citadel at Palmyra. According to Sempronius' message they have adequate of food and water and as long as Artaxes doesn't get hold of any siege equipment then they should be able to hold the citadel for a while yet. Of course, we can assume that our Parthian friends had some advance warning of Artaxes' intentions. Even if they didn't, word will have reached them a matter of days after it reached us. So at best we have the slimmest of head starts, gentlemen. We must send help to King Vabathus.'

Amatius shook his head. 'But, sir, the army is not ready. The other legions haven't even left their bases yet. Even the Tenth is not prepared to march. Many of my men are on detached duties and it will take several days to concentrate the legion. It's the same with most of the auxiliary cohorts. Some of them have only just arrived here.'

'There is one cohort that is ready to move,' Longinus responded. 'The Second Illyrian. Is that not so, Prefect?'

Macro started and then leaned forward a little as he nodded. 'My lads could be on the road to Palmyra within the hour, sir. We could reach Palmyra in ten days if we went flat out.'

'Good. Then that's what we'll do,' Longinus decided. 'The Second Illyrian will make for Palmyra immediately while the rest of the army prepares to march. The other legions will follow us the moment they are ready to move.'

'That's all very well, sir,' said Cato, 'but what exactly is the Second Illyrian supposed to do when it reaches Palmyra? We'll be outnumbered, and the chances are that the rebels will hold the city walls. How are we going to help those trapped in the citadel?'

'Your job is to reinforce them, Centurion. Help Vabathus hold out until the main force arrives.'

'But, sir, even if we can gain entrance to the city, we'll have to cut our way through hostile streets to the citadel.'

'Yes, I imagine so.'

Cato looked at the governor helplessly. Clearly the man had no idea what he was asking of the Second Illyrian.

Macro came to his support. 'The lad's right, sir. It can't be done. Not by one cohort.'

Longinus smiled. 'Which is why I'm not just sending the Second Illyrian. I'm not a fool, Macro. I know how difficult a task this is. I'll not send anyone on a suicide mission. That would not look good back in Rome. So, in addition to the Second Illyrian I'm sending a cohort of the Tenth Legion, together with their cavalry scouts. Since Centurion Castor has been killed on detached duty his cohort needs a new commander. I've decided that you're the best man for the job. You will also command the relief force.'

'And who will lead the Second Illyrian?' asked Macro.

Longinus gestured towards Cato. 'Your adjutant. He will be acting prefect until the crisis is over.'

'Him?' Amatius raised his eyebrows. 'But he's too young. Too inexperienced. Let Macro remain in command of his auxiliaries, sir, and I'll find an officer from within the legion to replace Centurion Castor.'

'No, I've made my decision. Macro is the best man available. Besides, there's no time to debate the issue. Castor's cohort and the Second Illyrian are to set off at once. Those are my orders, gentlemen. My clerks will give you your instructions before you leave the camp, Macro. The rest of you will have your orders as soon as they are drafted. Dismissed.'

'What the hell do you make of all that?' Macro jerked his thumb back in the direction of the governor's house as he and Cato strode down the street. 'Sending an advance column to save the king of Palmyra's arse is about as stupid an idea as I have ever heard.'

'Then why didn't you say so?'

Macro glanced at his friend sharply. 'We don't make policy, Cato, we just obey orders. Besides, it might just work. If we can find a way through to the citadel.'

'If?' Cato shook his head. 'That's a bloody big if.'

Macro was silent for a moment and then forced a laugh. 'Well, you heard him, Cato. If there's anyone who can do this, it's me. Best man for the job. His exact words.'

'You really think so?'

Macro pursed his lips. 'It would be nice if it was true. Perhaps Longinus thinks it's true.'

'Perhaps,' Cato replied flatly. 'And perhaps Longinus thinks that this might be the best chance he has of getting rid of us.'

'Eh?'

'You have to admire the way he thinks,' Cato continued. 'It would have been easy to send us to certain death, by just dispatching the Second Illyrian to Palmyra. And he was right, Narcissus would have seen through it in an instant. The deliberately arranged destruction of his two agents in Syria would have confirmed his suspicions about Longinus. This way he can argue that he sent a force strong enough for the job. Who in Rome would doubt that a cohort of legionaries was not sufficient for the task? If we succeed he reaps the rewards of acting swiftly and decisively. If we don't, then we'll be tarred with the brush of failure. That's even if we survive. And of course, our destruction will add weight to his request for those

58

reinforcements he has been angling for all along. Oh, he's a shrewd one, that Longinus.'

Macro suddenly stopped and turned to face his companion. 'Cato, did you really just think all that up?'

Cato looked bemused. 'It seems to make sense.'

'Really?' Macro sighed. 'You know, it is also possible that Longinus thinks that this might work. That we might arrive with enough force to save the king and hold out until the rest of the army arrives.'

'Assuming that Longinus and the army set off in time to rescue us.'

'Bloody hell, Cato!' Macro cried out in bewilderment. 'Why is everything a conspiracy to you? Why do you assume that everyone above the rank of centurion is scheming to become emperor?'

People in the street were looking in their direction and Cato hissed, 'Keep it down!'

'Or what? Someone will report us to Narcissus' agents? Cato, we *are* his bloody agents. So I'll say what I damn well please. Why do you think every man in the Roman senate is involved in a conspiracy?'

'How do you know that they aren't?'

'Oh, come on!' Macro fumed, and then started marching off down the street again. 'We haven't got time for this. Let's go.'

They walked on in silence for a moment before Macro clicked his fingers. 'Well, what about Vespasian then?'

Cato recalled the legate they had served under in the Second Legion during the invasion of Britain. Vespasian's family had only been elevated to senatorial rank in recent years, and so he had a measure of understanding of the men he commanded. 'What about him?'

'He was as straight as they come. A soldier to the bone that one. Not a grain of politician in him.'

Cato thought a moment and then shook his head. 'He's an aristocrat, like the rest of them. They are breastfed on politics. But I agree with you. He seemed straightforward enough. Even so, I shouldn't wonder if even Vespasian surprised us all in the end.'

Macro snorted with derision and they continued their fast-paced march back to the camp in silence.

The instant they arrived Macro summoned his centurions and explained the situation to them, and confirmed Cato's temporary appointment as prefect.

'I'll see you on the track outside the camp. Make 'em travel light. Weapons, minimal kit and rations only. Spare rations can be carried on the light carts.'

'Yes, sir. I understand. They'll have what they need.'

'Right then.' Macro thumped Cato gently on the shoulder. 'Time for me to rejoin the Eagles.'

He left his subordinate to give the orders for the men to make ready to leave the camp and went to take up his command of Castor's cohort of the Tenth Legion. The governor's clerk was waiting for him outside the headquarters tent. He had run hard from the general's house in the city and was panting for breath as he handed a sealed tablet to Macro.

'Your authority to assume command, sir . . . and the general's orders.'

Macro nodded curtly and entered the tent. Inside, a pair of veterans sat on stools at their desks and hurriedly tried to look busy as the officer entered. Macro pointed to the nearest man.

'You! Fetch my officers. I want them here at once. Tell them the cohort has a new commander. And you, get word to their optios, and tell them to ready the men for a hard march and' – he grinned – 'an even harder fight.'

As soon as the men were formed up Cato made a close inspection of each century. The man he had selected as his adjutant, Centurion Parmenion, the oldest and most experienced of the auxiliary officers, marched at his shoulder with a tablet and stylus, ready to take notes for his commander. It was funny, Cato mused. Only this morning he had been in Parmenion's job, and well knew the burdens that his replacement had taken on. But it was nothing compared to the weight of responsibility that had now landed on Cato's shoulders. More than eight hundred men now looked to him and he would be directly compared to Macro in their judgement of him. It would be a hard standard to live up to, he reflected grimly. Still, it was not as if he was a new commander, freshly appointed to the cohort, and anxious to prove himself. He had served with the Second Illyrian for nearly a year and had fought alongside most of them. So they knew him well enough and accepted him. But he was aware that they would be measuring him by a new standard and watching him closely now that he was the prefect of the cohort, albeit temporarily.

Cato's eye was drawn to a man just ahead of him, swaying slightly as he stood in line. He quickened his step and drew up suddenly in front of the auxiliary.

'Name?'

The auxiliary, an older man whom Cato recognised as one of the new recruits Macro had brought in, stiffened and tried to stand as erect and still as he could, but the raw reek of cheap wine gave him away.

'Publius Galenus, sir.'

'Well, Galenus, it appears that you are not quite sober.'

'No, sir.'

'You are aware that being drunk on duty is an offence.'

'Yes, sir.'

'In which case, you're pulling extra fatigues for a week and will be docked ten days' pay.'

'That ain't fair, sir,' Galenus grumbled. 'I wasn't on duty an hour ago. None of us were. We was all looking forward to a night on the town and I decided to get some drink in early – you know what crooks them local wine merchants are – then we get the call to arms, and, well . . .' he glanced at Cato, 'here we are, sir.'

'Indeed.'

For a moment Cato was about to cancel the man's punishment. Galenus had a point. He could hardly be blamed for the vagaries of military timing. But then, Cato had already spoken and to change his mind would be an admission of indecision. He wondered briefly what Macro would do and the answer was clear.

'Parmenion. Mark this man down for fatigues and the fine. Drunk on duty is the offence, whatever the circumstances.'

Galenus frowned blearily. 'But that ain't fair, sir.'

Cato continued to address Centurion Parmenion. 'Add ten nights on double watch for insubordination.'

Galenus' jaw dropped open, then some reserve of self-control came to the rescue and he clamped it shut as Parmenion made notes on his wax tablet with swift strokes of his stylus. Cato strode on. He completed the inspection and was satisfied that every man was carrying only the necessary equipment and supplies, according to their orders. Then he mounted the horse that was being held for him by an orderly and trotted it up to the head of the column.

'Second Illyrian!' he called out, and paused for an instant to relish the fact that he was now Prefect Cato, about to lead his men to war. 'Advance!'

The auxiliary cohort tramped out of the camp gates and marched towards the road leading to Palmyra. It was not yet noon but the sun beat down on the parched earth without mercy and the familiar clinging dust was scraped up by the nailed boots of the soldiers and the hooves of the horses and hung in the air like a faint mist.

As they turned the corner of the fortress Cato saw that Macro's cohort was already formed up on the track, waiting. As the Second Illyrian marched up to join the end of the column Macro rode towards Cato and raised a hand in greeting.

'What kept you?'

Cato raised his eyebrows and replied good-humouredly. 'We came as fast as we could, sir.'

Macro frowned at his tone, and Cato realised that his friend was once again the consummate professional at the prospect of action.

'I'm sorry, sir. We won't delay you again.'

'Make sure you don't.' Macro turned and nodded down the track stretching out ahead of them. 'We're going to have the hardest of marches, and then a fight at the end of it, Cato. Make no mistake about it, this is going to be the toughest campaign we've ever known.'

CHAPTER SEVEN

Macro led his two cohorts at an unflagging pace into the parched hills east of Antioch. By day the sun blazed down mercilessly on the small column, and at night the temperature dropped sharply so that the men shivered as they gathered round their campfires and chewed on dried meat and hard bread. The first evening the men grumbled bitterly about having to sleep in the open and then after an uncomfortable night they were back on the road while the stars still glittered in the velvet darkness. For the first two days he permitted them only the briefest of rests at midday and by the time the column stopped, when there was no longer light to see the way ahead the men were too tired to complain about the lack of tents. They simply stumbled into rough sleeping lines, dropped their kit and curled up on the ground, falling asleep almost at once. There they lay, until stirred to take their turn on watch duty.

The orders from Longinus were explicit on the need for speed. Macro was to march for as many hours as he could, and was not to construct a marching camp at the end of each day. As a soldier who had many years of campaign experience Macro was wretchedly disturbed by the need to sacrifice security for celerity. In order to compensate for the lack of a ditch and rampart he doubled the watches every night and posted cavalry vedettes for good measure. The burden of extra watch-keeping duties compounded the exhaustion of the day's march and by the third day a small number of men had begun to straggle, and did not catch up with the main body until late in the evening.

'This can only get worse,' Cato muttered as he watched the dark figures of the last men to arrive fumble through the dark lines stretching out across the rock-strewn ground, searching for their units. 'In a day or two they will no longer be able to catch up with us. They'll be strung out along the route. Easy pickings for any bandits, or the enemy.'

'Can't be helped,' Macro replied, and then yawned as he eased himself back against his saddle bag and arranged his heavy military cloak across his body. 'There's bound to be a few slackers in any cohort. A few days of marching always finds them out.'

'Slackers?' Cato shook his head. 'I saw some good men fall out of the column this afternoon. If we keep this pace up then those who actually make it as far as Palmyra will be in no shape to fight.'

'Oh, they'll fight,' Macro replied confidently. 'Or they'll die.'

'I wish I shared your optimism.'

Macro turned towards Cato and in the faint loom of the stars Cato could see his friend's amused expression.

'What? What's so bloody funny?'

'Who said I was an optimist? I'm just telling you how it is. How it has always been for a soldier on campaign. You think we had it hard in Britain? That was a walk in the forum compared to the desert. This land is as much a danger to us as the enemy. Once we reach Chalcis we'll have over a hundred miles to go before we arrive at Palmyra.' Macro rolled on to his back and tucked an arm beneath his head. 'This is the easy part, Cato. You wait until we reach the open desert. Then you, and the men, will really have something to complain about. Almost no chance of finding any water on the way, according to the governor's instructions. The men will have to carry enough water to last five, maybe six, days when we leave Chalcis. I have no idea what condition they'll be in when we reach Palmyra. But I do know that they will have the fight of their lives.'

'Then it might be advisable to give them some opportunity to rest before they fight,' Cato persisted. 'These double watches are not helping things. We're still a long way from Palmyra.'

'Cato, you saw how easily that Parthian prince and his men slipped through our outposts and turned up on the governor's doorstep.' Macro jerked a thumb towards the horizon. 'Who's to say they're not out there watching us right now? Waiting for the chance to attack. I'll not take that risk. In fact,' he reflected, 'we'd better not have any more campfires from now on. Just in case the enemy are out there. I'd sooner the men were cold and tired than dead. Besides—' He broke off and yawned. 'We've got more immediate difficulties.'

'Oh?'

'Yes. The officers and lads of my cohort are not best pleased to have me appointed as their new commander. As if the execution of Crispus wasn't bad enough, they've had the former commander of Crispus' victim foisted on them. Bit of a slap in the face. Makes you wonder if the governor wanted to cause us even more trouble on the road to Palmyra.'

'I shouldn't be surprised,' Cato replied bleakly. 'Another twist of the knife. What have your lads been saying, then?'

'Nothing to my face. It's more the tone of their comments and the generally sour ambience whenever I'm around. Of course, I don't give a flying fuck about how they feel towards me. Just as long as they do as they're told. All the same, we'd better keep an eye out for any further trouble between the legionaries and the auxiliaries. Last thing we need is for them to be watching their backs when they should be looking out for the enemy.'

'Quite.' Cato took a last glance round the camp before he eased himself down on to the ground and tried to make himself comfortable under his cloak. But despite the heat of the day the nights were cold and he could not help shivering. He knew that it would be a while before he managed to get to sleep, if he ever did.

'Macro?'

'Hmm?' Macro grumbled drowsily. 'What? What is it?'

'What are your plans when we reach Palmyra?'

'Plans?' Macro paused before replying. 'Longinus did not have much to say on that front. Just that we are to cut through to the citadel and hold it until he arrives.'

'That's assuming that Artaxes and his followers haven't taken the citadel yet.'

'Yes.'

'And if they have?'

'Then we've pretty much had it. Our water will be finished by then so there'll be no possibility of retreat. We'll have to take Palmyra by ourselves, or surrender.' Macro chuckled. 'It's the same old story. Death or disgrace. Some choice, eh?'

'Some choice,' Cato agreed quietly.

'Still, nothing to be done about it,' Macro concluded. 'So do me a favour and shut up and get some sleep. We need all we can get.'

Macro turned his back to Cato and pulled his cloak tightly round his stocky body. A short time later he was asleep and his rumbling snores added to the more distant chorus of the other men, broken here and there by the low voices of the restless and the occasional snort and whinny from the horse lines. But there was no sleep for Cato as his mind dwelt on the situation. The odds were stacking up against them and while he understood the need for the governor to send a relief force to Palmyra it appeared to Cato that their mission was little more than a desperate gesture. King Vabathus might already be dead, along with the ambassador and his small retinue. Even now Artaxes could be cementing his grip on the throne, and throwing his kingdom open to Parthia. If that happened then the delicate balance of power that had kept the peace in the east of the Empire would be shattered. Parthia would be able to mass its fast-moving army on the very frontier of Syria and threaten Roman territory from Armenia to Egypt. Emperor Claudius would be forced to reinforce his eastern armies at huge expense, and strip legions from the Rhine frontier, already thinly stretched. That, or abandon huge swathes of land to Parthia and risk the ire of the mob and political rivals in Rome.

It could all have been avoided, Cato realised. If only Rome had been content to leave Palmyra as a buffer between the empire and Parthia then peace could have lasted, albeit an uneasy peace. But the moment the treaty had been signed with King Vabathus, a confrontation with Parthia was assured. Cato felt a cold rage grow within him as he contemplated the policymakers back in Rome, living lives of luxury far from the consequences of their power play. Perhaps they had calculated that their designs on Palmyra justified the risk of provoking the Parthians, as one might wager a stake on the roll of a dice. But here on the frontier that stake was measured in the lives of the men sleeping in the darkness all around Cato. Men whose endurance would be stretched to the limit in the days ahead, before they even had the chance to close with the enemy. If they won, then a token would be shifted fractionally on the map of the Empire back in Claudius' palace in Rome. If they lost, then the token would be casually swept from the board and discarded.

Cato smiled bitterly at the thought, and cursed himself for possessing this cruel streak of detachment that caused him to view his actions in the widest context. For a while he glanced at Macro's slumbering form with envy. Finally, a long time after almost all the other soldiers had fallen still and silent, Cato eventually drifted off into a troubled sleep on the cold, hard ground.

The next day the column left the hills and emerged on to the rolling dusty plain on the road to Chalcis. Despite Macro's concerns, they encountered only the usual trade caravans from which the men hurriedly bought fruit and wine at vastly inflated prices. All the while the number of stragglers increased and by the time they reached Chalcis, three days after leaving Antioch, Cato saw from his strength returns that eight men of the Second Illyrian had failed to reach the camp in time for that morning's roll-call. He sat in the shade of the palm trees that fringed the small lake on whose bank the town of Chalcis squatted. Like the other towns that had been founded on the ancient trade routes, Chalcis profited from levying taxes on the caravans of camels that passed through its territory, and its inhabitants lived with an enviable degree of comfort. But now, news of the revolt in Palmyra and rumours of the inevitable conflict between Rome and Parthia had unsettled the people and small crowds gathered to watch the Roman column as it marched up to the town and halted to rest and fill its canteens and spare waterskins at the lake.

Cato could well understand their anxiety. The isolation that made peace so profitable for Chalcis also made it vulnerable in time of war, and its strategic importance meant that it would be contested by both sides. The income from trade would dry up and the town faced hard times, if it survived at all. Cato focused his mind on the strength returns on the waxed slate that Centurion Parmenion had brought to him.

'Eight men now. I wonder how many more we will have lost by the time we reach Palmyra?'

'Shall I send a cavalry squadron back to round them up, sir?'

Cato considered this for a moment and shook his head. 'If they're able to, they'll find us. But I'll not lose any more men than I have to by sending out search parties. Mark them down as absent without leave. If they fail to catch up by tomorrow morning then put them down as deserters.'

'Very well, sir.' Parmenion scored a note on his tablet and Cato watched him for a moment before speaking in a low voice.

'What's the mood of our men?'

Parmenion looked up at his commander, then glanced round to make sure that they would not be overheard. 'Not too bad, considering.'

'Considering what?'

Parmenion nodded towards the legionaries sitting beneath the palms a short distance from the men and horses of the Second Illyrian. 'There's still plenty of bad blood over that business in Antioch. The legionaries are needling our lads at every opportunity. Frankly, they're spoiling for a fight.'

'Who, our men, or Macro's?'

'Both.' Parmenion wearily rubbed the bristles on his chin. 'Wouldn't take much to set them at each other's throats.'

'We must see that it doesn't happen,' Cato said firmly. 'I want you to pass the word on to the other centurions and their optios. We can't afford any trouble. I'll come down like a bloody avalanche on any man who causes a fight. Make sure that's understood.'

'Yes, sir.'

'Very well then, Parmenion. Carry on.'

His adjutant closed his wax tablets, saluted and then strode off towards the handful of mule carts that carried the cohort's records, pay chest and small stock of spare weapons and rations. A party of auxiliaries was busy loading the filled waterskins and baskets of fruit and dried meat bought from the market in Chalcis. Cato regarded them for a moment, and wondered briefly if he had allowed for adequate supplies to see his men across the desert to Palmyra. It had been a difficult calculation. Of all the supplies that a commander had to provide for his men, water was the most onerous, thanks to its weight, and propensity to find the means of spilling or leaking. If they carried too much water on the carts it would slow their progress. But if too little was loaded and the column was delayed by a sandstorm, or enemy action, then it would run out and the men would suffer the agonies of thirst that desert conditions swiftly made so acute.

A flash of red caught his eye and he saw Macro emerge from the city gate, striding back towards his column. As he reached the carts Macro caught sight of Cato and made directly for him.

'Don't get up!' he called out as Cato made to rise and stand formally at attention. A moment later he squatted down heavily beside

Cato and untied the chin straps of his helmet, removing it with a sigh of relief.

'Was that necessary?' Cato nodded. 'The helmet, I mean.'

'I think so.' Macro mopped his sweaty brow on the back of his forearm. 'There's bound to be some kid in Chalcis with a sling and Parthian sympathies. Why take the risk?'

'Fair enough. Any news from Palmyra?'

Macro had made it his priority to visit the ruling council of Chalcis the moment the column had arrived. He lowered his arm and nodded.

'A Greek merchant and his family arrived at dawn. The situation in Palmyra doesn't look good for our side. The king and his followers are still holding the citadel, while Artaxes controls the surrounding streets. Seems that he doesn't have full control over his men. They've started looting the city. That's why the merchant has fled the place. He has young daughters. Probably the wise thing to do.'

Cato nodded.

'He also provided me with a map of the city,' Macro continued as he pulled a flattened scroll of papyrus from his harness and unrolled it. Placing it on the ground he weighted the corners with stones while Cato leaned forward and briefly examined the diagram. It had clearly been drafted in a hurry and lacked any detail. Only the outline of the walls and the most important districts had been depicted.

'Not much to go on,' Cato ventured.

'Well, it's all we have, for now. The Greek merchant did his best for me.' Macro glanced up with a thin smile. 'Before you ask, I did put it to him that we needed someone with local knowledge and could use him as a guide.'

'What did he say?'

'Something colourful. Diligent as I have been in my studies of the language in recent months, it was a word I was unfamiliar with. But his response was, in a word, no.'

'A pity.'

'But he did tell me a bit about the ground.' Macro indicated the flattened semicircle of Palmyra's walls. 'The defences are in good order, he claims, so we will need to gain entrance by a gate. The citadel is here.' Macro tapped an arrangement of black boxes at the right of the diagram.

'Then we can skirt round the city and enter the citadel directly,' Cato observed hopefully.

'Sorry, sunshine. It ain't going to be that easy. The citadel is built on a low bluff of rock on the wall. There's no access there. There's only one entrance into the citadel inside Palmyra. According to the merchant the best way into the city for us is here, a gate on the east side of Palmyra. It's the most direct route to the entrance to the citadel.'

'That means going through the streets.' Cato shook his head as he considered the prospect. 'If we have to fight our way in, then the rebels will be able to hit us from all sides, and from the roofs. If they get any advance warning they can block our route. If we lose our direction . . .'

'I can imagine the details, thank you,' Macro responded tersely. 'But for now that's the only plan we have. Like it or bloody lump it.'

Cato raised his eyebrows in resignation, and then continued, 'Did your merchant have anything else to tell us?'

'I got as much from him as I could. The citadel is well fortified and the king's bodyguard are the pick of his army. Tough cases, every one of 'em. So says the Greek, but he's no soldier, so we'll have to take that comment with a pinch of salt. But there is one good piece of news. The Palmyran siege weapons are stored in a compound inside the citadel. So Artaxes is going to have to build his kit from scratch before he can manage an assault. Buys us a little more time at any rate?'

'What about the size of Artaxes' forces? What did the Greek know of their numbers?'

'He says that Artaxes has a huge army at his command.' Macro spat with contempt. 'It's probably the first mob the merchant has ever seen. He couldn't tell me if there was one thousand of them or ten thousand. He just didn't have a clue. But he did say that Artaxes is telling everyone that a Parthian army is on its way to help him, and when it arrives, then those in the citadel and anyone who does not swear an oath of loyalty to him will be put to death.'

'We can assume that it's true,' Cato reflected. 'After all, Longinus put a force into the field the moment he was aware of the situation. There's every reason to believe that the Parthians would do the same. In which case, it's all down to which side reaches Palmyra first.'

'My thoughts exactly.' Macro nodded, and rolled up his map. 'So we'd better get the lads back on the road as soon as we can.'

A short time later, the column resumed its march and the men could only glance wistfully at the sparkling surface of the lake as they marched along its bank. They had had only the briefest of opportunities to fill their canteens and rest in the shade of the palms and only a handful had had the chance to immerse themselves in the cool water before the orders to pick up their packs and fall in had been bellowed out, rousing the men from the comfortable shade of the trees. The people of Chalcis watched them for a while before drifting back to their homes to anxiously contemplate the future.

On the far side of the lake the route to Palmyra abruptly branched off through a strip of irrigated farmland, and then gave out on to the desert. Cato's heart sank as he contemplated the flat expanse of pallid yellow sand and rock that stretched ahead into the distance, where the horizon was lost in a shimmering band of hot air that looked like molten silver. The column marched on into the afternoon heat, gradually leaving behind the thin strip of palm-fringed green that marked the lake, until it too was swallowed up by the stifling air that wavered far off in every direction.

Parmenion took one last glance over his shoulder before he turned to Cato and grumbled, 'Five days of this, at least, before we reach Palmyra. When I get there, I'm going to make those rebel bastards pay for every step of the way.'

CHAPTER EIGHT

Each day began with the same ritual. At the first glimmer of light on the horizon the duty centurion of each cohort woke the other officers. They in turn moved down the lines of sleeping men, shouting the order to rise and prepare to march, pausing here and there to stick the boot into any man slow to respond. With groans and the stretching of cold, stiff limbs the men stood and shook off the sand that had blown over them during the night. They attached their equipment to their marching yokes and then ate a quick meal of dried meat and hard bread from the rations in their haversacks and washed it down with a few mouthfuls of water. Every centurion and optio was conscious of the need to make the water last as long as possible and closely supervised their men as they drank from their canteens.

Once the men had formed into their centuries there was a quick roll-call and then Macro gave the order to begin the day's march. As dawn lightened the sky the air was still and cool and the cohorts marched in an easy rhythm, the heavy crunch of their nailed boots accompanied by the irregular slap and jingle of loose equipment, and muted conversation. The early hours were the most comfortable time of the day to march and Macro deliberately kept the pace up, before the day's heat smothered the desert in its searing embrace. Before this campaign Cato had thought that dawn was the most beautiful time of the day. Now, as the sun rose over the horizon, casting long shadows across the desert plain, he quickly came to regard it as a source of torment.

Gradually the shadows shortened and the light strengthened into a dazzling glare that caused the men to squint their eyes and keep their gaze cast down as they tramped further into the wasteland. Then came the heat. Quickly overpowering the last of the cool dawn air, it wrapped itself around the men of the two cohorts. Now, seasoned veteran and fresh-faced recruit alike began to feel the weight of their equipment and their yokes pressed on to their shoulders as they set their expressions into grim masks and put one foot in front of the other and tried not to think of the remainder of the day stretching ahead of them. As the sun climbed higher and higher into the sky the men became drenched with perspiration that for many caused a hot prickling sensation under their military tunics which became unbearable as the day wore on.

Finally, as the sun neared its zenith, Macro called a halt and the men downed their yokes with weary sighs and groans, before slumping down and taking the midday drink from their canteens. Then they made what shade they could from their shields and cloaks and rested until the midday heat had passed, and the order was given to make ready to continue the march. Back on their feet, the men raised their yokes again and formed up on the track. Then, as the order was given, they shuffled forward into a leaden stride for the rest of the afternoon until the sun slipped towards the horizon. Only as the light faded did the day's march end.

On the third night after leaving Chalcis Cato organised the watches and then went to report to Macro. Several more of his men had fallen behind during the march and three of the cavalry horses had gone lame. Under normal circumstances the beasts would be slaughtered and the meat distributed to the men to cook. But since they were not construct-ing marching camps Macro had forbidden the lighting of any fires – not that much of a fire could be built from the pitiful stunted growths they had occasionally encountered beside the track – so the animals were killed and their carcasses left in the wake of the two cohorts.

Macro was standing on a small rise, a short distance from his men, surveying the ground ahead of them in the gathering dusk. He turned as he heard the sound of Cato's boots approaching. Forcing a smile on to his cracked lips Macro waved a greeting.

'Two more days of this, and it's over, Cato. Just two more days.'

'It'll be over one way or another.'

'True. But we'll deal with the situation in Palmyra when we get to it.'

Cato could sense that his friend was exhausted, and nodded. 'Of course. Let's just get through this.'

Macro stared at him a moment and then laughed at the concern in

Cato's tone. 'You sound like my mother. I'm all right, really.' He gazed back over the desert. 'I was just wondering why anyone would want to fight over possession of a land like this. It's a wasteland.'

'It's a wasteland with a city perched on top of a lucrative trade route right next to an oasis,' Cato replied.

Macro nodded slowly and then pursed his lips. 'Well, if you put it like that . . .'

A sudden burst of angry shouting caused them both to turn back towards their camp. Several men were clustered round the cart from which the canteens were being replenished. As the two officers watched, more men emerged from the surrounding dusk.

'Bugger! More trouble,' Macro sighed at the chorus of raised voices. 'Come on. Sound like that will carry a long way across the desert.'

They scrambled down from the low mound and ran across to the cart.

'Out of the way there!' Macro called out as loudly as he dared. In the gloom it was difficult for the men to make out his rank as he thrust his way through the crowd. Cato grabbed an arm and forcefully hauled a soldier out of Macro's path. 'Make way for your commanding officer, damn you!'

Ahead of him a handful of men were locked in a savage fight, fists and boots flailing at each other. Macro raised his vine staff and swung it out in an arc ahead of him. It connected with a sharp crack and a man fell back with a cry, hands clutched to his head.

'Stop this bloody nonsense at once!' Macro shouted briefly, and slashed his cane at two men who were still swinging their fists at each other. 'At once, I said!'

The fighting stopped abruptly and those involved drew apart as Macro stood his ground by the back of the cart and glared at the crowd, a mixture of auxiliaries and legionaries.

'What the hell is going on? Where's the optio in charge of the water distribution?'

'Here, sir.' An auxiliary officer rose up unsteadily from the ground.

'Report, man! What's the meaning of this?'

The optio stood to attention. He glanced quickly at the men surrounding him and swallowed nervously. 'Sir, there was a misunderstanding.'

Macro snorted with derision. 'I should fucking say so! Now what the hell is going on?'

The optio realised that there was no chance of keeping the situation a ranker affair and continued in a monotone.

'I was on duty, sir. Supervising the water rations. The canteen carriers from the Second Illyrian came up first, just ahead of the lads from the Tenth. As I start filling the canteens one of the legionaries pushes into the line and demands his section's share before I'd finished with my lads. I told him to wait his turn. He told me that legionaries come first, and that my lads would have to give way for . . . well, for real soldiers, he said.'

'Which man said this?'

The optio glanced over Macro's shoulder, but before he could identify the legionary the man stepped forward.

'It was me, sir.'

Macro turned to the man and quickly sized him up. 'And you are?'

'Decimus Tadius, sir. Sixth Century.'

'And what exactly did you think you were doing, soldier?'

'Sir, it was like he said. The legions always take the first share of whatever's going.'

'That applies to booty, Tadius, and you know it. Not rations. And certainly not rations in this situation. Every man gets his fair share, in his turn, while I'm in command. Whether he's an auxiliary or a legionary.' Macro stepped up to Tadius and rapped his vine cane on the man's segmented armour. 'Got that?'

'Yes, sir.'

'Good, because if you cause any more trouble, I'll chuck you out of my cohort and have you serve with the Second Illyrian. Then you might learn something.'

Tadius opened his mouth to protest.

'Don't!' Macro warned him. 'Now, the rest of you, get back in line and take your water in turn. Now move!'

'Wait,' Cato added softly to Tadius as the other men shuffled away. 'Not you, Tadius. Stand still.'

Macro growled. 'What are you doing, Cato? The matter's resolved.'

'Not yet, sir. This man disobeyed the optio's order. That's a clear breach of the regulations.'

Macro glanced round at the men and saw that the nearest were watching them curiously, while trying to appear as if they weren't. He eased himself closer to Cato and continued in an undertone, 'Look, it's over. No harm done. No point in making an issue of it.'

'We can't avoid it, sir. He defied a superior officer in front of witnesses. We can't allow that to pass. He has to be punished.'

Macro sighed with exasperation. 'Listen, Cato. I haven't got time for this. And we've all got enough on our plates without having to worry about some kind of field punishment.'

'Nevertheless, I insist that this man is punished, according to the regulations.'

Macro rubbed his brow irritably and then hissed, 'Very well then.' He turned to Tadius and raised his voice. 'Legionary Tadius!'

'Yes, sir.'

Macro thought quickly. A fine, fatigues or a flogging would be pointless here in the desert. There was only one punishment fit for the situation, and one that Tadius would feel keenly. 'You are denied a day's water rations. Return to your century.'

Tadius swallowed hard and replied through gritted teeth. 'Yes, sir.' Then he saluted and, slinging his canteen across his shoulder, turned and strode stiffly away, every step betraying his rage and sense of injustice. Macro nodded to the optio by the water cart.

'Carry on.'

As the meagre measures of water were poured into the proffered canteens Macro beckoned to Cato and began to walk away from the line of men. When they were safely out of earshot he stopped and faced his friend with a fierce expression.

'What the hell was that about?'

'Discipline, sir.'

'You can drop the "sir" routine when the men aren't listening, Cato.'

'All right then.' Cato nodded. 'I can't understand you. When did you ever let a man get away with something like that? If we were back in camp you'd have Tadius digging shit out of latrines for the rest of his life.'

'I might,' Macro conceded. 'But we're not in camp. We're about as far out on a limb as we can be. There's enough bad feeling between your lads and mine already without fanning the flames any further.'

'Your lads and mine?' Cato repeated. 'You make it sound as if we're not on the same side.'

'That's the point. If these men see themselves as enemies then we're in deep trouble the moment any real foes turn up. Petty grievances are a luxury we can't afford.'

'And what about discipline?'

'Sometimes you have to compromise. Anyway, you've taken care of the discipline, it would seem.' Macro sighed. 'If a day without water doesn't kill Tadius, then you will have made yourself an enemy for life. Congratulations.'

Cato was about to reply when there was a shout from the camp. 'Cavalry patrol coming in!'

Macro shook his head wearily. 'Will I get no bloody rest tonight? Come on, something's up.'

The sound of hooves drumming across the desert announced the return of one of Cato's cavalry patrols and the two officers hurried over to where the decurion and his men were reining in at the edge of the column's sleeping lines.

'Where's the prefect?' the decurion called out anxiously.

Cato raised a hand. 'Over here. What's happened?'

'Beg to report, we've sighted a large force of mounted men, sir.' The decurion was breathing heavily as he steadied his mount, still snorting for breath after its gallop back to the camp. 'To the south.'

'How far from here?' Macro snapped.

'No more than two miles, sir. Seemed to be heading towards us.'

'Could you identify them?'

'Too dark, sir. I watched long enough to gauge their heading, then came to report. I'm sure they didn't see us.'

Cato interrupted. 'Mounted men, you say? Horse or camel?'

The decurion paused for a moment. 'Bit of both, sir.'

'Then it's likely to be a force from Palmyra, rather than Parthians. Parthians are supposed to favour horses.' Cato glanced at Macro. 'According to my sources, sir.'

'Your sources?'

'What I read in the library at Antioch.'

'Then it's bound to be true,' Macro grumbled sarcastically. 'Right, we

77

haven't time to get out of their way. So we'll have to lie low and keep quiet until they have passed.'

'And if they ride right up to us?' asked Cato.

'Then we give them the surprise of their bloody lives.'

Cato recalled the mounted patrols and sent the cavalry back down the track to hide in a small depression the column had marched through before halting for the night. If there was a fight the Romans could not risk confusing their cavalry with the approaching horsemen in the darkness. When they heard a bucina signal they were to rejoin the column. Meanwhile the auxiliary and legionary infantry put on their armour and drew their swords before lying down beside their shields. If it came to a fight, then this would be a confused affair at close quarters. Javelins would be too cumbersome, so the short sword favoured by the Roman army would settle the affair. The officers, crouching low, passed along their lines harshly whispering to their men the need to keep still and silent and not to move a muscle unless an order was given. Macro and Cato crept a short distance forward, in the direction of the approaching horsemen, and squatted down, straining their eyes as they scanned the almost featureless landscape to their front.

'If it is the enemy,' Macro said softly, 'we're only going to have one chance to hit them hard. If they can break away from us in good order, then the column's going to be arrow fodder come first light.'

'I know.'

'So if the moment comes, you and your men go in hard.'

'Trust me, Macro. I know my job.'

The older officer turned to his young friend and grinned. By the dim light of the stars his teeth seemed inordinately white in the muted dark shades of the night. He clapped Cato on the shoulder. 'Of course you know your job. You learned from the best.'

They both chuckled for a moment and Cato felt a little of the nervous tension drain from his body. If it did come to a fight, there was no man better to have at his side in a battle than Centurion Macro. Then he froze, squinting out across the desert.

'There!' He leaned closer so that Macro could follow the direction indicated and thrust his finger towards the horizon. At first Macro could see nothing. He blinked to clear his eyes and stared again.

'Can't see a thing. Are you sure?'

'Of course I am,' Cato responded irritably. 'Use your eyes.'

This time Macro saw them, or rather he saw the dark smudge emerging from the greater gloom no more than half a mile off. As the detail began to resolve he could even see the faint penumbra of sand kicked up by the horses' hooves. As the column approached something else occurred to Macro.

'They're quiet,' he whispered. 'They move like ghosts.'

For a moment, a chill gripped Macro's spine at the thought. There had certainly been enough blood spilt across this land for it to be haunted by hosts of the spirits of the dead.

'Relax. They're alive enough, for now,' Cato replied softly. 'They're quiet all right. The question is, what the hell are they doing out here? And why move after dark? They're not part of a caravan, that's for sure. Given the situation, they're almost certainly hostile.'

'How can we be sure?'

'We're the only Romans out here, and I'd have thought any friends we have are bottled up in the citadel at Palmyra. Besides . . .' A nasty thought struck him. 'It's almost as if they're looking for something. Us perhaps. In which case, I doubt they're friendly.'

'Us? How could they be looking for us? They can't possibly know we're here. Not yet.'

'Why not? Someone at Chalcis could easily have ridden ahead to raise the alarm.'

'Shit, you're right.' Macro ground his fist into the sand. Then he glanced at Cato. 'If they're looking for us then why aren't there any scouts?'

Cato thought for a moment. 'Could be that they don't think we've advanced this far yet. Anyway.' Cato nudged him. 'They're coming our way. We have to get back to the column.'

The two officers rose into a low crouch and worked their way back to their men, taking care not to disturb too much sand and betray their presence. Macro stole back towards his legionaries as Cato lay down beside his standard-bearer, drew his sword and pulled his shield up beside his body. He glanced round and saw that his men were as flat to the ground as they could be and in the darkness there was every chance that they would be missed by the horsemen, provided the latter did not pass too close or, worse, stumble upon the concealed Romans. Cato's heart was beating like a hammer and his excited senses were overwhelmed by the sight, sound and smell of the cold desert night. For a moment there was nothing, and then the faintest sound of muffled hooves before the head of the column of horsemen was visible against the faintly lighter horizon.

One of his men muttered something close by and Cato swivelled his head round to glare in that direction, and let a faint sound escape through his clenched teeth. 'Shhh.' If he discovered who the man was later, he thought furiously, he'd have him beaten. If they both survived the night.

Now Cato could hear the creak of saddles and straps and the snorts and champ of the horses, as the riders closed on the Romans at an angle. Cato frantically tried to calculate their path and realised, with a sick feeling of inevitability, that they were riding straight at Macro and his cohort to Cato's left.

'Shit,' he muttered under his breath, and then raged at himself for making the sound. He clamped his lips shut and tightened his grasp on his sword and shield. On they came, looming out of the dark so that now he could clearly see the individual details of helmets, spears and shields in silhouette. There was even the soft sound of muted conversation as they approached the waiting Romans.

A horse suddenly whinnied at the front of the column and reared up, nearly throwing its rider. A cry of pain split the darkness and Cato realised that the horse had stepped on a Roman.

'Get up and kill them!' Macro bellowed, and then a dark wave of armoured men suddenly rose from the desert and charged towards the horsemen with a deafening roar.

CHAPTER NINE

Cato thrust himself up from the ground and filled his lungs. 'Second Illyrian! Charge!'

There was no attempt to fight as a cohort. The auxiliaries just swarmed forward, racing towards the reeling horsemen, knowing that they must be given no chance to recover. For a moment the riders sat in the saddles, stunned into immobility as the Romans erupted from the still desert to their front and flank. Cato quickly glanced round to make sure that his standard-bearer and the other men were with him, and then threw himself towards the nearest horseman. He was close enough to see the dark, beard-fringed face of the rider staring down at him. Then the man uttered some curse in his tongue and hefted his spear, flicking it up into an overhand grip. With a last spurt, Cato sprinted inside the reach of the spear and slammed his shield up into the man's side as he thrust his sword into the horse's belly and ripped it free in a hot rush of blood, black as pitch in the darkness. The rider swayed for a moment and was thrown from his saddle as the wounded animal lurched away from Cato.

'Go for the horses!' Cato shouted out. 'Kill the horses!'

It infuriated him that he hadn't thought to give the order earlier, when the men were being readied. If these were Parthians, or Palmyran rebels, then they would stand less chance fighting on foot. If they managed to cut their way out and use their bows then it was a different matter. Some of the men nearest to Cato followed his lead and stabbed their blades into the nearest animal's vitals, or hacked at the tendons of the legs causing the stricken beasts to collapse into the dust that swirled around the vicious mêlée. Cato pressed on warily, glancing quickly around him to make sure that he was not knocked down and trampled. He felt a sudden blast of warm air and turned just in time to see a horse's head loom over his right shoulder. The rider was leaning forward in his saddle, sword rising. Cato swung round, slamming the rim of his shield up under the horse's muzzle. As the beast reared, the rider's blade swished through the air above Cato's head, rustling briefly through the top of his horsehair crest. Cato punched his blade up at an angle, through the loose robes, into the man's side, cracking a rib before the point sliced through a lung and into his heart. The man groaned and slumped over his saddle, the reins dropping from his fingers as the horse swerved away from Cato into the jostling press of the other mounts and their riders.

He drew back a few paces and saw the dim outline of the standard a short distance away across the heads of his men.

'Standard-bearer! On me!'

As he waited for the man to join him Cato glanced round at the fight. From the little that he could make out, the Romans were having the best of it. Macro and his cohort had smashed into the head of the column and rolled it back up, while the Second Illyrian had charged at an angle into the flank. Caught from two directions the horsemen had no chance of forming up to fight back, and were simply trying to survive the onslaught of the infantrymen swirling around the sides of their horses, hacking and slashing at man and beast alike. This was not the style of fighting they were accustomed to, or even remotely wished to engage in. They were at a disadvantage and unless they could find some way to break away from the Romans they would be cut to pieces. For their part, the infantrymen were relishing the chance to butcher these horse-archers whose favoured method of fighting seemed unmanly and unfair.

Cato glanced to his right and saw that the tail end of the enemy column was slipping away from his men, galloping off into the night.

'Keep at 'em!' he shouted. 'Push on! Get stuck in, lads!'

With a nod to the standard-bearer, he took a breath, gritted his teeth, and surged forward into the fight once again. The auxiliaries followed close on his heels as they joined the first wave of their comrades. The fresh weight of men carved a new path through the horsemen, breaking them up into small pockets that were set upon from all sides. From somewhere to his left Cato heard Macro shouting to his men.

'Finish them! Finish the bastards! Don't let them get away!'

Cato picked his way through the bodies on the ground. Some horses were dead, but many were wounded, and they lashed out with their hooves as their shrill whinnies of agony and terror filled the air, adding to the scrape and ringing of weapons and the cries of men. Ahead Cato saw his men attacking a group of riders and he hurried over to join the fight. Pushing his way into a space he crouched to lower his centre of balance and stepped forward behind his shield, sword raised to one side. The remaining horsemen had recovered from their surprise and held shields and swords ready to take on their attackers. In front of Cato a man on a horse larger and more powerful than the others was skilfully wheeling it about as he slashed at any of the auxiliaries that came in reach. As Cato tensed his muscles and edged closer the rider leaned to one side and his blade arced round, whirring through the air before it struck the raised arm of one of Cato's men, severing it just below the elbow. The man fell back with a shriek as his sword arm, still clutching the sword, tumbled to the ground at his feet.

The rider shouted an order over his shoulder and several of his comrades wheeled their mounts about and spurred them on, riding straight at Cato and his standard-bearer.

'Oh, shit!' the standard-bearer just had time to mutter before the enemy were on them. Cato threw his shield up and an instant later was hurled to one side as the breast of the big horse smashed into the front of it. The blow stunned Cato's left arm right up to the shoulder and the shield slipped from his fingers. The blow took a fraction of the pace off the horse, but it was enough. Behind Cato, the standard-bearer dropped to one knee and lowered the sharpened tip of the standard towards it. The beast had no chance to avoid the point and ploughed straight on to it, taking the head of the standard in the breast, snapping the cross-piece as the shaft pierced its body. It shuddered and then toppled to the side. With a curse the rider threw himself clear, and on to Cato. Both men crashed heavily to the ground and the impact drove the breath from Cato in an explosive gasp. Around them, the other horsemen were desperately trying to drive their mounts through the loose ranks of the auxiliaries and there was no one to pay any attention to the prefect struggling in the dust with one of the horsemen.

The man's breath blasted over Cato's face as he pressed Cato's chest back with his forearm while the other hand released its grip on his sword and went for the dagger strapped at his side. Cato's right hand still grasped his sword but he could not bring the point to bear and instead hammered the pommel into the man's side. For the first time he saw that the man was wearing some kind of cap rather than a helmet and his eyes were fierce with hate and a desire to kill his Roman enemy. There was a rasp as the dagger was drawn and Cato knew he had only an instant to save himself. Tensing his neck muscles, he threw his head up as hard as he could. The man's eyes widened in surprise and the snarl died on his lips as the iron rim of Cato's helmet smashed the bridge of his nose and crushed one of his eyes. The man howled and instinctively relaxed the pressure of his forearm. Cato thrust up with his right knee and threw his fist at the man's cheek for good measure. The blow connected with a jarring thud and the rider rolled to one side with a deep groan of agony. Cato thrust him away and scrambled back on to his feet. His heart was pounding wildly and he was not thinking clearly any more. The instinct to fight and kill had taken over. He stepped towards the man groaning on the ground and drew his sword back for the killing blow. As he did so, he sensed rather than saw a movement at the corner of his eye: a figure charging towards him, the dull gleam of a blade in the starlight and a feral growl in the man's throat. Cato whirled round towards the new threat, snapping his sword point out towards the figure. The tip of the blade caught the man high, just above the edge of his chain mail, shattering his collarbone and cutting clean through his flesh to burst through his shoulder.

There was a dreadful pause as Cato stared into the face of the man, who was looking back, with shocked wide eyes, from inside a Roman helmet. Cato gasped, and yanked his weapon free, as if he could undo the blow if he moved fast enough. The blade came out with a jerk, a sucking sound and a rush of blood as the auxiliary sank to his knees, staring at Cato with a puzzled expression. He shook his head slowly and sank back on to the ground.

Cato stood over him, holding his dripping sword as his other hand momentarily flashed up in front of his face, as if to protect it. Then the moment of sick panic passed and he hurriedly looked round. The nearest auxiliaries had their backs to him as they grabbed a rider and hauled him from his saddle. No one had seen him, then. Cato swallowed, and knelt down, stabbing his sword into the sand where it would be ready to snatch up if he needed it. He hurriedly undid the man's neck scarf and pressed it against the blood gushing from the wound. The man cried out as he felt the pressure and his hand grasped Cato's wrist like an iron manacle.

'Fuck, it hurts,' he moaned through clenched teeth.

'Let go of me,' Cato growled. 'I'm trying to help you. You're injured. If I can't staunch the wound, you'll bleed to death.'

The man nodded and released his grip, before his eyes widened suddenly and he stared at Cato and hissed, 'It was you . . .'

'Quiet,' Cato said urgently. 'Save your breath.'

'It was you,' the man repeated, then his eyes clenched shut and he slumped back, moaning. Cato crouched over him, pressing the scarf on to the wound with one hand while he kept his sword ready with the other. Glancing round he saw that the surviving horsemen were in full flight, and only a handful were still hemmed in by the auxiliaries, desperately wheeling their mounts one way then another as they tried to parry the thrusts of the men around them. It was an unequal duel, and the last rider was cut down moments later. The auxiliaries raised their swords and jeered as the sound of hooves receded into the night.

'Over here!' Cato shouted at the nearest of his men. 'On me!'

Several trotted over and Cato indicated the man on the ground. 'This man is wounded. Get him to the carts.'

'Yes, sir.'

As the auxiliary lowered his weapons to tend to his comrade Cato scrambled to his feet and hurried away. Around him the rest of the cohort was busy finishing off the enemy wounded and looting the bodies. Cato cupped a hand to his mouth.

'Centurion Parmenion!'

He called out again before Parmenion replied and came running towards him. The centurion was hurriedly tying off a strip of dressing round his sword arm as he reached Cato.

'How bad's the wound?' Cato asked.

'Flesh wound, sir. I can still swing a sword. Which is more than can be said for those bloody horsemen. They've bolted like rabbits.'

'For now,' Cato conceded. 'But they may yet cause us trouble.'

'You really think so, sir?'

The surprised tone was tinged with disbelief and Cato irritably drew a breath. 'Let's not take the risk, all right? Now I want our wounded collected and made as comfortable as possible. The cohort is to form up round them. Understand?'

'Yes, sir.'

'Any sign of Centurion Macro?'

'Haven't seen him, sir. But I heard him.' Parmenion pointed over his shoulder.

'Hard not to,' Cato muttered and patted his subordinate on his shoulder. 'Carry on.'

He set off across the site of the skirmish, stepping round the bodies of men and horses littering the ground. The first few legionaries he encountered were still dazed by the fast and furious fight and had no idea where their commander was. With a growing sense of frustration Cato pressed on until he found one of Macro's centurions.

'What the hell's going on?' Cato asked angrily. 'Why aren't you re-forming your men?'

'We've beaten them, sir. I don't see the need . . .'

'Where's Macro?'

'By the standard, sir. There.'

'Fine.' Cato nodded as he picked out the faint shape of the cohort's standard-bearer. 'Now form your men up, Centurion. Quick as you can.' Cato pushed past the man and strode on.

'Centurion Macro? Are you there, sir?'

'Cato!' A bearlike shape loomed out of the darkness as Macro came over to him. 'By the Gods, we gave them a damn fine pasting! Must have taken down half of them at least.'

'Maybe, but it's the other half than concerns me.'

'They've run for it, lad!' Macro laughed jubilantly. 'I doubt they'll stop until dawn.'

'They'll stop long before then,' Cato replied quietly. He pointed to one of the bodies of the horsemen sprawled beside his mount a short distance away. 'See. This one has a bow case. There's plenty like him out there.'

Macro examined the body and prodded it with his toe. 'Parthian?'

Cato glanced at the loosely robed corpse. A conical helmet with a twisted fabric rim lay near the head. 'Could be. But he's more likely to be one of the rebels from Palmyra. The Parthians can't be on the scene yet,' he added cautiously. 'Surely?'

Macro tipped his head to one side. 'Maybe . . . I hope not, or we're really in the shit.'

'Either way we're dealing with the same type of horseman and the same tactics. We may have surprised them, but the moment they reach a safe distance and re-form they will come after us.'

'Come after us?' Macro shook his head. 'After that hiding we gave 'em? I don't think so.'

'Macro, now that the element of surprise is gone, they can use their bows and pick us off at will.' Cato slapped his hand against his thigh. 'If only we had got them all.'

'We did well enough,' Macro insisted. 'Still, better get my lads formed up. Just in case. Better if we put the cohorts together, with the wounded in the middle.'

'I think that would be wise, sir. I'll fetch my men.'

'What about our cavalry?'

Cato thought for a moment. 'Better leave them where they are for now. There's still the risk of confusing them with those horse-archers. If we need them, we can call on them quick enough.'

'Good. Then we'd better get moving.'

The centurions and optios called their men together and the ranks formed behind their standards while those detailed to move the injured to safety carried them towards the slight fold in the ground that Macro had chosen as the position where the two cohorts would wait for daylight. If there was an attack then the enemy would have to close the range to see their target. They might even venture within reach of the cohort's javelins and slings where they would pay the price soon enough, Macro mused grimly. While the wounded were laid down in the centre of the shallow bowl of dust and rock others drew the supply carts in. Then the two cohorts formed into a defensive box and sheltered behind their shields as they stared out into the desert, wrapped in darkness.

Macro and Cato stood on the side facing the direction the enemy had retreated and shared the tense anticipation of those around them. The men had been ordered to stand in silence and the only noise came from those wounded who could not contain their pain. The occasional groan or gasping cry of agony wore away at the nerves of the other men so that they eventually fell to cursing their injured comrades.

As soon as that thought occurred to him, Cato vividly recalled the auxiliary he had wounded, and the sick feeling of guilt welled up inside him again. He wondered if he should say anything to Macro. It had been an accident, he reassured himself. But even so, it was a tragic mistake, one that no officer with battle experience could be forgiven. After a while Cato wondered if the man was still alive. If he was, had he told his comrades about the officer who had stabbed him in a blind panic? For an instant Cato wished the man dead. Then at once he cursed himself for the thought. But the urge to know the man's condition was irresistible and in the last hour before dawn he turned to Macro.

'Sir, if I may, I'd like to check on my injured.'

Macro looked at him curiously. 'Now? Why?'

Cato forced himself to remain as calm as he could. 'While I'm acting prefect, I need to ensure that the men get what they need. That includes seeing to the comfort of the wounded, sir.'

'Yes . . . I suppose so. Go on then, but be as quick as you can.'

Cato tried to hide his relief as he stole away from Macro and quietly made his way towards the wounded lying in rows beside the supply carts.

CHAPTER TEN

'What's the butcher's bill?' Cato asked the cohort's surgeon, a thin Greek only a few months away from discharge and a comfortable retirement. Themocrites stood up, wiping his bloodied hands on a rag before he saluted his prefect.

'Four dead so far, sir.' The surgeon gestured to the men around him. 'Eighteen wounded. Three almost certainly will die, but the rest will recover. Most of them will be walking wounded.'

'I see.' Cato nodded. 'Show me the men with the mortal wounds.'

'Yes, sir.' Themocrites' eyes flickered with surprise. Then he beckoned Cato. 'This way.'

He led Cato to the end of the line of men lying on the sand. Most were still and quiet but some groaned and cried out at the agony of their injuries. The surgeon's small section of medical orderlies crouched amongst them, doing their best to dress wounds, tie splints to shattered limbs and staunch the flow of blood from wounds. The most severely wounded lay a short distance from the others. One man lay still, his breath coming in faint, fluttering gasps. One of Themocrites' orderlies was watching over the other two. As soon as he became aware of the officers' approach he stood up smartly.

'Report,' said Cato.

'Lost one of them a short time ago, sir. He bled to death. The other's not long for this world.'

He pointed to the man at his feet and in the gloom Cato could just make out the features of the man he had wounded. His heart fluttered wildly for a moment and he felt himself flush with shame and guilt, and gave silent thanks that it was still night and his expression would be hard to read by the pale gloom of the stars. He was aware that the orderly was watching him fixedly.

He cleared his throat and continued, 'What's this man's name?'

The orderly paused a moment before replying, 'Gaius Primus, sir.'

Cato squatted down beside the man and hesitated a moment before he patted his unwounded shoulder. The soldier started and his head jerked off the ground as he stared wide-eyed at Cato.

Cato forced a smile on to his lips. 'Don't worry, Primus. You'll be taken care of. I swear it.'

The auxiliary flinched from his superior's touch at the words. A wave of cold fury hit Cato as he cursed his thoughtlessness. *That could have been better worded.* He tried to inject a reassuring tone into his voice as he continued. 'You will be looked after.'

'You . . .' Primus muttered, and then winced as a wave of agony swept through him, causing him to clench his teeth as he fought to resist it. His hand suddenly grasped Cato's wrist and his fingers closed round the flesh like a manacle. As the auxiliary endured the agony Cato tried to pull himself free, but couldn't without an unseemly use of force in front of the medical orderly. He gently started to prise the fingers off, marvelling at the power in the wounded man's grip.

There was a sudden whirr and something landed in the sand close to Cato with a sharp thud. He glanced round and saw the shaft of an arrow sprouting up from the ground no more than a sword's length from his boot.

The orderly recoiled in fear as Cato instantly realised the danger they were all in. There was no time for Primus any more as Cato ripped his hand free and stood up.

'Incoming arrows! Take cover!'

The air was suddenly filled with a sound like leaves rustling in a high wind as the men scrambled to take cover beneath their shields. Cato snatched his up and swiftly raised it over his head as he shouted the order again. All around him the thin dark shafts sprouted up like stalks of wheat, some punching into the shields with splintering cracks. A sharp cry told of one auxiliary who had failed to act in time. Cato glanced round and saw that the wounded men and the medical orderlies were helpless under the barrage of missiles. Even as he watched, two of the injured were hit. One was struck in the forehead and the barbed head punched through his skull into his brain, silencing his moans at once. Cato beckoned to the nearest men.

'You! Shelter our wounded! Move yourselves!'

The men reluctantly crept towards the line of wounded and dead and covered themselves and an injured comrade with their shields as best they could. Once he saw that the orderlies and their charges were protected Cato returned to the rest of his men. They were already formed up when the order was given and had responded quickly, kneeling down and sheltering behind their shields.

'Centurion Parmenion!'

'Sir?' the adjutant's voice called back from nearby.

'On me!'

A dark shape scurried across the sand towards him.

'Parmenion. Take over. I'm going to find Macro. We need to pull the men in. Make a smaller target. You take over here.'

'Yes, sir.'

Cato crept down the lines of his men until he came to the first of Macro's legionaries and then edged along behind them towards the standard. The earlier volleys of arrows had become a steady shower, rattling like hail as the horse-archers nocked, aimed and loosed shafts at different speeds. Over the shields and helmet of the legionaries Cato could just make out the flitting shapes of the enemy as they rode along the face of the Roman square, shooting their arrows. It occurred to Cato that they might just as easily stand their ground, or even dismount, to aim at the two cohorts. They must be fighting the only way they knew how, he reasoned. But they were safe enough while they remained out of javelin range. As soon as they realised that, the Romans would be in trouble, and when dawn broke in a few hours' time the horse-archers would have an easy target.

When he reached Macro, squatting by the standard, Cato saluted.

'Hot work!' Macro grinned ruefully. 'Seems like it's their turn to stick the boot in.'

'Yes, sir. We have to do something about it, before they realise just how much of an advantage they have.'

'Do something?' Macro pursed his lips for a moment. 'Very well. We'll double the ranks up.'

'Yes, sir. That would be best,' Cato concurred and nodded towards the carts. 'And we might use some sling shot to discourage them.'

'Yes. Yes, good idea. I'll get some of my lads on to it.'

'How long do you think they'll keep peppering us with arrows?' asked Cato as one glanced off his shield with a sharp thud.

'Till they run out, I imagine.'

'That's helpful.'

'If you will ask a stupid question.' Macro shook his head mockingly. 'Anyway, you know the score. The archers are trying to soften us up. As long as we keep formation we'll survive. If we don't, then they'll ride over us and cut us to pieces.'

'Shall I give the signal for our cavalry to move in, sir?'

'Not yet. Not until there's enough light for us to see who is who. I don't want any of our lads taking on their own side by mistake.'

'Yes, sir.' Cato nodded. 'Right, I'd better get back to my men.'

As soon as he returned to his cohort Cato passed on the orders, and once the centuries had formed four lines of men they slowly drew back into a tight shield wall around the carts and the injured, whose number gradually swelled as the night drew on. Macro issued the slings to one section in each of his centuries, and the legionaries, having no clear sight of the horse-archers, whirled the leather thongs and released the shot in a shallow arc over the heads of their comrades in the general direction of the enemy. In the dark it was impossible to tell where the lead shot fell, or whether any of the horsemen were hit, but Cato hoped that it might at least help to keep them at a distance and unsettle their aim. The barrage of barbed missiles slackened as the enemy decided to conserve what was left of their arrows, and both sides exchanged occasional shots while the night crawled towards the coming dawn.

As the pallid pearl hue thickened along the eastern horizon Cato's keen eyes peered over the rim of his shield as he scanned the surrounding desert. The horse-archers were easily visible now, and as the light grew he was able to pick out ever more detail in the scattered screen of riders surrounding the two cohorts. Now Cato could see that their clothes and accoutrements were subtly different from those of the Parthians he had fought the year before. They were Palmyran troops, then.

There was a sick tremor of anxiety in his stomach as he wondered if these men might be loyalists, sent by the king to seek help from the Romans. If that was the case, Cato's thoughts raced on, then there had been a tragic mistake in the confusion of the night's encounter. The man he had wounded would be merely one of many who had been needlessly injured or killed. The dread thought passed almost as quickly as it had arisen. There was little chance of the Roman infantry's being mistaken for anything else and the horsemen had made no attempt to call off their attack. They were clearly hostile: followers of the traitor Artaxes and his Parthian allies.

As pale light spilled across the desert, the horsemen began to shoot more arrows, aiming high so that the shafts rose gracefully up, hung for an instant, and then plunged down at a steep angle on to the Romans. Although the auxiliaries and legionaries were well sheltered by their shields, the cart mules were not, and as Cato watched they were struck down, one after another, with pitiful shrill brays of shock and pain as the arrow heads whacked through their hides and punched deep into the flesh beneath. However, the enemy did not have things all their own way, Cato noted, as he saw one of the horse-archers suddenly thrown back in his saddle, his bow dropping from his fingers as a lead shot struck his head, killing him instantly. The body toppled from the saddle on to the ground in a small explosion of dust, and those Romans who saw it gave a lusty cheer.

'A fine shot!' Macro bellowed from the other end of the square. 'A denarius for that man, and any others you knock down!'

The offer of a reward had its effect as the slingers released their shots even more swiftly and the horsemen immediately shied away to a much greater range where their fire could not be so accurate. Cato noticed that the enemy's barrage slackened until there were clear intervals between each handful of arrows. Finally, as the sun rose over the horizon and cast long shadows across the desert, the enemy archers ceased their shooting altogether and retired a short distance to dismount and rest their horses as they took a quick meal from their saddlebags.

'Seems we have something of a stand-off,' Parmenion muttered. 'They can't crack us and we can't get at them. Not until our cavalry is ordered forward.'

'Yes, it's about time for that.' Cato turned towards Macro and waved an arm to attract his friend's attention. As soon as Macro saw him, he gave Cato the thumbs-up. Cato pointed to the two bucinators standing just behind the Second Illyrian's standard and Macro nodded deliberately as he grasped Cato's intention. Cato turned towards his bucinators, but before he could give the order Parmenion grasped his arm.

'Sir! They're moving.'

Cato swung round and saw that the enemy riders had thrown down their rations and were hurriedly scrambling back into their saddles and snatching the bows from their cases.

'Looks like they're going to charge us after all.'

'Let 'em try it,' Centurion Parmenion growled. 'They'll not break into the square. Not in a fair fight.'

Cato smiled briefly. Parmenion clearly belonged to that element of the Roman military that held the view that archers were cowards. For his part Cato saw them as merely another means of waging war. Archers had their limitations as well as their advantages. Unfortunately, the present circumstances favoured their advantages.

'Close up!' Cato shouted. 'Front rank! Present javelins! Prepare to receive cavalry!'

Around him the auxiliaries and legionaries braced themselves with grim expressions as they stared at the enemy, still hurriedly mounting up and forming into loose bodies of men amid swirls of dust. As the riders gathered together, behind their serpent standards, Cato frowned.

'What the hell?'

Parmenion squinted over the ranks of the auxiliaries standing silently in front of the two officers. 'They're facing the other way. Why?'

Cato shook his head. This was strange. They were forming up quickly, as if to charge, but away from the two Roman cohorts. What was happening? Just then, the faint, strident blasts of a horn sounded in the mid-distance, from beyond the enemy horsemen.

'Reinforcements?' Parmenion wondered hopefully. 'Ours or theirs?'

'Not ours. We're the only body of Roman soldiers for a hundred miles around.'

More horns sounded, and then there was a reply from the men who had been attacking the two cohorts a moment earlier – a clear sharp note of defiance. And then they charged away from the Romans in a cloud of dust kicked up by the thundering hooves of their mounts. The Roman troops gazed after them in amazement. Macro hurried across the square to Cato.

'What the fuck is going on?'

'No idea, sir. Only that there's more horsemen out there. Might be more hostiles and those men have gone to join them, or, if we're lucky, someone's come to help us. Either way, we should call in our cavalry.'

'You're right. Do it now.'

'Yes, sir.' Cato turned to give the order to the bucinators carrying the large curved brass horns. They took a breath, puffed their cheeks and a moment later the signal blasted out. They repeated it twice before lowering their instruments and then all eyes turned back towards the receding wave of enemy horsemen. Thanks to the red-hued cloud of dust they had kicked up it was hard to pick out any detail and only once in a while could the dim figures be seen amid the sandy haze. But the sound of horns, and the faint clash of weapons and shouted war cries that carried back to Roman ears, told their own story.

'Who the hell is attacking them?' asked Macro. 'I thought we were the only Romans out here?'

'Perhaps Longinus has sent a cavalry column out after us,' Centurion Parmenion suggested hopefully.

'Maybe,' said Cato. 'But I doubt it.'

'Then who is it, sir?'

'We'll know soon enough.'

As the three officers and their men continued to watch in silence, the distant fight raged on. Occasionally a figure would flee from the fight and burst free of the obscuring dust cloud to race off over the desert. Here and there a riderless horse emerged and trotted aimlessly away. At length the sounds of battle died away and then there was quiet, as the sun rose low in the sky and its blood-red beams streamed over the landscape.

Parmenion turned and called out, 'Here come our boys!'

The Second Illyrian's four cavalry squadrons were galloping towards the two cohorts, armour glinting in the early morning light. Cato spared them a brief glance and then turned back. He took a sharp breath.

'Look!'

Macro and Parmenion faced round as they followed the direction of Cato's outstretched finger.

A rider had emerged from the slowly settling cloud of dust. He was dressed in black and the first rays of the rising sun played off the silver ornaments of his harness and coned helmet. Reining his horse in, he stopped to examine the Roman soldiers before him, still formed into a square. Then more figures resolved into sharp outlines behind him as other mounted men appeared. Still more rode out of the dust until at last Cato calculated that the man must have at least a hundred followers. They rode forward and stopped behind their leader and stared at the Romans.

'Great,' Macro muttered. 'Now what? Hostiles?'

Cato scratched his chin. 'Out here? More than likely. However, they've seen off those horse-archers. Let's hope that my enemy's enemy really is my friend.'

A moment later their leader raised his arm and gestured to his men to follow him as he rode steadily towards the two Roman cohorts.

CHAPTER ELEVEN

Macro cupped a hand to his mouth and shouted, in Greek, across the intervening ground. 'That's close enough! Stop right there!'

The leader of the approaching horsemen raised a hand to halt his followers and then continued to walk his horse defiantly towards the line of Roman shields. For a moment Macro wondered if the man did not understand Greek. It was unlikely, he reasoned, since Greek was commonly spoken across the east, even here where the native tongue was Aramaic. Close by Macro, one of the legionaries armed with a sling began to swing it round in an arc and let the whirring disc of leather thong and weighted pouch rise up over his head.

'Lower that sling!' Macro barked at him. 'No one is to take a shot at him until I give the order! The denarius bounty is temporarily revoked.'

Most of the men laughed at that, especially those who had not been given a chance to swap shield for sling. Cato had often wondered at the pleasure soldiers took in the frustration of their comrades and he shook his head with a wry expression. The legionary dropped his wrist and the sling shot thudded on to the ground. Once again silence settled over the Roman lines as the lone horseman continued towards them, openly contemptuous of Macro's earlier instruction.

'Cocky little bugger, isn't he?'

'Well, at least he isn't ordering his men to attack us.'

Macro jerked his thumb towards the cavalry approaching from the other direction. 'And why would he, with our lads on the way?'

'He doesn't look like the kind of man who is afraid of Roman cavalry.'

Macro shrugged. 'We'll see.'

He stepped forward, out from the ranks of the square, and stabbed his finger at the horseman, now no more than fifty feet away.

'Stop there! I'll not warn you again!'

At last, the rider pulled on his reins and halted his mount. For a moment there was silence as he surveyed the Roman soldiers with a fierce gaze. Cato saw that his dark robes were of a fine material, silk possibly, that rippled and billowed gently as the horse stamped a foot on the ground. He seemed to be a large man beneath his robes, and his face was broad and strong and fringed with a dark, neatly trimmed beard. He was perhaps a few years younger than Macro. His eyes flickered towards Macro and fixed on the stocky Roman officer.

'And who are you?' he called out in Greek. 'Besides being Romans.'

The voice was rich and deep with no trace of an accent.

'Centurion Macro, Fourth Cohort, Tenth Legion. Commander of the relief column sent to help his majesty King Vabathus, ally of Rome.'

'Ally of Rome?' The horseman's eyebrows rose sardonically. 'Lapdog of Rome, more like.'

Macro ignored the gibe. 'Who might you be then, sunshine?'

'Sunshine?' The man was momentarily taken aback by the idiom. 'I am Balthus, prince of Palmyra, and these . . .' He gestured back towards his waiting followers. 'This is my retinue, hunters mostly. Less than a month ago we hunted deer and wolves in the hills. Today we hunt traitors, and the enemies of Palmyra. Like the dogs we left in the sand back there.' He nodded over his shoulder.

Macro held out a hand. 'Then we are friends, Prince.'

'Friends?' Balthus snorted and spat on to the ground. 'Rome is no friend of Palmyra.'

Cato coughed and called out, 'But she is no enemy either. Unlike Parthia, and those in your city who would sell Palmyra into Parthian domination.'

There was a pause as Balthus glared at Cato before he spoke. 'That we shall see, Roman. It is no secret that your emperor covets Palmyra, as a thief covets the property of others.'

Macro shook his head. 'Now, steady on, friend. We ain't thieves. We're here to help your king. To save him from those who seek to betray him to Parthia.'

'Really?' Balthus smiled mockingly. 'And how do you propose to save him with this meagre force?'

Macro puffed out his chest. 'We're more than enough to do the job.'

'I think not, Centurion. It was *you* who needed rescuing just a moment ago. If I had not intervened then surely it would have been only a matter of time before you were destroyed by those traitors.'

'No. We had the matter in hand. We were just waiting for first light before calling in our cavalry.' Macro gestured to the men of the Second Illyrian galloping towards them.

Behind the front rank of auxiliaries, Cato turned to Parmenion and muttered, 'Better send a runner to Centurion Aquila. Don't want our cavalry getting the wrong end of the stick.'

'Yes, sir.'

As Parmenion hurried off to give the orders Cato stepped out from the line of his auxiliaries and joined Macro just as Balthus shook his head and laughed.

'Roman cavalry . . . I don't think they would have made much of a difference.'

Macro flushed angrily and took a step towards Balthus. 'Now, look here, we could have taken care of ourselves.'

Even though he shared his friend's sense of wounded pride Cato knew this was neither the time nor the place to take umbrage, and he cleared his throat loudly. So loudly that both Balthus and Macro turned to look at him.

'Quite finished?' Macro growled.

'Sorry, sir. It's the dust. Anyway, I think we've established that we're on the same side as the prince. It's time we discussed the situation in Palmyra with him.'

'It is?'

'Yes.' Cato nodded quickly. 'Most definitely, sir.'

Macro stared at Cato for a moment and then turned back to Prince Balthus. 'Very well. If you tell your followers to dismount, I'll order my men to stand down, then we can talk a bit more calmly.'

Balthus nodded. 'That would be best, Centurion.'

He turned round and called out to his followers. A moment later, the riders slipped down from their saddles and squatted quietly by their horses, ready to remount the instant their leader gave the order. Still, Macro reasoned, they were acting in good faith, and he turned to his own men and bellowed the order to stand down. The men lowered their shields and javelins and kept a wary eye on the Palmyrans as the latter reached into their saddlebags for a scrap of bread or dried meat to chew on as they waited for further orders. A short distance from the square, Centurion Aquila had halted his men and they too dismounted as they rejoined their comrades. The tension between the two small forces was still quite palpable. Cato smiled faintly. At least it took the edge off the ongoing hostility between the legionaries and the auxiliaries, for the moment.

Prince Balthus slid off his horse and beckoned to one of his men to look after the beast before he turned to stride across the sand towards the two Roman officers. He stopped before them and appraised them carefully with his dark eyes, then squatted down, gesturing for them to do the same. Macro frowned, unused and unwilling to accept authority from anyone who wasn't Roman. Cato lowered himself to the ground and crossed his legs and, with a weary sigh, Macro followed suit.

'So,' Balthus began, 'this is how Rome honours its treaty with my father. At his time of need, your governor sends him a mere handful of men to restore his kingdom. I warned him not to trust Rome.'

'We are the advance force,' Macro explained tersely. 'General Longinus will march on Palmyra the moment the rest of his army has formed up.'

'And what is this advance force expected to achieve, precisely?'

'Our orders are to break through to the citadel and protect the king and the Roman citizens there, until the rest of the army arrives.'

'I see.' Balthus nodded. 'The Roman reputation for meticulous planning is clearly well deserved.'

Cato winced at the man's ironic tone, while Macro's frown deepened.

'How do you intend to enter the city?' Balthus continued. 'What route do you intend to take through the streets to the citadel?'

'We'll deal with that when we get there.'

'Although,' Cato intervened, 'we would, of course, be grateful if you could offer us any advice, or assistance, in carrying through our orders.'

'I'm sure a man can rely on Roman gratitude every bit as much as he can on Roman promises to help him.' Before Macro could react, Balthus continued smoothly, 'I will help you reach the citadel. But there are conditions.'

'Conditions?' Macro responded warily. 'What conditions?'

'First, that I will lead the relief column, until it is safely within the citadel.'

Macro shook his head. 'No. It's my command. There's no question of my giving it up.'

'Centurion, right now you need my help rather more than I need yours. Without my men I doubt you'll even reach Palmyra, let alone fight your way through to the citadel. If you encounter any more horse-archers then I fear that you and your men would succumb to the fate I saved you from just now.'

He paused to let his words sink in, and allow time for the two Roman officers to realise that he spoke the truth. Then he continued.

'So I will lead this column. You will obey my orders, and when we reach the citadel you can assume command of your men again.'

Macro smiled. 'I'm sure your father will appreciate the gesture. His faithful son coming to the rescue, at the head of my men. That's bound to make you look good in his eyes.'

'Of course. I will need the trappings of loyalty if I am to make the most of being his successor.'

'His successor?' Macro was taken aback. 'But you're the second son. You're not his heir.'

'Not yet.' Balthus smiled.

'I assume that's another of your conditions?' Cato asked quietly. 'You want Rome to confirm you as the successor.'

'Yes. And there's more.' He lowered his voice. 'I want Artaxes executed the moment the revolt has been crushed, assuming he is captured.'

'I doubt you'll find any opposition to that demand in Rome,' said Macro.

'And I also want my older brother sent into exile.'

'Exile?' Cato raised his eyebrows. 'Why? Your older brother is in the citadel with the king. He's a loyalist.'

'Yes, it's too bad. But Amethus is also a fool.'

Macro shook his head. 'I don't know about that. Foolishness is no bar to kingship as far as I know. Although there are exceptions.'

'Quite. I am no fool, Centurion, and in the interests of Rome and Palmyra, it is best that I succeed my father.' A ruthless hunger filled the prince's eyes as he continued. 'Once this revolt is over, I will become the king. Naturally I may honour his treaty with Rome, with some modifications.'

'Oh yes, naturally.'

Balthus ignored Macro's sarcastic tone and eased himself back. 'Those are my terms. They are not open to negotiation.'

Macro pursed his lips as he considered the offer. Then Cato intervened. 'They sound fair enough, sir.'

Macro thought a moment before he replied. 'Maybe. But I can't go and make deals like this without the approval of Longinus. All I can give you is my word that I will present your case to my superiors. Is that acceptable?'

Balthus shrugged. 'I'll take your word, Centurion. The word of a Roman officer is good enough for me. In return, my men and I will escort you to Palmyra and guide you through to the citadel, and then you will take command.'

'All right.' Macro nodded, and offered his hand. 'I agree.'

A smile flickered across Prince Balthus' lips as he clasped the Roman officer's hand and sealed the deal. Then he rose to his feet with a swift shimmer of his dark, gleaming robes. 'Then you had better prepare your men to march, Centurion. The dawn is already on us and we must cover as many miles as we can before midday.'

Macro and Cato scrambled to their feet and bowed their heads as the Palmyran prince swirled round and strode back towards his men. Macro waited until Balthus was out of earshot and then said quietly. 'Well? What do you think?'

'The arrangement is as good as we could get.'

Macro looked at his friend. 'But?'

'I don't trust him.'

'Me neither.' Macro stared after Balthus a moment longer and then puffed out his cheeks. 'Well, let's get the men formed up for the day's march.'

After a brief rest to eat the morning's rations the wounded were loaded on to the carts and the surviving mules were harnessed into their yokes. Several had been killed or crippled by the arrows and horses were taken from one of the cavalry columns to serve in their place. Prince Balthus and his men had already seized the handful of enemy mounts remaining on the battlefield as spoils of war. The dead were hurriedly buried in a shallow grave, which was covered with rocks to spare the bodies the indignity of being worried by carrion and other scavengers. Then the two cohorts formed up: the legionaries at the front, followed by the carts, and then the auxiliaries, with the cavalry squadrons riding ahead on both flanks. When every man was in place, Macro glanced back down the column and muttered, 'They're good men. You'd never think they had just been in a fight. We'll show that prince what real soldiers can do when we reach Palmyra.'

'Yes, sir,' Cato responded. He continued evenly, 'Meanwhile, we need him and his men. They're our best chance of seeing this through.'

Macro shook his head. 'Cato, my lad, I'm as aware of the situation as you are. I'll be on my best behaviour.'

'Oh, I didn't mean you, sir.' Cato was embarrassed. 'I was referring to the men. We're going to have to watch them. Make sure they don't cause any trouble with the locals. If Balthus is anything to go by then we can't count on the warmest of welcomes when we get to Palmyra, whether they are our allies or not.'

'No.' Macro sighed deeply. 'And on that heart-warming note, let's get moving.'

The column trudged forward, towards the waiting Palmyran horsemen. A moment later, Balthus shouted an order and his men spread out in a thin screen ahead of the column and headed across the desert towards the distant city. The track took them past the site of the skirmish the Palmyrans had fought with the horse-archers at dawn and the Romans glanced curiously at the scores of bodies of men and horses littering the stony desert.

Cato felt a chill in his spine as he looked over the scattered corpses. 'Curious, don't you think?'

'What?' Macro turned towards his friend. 'What's curious?'

'There were no prisoners. No sign of any seriously wounded amongst Balthus' men.'

'So? They caught them on the hop, and gave them a good kicking.'

'I know,' Cato agreed. 'But surely some of the rebels would have surrendered, and there must have been some casualties amongst Balthus' men. So, where are they?'

Both officers glanced back to the dead men lying in the glare of the early morning sun. Macro spoke first.

'It seems our man Balthus is an even more ruthless bastard than I thought.'

Cato nodded. 'Just as long as he's our ruthless bastard.'

'And if he isn't?'

'Then the situation in Palmyra has every chance of becoming our worst nightmare,' Cato said quietly.

CHAPTER TWELVE

'Q uite a view,' Macro said as he reached for his canteen and took a small swig.

Balthus and Cato were lying next to him, in the shadow cast by a stunted bush that grew along the long ridge overlooking Palmyra. Below them the rocky slope fell away until it met the plain which stretched away to the oasis that gave the city its name, and its wealth. Beyond the city lay a dense belt of palm trees and patches of irrigated farmland. To the south was a shallow vale scattered with tombs in the form of small towers. The gleaming walls of the city looped round the domes and tiled roofs of its dwellings and public buildings, built in the familiar Greek style. The main market, courts and temples stood to the west of the city, while at the eastern end a large walled enclosure dominated the surrounding buildings from the top of an expanse of higher ground. Cato pointed it out.

'Is that the citadel?'

Balthus nodded.

'What's the best way to get to it?'

'The east gate. There, see?'

'Yes . . .' Cato strained his eyes. 'Yes, I've got it.'

The gate was built into the wall without towers and only the thin ribbon of morning visitors to the city revealed its presence to Cato. Hardly a formidable defence, Cato decided. Inside the eastern gate the buildings sprawled low and it was clear this was the poorest quarter of the city. Cato's suspicions were instantly aroused.

'Won't the streets be narrow there?'

'Yes,' Balthus conceded. 'But it is the most direct route to the citadel, and the main barracks and palaces are at the other end of the city. If we can gain entrance by the eastern gate before the alarm is given, and move fast, we should be able to break through the surrounding line of rebels and reach the citadel.'

'*If* we can get in,' Cato stressed. 'We have to make sure that there are as few men as possible defending the gate when the column attacks. Which means there'll need to be a diversion. The garrison in the citadel will need to make a sortie.'

'Sortie?' Macro turned on Cato. 'Have you forgotten? They're outnumbered and under siege.'

'I know. But they must draw the enemy's attention away from the gate if there's to be any chance of the relief column cutting its way through to the citadel.'

Balthus nodded. 'He is right, Centurion Macro. We must get the garrison to help us.'

'Really?' Macro moistened his lips. 'You make it sound easy.'

Balthus smiled at him. 'Surely the soldiers of the great Roman Empire will not baulk at such a minor challenge?'

'They will not,' Macro replied firmly. 'So how do we get to the gate without attracting attention? There's too little cover down on the plain. We'll have to approach under cover of darkness.'

'Of course we will, Centurion.' A frown briefly flickered across the prince's face. 'As I was about to say. We'll follow the ridge round to that point there.' He indicated a low spur that projected into the plain, no more than two miles from the curve of the wall on the northern side of the city. 'We'll have to muffle the horses' hooves with rags and abandon your carts there. We cannot afford to be given away by the sound of wheels or the squeal of an axle.'

'What about our wounded?' asked Cato. 'We're not leaving them behind.'

'They will slow us down. And what if one of them should cry out in pain? You would risk the rest of your men for the sake of a useless injured soldier?'

'We're not leaving them behind,' Cato repeated forcefully. 'And they know better than to put the lives of their comrades at risk. They won't make any noise.'

Balthus' gaze switched to Macro. 'Is this your will, Centurion?'

'It is. Just as Cato said.'

'Very well. But if our approach is detected, and we have to escape, then my men and I will be forced to fend for ourselves.'

'I expected nothing less, Prince.'

'Just as long as we understand each other, Roman.'

'I don't think there's any doubt about that,' Macro concluded, and eased himself back from the shrub, towards the slope behind them. 'Come on, we'd better rejoin the column.'

The three men crept out of sight of the city and then descended to the men behind the ridge. The infantry had been permitted to fall out of line and were resting in whatever shade they could find, or had made their own by hanging their cloaks over their yokes and javelins. The horsemen, Roman and Palmyran alike, sat in the shade of their mounts, holding the reins in one hand. They had approached the ridge early in the morning and halted while the three commanders ascended the slope to reconnoitre. When they had rejoined their men the column trudged forward again, moving behind the line of the ridge until they reached the spur, where they halted, shortly before noon.

'Why are we stopping?' Macro demanded.

'Look.' Balthus gestured to the dust cloud hanging over the column. 'We can't afford to give any sign of our presence. The ridge is high enough to conceal us from the watchmen on the walls of the city, but once we climb across the ridge they might see any dust we kick up. So, we must stop and wait until dusk before moving on again.'

'Very well,' Macro conceded. 'Until dusk.'

When a watch had been posted up on the ridge they rested under the glare of the midday sun, and once the blazing orb had sunk sufficiently from its zenith Macro gave the orders for the men to prepare for the night march to the east gate. All portable equipment was removed from the carts and distributed to the legionaries and auxiliaries. The small stock of construction timber and spare javelin shafts was used to make stretchers for the wounded and several assault ladders. Meanwhile, Cato gave orders for his cavalrymen to bind the hooves of their mounts with strips of cloth cut from their cloaks.

'You won't be needing them tonight.' He forced himself to smile at Centurion Aquila and the other cavalry officers. 'If we succeed, there's a nice warm billet waiting for you in the citadel at Palmyra. If we fail, well, I doubt we'll need our cloaks in Hades.'

A lame joke, he knew, but his officers smiled appreciatively enough. Despite his youth Cato had led men long enough to know the value of a light touch and apparent fearlessness. He left Aquila to carry out his instructions and returned to Macro. There was one last task to organise. A message had to be got through the enemy's lines so that the king and his followers were ready to admit the small relief column into the citadel. It was obvious that one of Balthus' men would have to be the courier and once again the two Roman officers were instinctively distrustful of their new ally.

'I don't like it,' Macro grumbled. 'I know he helped us out with those horse-archers, but I still find it hard to turn my back towards the man. And the moment we head towards the gate, we're in his hands. If he should betray us, we've had it.'

'True.' Cato nodded. 'But there's no reason why he should betray us. He has as much at stake as we do in seeing that the revolt is put down. My main worry is that the Parthians might cut a better deal with him than Rome can. I think you're right. We have to watch our backs.'

'Fine words don't make fine actions, Cato. What are we going to do about it?'

Cato thought for a moment, and did not like what seemed to be the best course of action. In fact, the prospect of what he was about to suggest terrified him. Yet, at the same time, there was a peculiar thrill at the danger of it all, and he realised – quite suddenly – that he was getting a taste for taking risks. There was some perverse facet of his nature that craved danger, and he wondered if this desire was so strong that it threatened to corrupt his reason. He felt a wave of revulsion and contempt for himself. If that were true then he had no right to command other men; to have responsibility for their lives. They would be safer under another man's command. That thought made his decision much easier.

'If we don't trust Balthus, we should send one of our men in with his courier. Just to make sure he doesn't go astray, and that the citadel's defenders are ready for us.'

Macro considered the suggestion for a moment and then looked at Cato with a sad, weary expression. 'I know what you're going to say. I know it before you even open your mouth. You're not going. Your men need you. Frankly, I need you. There's going to be action tonight, and I would feel easier about it if I knew the Second Illyrian was safe in your hands.'

Cato stared at his friend for a moment and his heart filled with affection for the gruff, honest man who had taught him how to be a soldier, and how to be a leader of men. Macro was Cato's ideal. He was the true measure of a soldier in Cato's eyes, and the thought that Macro depended on him was an accolade far beyond praise from the veteran. Cato bit back on his pride and affection.

'Centurion Parmenion can lead the men as well as me.'

'No.' Macro shook his head and then grinned. 'He can do it better. I just don't like to be shown up. Far better to have you to compete against.'

They laughed, and then Cato continued, 'I have to go. To make sure that everything is ready from the other end. If we're going to be betrayed, better to lose me than both cohorts.'

'How will I know if it's safe to go through with Balthus' plan?'

'I've thought of that. If I make it through to the citadel then I'll have them light a beacon in the highest tower. You and Balthus rush the gate the moment you see it. If there's no signal by first light, then you'll have to accept that I've failed. Is that all right, sir?' The deferential tone was deliberate. Cato knew that the final decision was Macro's alone and if he refused then there was no further debating the matter.

Macro rubbed the bristles on his cheek. 'Very well. Give Parmenion his orders and then report to me. I'll be with our friend the prince, deciding on our message to the king.'

By the time Cato rejoined Macro the sun was low on the horizon and the evening shadows were creeping across the plain. One of Balthus' men was standing with his prince and Macro, holding some dark robes over his arm.

'This is Carpex, one of my household slaves,' Balthus explained. 'He is as loyal a man as you can find.'

'For a slave,' said Macro.

'Yes. But I would trust him with my life,' Balthus said.

'That's good. Because that's exactly what we are trusting him with. Yours, and ours.'

Carpex gestured to the robes as he addressed Cato. 'You'll need to wear these, master. Better leave your armour and keep your weapons covered. The rest of your equipment has to be left behind.'

'How are we going to get through to the citadel?' Cato asked.

'There is a way,' said Balthus. 'A tunnel leading from one of the city's drains into the old stables of the citadel. They use the building as a barracks now, but Carpex and I discovered it when we were boys, and used to hide there to escape punishment.'

'How mischievous of you,' said Macro. 'And when did you last use this tunnel?'

'Ten years ago.' Balthus pursed his lips. 'Maybe more.'

'I see. So there's no guarantee it hasn't been blocked up, or filled in, then?'

'It's still there as far as I know.'

'And if it isn't?' asked Cato.

'Then we will have to try some other way.'

'Fair enough.' Cato nodded. 'We'll have to deal with that problem if it arises.'

Macro shook his head. 'That's madness.'

'Perhaps,' Cato admitted. 'But sometimes madness is all that's left.'

'Oh, how very sage.'

Cato shrugged and turned to the prince's slave. 'Where's the message?'

Balthus pulled a waxed slate from his robes and handed it to Cato. 'Here.'

'Is it, er, sufficiently clear?' Cato asked Macro.

His friend smiled. 'It says all that it needs to. No surprises.'

'Good,' Cato replied and tucked the waxed tablet into his haversack. Then he removed his helmet, cape, harness and armour and handed them to Macro, before leaning down to remove his silvered greaves. By the time he had put on the robes and fastened the band round his headdress he no longer looked so Roman, and he hoped that he would pass as a Palmyran subject – in the dark at least. As the sun eased itself down towards the horizon, Cato and Macro sat a short distance up the slope from the rest of the men. Almost as soon as he had propped himself up against a boulder, Macro fell asleep. His head lolled on his chest and he began to snore. Cato could not help smiling. Tired as his body was he could never sleep on the eve of any action, and his mind raced through seemingly disparate trains of thought. Now that the first thrill at the prospect of danger was over, Cato found that he was trembling and was

110

aware that his knee was twitching in a frantic rhythm. He stared at it in surprise and had to force himself to stop the nervous tic.

Then, for no accountable reason, the image of the man he had wounded flashed into his mind. He could see every detail of the fearful surprise in Primus' expression as the blade lodged deep in his shoulder. Primus had slipped into unconsciousness and died the day before, and was buried back in the desert under a pile of rocks to stop wild animals digging up his body. Cato had not seen him since the night of the fight, yet he was haunted by the image of the man he had wounded. At length he could bear it no longer and he nudged Macro.

'Hey, wake up.'

'Hmmm?' Macro mumbled, smacking his lips and turning slightly away from Cato. 'Fuck off, I'm asleep.'

'No you're not. Come on, wake up. I need to talk. Sir?' Cato shook his shoulder gently.

Macro stirred, blinked and eased himself up from the rock, wincing at the stiffness in his back. 'What? What is it, Cato?'

Now that he had his friend's attention Cato was not sure where to begin. He swallowed nervously. 'Something happened the other night. When we ambushed the horse-archers. Something I haven't told you about.'

'Oh? Well, what is it?'

Cato breathed deeply and made himself confess. 'During the fight, I . . . I wounded one of my men. Ran him through with my sword.'

Macro stared at him for a moment, then rubbed his eyes. 'You did what?'

'I wounded one of my auxiliaries.'

'Is he dead?'

'Yes.'

'Did he recognise you?'

'Yes.' Cato recalled the man's accusing look, and shook off the memory with difficulty. 'I'm sure of it.'

'Did he tell anyone about it?'

'I don't know.'

'Hmmm. Awkward. Normally it would just be one of those things. Accidents happen in the heat of battle, especially at night. But it still needs to be accounted for. It won't look good on your record if there's

111

any kind of enquiry. Even if there isn't, word will get round, assuming the man spoke to anyone. You know how it is with the army's rumour mill. That's not going to go down well with your men. Nor mine, come to that. Not while the memory of that incident back at Antioch preys on their minds.'

'But it was an accident,' Cato protested. 'It was dark. It was during a fight. I didn't mean to do it.'

'I know that, lad. Trouble is that the boys in the Tenth Legion won't see it that way. They'll say that Crispus killed his man by accident and was executed for it. They're bound to ask why you shouldn't suffer the same fate. I know the circumstances are quite different, but that's the kind of detail that men ignore when they nurse a grievance and are out for revenge.'

Cato was silent for a moment before he looked earnestly at his friend. 'What can I do?'

'Not much. If Primus died without spilling his guts then you're in the clear.' Macro paused, and smiled. 'Well, hardly that. Knowing you as I do, you'll carry the burden of guilt with you to the grave. If Primus talked, then you'll be treated like a leper. Worse, you'll have to watch your back.'

Cato felt sick at the prospect of being an outcast amongst his army comrades. He swallowed. 'I'd better make a clean breast of it, before any rumours start circulating. For the good of the cohort.'

'Shit, Cato, there's no need to play the heroic martyr just yet,' Macro responded irritably. 'Just wait a while. You'll soon find out if he talked. Meanwhile it would be better for you if you didn't torment yourself over it.' Macro thought a moment and pointed a finger at Cato. 'Is that what this is about?'

'What?'

'You volunteering to get this message through to the king.'

'No. It has nothing to do with that.'

Macro stared at him for an instant and then shrugged. 'If you say so. Just don't go and get yourself killed out of some perverse sense of righting a wrong. I know you, Cato.'

'Don't worry. I have no intention of throwing my life away.'

'All right, then.' Macro was not wholly convinced. 'Just be careful, eh?'

Cato was watching two figures climbing the slope towards them: Balthus and Carpex. The two Romans clambered to their feet and bowed their heads in greeting.

'It's time,' Balthus announced to Cato. 'You must follow my man and do exactly as he says. There is a way into the citadel, but you must trust him, and obey. Do not speak, even in Greek, for your accent will betray you. And don't forget the signal. We will not enter the city if we do not see it.'

'I understand.'

'Well then, much as it pains me to say it, Roman, I wish you good luck.'

'Thank you.' Cato turned to Macro. 'I'll see you in the citadel later on, sir.'

'Of course you will.' Macro smiled and slapped him on the shoulder. 'As the prince says, good luck.'

'Thank you, sir,' Cato said solemnly and then turned to follow Carpex up towards the ridge.

CHAPTER THIRTEEN

They crossed the ridge and descended the far side, keeping behind the line of the rocky spur that jutted out into the plain towards Palmyra. The sun set behind the ridge and they walked in silence as the shadows thickened about them in the gathering dusk. Cato followed Carpex closely, keeping a wary eye on the ground ahead of them, looking for any signs of human habitation or enemy patrols. But the landscape this side of the city was mainly barren and deserted and only a handful of the creatures of the desert were abroad. A jackal, startled by the two men, scrambled away into some low brush with a shrill yipping noise. Overhead a vulture spiralled lazily in the sky and Cato could not help thinking that both animals would quickly grow fat on the flesh of dead men in the days to come.

As the last glimmer of light faded in the sky they reached the end of the spur and paused as they caught sight of the twinkling lamps strung along the wall of the city and burning faintly in the windows and on the flat roofs of the buildings beyond. A number of fires burned outside the gates where travellers and merchants camped for the night, continuing about their business despite the power struggle taking place within Palmyra. The bulk of the citadel loomed over the eastern side of the city and Cato touched his companion on the shoulder.

'Which way now?'

Carpex pointed out a shallow depression that snaked from the hills and across the plain towards the city. In the few days each year that rain fell this was one of the streams that fed off the hills and into the oasis. But now it was quite dry and provided ample cover for their approach.

'Stay behind me, master. If we encounter anyone, not a word, eh?'

'I know. Let's go.'

They trotted towards the lip of the narrow water channel and slid down on to the bed. The ground was smooth and hard and they made hardly a sound as they padded quickly along, following the course of the channel. Once Cato thought he heard voices, and stopped Carpex until he was sure there was nothing, and then they cautiously continued forward again. After they had gone perhaps three miles, as Cato calculated it, the narrowing course of the dried-up bed of the stream petered out and they emerged on to the plain no more than half a mile from the city. Just ahead, a grove of palms marked the spot where the flow of water ended its journey from the hills and Carpex beckoned to Cato to follow him to the tall, thin trunks curving up towards the spiky fronds above. There was a faint evening breeze which ruffled the long leaves so that they rustled as the two men crept into the shadows beneath and cautiously made their way through the husked trunks to the far side of the grove.

Carpex suddenly crouched down and bade Cato to do the same. As Cato shuffled to his side Carpex turned to him with a fierce glare and touched a finger to his lips. No more than thirty paces away, where the palm trees were more stunted and dispersed, the unmistakable silhouettes of several camels knelt on the ground. A short distance beyond there was a dark huddle of men sitting under the stars speaking Aramaic in muted voices.

'Rebels?' Cato whispered.

Carpex shook his head. 'Merchants.' He tilted his head to one side for a moment to listen before he continued, 'They're complaining about the way the uprising is interfering with their trade.'

Cato grunted lightly. 'I wish I had their problems. What do we do? We have to get round them.'

'Yes. This way.' Carpex lowered himself to the ground and crept along the fringe of the trees on all fours, careful not to disturb the dried fronds that had fallen from the palms. He paused and glanced back at Cato, whispering, 'Go carefully, Roman. There may be scorpions, or snakes hunting in the darkness.'

'Snakes?'

'Yes, vipers. Now come!'

Cato followed him, trying not to flinch at the thought of any lethal reptiles or insects that might lie in his path. He cast wary glances towards the camels and the men slightly further off. Once he froze as a camel turned to him, jaws working casually, and grunted. It soon lost interest, and turned back and chewed contentedly. As soon as they were a safe distance from the traders they stood up again and continued towards the city. To their left was the track leading east towards Parthia and Carpex angled towards it. Cato grasped his arm.

'Why this route? We're bound to be seen.'

'Of course. This way we could be anybody travelling to Palmyra. If we're seen coming from the hills to the north, we might cause suspicion. Trust me, master.'

Cato took a deep breath and nodded. 'Looks like I'll have to.'

'Yes. Now please – no more talking.'

As soon as they reached the track they followed it towards the city. A short distance along it they passed a long caravan heading in the opposite direction, making the most of the comfort of the cool night air to begin their journey. Carpex exchanged a few comments with some of the drivers as they passed by and once the tail of the caravan was behind them he turned to Cato.

'It seems that the merchants are sending their most valuable stock out of the city. Many of the wealthiest families have already left. They're fearful that there will be a big battle, master. Perhaps they have already heard that your governor Longinus is coming with his legions?'

Cato nodded. If it came to battle, or a siege, then it would be the people of Palmyra who suffered most. He could understand their desire to get away until the fighting was over. As ever the poor, who had no other home, nor the means to support themselves, were condemned to remain behind and weather the bloody tempest that was about to break over their city.

As they approached the eastern gate, Cato could see that there was still a handful of people sitting or sleeping on the ground either side of the route. Even with the revolt, some of the locals still dared to go in and out of the city, tending to their smallholdings or making sure their goats remained safe. The gate itself was open, but heavily guarded by armed men who prevented access during the hours of the night. By the light of the torches burning in brackets above the gate, and the braziers on either side, Cato could see that they wore scale armour over loose robes and baggy leggings. Each wore a conical helmet and was equipped with a round shield and a spear. They barred the way into the city.

'What now?' Cato muttered.

'You do as I say, master. Remember?'

Cato nodded.

'Follow my lead and do not speak. When we reach the gate I will say who I am. It is likely that I will be recognised in any case. I will tell them that you are another slave who escaped from Prince Balthus' retinue with me. I will tell them that the camp of my master is a short distance away to the east. I will say that I will tell them precisely where it is only when I am given a reward for the information I have for Prince Artaxes. They will admit us, and escort us through the gate to find the prince. Once inside we will be in the slum quarter of the city. The streets are narrow and winding. When I tell you, we run and you follow me. We will easily outstrip them and lose them in the streets, but you must not lose sight of me, master, or you'll get lost, and be sure to fall into their hands.'

'That's your plan?' Cato whispered furiously. 'What if it doesn't work?'

'Have you got a better idea, master?' Carpex responded testily.

Cato nodded vigorously. 'We should get the fuck out of here and think of a proper plan.' But it was already too late. There was no time to do anything else. 'What if they send for someone instead of escorting us into the city? What then?'

'Then?' Carpex looked surprised. 'Then we are sure to be discovered for what we are, master, and we'll be executed.'

Cato shook his head in wonder at the desperate nature of his companion's ruse, and despair that there was no way out of it now. They were close enough to the men guarding the gates to be seen in the loom of their torches, and to turn round would provoke their instant suspicion. Cato swallowed nervously and hoped that his headpiece would hide his Roman features in the darkness.

Carpex quickened his pace and, with a nervous glance over his shoulder, hurried up to the east gate, with Cato close behind him.

They were instantly seen by some of the guards, who lowered their spears and pointed the tips at the two figures coming towards them. A harsh shout split the darkness and the remaining guards scrambled to their feet, weapons at the ready as Carpex and Cato stopped a short distance away. One of the rebels came forward, shouting at them. Carpex raised his hands and dropped to his knees and began speaking in a frightened rush. Cato knelt down behind him, head lowered, adopting what he hoped was an obeisant slave posture. The exchange between Carpex and the guard continued for a little longer, and the tone of the other man's voice changed from hostile to surprised and then excited as he beckoned to Carpex to stand up and follow him. Cato scrambled to his feet and stayed as close to the slave as possible as they were led past the other men and through the gateway.

Inside, by the light of more torches, he could see an ancient street, edged with refuse, leading away between grimy buildings. After several days in the desert the close, fetid smell of the city hit his nostrils like a blow and he instinctively wrinkled his nose. The officer in charge of the gate lit a small torch and led them up the street at a fast pace. Carpex and Cato followed, and then came two more men, carrying spears, and wearing scale armour and helmets. The trick of it, Cato knew, was to make their break fast enough to get out of range of a spear thrust, or even a throw, if the guards were sufficiently alert to chance such a thing after their fleeing prisoners. The street bent round a public well, and then began to climb gently at an angle to where Cato assumed the citadel must be. All the time he watched Carpex closely, muscles tensed and ready to flee. Twenty paces on a narrow alley opened up to their left and Carpex edged slightly towards that side of the street as they approached. As they drew level, Carpex stumbled on to his hands and knees with a cry of pain. The leader turned, frowned, and called back to his men as he continued up the street. One of the guards strode past the slave and halted a few paces further on to watch Cato. The other guard reached down and roughly pulled Carpex to his feet.

Carpex came up fast, hurling a handful of gravel and filth into the face of the guard. The man instinctively flinched back with a surprised gasp.

'Run!' Carpex shouted in Greek and leaped for the entrance to the alley as Cato sprinted after him. The moment they left the light cast by the officer's torch they were plunged into darkness. The alley was narrow, scarcely wide enough for two men to walk down it abreast, and the intensity of the smell of rotten food, shit and sweat was overpowering as Cato and Carpex stumbled and slithered past dark doorways and shuttered windows. Behind them the officer shouted orders to his men and then there was a glimmer of light behind the two fugitives as the guards thrust their way into the alley.

'Move!' Carpex dragged Cato behind him as they ran on. Glancing back over his shoulder Cato saw the officer leading the pursuit, torch held high and flaring brightly in the confined space, casting a red hue over the guards and the squalid surroundings. The officer shouted and thrust an arm towards the two fugitives.

'Stay close!' Carpex hissed, and they scrambled on, keeping to the middle of the alley in a bid to stay clear of any obstacles leaning against the walls close by on either side. Behind them Cato could hear the clatter and thud of the guards' boots as they tried to run down their prey. Carpex slithered and lost his balance, nearly fell, but managed to keep going as Cato almost ran into the back of him.

'They're gaining!' Cato said through gritted teeth. 'We have to do something.'

'Just keep running!' Carpex gasped. 'We'll lose them. Trust me!'

But Cato was already sure the attempt to stay ahead of the enemy was bound to fail. There were too many obstacles in the street. Sooner or later they would fall headlong and be caught. Ahead he could just make out a change in the shadows as the alley bent sharply to the left. As Carpex scrambled round the corner Cato knew that he must act, or they were doomed, and the men of both cohorts along with them. He grasped Carpex's arm. 'Wait there!' He pointed to the middle of the alley, a few paces on from the corner. Then, snatching his robes aside, Cato drew his sword and flattened himself into the nearest doorway. His heart was pounding so loudly in his ears that it was difficult to clearly make out the approaching footsteps. He knew there would be only one chance to turn on his pursuers. Cato must strike hard and fast, just as Macro would in the same situation. He took a deep breath, filling his lungs, as the flickering red glow of the torch flared on the walls in the angle of the corner.

Then the gloom of the alley was brilliantly illuminated as the torch burst round the end of the wall Cato was pressed into. The officer caught sight of Carpex at once and shouted with triumph as he ran towards the slave. The first of his men appeared a moment later, just as their officer passed Cato. With as loud a roar as he could manage Cato sprang out, sword held high, tip pointed towards the face of the guard.

There was no pause as he slammed his sword arm out, taking the man in the cheek just below his left eye. The blade cut through flesh and muscle before shattering the bone beneath and driving deep into the skull. Instantly Cato withdrew the sword with a savage wrench and swirled round in one movement, still roaring at the top of his voice. The rebel officer had half turned, his face a mask of surprise and fear in the red glow of the torch. Then the edge of Cato's sword cut into his neck, between the mail shirt and the rim of his helmet. The blow had been directed with all the strength at Cato's command and it carved diagonally through the neck and split the collarbone before it hit the officer's spine, and stopped. His legs gave out and he slumped to his knees with a puzzled expression, just before he died.

A thud from behind caused Cato to turn back, pulling his blade free. The first guard's body had just hit the ground, the legs kicking out in a savage spasm, as the second guard ran into sight. He stopped as he made to change direction round the corner, but the sight of his two stricken comrades, and Cato looming over them, slightly crouched and ready to spring as he raised his dripping blade, was too much. He backed away frantically, back round the corner and out of sight, then Cato heard his footsteps sprinting away as the man cried out in alarm and terror.

There was no time to take any satisfaction in his small victory and Cato quickly wiped the blood from his sword on the edge of his cloak, and beckoned to Carpex.

'Take off your robe. Put on the officer's kit.'

'What?' Carpex still looked stunned in the light of the torch guttering amongst the filth on the ground.

'Put it on now,' Cato ordered harshly as he cast his robe aside and leaned over the body of the guard. He untied the chin straps and pulled the helmet and the liner off the man's head, and then undid the sword belt. Glancing round he saw that Carpex had knelt down and after a brief, reluctant pause was beginning to do the same to the rebel officer. The guard was wearing chain mail, and as ever the awkward metal rings were difficult to wriggle over the chest, shoulders and head and Cato had to wrench furiously at the mail to get it free. At once he gathered it up over his head and thrusting his arms through he let the mail slide heavily over his body. He picked up the liner and jammed it on his head before putting on the conical helmet and tying the chin straps. Carpex was still struggling to get into his mail and Cato quickly helped him. A moment later Cato picked up the torch and handed it to the slave before he bent down and retrieved the guard's spear.

'At least now we shouldn't attract too much unwanted attention. Now, get us to that tunnel, Carpex.'

The slave turned and trotted down the alley. Cato followed, sticking close to his companion so that he could see the way ahead lit by the torch. Carpex led them through the twisting network of old streets unerringly, even though it was night. Not once did they see any sign of the inhabitants and Cato guessed that they must be sheltering anxiously behind their locked doors, praying that the rebels would ignore them. At length, they entered a slightly wider thoroughfare that ended in a market square where the traders' stalls stood bare. A voice grumbled from the shadows, and as Cato and Carpex turned to the sound they saw a figure a short distance off. Before they could react the man turned and disappeared. The sound of footsteps padded away into the night.

'Must have been a beggar,' Carpex suggested softly. 'They sometimes sleep in the markets. Anyway, look there, master.' Carpex indicated a stone structure in the centre of the square with a low arched doorway.

'What is it?'

'One of the entrances to the city's sewers. The engineers use it from time to time, but it's nearly always locked.' Carpex smiled. 'At least that's what they think.'

'Locked?' Cato shook his head in frustration as they approached the heavy studded door set into the stone archway. 'What now?'

'Just watch,' said Carpex as he examined the iron bracket where the bar slid into the masonry. Drawing his dagger, Carpex scraped some of the filth away from the edges of the stones and then inserted the blade in the gap where the mortar should have been. He wriggled the blade for a moment until a square-edged piece of stone began to come out. As soon as he could grasp its edges Carpex pulled it free and placed it carefully on the ground. The bolt was exposed and now Carpex could open the locked door. The bottom grated over the flagstone and then there was a groan of protest from the hinges. Both men winced, waited a moment for a reaction, and then slid through the gap.

'How did you know about the door?' asked Cato when they were inside.

'I arranged it that way, so the prince and I could slip in and out of the sewage tunnels without anyone's knowing. If you don't look at that piece of stone carefully you'd never know it could be moved. Come on.'

Carpex ducked under the low ceiling, lighting his way with the torch held out ahead of him. Cato followed. Just inside was a small stone platform, with several stained steps leading down towards the tunnel.

'Better shut the door, master.'

Cato eased it back into its frame, keeping the noise from the hinges as quiet and gradual as possible. Then he nodded to Carpex. 'There. Now let's go.'

The steps were dry at the top, but the last few were slimy and Cato trod warily as they descended through a small arch into the tunnel. His nose wrinkled at the stench as they paused in the light of the torch. The sewer stretched out on either side as far as Cato could see by the wavering glow of the small flame. The steps disappeared into the slowly flowing current of fouled water and after a small hesitation Carpex stepped down into the flow. It came halfway up his calves as he headed to their right, in the direction of the current. With a grimace, Cato followed him. The thick atmosphere was filled with the tang of shit and piss and Cato had to swallow hard as he fought the impulse to be sick.

'How far have we got to go?'

'A few hundred paces, master. Then we're beneath the citadel.'

They had waded no more than fifty yards when both men heard a muffled squeal of iron hinges, and they paused to look back down the tunnel. The sound of voices echoed off the rough stonework and a moment later a red glow marked the low arch where the steps led up to the entrance.

'Shit,' Cato muttered. 'That beggar must have found someone. That was quick. The other guard must have alerted the whole town.'

'What do we do?'

'Could you find your way from here in the dark?'

'No.'

'Then we have to go on! Fast!'

They moved on, splashing through the filthy stream in the wildly flaring glow of Carpex's torch. Then behind them came a shout, harsh and immediate in the closed tunnel, and the churning rush of several men coming after the two fugitives.

'How much further?' Cato gasped.

'Not far. Just up ahead, a tunnel branches to the right.'

Cato glanced up and scanned the side of the tunnel. The black mouth of an opening loomed up at the limit of the orange bloom cast by the torch.

'I see it!'

They splashed up to the junction and turned into the side tunnel.

'What now?'

'Follow it for a short stretch, until there's a curve, then there's the spur going towards the old stables of the citadel.'

'Right.' Cato followed the slave as he surged on. The pursuers were lost from sight for a moment, and even the sound of their progress had diminished now that Cato and Carpex were in the new stretch of tunnel. But all too quickly the entrance behind them was illuminated by a growing glow and a moment later the rebels had followed them into the side tunnel. Just ahead Cato could see the tunnel begin to curve, as Carpex had said it would. As they splashed round the bend the pursuers were again lost from view and then Carpex pointed.

'There! See!'

A small passage opened on to the main sewer, perhaps just over half the height of the tunnel they were in. As they reached it Cato glanced in and saw that the spur sloped gently up.

'Where does it go?'

'Directly to the barracks, master. It ends just below a grille.'

'Right.' Cato took the torch from the slave and thrust him into the small opening. 'You first. Go as fast as you can. But you stop the moment we hear the rebels.'

Carpex nodded and ducked down as he scrambled up the tunnel. Cato swung the torch underarm and then lobbed it as far down the tunnel as he could. It flared through the dark air, bounced off the wall in a shower of sparks and then fell into the stinking current, hissed a moment and died, pitching the tunnel into darkness. Cato felt for the rim of the entrance to the side tunnel and bent down to ease his way into it. There was no way of walking, or even crouching, and he went down on hands and knees. There was only a trickle on the sloping floor, but it was covered with slime and small pieces of rubble. Ahead of him he could hear Carpex grunting and scrabbling up the slope. His breaths came in strained gasps and the weight of the chain mail was quickly exhausting him. They had gone perhaps thirty feet when the sounds of their pursuers reached Cato's ears.

'Carpex!' he hissed as loudly as he dared. 'Stop!'

The small passage fell silent as they froze and Cato struggled to control his breathing as the rebels approached the end of the tunnel. The entrance gleamed briefly, and then they had passed it. Cato waited a little longer and then whispered, 'Go.'

On they went, climbing the spur in the pitch darkness, until Cato heard the sound of the rebels coming back down the tunnel. A voice called out and then there came the sounds of men scurrying up the small passage behind them. There was no longer any need for quiet and Cato called out to Carpex.

'They're on to us! Move yourself!'

They hurried forward, ignoring the stench and the muck beneath their hands and legs as they moved on all fours. Behind them, their pursuers, aided by the light cast by their torches, came on swiftly, their grunts and shouts carrying up the narrow tunnel as if they were breathing down Cato's neck. Then he was aware of the faint details in the walls ahead of him and realised that the rebels were closing on him. If they should catch up before Cato and Carpex reached the end of the passage there was no chance of being able to turn and hold them off. All Cato had was a sword. He had glimpsed at least one spear amongst the men following him. They could easily outreach him and he had no room to move to avoid being skewered.

The tunnel began to flatten out and Cato was aware of voices ahead of him. 'Almost there!' Carpex called back.

Cato glanced over his shoulder and saw, perhaps only fifteen paces behind him, the torch of the first of their pursuers, and the grimly determined expression of the man behind it as he scuttled forward.

The voices above them quickly grew louder and then Cato saw a dim shaft of light shining down into the tunnel just ahead. Carpex hurled himself forward to cover the last few yards and then he rose up and grasped the iron bars of the grille above him and thrust. The grille did not budge, and as Cato reached him he too straightened up and pushed with all his strength, gashing one hand on a broken prong. A small trickle of mortar fell on them and then with a sudden scraping rush the grille gave and toppled on to the floor of the room above with a crash. Carpex clambered up, grasping the edge of the hole as he dragged himself up and then rolled to one side. Cato cast a glance down the tunnel and saw that the nearest rebel was almost on him, and had dropped his torch and drawn his sword as he came on, teeth clenched, intent on getting his kill.

There was a sudden roar of surprised voices in the room above and Carpex screamed. But Cato thrust himself up through the hole, heedless of the danger, to escape from the murderous intent of the man coming along the tunnel. With a grunt of supreme effort he drew himself up through the opening. His torso was halfway through when he saw Carpex sprawled on the flagstones beside him. The slave wore a dazed expression and blood was oozing from his mouth. Around them, a crowd of men in blue tunics was closing in, shouting furiously. Several were armed and one leaped forward, sword raised as he made to smash the blade into Cato's head.

'Don't!' Cato screamed out in Latin, throwing his arm up in an effort to protect himself as the blade swept down. 'I'm a Roman!'

CHAPTER FOURTEEN

As soon as night had fallen Macro and Prince Balthus led their column along a less direct route than Cato and Carpex had taken. The Roman cavalry and Palmyran horsemen marched on foot, leading their mounts, whose hooves had been muffled by strips of cloth. The infantry had been ordered to leave their packs in a cave at the base of the hill and marched in a broken step carrying just their weapons in addition to their armour. All items of loose kit had been tied down so that the men might march as quietly as possible and all talk had been forbidden. The centurions and optios marched alongside their men, ears pricked for the slightest infraction of orders, which would result in a beating for any man they overheard.

As the column shuffled along in silence Macro could not help taking a great deal of pride in their achievement. They had crossed a wasteland and fought off an enemy to get this far and now their goal was in sight. However, unless Cato made it through to the garrison of the citadel, and then managed to persuade them to create a diversion so that Macro and the others could enter the city, this was almost as close to their goal as they would ever be. As he thought of his young friend, Macro once again regretted giving him permission to go with Balthus' slave. There were many other officers who would have done just as well, and Cato was needed by the men of his cohort. In truth, Macro realised as he pondered his decision, he too needed Cato in situations like this where timing, judgement and the ability to think on your feet were vital qualities. In a straightforward stand-up fight with an enemy Macro was in his element and there were few men in the legions who could match him as a battlefield leader. He was as strong and brutal as he was courageous and when the eager anticipation of battle flowed like fire through his veins he was open enough to admit that he actually enjoyed the prospect. Unlike Cato, who saw it as a necessary means to an end.

Or at least Cato used to see it that way, Macro reflected with a concerned expression. Earlier that day, for the first time, he had seen the excited glint in Cato's eye when he had insisted on accompanying Balthus' slave into Palmyra. It was a ludicrously dangerous task to volunteer for and Macro could not help worrying for his friend's safety. Not just because Cato would be venturing into the heart of an enemy-controlled city, but mostly because Macro was not convinced that Cato was a natural fighter. There was too much of the thinker in the lad, Macro mused regretfully. Filling his head with fancy philosophies read in obscure scrolls served no practical purpose, nor even provided much in the way of entertainment, unlike the comedy plays that were Macro's main pleasure.

In the years since Cato had taught him to read, Macro had mostly used his new skill to fulfil the tedious demands of military bureaucracy. But in recent months, thanks to the peaceful and pleasant posting to Antioch, Macro had begun to read for pleasure. Quietly putting aside the Latin translations of Socrates and Aristotle that Cato had dug out of the local library, Macro devoted his reading hours to comedies amongst other more racy material and had been working his way through the plays of Plautius before the present crisis with Parthia had blown up and brought him here to Palmyra.

Macro's mind snapped back to the present as one of the scouts came scrambling along the edge of the spur that projected into the plain. He raised his hand to halt the men behind him and the column awkwardly stumbled to a halt in the darkness. The scout was from one of the Second Illyrian's cavalry squadrons and he saluted as he made his report. Macro stopped him at once.

'Speak in Greek,' he nodded towards Balthus, 'so that we both understand.'

'Yes, sir.' The scout, like most troops stationed in the eastern Empire, spoke Greek first, and Latin as much as the army required him to. He pointed over the end of the spur. 'We've come across an enemy patrol in that direction, sir. No more than half a mile from the tip of the spur. By a few palm trees.'

'How many?'

'No more than twenty, sir.'

'Which direction are they headed?'

'They're not heading anywhere, sir. They seem to have stopped for the night. Most of them seem to be asleep, but there's two on watch.'

'Damn,' Macro muttered. The rebel patrol had camped right across his line of advance.

'We could go round them,' Balthus suggested. 'March out from the spur for half a mile and then try to cut round.'

Macro shook his head. 'That'd take too long. We have to get into the city before first light. Besides,' he turned towards the open landscape beyond the end of the spur, 'we'd have to go further out to be sure that they didn't see us. If they did, you can be sure that their first act would be to alert their friends in Palmyra. And even if they didn't spot us, we'd have to cross a lot of ground before we could resume our approach to the eastern gate. There are bound to be some shepherds, merchants or travellers out there on the plain. Any one of them could raise the alarm.'

'A fair point, Centurion. What do you suggest we do?'

Macro thought a moment. 'We'd better take the direct route. It would be swiftest and safest, provided we eliminate that patrol first.'

'Eliminate the patrol?' The surprise in the prince's tone was clear.

'Yes. It must be done quickly. We can catch and kill them all before they have a chance to send someone to raise the alarm. This is where your boys come in.'

'What are you talking about?'

'We send them out either side of the camp. When they're in position, they can mount up, ride in and finish the rebels off before they can get in their saddles. None of them can be allowed to escape. Be clear on that.'

'Don't worry, Roman. I know the stakes.' Balthus paused a moment before continuing, 'But what if some of them do escape and raise the alarm? What then?'

'Then we must decide whether we fall back to the hills and wait for another opportunity to enter the city, which, frankly, I doubt we'll get once the rebels are alerted to our presence close to Palmyra. In all likelihood, they'll make it a priority to hunt us down and destroy us. Or,' Macro watched the prince's face closely, 'we continue with the attack and get stuck into the rebels before they have much of a chance to react. Of course, if they manage to hold the gate then it will all have been for nothing. So, that's the choice, if any of that patrol escapes the net. What would you do?'

Macro had already made up his mind, but he was curious to take the measure of Balthus. Would the prince of Palmyra fight, or would he flee? Balthus responded without any hesitation.

'If any escape, then I say we advance on Palmyra as fast as we can.' Balthus tapped his chest. 'And since I am in command until we reach the citadel, that is what we will do.'

Macro smiled. 'A man after my own heart. Right, I expect you will want to give the orders to your men for the attack on that patrol.'

Balthus nodded and turned away, striding across the desert to the dark line of his men stretched out a short distance from the Roman column. Macro watched him for a moment and then returned to the head of his column and took the leading century, under Centurion Horatius, from his cohort forward, following the scout towards the enemy patrol, moving as stealthily as possible. To his left the Palmyran horsemen moved out, away from the spur and into the desert, to encircle the rebels. To Macro's right the crest of the spur gradually sloped down to the plain and ended in a jumble of boulders at its tip. A short distance beyond he saw the dark outline of the fronds of the palm trees against the starlit sky.

'Halt here,' Macro whispered to the centurion behind him, and crept forward as the order was quietly relayed down the line of dark figures. He caught up with the scout and tapped him on the shoulder. 'This is close enough.'

The scout nodded and lowered himself to the ground. A moment later Macro lay beside him and squinted into the darkness. The trees were clear enough, as were the horses tethered beneath them. Around them, huddled on the ground, were the rebels. As the scout had reported, most were lying down, but a handful sat together and Macro could just hear snatches of their conversation. They sounded good-humoured enough and it was clear that they weren't expecting any trouble. Two men squatted in the desert on either side of the camp, keeping watch.

Macro eased himself into a more comfortable position and whispered softly to the scout, 'Get back to Centurion Horatius and tell him that all's well. The enemy are still here and Balthus should take them by surprise. Tell him that I want his men ready to come forward the moment the attack begins.'

'Yes, sir.'

'Off you go.'

The scout nodded his head and then crept off through the rocks, leaving Macro to watch the enemy alone. The delay was frustrating but it should not set them back too long, he hoped. Otherwise Cato might light his beacon and have the garrison launch a costly and pointless diversionary attack. Assuming Cato had actually got through to the garrison, Macro reminded himself. He settled down to watch the rebel patrol, occasionally glancing out into the night for any sign of Balthus and his men. But there was nothing. After a while Macro grew fretful and hissed impatiently through his clenched teeth.

'Come on . . . come on. Haven't got all bloody night . . . Where the hell are you?'

As he heaped curses on to the head of the Palmyran prince, one of the rebels who was still awake, talking with his companions, eased himself off the ground and started walking slowly in Macro's direction.

'Oh, great,' Macro muttered. 'Fine time to have a crap.'

His irritation turned to anxiety as the figure continued towards Macro's position. If he continued on his course he would walk right up to Macro and trip over him. Macro flattened himself to the ground and reached a hand down to his sword handle. He could hear the man's footsteps now: a soft scraping shuffle over the stony ground. Someone called out to him from the camp and the man shouted back an angry response and his comrades laughed. Macro was lying between a large boulder and a stunted shrub and he peered through the skein of small spidery branches as the man approached. He cast about a moment before settling on a rock no more than ten feet from Macro, where he could squat out of sight of his comrades. Pulling up his robes he crouched down and stuck his backside out in Macro's direction. With a grunt he began his movements and Macro instantly wished that the man's diet had not left him with such loose bowels. A foul odour filled the air and Macro's nose wrinkled with disgust. At length the man finished and looked around for something to wipe his backside. He turned towards Macro and froze.

130

There was a pause as neither man moved, then the rebel rose up to his full height, still staring in Macro's direction. Hardly daring to breathe, Macro released his grip on his sword handle and groped for the nearest sizeable rock. His fingers grazed over one that would fit in his hand comfortably and closed round it as the rebel took a hesitant step towards him, and muttered an exclamation.

Macro burst from cover, throwing the rock as hard as he could, and then snatched out his sword as he hurled himself towards the rebel. The rock struck the man on the side of his jaw and glanced off, but the impact stunned him for the instant that it took Macro to cannon into his body, ramming home his sword into the man's stomach as they slammed on to the ground. Macro landed heavily on the rebel, driving the breath from him in a harsh gasp. The blade drove up under the man's ribs, into vital organs. He squirmed, gasping for breath so that Macro feared he might cry out a warning before he died.

'Oh no you don't,' Macro hissed, clamping his hand over the man's mouth and pressing down. With a last reserve of his failing strength the rebel writhed and bucked, trying to dislodge the Roman, but Macro fought back, working his blade furiously inside the man's chest. Then the rebel slumped, inert, his eyes staring blindly at the stars. Macro continued to hold him down a moment longer until he was quite certain that the man was dead, and then relaxed his grip, removing his hand from the slack jaw. He rolled away from the body, wrenching his blade free as he lay and caught his breath. It was a moment before he was aware of the smell and realised he was on the spot where the man had been squatting a moment earlier.

'Shit,' he grumbled. 'How fucking lovely.'

He leaned towards the body, cut a strip off the man's tunic and did his best to clean off the filth as he continued to keep watch for any sign of Balthus and his men. This was getting beyond a joke, he thought bitterly. If Balthus didn't make his move now it would be too late to arrive before the gate under the cover of darkness. A voice called out from the camp. Macro kept still, until the man called out again. This was not good, he realised. If there was no reply from the rocks the rebels were bound to send someone over to look. Macro hurriedly untied his helmet and lowered it to the ground. Then he rose up cautiously, looking over the rock towards the camp. When the rebel called out a third time, the anxiety clear in his tone, Macro stood up a little further and waved his hand. To his relief the men waiting for their companion to return laughed and settled back down to their conversation.

Barely had Macro resumed his position behind the rock when there was a sudden thrumming of hooves and dark shapes rushed out of the night towards the rebel patrol's camp. The dull whack of arrows striking home sounded above the thud of hooves, and the snorts and whinnying of frightened horses. Then the cries of the wounded and the shouts of alarm split the night as the first blades clashed with a series of sharp ringing blows. There was no need to conceal himself any longer and Macro emerged from the rocks and watched from a safe distance as Balthus and his men swirled through the palm trees and cut down any man they found on the ground.

'Sir?' Centurion Horatius called out as he led his men through the rocks towards Macro. 'Sir, are you there?'

'Over here!' Macro raised his arm and the centurion and his legionaries came jogging towards him. 'Form two lines here. We're not taking part in this. We're just here to prevent any rebels running for it in this direction.'

'Yes, sir.' Horatius sniffed, then grimaced before he saluted and strode off to pass on the orders to his century. Macro turned to watch the attack on the rebels. It was all but over. The riders were no longer charging across the campsite, but picking their way over the bodies, pausing to finish off the wounded and any who were cowering on the ground trying to surrender. There could be no prisoners taken tonight. They would only hold the column up and provide the added inconvenience of having to be guarded, not to mention the danger that they might give the column away as it approached the city and lay in wait for the chance to assault the eastern gate.

'Right, it's all over,' Macro announced. 'Send a runner back for the rest of the column. It's time we got moving again.'

A rider approached from the sparse spread of palm trees and Macro guessed it was Balthus.

'The way is clear, Centurion. None of the rebels escaped my men. They're all dead.'

'Good job,' Macro conceded. 'I suggest we continue the advance immediately, Prince.'

132

It was the first time that Macro had shown any sign of deference to Balthus and the latter paused a moment to take in the implied praise and respect. He nodded to Macro. 'I agree. Now that we have reached the plain, my men will spread out and screen our approach to the gate. There shouldn't be any more delays.'

'That's good,' said Macro. 'We can't stop for anything until we are in position to wait for Cato's signal.'

'Very well, Centurion. I shall let my men know.' He paused. 'By the way, where is that stink coming from?'

'Stink?' Macro responded testily. 'What stink?'

Balthus wheeled his mount round and trotted back towards his men. Macro stared at them a moment, impressed by the ruthless speed with which they had struck and wiped out the patrol. With a few thousand such men in the service of Rome there was no telling what might be achieved on the eastern frontier of the Empire. Their skill with bow and sword while mounted was matchless. Only the Parthians were better at this highly mobile form of warfare, and even then, Macro decided, the men of Palmyra must surely give a good account of themselves when they fought Parthian troops. As the uneven footsteps of the rest of his men reached Macro's ears he shrugged off his speculative frame of mind with a slight smile. He was thinking a good deal too much since he had met Cato. Especially when there was soldiering to be done.

'Column!' he called out as loudly as he dared. 'Advance!'

The men of the two cohorts emerged from the rocks like a black snake. They marched quickly past the site of the butchered patrol and followed in the wake of Balthus and his men as they headed directly for the east gate of Palmyra. They met no more rebels, and startled only a young shepherd boy, who immediately took off into the night with his small flock of sheep, which bleated irritably as they fled.

By the time they drew close to the city, Macro and his men were exhausted. Marching at night was always more tiring than during daylight, with the added burden of the strain on eyes and ears as they watched for any sign of the enemy, or an ambush. Balthus halted his riders and dispersed them to the flanks as Macro came up with his infantry. The men were quietly ordered to lie down and remain still and silent until the order to attack was given. Macro and Balthus crept a short distance ahead of their men and crouched down no more than a quarter of a mile from the gate. The walls of the city now loomed dark and tall and torches flickered along its length as the men on watch duty moved slowly between the towers watching for trouble.

The citadel was visible in the distance and Macro could just make out the tallest of its towers. If Cato had got through, that would be where the signal was shown, and Macro kept his eye fixed to the spot. The night gradually wore on and there was no sign of a signal. Balthus stirred and turned towards Macro.

'Perhaps your comrade, and my slave, failed to get through.'

'Give the lad a chance,' Macro responded. 'Cato can do it. He always does.'

Balthus stared at him a moment before he continued, 'You think highly of that young officer.'

'Yes. Yes, I do. He's a rare one, is Cato. He won't let us down.'

'I hope not, Centurion. It all depends on him now.'

'I know,' Macro replied softly, and they both gazed towards the city walls as they waited, and wondered what had become of Carpex and Cato.

CHAPTER FIFTEEN

'R oman?' asked the soldier in Greek as he lowered his sword. 'What in Hades is a Roman doing popping up out of our sewer?'

'Just get me out of here,' Cato snapped, hearing the laboured breathing and scraping in the tunnel as the rebels came after him.

The Palmyran soldier paused a moment, as his comrades came hurrying over. Then the soldier sheathed his sword, grasped Cato's arm and hauled him up through the grating and into the barrack room, still watching him suspiciously. He gestured to Carpex lying stunned in the gutter that ran through the room and fed into the drain. 'Well, he's certainly no Roman.'

'Explain later,' Cato gasped and pointed back into the tunnel. 'Rebels, down there.'

'A likely story,' someone snorted derisively. 'They're bloody spies, the pair of them. Silence his tongue, Archelaus.'

The man who had felled Carpex and hauled Cato out of the sewer reached for his sword, and then paused, staring into the hole. Cato glanced down and saw the glow of a torch, and then the tip of a spear came into view. The Greek called Archelaus snatched out his sword and took a step back as he called out to his comrades, 'He's right! There's someone in there. Arm yourselves!'

At once the barrack room was a mass of rushing figures as those who had not yet taken up their weapons ran back to their bunks to get them. The spear tip rose through the hole, a hand gripped the rim, and a moment later a helmeted head appeared above the floor. Archelaus leaped forward and cut down savagely with his falcata. There was a dull ring and a crunch as the blade cut through the helmet and the skull beneath, lodging just above the rebel's brow. His eyes were wide and startled for an instant before a sheet of blood obscured his face. Archelaus pressed a foot on the man's shoulder and yanked his blade

135

free, and the body and spear dropped out of sight. There was a loud shout of rage from the tunnel, but none of the pursuers dared to take the place of the first man.

Cato pointed to a cauldron suspended over an iron stove in the side of the room used as the soldier's mess. Wisps of steam curled up from the lip of the cauldron.

'Use that! Get the cauldron over here!'

'But that's our stew,' one of the soldiers protested. 'It's almost ready to eat.'

Cato scrambled up to his feet, and rose to his full height as he snapped out the order. 'You and you, get it over here, now!'

The two men turned to Archelaus with a questioning look and he waved his dripping blade at them. 'Do it!'

The two men hurried over to the cauldron and picking up rags they grasped the heavy iron handles and lifted it off the stove, grunting with the effort as they struggled towards the drain with their burden. As one of the Greek mercenaries leaned over the hole the head of a spear shot up at his face, and he threw himself back just in time to avoid a terrible wound. As soon as the men with the cauldron reached the edge they set it down and grasped the rim with their rags, straining as they tipped the cauldron. The steaming liquid and some lumps of meat sloshed over, most of it going straight down into the sewer in a thick brown gush. At once there were several agonised screams, and the glow from the torch blinked out. A puff of steam came up through the hole with the cries of pain and rage. Then they heard the rebels scrambling down the tunnel, before anything else was poured on them.

Archelaus let out a loud laugh. 'That's cooked 'em nicely! Now get the grille back in place, and you, Croton, keep a watch on it.' The Greek glanced at Carpex, who had propped himself up on an elbow and was shaking his head. 'Sorry about that, friend, but if you will pop your head up out of a sewer unannounced, that's your own lookout.'

Carpex looked up at him, winced and then let out a low groan. Archelaus saw the slave brand on his forehead and turned to Cato. 'This one yours, Roman?'

'No. He belongs to Prince Balthus. The prince told him to guide me into the citadel. We carry a message for the king. I have to speak to him at once.'

'Not so fast.' Archelaus held up a hand. 'First, tell me who you are, and what's going on here.'

Cato restrained the impulse to shout at the man and demand to be taken to the king. He took a deep breath to calm his frustration. 'I'm the prefect of the Second Illyrian cohort. Part of a relief column sent by the governor of Syria. The rest of the force is outside the city waiting for a signal to assault the eastern gate and cut their way through to the citadel. Now, if that's enough for you, I must see your king.'

The Greek mercenary narrowed his eyes. 'That's quite a story. Under normal circumstances I wouldn't believe a word of it. But the unusual nature of your appearance seems to support your tale. Just as well we had come off watch, otherwise there would have been no one here to help you.' Archelaus turned to the hole. 'And now it seems that you have shown the rebels a way into the citadel. Well, that's sorted out easily enough. You!' He pointed to one of his men. 'Get some rubble into that tunnel. Fill it up and then cover the grille over with something heavy. Come, Roman, you'd better follow me.'

He made to help Carpex back on to his feet then sniffed distastefully. 'Better get rid of those robes first though, eh?'

Cato was all for seeing the king immediately, but realised that some modicum of formality had to be maintained if he was to create a favourable impression. Once they had cast aside their soiled outer clothes and cleaned as much of the sewer filth off their bodies as quickly as they could, they followed Archelaus from the barracks. The room they had entered from the sewers proved to be one of ten that opened on to a courtyard behind the royal quarters of the citadel. In a more peaceful era the barracks had once accommodated some of the finest horses in the eastern world. Now people slept and sat in clusters where the horses once exercised. The sound of coughing and muted snatches of conversation punctuated the quiet of the night.

'Who are these people?' Cato asked.

'Some are from the palace. But most of them are loyalists who fled to the citadel when the revolt broke out. We took as many as we could before the king ordered the gates closed. There was no room for any more.'

'There were others?'

'Hundreds. Trapped outside when the rebels closed in on the citadel.'

'What happened to them?'

'What do you think?' Archelaus replied harshly. 'Want me to draw you a picture? Let's just say Prince Artaxes won't be remembered for his merciful nature.'

They walked in silence for a moment, picking a path through the refugees, before Cato spoke again.

'What's the situation here? The message we got in Antioch was that you were holding your own.'

'That's true enough,' Archelaus responded. 'The rebels aren't going to get through the walls any time soon. We've more than enough men here to keep them at bay. And we have enough food for a few days yet. The only problem is water. There are two cisterns under the royal quarters, there.' He pointed towards the colonnaded building with a tower at each corner ahead of them. Next to it was the Temple of Bel, surrounded by a high curtain wall to prevent impious eyes from gazing upon the shrine of Palmyra's most powerful deity. Archelaus continued, 'Both were supposed to be kept filled to capacity, for emergencies. Turns out that the water in one has been fouled and the other was only half full. There wouldn't be much difficulty if we had to supply the current garrison.'

'How many men under arms do you have?' Cato asked.

'The royal guard numbered nearly five hundred when the revolt broke out. We lost over a hundred when we escaped from the palace, and fought our way across the city to the citadel. We've lost more in the days since then. Now?' He thought for a moment. 'There's nearly three hundred and fifty of us left. My syntagma suffered the heaviest casualties in the fight to reach the citadel.'

'Syntagma?'

'The royal guard is made up of two syntagmata. Each one has two hundred and forty men in it, or did before the revolt flared up. Each syntagma has four tetrarchies of sixty men. That's what I command.' He jabbed a thumb at his chest. 'I'm a tetrarch.'

'I see.' Cato nodded. 'Any other men on your strength, apart from the king's bodyguard?'

Archelaus shrugged dismissively. 'A handful of nobles and their retinues. Personally, I think they're more danger to us than to the rebels. Then there's a half-century of auxiliaries who were guarding the

Roman ambassador and his family and staff. So we have just over four hundred effectives, and at least five hundred civvies.'

Cato thought for a moment. If all went well this night the garrison was about to be swelled by over a thousand Roman soldiers and Prince Balthus' companions, not to mention all their horses. He turned to Archelaus. 'How long will the water last?'

'Another twenty days or so. At the rate we're rationing it. Oh . . .' He paused mid-stride and looked at Cato. 'That's before your relief column joins us.'

'On current form that water is going to run out in less than ten days.'

'Great,' Archelaus muttered as he resumed his course towards the royal quarters. 'I can imagine how delighted the king is going to be when he works that one out.'

As they approached the royal quarters the guards at the entrance rose from the benches either side of the bronze doors and stood to, spears in hand. One of them stepped forward into Archelaus' path and saluted. He glanced over at Cato and Carpex before turning back to the tetrarch.

'Your business, sir?'

'These two just entered the citadel. They claim they have a message for the king.'

'The king's asleep, sir.'

'I can imagine.' Archelaus smiled thinly. 'It's the middle of the night. But these men must see him urgently.'

The guard shifted uncomfortably and then made a decision. 'I'll send a man to his chamberlain, sir.'

'Then do it quickly!' Cato snapped in exasperation. 'There's no time to lose.'

The guard stared at Cato for a moment, wrinkled his nose, and then looked to Archelaus. The latter nodded.

'Do as he says.'

'Yes, sir.'

The guard gestured to one of his comrades and the man turned, heaved one of the doors open a little way and slipped through the gap. There was a tense silence as the men waited for a response from within. Cato turned away and glanced round the courtyard. Beyond the dense clusters of refugees the walls rose up tall and dark. Along the battlements he could see the dark figures of sentries keeping watch on the approaches to the citadel. A handful of torches flickered on each of the towers, but the sentries kept their distance from the light they cast, not wanting to make a target of themselves. Cato was reassured by the strength of the fortifications, but the fine walls would be no use at all once the water ran out. Then the defenders would have to choose between dying of thirst, surrendering to the rebels – to be massacred – or mounting a desperate attempt to escape from the city, unless the governor of Syria and his army could reach Palmyra before any such choice had to be made.

The sound of footsteps approaching caused Cato to turn and he saw the bronze door swing open to reveal, by the light of the oil lamps burning within, a guard and another man, tall and thin with a straggling grey beard. He stared at Cato for a moment, and then turned to Carpex. A flicker of recognition crossed his features before he addressed the slave in Greek.

'Well, Carpex, how does your master? Still busy hunting with his drunken friends?'

Carpex gave a deep bow. 'My master is outside the city, waiting to come to the aid of his father.'

'Really? Has he run out of drinking money so soon?'

Carpex made to reply, thought better of it, and remained with bowed head as the chamberlain turned his attention back to Cato. 'You must be the Roman. I think you had better explain what you are doing here.'

Cato took a deep breath. 'There's no time for detail. A Roman relief column is outside the city waiting for the signal to force its way in through your east gate. But first you must draw the attention of the rebels away from the gate. Then the signal can be given.'

The chamberlain stared at him for a moment. 'You had better come in. That dog of a slave can remain here.'

'Yes, master,' Carpex muttered and bowed even lower.

'What about me, sir?' asked Archelaus.

The chamberlain dismissed him with a casual wave of the hand. 'You may return to your barracks, Tetrarch. Roman, follow me.'

The chamberlain led Cato through the bronze doors into a short corridor. The floors were laid with red-streaked marble and the walls were covered with paintings of galloping horses, as if they were in a race. The corridor was short, and emerged through an arch into a large paved area. A two-storey portico ran round the edge and torches flickered from wall brackets at regular intervals. To one side a set of comfortable dining couches were arranged about a large table bearing the remains of a small feast. Several slaves were engaged in clearing away the platters and goblets while some more waited on the handful of guests still drinking. Their conversation and muted laughter drifted across the open area as the chamberlain escorted Cato towards some steps that climbed towards what looked to be a large hall. Inside the entrance was a large vestibule and the chamberlain pointed to one of the stone benches lining the waiting area. 'Sit there.'

Cato did as he was told as the chamberlain continued through into the main hall and shut the door behind him. For a while there was silence and Cato fretted furiously at the delay, knowing that Macro and the others were outside the city anxiously waiting for his signal. Then he heard voices inside, a conversation that he could not quite make out. The door opened and the chamberlain beckoned to him.

'Inside.'

Cato did his best not to be even further irritated by the man's curt manner, and strode through into the hall. It was a large square chamber. Not by any means the audience chamber of a rich and powerful king, but then this was not Vabathus' palace, only his refuge. The walls were plain and high, and the floor unostentatiously paved, as the earlier corridor had been. A number of chairs had been arranged in a semicircle at the far end of the hall and two men were already seated there. The chamberlain led Cato to the open space in front of the men and then took his seat to one side. A large, overweight man who looked to be in his late fifties with grey hair and a tired expression sat in the largest chair. He wore a plain white tunic and sandals, and a cloak hung over his shoulders. The other man wore a tunic with a broad red stripe running down the middle. He was younger, no more than forty, and wiry, with the haughty bearing of a Roman aristocrat, and Cato knew at once that he must be the ambassador, Lucius Sempronius.

Cato stood to attention as Sempronius cleared his throat and began to speak.

'You have a message for us?'

'For the king, yes.'

Sempronius smiled. 'Of course, for the king. Let me have it.'

Cato paused, glancing towards Vabathus, waiting for any sign of approval, but Vabathus just stared back blankly and so Cato took the waxed slate from his haversack and walked over to give it to the Roman ambassador. 'From Prince Balthus, and my commander, Centurion Macro of the Tenth Legion.'

'And you are?'

'Quintus Licinius Cato, sir. Acting prefect of the Second Illyrian cohort.'

Sempronius weighed him up. 'Acting prefect, eh? Rather young for such a responsibility, I would say,' he added with a touch of suspicion in his tone.

'The governor was forced to send the two units he had ready, sir,' Cato explained with all the patience he could muster. 'Centurion Macro was seconded to the Tenth Legion from the Second Illyrian, for the duration of the present emergency. I was his adjutant and second-in-command.'

'I see. Well, needs must, I suppose.' Sempronius pursed his lips briefly. 'Obviously my message got through to Longinus. I assume he is hot on the heels of your two cohorts with the rest of his army?'

'I have no idea, sir. He said he would come as soon as possible. In the meantime, my cohort and that of Centurion Macro were sent ahead to bolster the garrison here. We joined forces with Prince Balthus and his men. They're approaching the eastern gate even as I speak, and—'

'Balthus?' The king stirred. 'What good will that fool do? I have no use for a drunkard who spends his life hunting and whoring. I'll have nothing to do with him. Send him away.' He looked through Cato for a moment and continued quietly, 'Of all my sons, why couldn't it have been Balthus who betrayed me? I would have shed no tears over that wastrel . . .'

The king frowned and lowered his head, staring at his feet. Cato glanced towards the ambassador for a cue on how to respond but Sempronius shook his head. There was a brief silence before Sempronius coughed and nodded to Cato. 'Please continue.'

Given the king's previous reaction Cato decided not to mention his son again. 'My superiors have asked me to request the garrison of the citadel to make a diversionary attack to draw forces away from the eastern gate. We have to do it as soon as possible if they are to stand any chance of breaking through to us, sir. They will be watching for my signal. A beacon on the highest tower of the citadel.' Cato switched to Latin, lowered his voice and continued urgently. 'Sir, I beg you. Use whatever influence you have here to begin the feint. Unless Centurion Macro can fight his way through the city he will be cut to pieces outside the walls of Palmyra.'

Sempronius nodded and spoke calmly. 'I will see to it that the orders are given, Prefect Cato. You have my word.' The ambassador switched back into Greek and turned to the chamberlain, who had been sitting in silence during the exchanges.

'Thermon, my friend, you heard it all. You must summon the commander of the garrison. The attack must begin as soon as possible. On the king's orders, understand?'

The chamberlain nodded, and turned to the king. 'Your majesty?'

'What?' Vabathus looked up wearily and saw that they were waiting for his response. He waved a hand flaccidly. 'Do as you wish.'

The chamberlain bowed and quickly backed out of the room as Sempronius beckoned to Cato.

'Prefect, I understand you have one of the prince's slaves with you.'

'Yes, sir.'

'Have him take you to the gate tower. There is a signal station there. You may light your beacon the moment the garrison begins its attack. Then,' he nodded to Cato's bloodied hand, 'you'd better get that seen to.'

CHAPTER SIXTEEN

'There's the signal!' Balthus rose quickly to his feet and stared towards the tower.

'Hmmm?' Macro mumbled, as he stirred from the spot where he had been resting. He had very nearly committed the unforgivable sin of falling asleep on duty. What the hell had come over him? Macro briefly discounted the lost sleep of the last days of the march from Antioch. He had marched and fought in more difficult campaigns before without letting exhaustion get the better of him. Perhaps it was just age, he mused sadly as he scrambled to his feet and stood beside the prince. Balthus pointed over the wall and the sprawl of the city towards the citadel. Above the torches that flickered along the ramparts was a brighter blaze that flared with greater intensity even as Macro picked it out.

'Are you sure that's the one?' asked Macro.

'I'm certain of it.'

'Then let's get moving.' Macro turned round to the officers who had been sitting on the ground, but now approached in response to Balthus' excited cry. Macro drew himself up to his full height, and rubbed his buttocks where they had grown numb as he sat waiting.

'Gentlemen, this is going to be swift and bloody. You have your orders; make sure you follow them precisely. I don't want any confusion when the attack goes in. Get the lads up and let's get moving.'

He exchanged a salute with his officers and returned to the side of Prince Balthus. 'We'll follow your men the moment you begin the attack. Good luck . . . sir.'

Balthus grinned as he patted Macro on the shoulder. 'Luck has never been my problem, Roman, so you can have my share of it tonight.'

With a swirl of his robes, Balthus turned and ran to his horse, snatched the reins from the hand of the auxiliary who was holding it ready, and threw himself up into the saddle. In the darkness behind him the rest of his retinue mounted and when Balthus saw that they were ready he drew his curved blade and raised it above his head, calling out a command to get their attention. He paused a moment and then swept his sword towards the city gate with a strident shout. With a chorus of cries his men urged their mounts into a gallop and a dark tide of horsemen surged out of the desert night towards the eastern gate of Palmyra.

The moment the charge began Macro filled his lungs and bellowed the order for his two cohorts to advance. As they followed the horsemen at a steady trot Macro saw fire arrows arc down from the distant ramparts of the citadel and realised that the diversionary attack was under way. His heart was lifted by the knowledge that Cato had succeeded in getting through. Macro and his men had concealed themselves no more than a quarter of a mile from the eastern gate in order to reach it before the enemy could react, but he knew that the plan would only work if Balthus and his men moved quickly.

Ahead, by the light of the torches burning above the gate, he saw the first of the rebels fall to the arrows of the mounted archers. Some of the men guarding the gate snatched up spears and shields and stood their ground. A handful of others fled for the safety of the city, while a handful of men appeared along the wall, alerted by the thunder of hoofbeats rushing towards the gate. The more courageous of those who remained raised their shields to protect them from the arrows shooting out of the mass of horsemen. A rebel officer, with commendable presence of mind, called on them to form ranks, and before the horsemen could reach the gate they were confronted by a small wall of shields between which spears angled towards Balthus and his men, causing them to swerve aside.

Macro drew his sword and shouted over his shoulder, 'Charge!'

The men broke into a run behind him, breathing hard as their equipment chinked and their iron-shod boots pounded over the hard ground. While Balthus and his men closed round the band of soldiers defending the gate, slashing and hacking at their shields and the shafts of their spears, behind them the doors were slowly being closed as the men inside the city heaved against the heavy slabs of studded timber. Macro watched in desperation as he sprinted forward, already passing through

145

the rearmost riders of the prince's force, steadying their horses as they raised their bows and traded shots with the archers on the battlements above the gate. Macro dodged round the back of a rearing horse, its rider grappling with the shaft of an arrow that pinned his leg to the saddle. Swerving through the other horses, Macro and the leading century of legionaries raced towards the gate. A gap opened ahead of him and Macro saw the last few defenders backing through the small space that remained behind them.

Macro gritted his teeth and ran for all he was worth, heart pounding wildly as he burst through the loose maul of horsemen and charged across the strip of open ground that separated them from the rebels. With a deep roar he hurled himself at the last three still outside the gate. They started at the sound of his war cry but stood their ground and lowered their spears, ready to thrust. Macro raised his shield and swung it across to cover his body and felt the tip of a spear glance aside as he struck the shaft of another with his sword, knocking the point away and down where it could not harm him. The third man just had time to stab his spear towards the centurion's face and Macro snatched his head down, wincing as the spear tip glanced off the side of his helmet just above the ear guard. Then he cannoned into the nearest of them, shield to shield, and flung the man back against the outer surface of one of the doors. The impetus of his charge had carried Macro past the next man, and now he slashed his sword to the right, behind him, and caught the rebel across the back of the shoulders, on his scaled armour. The blade of the short sword did not cut through, but the savage impact of the blow drove the breath from his lungs and stunned him, long enough for one of the legionaries following Macro to batter him on the helmet, driving him on to his knees, where a final downward thrust stabbed through his neck into his heart.

The last of the defenders had dropped his spear in his desperation to slip through the narrow opening that remained. Macro pounced on the weapon and stabbed it through the gap between the edges of the doors. They jarred on the spear shaft, which started to bend so that Macro feared it would snap. He stabbed his sword into the side of the man still standing pressed against the timber, and then threw his weight against the other door.

'On me!' he bellowed over his shoulder. 'Force the gate!'

More legionaries arrived and thrust themselves against the hard wooden surface, and more men pushed into their backs, boots scrabbling for purchase as they heaved against the doors. On either side, the ladder parties had reached the wall and were raising their assault ladders towards the battlements. Macro could hear the shouts from inside the wall as the rebel officers urged their men on, desperately struggling to close the gate and deny their enemy access to the city.

'Come on!' Macro roared. 'Heave, you bastards! Put your backs into it!' All around him the tightly packed legionaries grunted with the effort of pressing against the doors with all their might. For a moment the timbers inched towards them and Macro watched in alarm as the gap narrowed so that no man could squeeze through. Then, as even more legionaries arrived, and one of the optios began to call time, the Romans checked the efforts of the defenders. The heavy doors were still, caught between the desperate scrums of defenders and attackers. On either side Macro saw the first of the legionaries climbing up the assault ladders. The man was caught in the dull orange pools of light cast by the torches on the wall and was picked off at once by the archers above the gate, tumbling back from the ladders, pierced with the dark shafts of arrows. But the next man was already clambering up the ladder an instant later, one-handed as he covered himself as best he could with his shield as he climbed.

Macro felt the door he was leaning against shift a little and glancing towards the slim gap between the edges he saw that it was wider, and then widening perceptibly. His heart swelled with triumph and elation and he shouted encouragement to the men packed around him, gasping from their desperate efforts to force the gate open.

'It's giving! Keep at it, lads! Heave!'

Macro's feet were solidly braced on the worn slabs of paving as his legs strained with every fibre of his strength. Slowly, but surely, the Romans gained ground as the heavy iron hinges groaned under the pressures being applied to the doors. The narrow gap continued to open and now Macro could see through it to the packed ranks of the rebels inside the city. The nearest of them saw him at the same time, and leaped for the gap, stabbing at Macro with a long finely wrought blade. Macro threw his head to the side as the tip shot past his cheek guard, and was then whipped back.

'Shit,' he hissed through clenched teeth. 'That was too close.'

He kept his distance from the edge of the door and threw his shoulder against the timber once again. 'Keep it going, lads! Almost there!'

The pressure on the gate was remorseless and the Romans gained ground steadily. As the gap opened up enough for a man to pass, Macro ordered some of the nearest men to guard it, but not rush through. They must hit the rebels in a solid wave, with the full weight of the following ranks behind them, not in a fine dribble of individuals who were sure to be isolated and cut down within moments of entering Palmyra.

One of the legionaries hurled a javelin through the growing gap and then the air was filled with an exchange of missiles: more javelins, arrows, sling shot and rocks. Now three men in close formation could fill the gap and the legionaries locked their shields to prevent any attempt to injure the men still heaving at the doors. The time to charge was close and Macro thrust himself away from the timber.

'Make way there! You, take my place!'

He pushed his way across to the men forming up in front of the gap and readied his sword.

'On my command . . . !'

Around him the legionaries braced themselves, shields up, heads down, sword hands clamped tightly round the handles. Macro drew a deep breath.

'Charge!'

He let out an animal roar and it was instantly drowned in a deafening storm of noise as the other men joined in and the legionaries surged forward into the city. As soon as the charge burst upon them the defenders abandoned the gate and without the pressure from behind the doors swung back at speed and crashed against the walls, crushing one of the rebels who had not managed to move away fast enough. The officer in charge of defending the gate had assembled perhaps fifty men ready to countercharge the moment the Romans entered and now they let out a war cry of their own and surged forward behind their lighter, round shields. A handful of defenders found themselves caught between the two opposing waves of screaming men and were trampled underfoot or crushed as they came together in a rippling crash of wood and metal and flesh.

Macro was in the second rank of the century leading the assault and for a moment his instincts told him to thrust his way through to the front and lead his men into the fight. Then cold reason asserted itself. He was in command of over a thousand men. Their survival depended on him and it would be worse than reckless to throw away his life in this skirmish: it would be criminally self-indulgent. He took a deep breath, sheathed his sword and withdrew a short distance from the fighting. He looked round and up and saw that the flanking centuries had found their way on to the walls either side of the gate and were clearing the ramparts of rebels while the rest of the column made ready to pass through below them. He sensed a shadow suddenly looming at his shoulder and swung round to see Balthus swinging himself down from the saddle of his horse.

'Truly, the men of the legions fight like lions.'

The remark was sincere and Macro felt proud, and human enough to admit to a passing moment of smugness after the humiliation of being rescued by the prince and his retinue. Then the feeling fell away and he glanced up the street, over the heads of the fighting men, in the direction of the citadel.

'The action's barely begun, sir. We've a way to go yet.'

Balthus' smile faded. 'Yes. As soon as you have cleared the rebels from around the gate, I will lead the way.'

'Very well. Now, if you'll excuse me.' Macro turned and strode towards the fighting. He could see that his men had the upper hand. It was no surprise. The rebels were brave enough, but their weapons and armour were light and unequal to the task. The legionaries presented a wall of broad shields to the defenders, occasionally punching them forward when an enemy came too close. In between the shields the blades of short swords flickered in and out like silver tongues, stabbing and cutting at the press of rebel bodies, forcing them up the street. Men began to fall back, then turn and run, ducking into the side streets to escape the Roman onslaught. Macro nodded with satisfaction as the legionaries cut down the last of the rebels still brave or foolish enough to fight on, and then the street was in their hands.

'First century! Re-form ranks!' Centurion Horatius bellowed, and the remaining men formed a column four abreast, facing up the street.

As the next century entered the gate, Macro ordered their

commander to form up behind Horatius' men, then turned back to Prince Balthus.

'Sir, I'll need your men in small parties in between each of my centuries.'

'Why?'

Macro indicated the buildings crowding the street on either side. 'I've seen street fighting before. As we go deeper into the city, the rebels are going to regroup and attack us again. From the alleys, and up there on the roofs. Your men are fine shots. They proved that the other day.' He flashed a smile. 'They're the best chance we have of picking off the attackers, and discouraging them from getting too close.'

Balthus nodded. 'I understand. I will give the order.'

'They will need to dismount, and hand their horses over to my cavalry.'

Balthus' dark eyes flashed suspiciously in the torchlit street. 'My followers do not part with their horses lightly, Centurion.'

'I know that well enough, sir. But I give my word, they will be protected by my men.'

'Your word. Very well, I will order it.' Balthus turned away and strode out of the gate. Macro climbed the stairs inside the gate tower and called out to the commanders of the flank centuries to join him. As they picked their way along the battlements Macro glanced over the bodies sprawled around him and could easily imagine the bloody scramble for possession of the gatehouse and the nearest stretches of the city's wall. Once the two centurions were with him Macro gave them their orders.

'You're to guard our flanks until the last of the auxiliaries are inside the city. Then you become the rear guard. Keep your men formed up and stay on the street. You will not stop to engage any rebels. You will ignore any attacks from alleys and side streets. If the column is forced to stop then the initiative goes to the other side. If that happens, we're as good as dead. Is that clear?'

'Yes, sir,' the centurions chorused.

'Good. And by the way.' Macro gestured to the evidence of the bloody struggle around them. 'Good job.'

'Yes, sir. Thank you, sir.'

By the time Macro returned to the street, the first of Balthus' men

150

had positioned themselves at the rear of the first century, bows at the ready. Balthus had joined them, armed with his own bow, gaudily decorated, but quite deadly, Macro realised. He strode over to join the prince.

'All set?'

'Yes, Centurion. We head up that street, as far as the market, then left through the arch on to the way that leads to the citadel.'

'Very well.' Macro cupped his hand to his mouth. 'Column! . . . Advance!'

Even in the brief time it had taken to re-form the column the rebels had appeared at the far end of the street, and as the Roman vanguard tramped forward the first arrows cracked into the shields of the front rank. Balthus' men shot back at once and the rebels scurried for cover as the missiles arced towards them.

'Now we're in for trouble,' Macro growled.

Balthus looked at him. 'Why?'

'You'll see.' Macro's gaze flickered over the buildings lining the street ahead of them. Then he saw a faint blur of movement from one of the roofs and he stabbed a finger towards the spot. 'Up there!'

As the column approached the place where the arrows shot by Balthus' men lay on the paved surface of the street, a lump of masonry was hurled down from an overlooking building. Macro shouted a warning, too late to prevent its smashing down on to the shoulder of the first century's standard-bearer. The blow drove the man down on to his knees. He groaned and tried to keep the heavy shaft held up with his other hand, but the standard tottered a moment and began to fall to the side. Macro leaped towards the man and snatched the standard from his grasp before it hit the ground. He turned and gestured towards two of the men following him.

'You, take over the standard. And you help the bearer to the rear.'

The man chosen to take the standard was a wiry youth, whose expression openly betrayed his pride at being entrusted with the task.

'You know the score,' Macro said tersely. 'Keep it up where the men can see it, and defend it with your life.'

'Yes, sir.'

'Then carry on.' Macro nodded towards the first century marching steadily up the street. 'Don't fall behind.'

As the legionary scurried forward someone shouted a warning as more masonry was thrown down from the roofs on either side.

'Shields!' Macro shouted. 'Raise shields overhead!'

His men lifted their shields and formed a loosely interlocking protective screen over their heads. Balthus' men had no such protection, but in any case they were busy taking shots at any figures that became visible on the roofs. The first of them suddenly cried out and crumpled to the ground close by Macro, felled by a sling shot. There was no time to check if his wound was fatal as the column moved on. Ahead Macro could just make out the place where the street opened out on to the market. A file of rebel soldiers trotted into view and quickly formed up, locking their shields and presenting their sturdy spears to the Romans as they paced towards the end of the street and filled the gap. Macro drew Balthus' attention to the men ahead and the prince rattled out a quick series of orders. His men instantly turned their attention towards the men blocking the route and began to loose arrows in their direction. But these rebels were part of Palmyra's small but effective army; a contingent that had betrayed their king. Like the Romans they raised their shields and the arrows clanged off the bronzed surfaces.

'Spearmen to your front!' Macro warned.

The spearmen were packed tightly into the width of the street and came on steadily, at a pace called out by their officer. The legionaries advanced on them without faltering, shields held out and swords raised to the horizontal, ready to thrust. One of the men began to beat the side of his blade against the shield trim and within moments the rest of the leading century followed suit and the rhythmic metallic clank echoed off the walls on either side. As the Roman column advanced Macro glanced warily down each alley they passed, and saw occasional fleeting movements in the dark shadows. Every so often an arrow or a stone would fly out and clatter off a shield or the armour of one of Macro's men. They were more of a nuisance than a danger and it was only the handful of the enemy who had reached the roofs of the houses lining the street who presented a real threat as they continued to hurl missiles down on the column tramping up the street.

As the gap between the two sides narrowed Macro forced his way through the ranks of the first century until he marched only a few ranks back from the front. He drew his sword, raised it to hip level and joined in with his men as they continued to rap their blades against the edges of their shields. Ahead, the small enemy force, armour glinting faintly in the flickering glow of the torches held by a handful of men on either side, suddenly checked their pace and hefted their spears up and changed to an overhand grip, ready to stab with the sharp points. Macro and his men responded by raising their shields a little higher so that they were now peering over the rims as they came on. Then they were within striking range and the rebel soldiers shouted their war cries as they stabbed their spears at the Romans. The legionaries instinctively lowered their heads so the only targets were the crests of their helmets and the broad, curved surfaces of the shields. The savagely sharp spearheads thudded into the shields or glanced harmlessly off helmets as the Romans pressed ahead and closed to sword's length before rushing forward with a loud roar. Shield crashed against shield and then the Romans hacked at the spear shafts, battering them down before turning on the rebels and striking at them with ruthless and brutal abandon.

'Stick it to 'em, lads!' Macro shouted. 'Go in hard and fast!'

Against other enemies the trained spearmen might well have prevailed, but the legionaries had thrust the spears aside and closed the gap and now the spears were almost worse than useless. Some of the rebels wisely cast theirs down, or hurled them forward into the Roman ranks, before drawing their swords. Macro saw that they were armed with falcatas, short, down-curved swords with heavy blades that were lethal cutting weapons. There was a continuous chorus of thuds as shield slammed against shield and then the men of both sides began the bloody work of hacking and stabbing at each other whenever a gap appeared between the shields. As he heaved his weight behind the men in the front rank Macro noted that the rebel's swords had an unexpected advantage in close combat. The downward curve at the heavy end of the blade could only strike over the rim of a shield by a small distance, but it was lethal enough if the man behind the shield had his head raised far enough to peer over the top. Just ahead of Macro there was a sharp metallic crack as a falcata cut through the helmet of a legionary and cleaved his skull. The man dropped like a sack of wet barley and his sword clattered to the ground, his shield falling back to cover the body.

At once Macro rushed over the corpse to fill the gap and straightened his arm to stab at the man who had killed the legionary.

The rebel saw the glint of the blade and threw his shield up just in time to deflect the blow and then Macro's heavy legionary shield slammed into him, and the rebel staggered back a step. The rearmost ranks of both sides surged forward, pressing together the men who had been exchanging blows. Now it was almost impossible to fight and Macro leaned into his shield and pushed, gritting his teeth as he braced his booted feet and heaved. Around him other men grunted and strained as they sought to push the enemy back. From just the other side of his shield Macro could hear the laboured breathing of the man he had tried to kill. Now neither could strike, and the bitter skirmish was a simple test of strength and numbers.

'Shove harder, you bastards!' Macro called out to his men. 'Heave!'

For a moment neither side gave any ground, and then, slowly at first, the nailed boots and weight of the Roman side began to tell and Macro took a pace forward and threw his weight ahead again. Another step was won, then another, and then the Romans were steadily pushing the enemy up the street towards the market. They were still subjected to a steady barrage of missiles from the roofs and the ends of adjoining alleys, while Balthus and his archers did their best to force the enemy to keep their heads down.

'Keep going!'

Macro glanced up over his shield rim and saw that the enemy had been forced back into the market. He ducked down again and continued to press forward. There was little attempt to resist the Roman column now and the rebels began to peel away from the rear ranks and scatter amongst the empty market stalls. The rebel officer bellowed angrily at them, until his voice was suddenly cut off as an arrow punched through his throat. He dropped his sword and staggered back, pulling at the barbed shaft until it snapped and the blood coursed from his arteries and he fell to the ground, senseless. His men broke and ran, sprinting across the market away from the Romans. Balthus and his archers loosed a few arrows after them and then turned their attention back to the remaining rebels on the rooftops. The leading section of legionaries started after the fleeing rebels.

'Leave them!' Macro roared. 'Or I'll have your guts for bootlaces!'

The men stopped at once and hurried back to rejoin their comrades, with sheepish grins as their friends jeered them.

'That's enough,' Macro ordered. 'Close up and bear left. Over there.' Macro raised his sword and pointed towards an arched entrance to the market square. The column quickly dressed its ranks and began to march up the widest passage between the bare market stalls. Macro, breathing heavily, stood to one side for a moment to watch the men pass. In the open space there was a faint loom cast by the stars and a fine crescent moon, enough light for the men to see their surroundings and to fight by. Some distance beyond the arch, in the direction of the citadel, the sky was stained red and orange by a fire burning out of sight and Macro felt his stomach tighten. The sounds of fighting drifted on the night air.

'That must be the diversionary attack.'

Macro started and turned and saw that Balthus was standing at his shoulder.

'You move bloody quietly,' Macro muttered with relief. 'Good thing you're on our side.'

Balthus stared at him a second. 'For the moment. At least until Artaxes is dealt with and the Parthians have left my people alone.'

'And after that?'

'After that?' Balthus smiled thinly. 'After that we shall see.'

Macro nodded. 'All right. So that's how things stand. But for now . . .'

His attention was drawn by a sudden chorus of shouts and as he turned round to gaze across the market square he saw a dark mass of figures spilling down the street that led to the citadel.

Macro cupped a hand to his mouth to shout his orders. 'Column! Halt! Shields up! Prepare to receive enemy charge! Balthus, shoot 'em down!'

CHAPTER SEVENTEEN

The suite of rooms set aside for guests of the king had been turned into a makeshift hospital for the garrison's wounded. As Cato entered the small courtyard he saw that most of the rooms were already filled with men lying on sleeping mats, or simple beds of straw. Some slept soundly, others muttered in delirious tones and a few moaned or cried out in pain. A handful of orderlies and women were attending to their needs as best they could. Cato immediately felt as if he had little right to be there. He glanced down at the deep cut that ran across the palm of his left hand. The blood had slowed and was congealing in the filthy puckered lips of the wound. Even though it throbbed painfully Cato felt shamed by the insignificance of his wound compared to those of the other men in the hospital. He frowned in self-contempt, and was about to turn and walk away when a figure emerged from a room a short distance in front of him.

'Here,' the soft voice of a woman called to him in Greek. 'Let me have a look at that.'

'What?' Cato looked up and saw her outline against the light of a stand of oil lamps burning further down the corridor.

'Your hand. Let me have a look at it.' She moved towards him.

'No, it's not necessary,' Cato responded quickly. 'I have to go.'

The woman moved quickly and took his elbow gently with one hand. 'Over here, under the lamp, where I can see it.'

Cato allowed himself to be steered down the colonnade that ran round the small courtyard and as they moved into the light he began to make her out in more detail. She was young with long dark hair tied back in a ponytail. Her body was slight beneath a simple stola of light brown, now patched with dark splashes and smears. As they stopped close to the yellow glow of the lamps and she bent her head to examine his hand Cato saw that there was a peak in her dark hair and her cheeks

156

had fine pronounced bones. Her eyes were grey and as she glanced up at him a smile flickered across her lips.

'Nasty.'

Cato stared at her in confusion. 'Sorry? I don't—'

'This cut. How did this happen? It's not a sword cut. I should know – I've seen enough of them in recent days.'

'Oh.' Cato tore his eyes away from her, discomfited by her direct gaze. 'I gashed it in a tunnel.'

'Gashed it in a tunnel?' She shook her head. 'Honestly, you boys never grow up. One scrape after another.'

Cato pulled his arm away from her and stiffened his spine so that he could look down at her from his full height. 'I'll deal with it myself, then.'

'Oh, come now!' She chuckled wearily. 'I was just joking. And now, seriously, I must see to that. The wound needs to be cleaned and dressed. Follow me.'

She turned, not waiting for him, and strode towards a doorway at the end of the colonnade. After an instant's hesitation Cato sighed and followed her. The door opened on to a room dominated by a large wooden table, streaked with blood. Some brass instruments on one end of the table gleamed in the wan light of a lamp holder. To one side stood a brazier in which a few embers still glowed. An iron pot rested above it and the air was filled with the acrid stench of pitch. Just visible in the gloom beneath the table was a large basket from which the curled fingers of a hand emerged, and the stump of another limb. Cato glanced away from it quickly as the woman beckoned him to a side table where she was pouring water into a basin.

'Here. Let me clean it.'

Cato stepped over to her and offered his hand over the basin. She pushed it into the water and then, raising it, she began to clean away the filth with a length of cloth. She glanced at him.

'You're no local boy, nor even a Greek mercenary. A Roman then.' She switched to Latin. 'I haven't seen you before. You're certainly not on the ambassador's staff. Who are you?'

Cato was tired and not in the mood to answer her queries. Even now the Greek mercenaries were quietly forming up behind the citadel gates ready to make their move and he wanted to be with them the moment the signal beacon was lit. Nevertheless there was no harm in talking to her while she saw to his injury.

'I'm with a relief force sent by the governor of Syria.'

She paused and looked at him with widened eyes. 'Then the message got through. Thank the Gods, we're saved.'

'Not quite,' said Cato. 'We're only the advance column. The rest of the army is some days behind us.'

'Oh.' She turned her attention back to Cato's hand and wiped the cloth a little deeper into the cut to clear out the remainder of the dirt that had worked its way in. Cato winced but forced himself to keep his hand still. He looked away from it, back at her face.

'How about you? What's a Roman woman doing here in Palmyra?'

She shrugged. 'I travel with my father.'

'And your father is?'

'Lucius Sempronius, the ambassador.'

Cato examined her more closely. The daughter of a senator no less, and here she was tending to the wounds of ordinary soldiers. 'What's your name?'

She looked at him and smiled, revealing neat white teeth. 'Julia. And yours?'

'Quintus Licinius Cato, prefect of the Second Illyrian. Well, acting prefect for the present.' Now it was Cato's turn to smile. 'But you can call me Cato.'

'I was going to. There's no point in standing on formalities here. Or at least I don't think there is, not when the rebels might take the place any day and put us all to the sword,' Julia added matter-of-factly as she took a fresh strip of cloth and dried his hand, dabbing the water off. She reached for a dressing from a basket and began to wrap it round Cato's hand. 'Prefect, you say? That's an important rank, is it not?'

Cato frowned. 'It is to me.'

'Aren't you rather young for such a position?'

'Yes,' Cato admitted, and then continued tersely: 'And isn't the daughter of a senator rather out of place looking after common soldiers?'

She tied off the dressing firmly, and gave it a short extra tug that made Cato grit his teeth to stop a gasp of pain. 'Clearly you are no common soldier, Prefect, but your manner is common. Discourteous, even.'

'I meant no offence.'

'Really?' She took a step back from him. 'Well, your wound is dressed, and I have done the job as well as any man here, for all the disadvantages conferred on me by my social station. Now, if you don't mind, Prefect, I'm busy.'

Cato flushed with irritation at her mood, and shame at his rudeness. She strode past him, out of the door and back into the corridor. He turned after her.

'Thank you . . . Julia.'

She paused a moment, her back stiffening, and then turned into one of the rooms and disappeared from sight.

Cato shook his head and muttered to himself, 'Oh, well done. Surrounded by enemies, and you go and make yourself another one.' He slapped his hand against his thigh, and gasped as pain shot up his arm. 'Shit!'

Grinding his teeth, he marched swiftly out of the hospital and made for the signal tower. Once he was satisfied that the men there understood that they must only make their signal to Macro once the diversionary sortie was well under way, Cato went to join the force assembled just inside the citadel's gateway. The commander of the garrison had allocated the task to one syntagma of the royal bodyguard and the men had gathered quietly in the glow of the torches flickering in iron brackets above the gate. They were heavily armoured and carried the same large round shields and stout spears of their forebears in the days of Alexander. The horsehair crests of their helmets did not appeal to Cato's eye, more used to the utilitarian helmets of Roman soldiers, but it added to their stature and made the body of men look quite formidable, Cato conceded.

'Ah! My friend from the sewer.'

Cato glanced towards the voice and saw an officer waving at him. 'Archelaus?'

'The same!' The Greek laughed. 'Come and join my men, and see how real warriors fight.'

'I have no shield or helmet.'

Archelaus turned to the nearest of his men. 'Bring some kit for our Roman friend.'

The man saluted and hurried off to the barracks as Archelaus offered his spear and shield to Cato. 'Here, I'll explain how we use these.'

Cato saw that the shield had a central strap which he slipped his arm through before grasping the handle near the edge. Unlike the Roman design this shield was purely for protection and could not be punched into the enemy. It provided good cover for his body and thighs and Cato hefted it experimentally until he felt confident about its weight and balance. Then he took the spear that Archelaus was holding ready. It was perhaps two foot longer than his height, with a sturdy shaft and a long, tear-shaped iron point. The other end was capped with a small iron spike. Cato closed his fingers round the leather hand grip and tested the weight. It was heavy, and was a thrusting weapon, unlike the legionary javelin which could serve as a missile as well as a spear.

'Hold it upright,' Archelaus explained. 'We keep it that way until we close on the enemy. Stops us from doing any harm to our comrades, and helps to break up any arrows or sling shot they send our way. When we close and the order is given to advance spears, the front rank goes ahead of the formation and switches to an overhand grip.' He took the spear from Cato and flicked it up into the air and caught it, his arm bent and the shaft angled forward so the point was at eye level. 'Stab from here, like this.' He thrust the spear forward in a powerful jab and then recovered it, ready to strike again. Then he changed his grip, lowered the end and handed it back to Cato. 'You have a go.'

Cato tried the overhand grip and stabbed at the air. He would have preferred to use his sword but could see the advantage in using the spear's greater reach to strike at the enemy. The man Archelaus had sent to the barracks returned with the spare equipment and Cato returned Archelaus' shield and sword. As soon as he had tied the chin straps of the helmet and taken up spear and shield the commander of the syntagma bellowed the order to close ranks. Cato noticed that some of the men in the line beside him were carrying small haversacks.

'Incendiary material,' Archelaus explained quietly, following the direction of the Roman's gaze. 'We're making for a ram the rebels are constructing in front of a temple on the other side of the agora. We're to set it on fire. The ram and anything else that might be of use to the rebels.'

The commander shouted another order as he stepped into the front

160

line of the formation. Several of the Greek mercenaries raised the locking bar of the gate and, bracing their legs, they heaved for all they were worth. The tall, studded timber doors protested on their hinges and eased open with a grating groan. The commander raised his spear above his head and looked over his shoulder to call out to his comrades.

'Advance!'

The front rank of the syntagma rippled forward ahead of the following men as the dense column tramped out through the gate. Cato marched at the side of Archelaus a few ranks back from the front and as they emerged from the gate his heart was beating wildly. Earlier he had doubted the need to join the diversionary attack, but it was vital that Macro's column managed to cut their way through to the citadel, and Cato felt an instinctive duty to do all that he could to help his friend, and the men of the Second Illyrian. So he lowered his head, gritted his teeth and tightened his grip on shield and spear as the column spilled out of the citadel and made its way towards the makeshift barricades the rebels had erected across the streets leading from the agora in front of the citadel.

'At the run!' the commander yelled and the men around Cato swiftly quickened their pace, sandalled feet pounding across the paving stones as their scabbards slapped against their thighs and their ragged breath was drawn with sharp gasps. Above the din of the charging men around him Cato heard the sharp cries of alarm from the rebel lines. Braziers burned behind the barricades and dark figures rose up along the defences, clearly visible as they readied their weapons and faced the men of the royal bodyguard charging towards them across the open expanse of the agora. In the open-sided precinct of a temple Cato saw the looming shape of the shelter being constructed for the battering ram, and above the buildings on either side he saw the first faint glow of the coming dawn and knew that time was running out for Macro and the relief column to cut their way into the city under the cover of night.

The commander of the syntagma was the first to reach the barricade of overturned wagons and timber that had been constructed across the open side of the precinct. He slammed his shield against an upended market stall and stabbed his spear over the top, attempting to skewer the nearest rebel. The man jumped back, ducking down behind his shield as he slashed his sword at the spear shaft, trying to knock it from the commander's grip. On either side more Greek mercenaries arrived at the barricade, stabbing at the men on the far side, and already the first of them had scrambled over the defences and dropped into a crouch on the far side, shield raised and spear poised to thrust. With a savage roar he slashed the spear around and cleared a space for his comrades to clamber across the barricade to join the attack. Cato kept his position at the shoulder of Archelaus as some of the bodyguards ahead of them paused to pull the barricade apart, wrenching loose timbers aside and heaving an overturned cart back on to its heavy wheels before rolling it aside. Cato looked over his shoulder, back towards the citadel. A small flame flared at the top of the signal tower and then there was a cloud of sparks whirling into the darkness before the fire caught and tongues of orange and red flickered in the darkness. The signal was given, then. Any moment now Macro and his column would begin their assault on the eastern gate and Cato quickly prayed to Fortuna that the diversionary attack had drawn the attention of the rebels away from the relief column.

The bodyguards had succeeded in opening a gap through the defences and worked hard to widen it as their comrades filtered through, feeding into the temple precinct on the other side. As Archelaus pressed forward Cato went with him, surging ahead with the other mercenaries. The small square in front of the temple was filled with a confused mass of dim figures locked in savage duels. The two sides were only clearly distinguishable by the crested helmets of the royal guardsmen and the conical helmets of the rebels.

'Cut 'em down!' shouted the commander.

Archelaus thrust his spear into the sky and added his excited encouragement. 'Come on, boys! Pike the bastards!'

He ran forward, lowering the tip of his spear, and thrust it into the back of a fleeing enemy. The man threw out his arms and his sword clattered to the ground a moment before his body. Cato moved into the mêlée, eyes flickering from side to side as he advanced, crouching slightly to spread his weight and make it harder for anyone to knock him down. There was a savage cry from his left and Cato just had time to throw his round shield up and out to block the sword blow which glanced off with a deafening clang. Cato swung round, stabbing out with his spear. The rebel parried it aside with a contemptuous laugh and struck at Cato again, and again, in a flurry of sword blows that drove him back step by step as he desperately blocked the attacks. There was no chance to use the spear and the weapon was little more than a burden in Cato's unpractised hand.

'Fuck this,' he growled, casting the spear aside and reaching for his sword. He drew the blade from its scabbard with a familiar scrape and hefted it at his side. 'Right then, now let's see how tough you are.'

He rode out another short flurry of blows, and then leaped forward, slamming his shield against the rebel's. The man stumbled back, off guard, and now Cato struck at him, thrusting at his face and then his exposed thigh, ripping through cloth and flesh. The rebel gasped with agony and staggered away, blood flowing from his wound. Cato rushed forward, throwing his weight behind his shield, and gritted his teeth just before the collision. The rebel crashed to the ground, and just managed to pull his shield up across his body as Cato stood over him, hacking savagely. As soon as he judged that the man had been stunned by the ferocity of his attack Cato paused, glanced down and saw the dark shape of the man's legs and feet below the rim of his shield. Cato stepped back a pace and hacked at the limbs. As the blade shattered a bone the rebel howled. Cato slashed at the writhing limbs a few more times until he was certain the man would pose no further threat, and then turned away, ignoring the screams of agony.

Around him he could make out enough detail to see that the fight was going their way. Only a handful of figures were still engaged in combat and the long dark shape of the nearly constructed ram housing loomed against the far side of the temple precinct. Cato took a deep breath and called out, 'Archelaus! Archelaus!'

'Here!' The reply was close by and a moment later a figure strode towards Cato. 'Still with us then, Roman.'

'Evidently.' Cato could not help returning the Greek's smile for an instant before he gestured to the ram housing. 'You'd better get your lads to work on that, before the enemy gathers enough men to counter-attack.'

'Yes, at once.' Archelaus turned and called for the men with the incendiary materials to gather round him. As soon as they had found Archelaus and Cato the small party picked its way through the last few groups of men still fighting. They made straight for the ram housing and

Cato saw that the timber structure was mounted on large solid wooden wheels. Much of the sturdy frame had already been covered with bales of hide stuffed with animal skins and rags to absorb the impact of any missiles dropped from the citadel gatehouse when the ram was ready to go into action. Inside, hanging from chains, was the long shaft of the ram itself.

Archelaus stopped to address the small group of men. 'Get as many fires lit as you can. I want this thing well ablaze before we have to retreat.'

The mercenaries lowered their shields and spears and dispersed themselves around the structure, beginning to gather any combustible material around the places they chose to make their fires. Each carried a tinderbox and one by one they set to work striking flints and blowing on the charred kindling inside.

As Cato and Archelaus waited, weapons held ready, the first of the small flames licked up and soon the immediate area was illuminated by small fires as sparks and smoke began to swirl through the darkness. For a moment Cato was satisfied that the enemy structure would soon be ablaze. But then, as the kindling began to burn itself out, he realised something was wrong.

'It's not catching alight.' Cato strode towards the ram housing and sheathed his sword. He reached out to touch the leather hides. 'They've been wetted down . . . soaked.' Cato turned back to Archelaus. 'Forget setting fire to it. Go for the cordage.'

The Greek officer nodded and switching his spear to his shield hand he drew his falcata and shouted an order to his men. 'Use your swords! Cut the ropes! Set fire to their stores!'

At once his men abandoned their failing flames and set about the thick coarse ropes from which the ram was suspended. The air was filled with the dull thud of swords striking the twisted hemp and Cato made himself keep his mouth shut as he willed them to work faster. But the night was already coming to an end, he knew, as he glanced at the sky lightening above the rooftops of Palmyra.

Around him the last of the enemy had been killed or sent running and there were no more sounds of clashing weapons in the temple precinct, no more shouted war cries or muttered oaths. Here and there a man groaned with pain, or called out pitifully for help. Cato strode back towards the ruined barricade and cocked an ear in the direction of the eastern gate. He was relieved to hear the sounds of distant fighting. Macro and the others had begun their attack, and with luck were fighting their way into the city.

A sudden shout of triumph and a dull thud drew Cato's attention back and he turned to see that the rear of the ram had been cut from its ropes and had fallen to the ground. Archelaus' men at once attacked the remaining ropes with a desperate frenzy of blows. Beyond the temple, in the heart of the city, horns sounded, urgently blasting deep notes to waken and summon the rebel soldiers to trap and slaughter the small band of the royal guard who had had the audacity to mount this sortie against the rebels' siege weapon.

'Time we got out of here,' Archelaus muttered. 'They'll be after us at any moment.'

The commander echoed his thoughts a moment later by ordering his men to quit the precinct and form up beyond the remains of the barricade. Archelaus' men abandoned the ram and hurried back towards the agora. Cato quickly inspected the damage. The ram was hanging by one length of cord, badly frayed from sword slashes. Elsewhere flames licked up from piles of hemp and timber. It would set the rebels back perhaps half a day, he estimated. Not much, but it would frustrate Prince Artaxes and his followers and raise the moral of those sheltering in the citadel.

'Prefect!'

Cato turned to see Archelaus beckoning to him in the thin light of the coming dawn. He left the ram housing and trotted back to join the mercenaries. The sound of fighting from the eastern gate had faded slightly and Cato fervently hoped that it was because Macro and his men had succeeded in penetrating the city. From the other direction the shouts of the rebels and the blasts of their horns and beating of drums drew closer. As soon as the last of the injured men had been helped into the formation, the commander gave the order to withdraw. In tight ranks the mercenaries marched at a steady pace across the agora towards the citadel gate. A small unit of the bodyguard stood there, defending the gate against any surprise attack from the rebels. Cato nodded with approval. That was the kind of cautious contingency he approved of. Clearly the commander of the syntagma was an experienced and capable officer.

165

They had covered over half the distance to the gate when the first of the rebel reinforcements appeared on the far side of the agora. More poured out of the other entrances on to the paved expanse and the commander gave the order for the mercenaries to quicken their pace. Glancing back, Cato could see that they would easily reach the gate before the rebels could mass enough men together to charge the retreating mercenaries. The gate would be shut before that happened. With a sick feeling Cato realised that it would also be shut in face of the relief column as they approached the citadel.

'Archelaus! We must stop.'

'Stop?' The Greek turned to stare at him as if Cato was mad. He nodded over his shoulder. 'In case you hadn't noticed . . .'

'We have to keep the gate open. We must leave a way in for the relief column.'

Archelaus frowned for a moment, then hissed through his teeth. 'You're right. Come with me.'

He forced a way through the ranks until they reached the commander of the formation.

'Sir!' Archelaus called out. 'We must halt.'

'Halt?' The commander shook his head. 'Why?'

Cato pushed forward. 'We have to keep the way to the citadel clear for the relief column.'

The commander thought for a moment and then shook his head. 'Too much of a risk. We have to look after ourselves. They'll have to fight their way to the gates.'

'No!' Cato snapped. 'You can't abandon them.'

'I'm sorry, Roman.'

'Damn you! We marched across a desert to help you. Good men have died for you.' Cato forced himself to calm down and muttered, 'Have you no shame?'

The commander rounded on him angrily, disrupting the march of his men so that they had to flow around the three officers. 'Listen, Roman, I don't take orders from you. I look after my men first, and then my employer. You're not even on my list of priorities.'

Cato glared at him, as his mind raced to come up with some way of persuading the mercenary commander to change his mind. 'Look, you need us. A thousand more men in the garrison could be the difference

166

between surviving until General Longinus arrives with his army, and being wiped out. And supposing you do abandon our relief column, and Longinus gets to hear about it? He'd have his revenge on you. Either way, you die if you don't help those men.' Cato thrust his arm towards the eastern gate.

The commander clenched his jaw for an instant and then shrugged wearily. 'It seems you leave me no choice, Prefect. Very well then.' He drew a sharp breath and bellowed, 'Halt! Form a line across the agora! Wounded to the citadel!'

The mercenaries halted abruptly, and then, cajoled by their officers, they spread across the open space and formed up facing the rebels surging towards them. They closed ranks until their shields overlapped and then raised their spears, resting the shafts on shield rims as the enemy drew closer. The commander gestured impatiently to Archelaus.

'Take ten men from the rear rank. Go and find the relief column, and tell them to get here as quick as they can. I will hold the way open for as long as I can, then . . .'

Cato slapped Archelaus on the shoulder before the commander could change his mind. 'Let's go!'

The small party peeled away from the syntagma and ran for the avenue that led towards the east gate. A loud cheer went up from the rebels as they broke into a charge, hurling themselves towards the thin line of Greek mercenaries with their deadly spears. Cato ignored them and ran into the avenue that led down from the citadel into the heart of the city. The avenue was broad and clear, and in the dimness of the gathering light he could see the sprawl of Palmyra's poorest quarter spread out before him. They trotted down the incline, eyes warily searching for any sign of the enemy. Ahead the route bent slightly and as they rounded the corner Cato saw the familiar oblong shapes of legionary shields marching up towards him. He could not resist letting out a cheer and waving his sword arm in greeting. Archelaus and the others followed suit as they ran towards the relief column.

Then Cato saw the archers behind the first century of Macro's cohort. He saw them raise their bows, take aim and loose a hail of arrows.

'Down!' he shouted to Archelaus, ducking behind his shield. The mercenaries followed suit, save one who paused too long to stare in bewilderment at the dark shafts streaking towards them. With a wet thwack an arrow slammed through his throat and burst out at the back of his neck. He reached for the shaft with a shocked expression etched on his face, and tried to speak, but couldn't as blood filled his throat.

Cato tore his eyes away and shouted down the alley, as loud as he could.

'Cease shooting! It's Prefect Cato!'

More arrows rattled off the paved avenue and the fronts of their shields. Then there was a gasp and Cato glanced round and saw Archelaus topple backwards on to the ground, an arrow shaft protruding from his chest, just below the shoulder.

'Cease shooting!' Cato cried out desperately.

CHAPTER EIGHTEEN

Macro felt a chill clamp round the back of his neck as he heard Cato's cry. Instantly, he turned and bellowed towards Balthus and his men. 'Stop! Cease shooting!' He gestured frantically towards the dim figures sheltering behind their round shields. 'They're on our side!'

Balthus lowered his bow and shouted an order to his men and they followed suit, easing the tension on the nocked arrows. Satisfied that the danger was over Macro thrust his way through the front ranks, and started running up the hill towards his friend, bellowing the order for the column to continue their advance towards the citadel.

'Cato! Cato! Where are you, lad?' Macro slowed as he approached the men warily rising up from behind their shields. One man was down, lying flat on his back and quite still, shot through the throat by an arrow. Another man lay on the ground clutching the shaft that had pierced his thigh. A third man was wounded in the shoulder and was being helped up by one of his comrades who had already pulled the arrow free.

'Cato?'

A face turned towards him, and in the growing light Macro felt a wave of relief wash through him as he recognised his friend. He forced a laugh. 'Might have guessed that you'd be lucky enough to dodge those arrows.'

Cato's expression remained grim. 'It's a bloody miracle that any of us are still standing.'

'Well,' Macro waved his hand dismissively, 'we were hardly expecting to see friendly faces before we reached the citadel. In any case, it's easy to mistake friend for foe in the darkness, as we all know.'

Cato stared coldly at him for a moment and Macro fervently wished he had not said what he had. He stepped forward and reached down towards the man Cato was helping. 'I'll take his other side.'

'No, wait.'

But Macro had already slipped his hand under the man's arm and lifted him with a powerful heave. The mercenary rose to his feet with an agonised groan and Macro saw that the stump of the shaft still protruded from the wound where it had snapped off.

'Ah, sorry, mate. Couldn't see it there.'

The mercenary clenched his teeth together and rolled his eyes as he fought back the agony burning through his shoulder.

Cato shook his head. 'Nice going, sir.'

'Only trying to help.' Macro's tone was momentarily surly. 'Anyway, what's the situation and what in the well are you doing wearing that get-up?'

'I'd hardly be able to sneak into Palmyra with full kit, would I? In any case,' Cato looked away as he supported Archelaus, 'I wanted to be there to make sure the relief column reached the citadel safely.'

Macro was deeply moved by his friend's concern for his safety, and then felt a surge of embarrassment. At once he tried to push the feeling aside before Cato could guess at it. He turned away to urge the relief column to pick up its pace before he could trust himself to address Cato again. 'These Greeks of yours look tough enough. I assume there's more like 'em in the citadel.'

'They're not my Greeks. These men are under the command of Archelaus,' Cato nodded towards the man he was helping.

'Archelaus, eh? Pleased to meet you.' Macro thrust out his hand, but the Greek, still clenching his teeth, glanced down at his wound and then back at Macro with raised eyebrows.

'Ah, yes. Sorry.' Macro smiled awkwardly. 'Good to meet you all the same.'

Cato grunted under his burden. 'Now the formalities are over, let's get to the citadel.'

'Yes, of course. These men can fall in with us.' Macro looked up the street as the sound of the fighting in the agora carried towards them. 'What's happening up ahead?'

'The king's bodyguard are keeping the citadel gates cleared for you,' Cato explained. 'But we must hurry. They won't be able to hold the rebels back for long.'

The column continued up the street, towards the sound of fighting. As they emerged into the agora Macro glanced to his right and saw the line of Greek mercenaries giving ground under pressure of the enemy hacking at them from beyond their shield wall. From the walls of the citadel, a steady barrage of arrows, javelins and ballista bolts rained down on the rebel horde, thinning their numbers as they surged towards the Greeks.

'Keep moving there!' Macro shouted at his men, who had slowed to take in the spectacle. 'It's not a bloody day at the circus! Shift yourselves!'

The column moved forward at a quick pace towards the open gate, where Macro stepped aside to wave his men on. Cato left two of Archelaus' men to help their officer to the hospital and then he joined Macro. Once the legionaries had passed through the gate, the mounted men followed: Balthus and his men, and then the squadrons from the Second Illyria. Centurion Parmenion marched at the head of the auxiliary infantry who formed the rearguard. As soon as he recognised Cato he smiled and saluted.

'Good to see you, sir.'

'And you, Centurion. How have the men fared?'

'We've had no problems, sir. The lads from the Tenth did most of the hard work. They took the gate and cleared a path through the rebels.' He glanced at Macro and continued in a gently grudging tone, 'They did a fine job, sir.'

Macro shrugged. 'Of course; they're legionaries. But the lads of the Second Illyrian could have done the job just as well,' he added tactfully. 'And we were helped by Balthus and his boys. A team effort all round, I'd say.'

Cato looked at him and smiled. 'You've become quite the diplomat.'

'Diplomat?' Macro frowned. 'Sod off. I'll leave that to the broad-stripers. I lack a smooth tongue and the necessary arse-licking skills.'

Cato laughed. 'An unsavoury image if ever there was one.'

Macro punched him on the shoulder. 'Fine. Let's drop the subject, eh? Hardly the time and place for smart words.'

'Very well, sir.'

Macro was about to reply when a fresh roar of cheering burst out from the enemy ranks. All three officers turned to see the right flank of the mercenaries' line crumple before the relentless pressure of the rebels. Already several of them had broken through and were ruthlessly cutting down the Greeks. More of them pressed on, exploiting the overlap, and

Cato could see that the royal bodyguards were in danger of being rolled up, surrounded and slaughtered. Macro's experienced eye read the situation at once.

'Cato, get your lads to plug the gap. Now.'

'Yes, sir.' Cato nodded and ran out a short distance to the side of the column, still marching towards the citadel gate. 'Second Illyrian! Halt! . . . Right face!'

The months of hard training that Macro and Cato had put them through paid off as the cohort moved from column to line in a few heartbeats. Cato paused for another breath and shouted the order. 'Open ranks by half-century!'

The men shuffled aside to create lanes through their lines, and when the manoeuvre was complete Cato drew his sword and swept it towards the failing Greek line. 'Advance!'

The Second Illyrian moved evenly across the agora, their ranks carefully watched and dressed by their officers as they closed on the mercenaries. The commander of the syntagma glanced back and saw the auxiliaries coming to his aid. He saw the gaps in the line and grasped Cato's intention immediately. Turning back to his men he cupped a hand to his mouth and bellowed, 'Fall back! Fall back to the citadel!'

The mercenaries began to back away from the rebels, stabbing their spears frantically to try to create a gap between them and their enemies. As soon as some were clear they turned and ran towards Cato's men, immediately endangering their slower comrades as the rebels swarmed into the gaps in the rapidly fragmenting line. A handful were cut off and overwhelmed, attacked from all sides as they desperately swirled round, trying to block the rebels' blows. Inevitably, a blade darted in, and as each man staggered back from the wound he was hacked to the ground in a flurry of sword blows and spear thrusts. The first of the mercenaries reached the approaching line of Roman troops and hurried through the gaps. Cato drew his sword once more and stepped into place alongside Parmenion in the middle of the line. As they paced forward across the paving stones Cato glanced to both sides, gauging the moment. As the last of the mercenaries passed through the gaps he shouted an order.

'Close ranks!'

The men on the rear rank hurriedly stepped round and forward to fill the gaps as the rebels raced towards them.

'Shields to the front!' Cato yelled, just before the impact, and at once the auxiliaries' broad shields swept round to confront the rebels with a wall of gleaming bosses. The sharp points of swords glinted brightly where they punctuated the line of shields. At the sight the rebels hesitated for a brief moment, and the charge immediately lost its impetus. The two lines came together in a rolling chorus of shield thudding against shield, swords striking home against hide-covered wood, and the brittle clatter of blade clashing against blade. Cato hunched down behind his borrowed shield and braced his legs. A blow thudded against the rim, driving it back against his helmet. Cato saw white briefly, blinked and then thrust his sword out. There was no contact and he snatched his sword arm back before any rebel could slash at his unprotected flesh. On either side men grunted as they struck out, some bellowing full-throated war cries, insults or defiance. Mingled with this were the gasps and groans of the wounded and dying. Cato concentrated on keeping his position in the front rank of his cohort, knowing full well that as long as the line held the Second Illyrian would hold their own, despite the unequal numbers.

The rebel charge had halted the Roman advance and now they stood, feet braced, punching out their shields as they stabbed at any of the enemy who dared to press their attack too closely. In the growing light Cato saw the glint of a blade rising in front of his shield and instinctively threw his sword up to block the blow. An instant later the heavy tip of a falcata crashed against his short sword, driving Cato's weapon down. His arm felt numb and Cato clenched his fist with all his strength to retain a firm grip on the handle. The falcata rose again, accompanied by a triumphant snarl from the rebel who was wielding the weapon. This time Cato was able to swing his shield up and punched it out to meet the sword as he swung his own blade in a short scything cut at the man's leading leg. The blow landed at the same time as the shield boss rang overhead and drove down on to Cato's helmet. As he went down on one knee he heard the rebel howl with pain and rage and Cato saw that the edge of his sword had cut deep into the man's thigh, severing muscles all the way to the bone. The man stumbled back and slumped to the ground as he dropped his weapon and clamped a hand over the wound, trying to stem the rush of blood. Then another man jumped in front of him and he was lost to Cato's view.

A hand gripped Cato's arm and pulled him on to his feet and back into the Roman formation. Cato glanced round and saw Parmenion.

'Are you injured, Prefect?'

'No.'

Parmenion nodded, then leaned to one side as a spear stabbed past his head. Cato cut down on the shaft, knocking it to the ground, and then slashed at the hand grasping it, smashing knuckles and cutting tendons, so that the spear fell from nerveless fingers.

'Give ground!' Cato ordered. 'Parmenion, call the pace.'

'One!' Parmenion shouted, and the cohort backed off a step. 'Two! One! Two!'

The Second Illyrian steadily withdrew towards the citadel and Cato eased his way back through the ranks to the side of the standard-bearer. A withdrawal was one of the most difficult manoeuvres to handle. If the formation faltered, or fell apart, then the Palmyran rebels would cut them to pieces. Cato saw that the last of the mercenaries had entered the citadel and Macro stood alone under the massive stone arch, beckoning to Cato. Beside him Parmenion continued to call the pace and the cohort edged slowly towards the gate. The left flank was protected by the towering wall and the archers and javelin throwers pelting the rebels from above. But the right of the line would soon have to fold back and the rebels would flow round the edge and surround the Romans just as they had the Greek mercenaries.

'Parmenion! On me!'

As soon as his second-in-command was at his side Cato indicated the right flank. 'I'll take command of the flank century. As soon as the left of the line reaches the gate you get them inside a century at a time. I'll cover you until it's our turn.'

'Yes, sir.' Parmenion nodded. 'Good luck, sir.'

'I'll need it.'

Cato ran down the rear of the cohort until he reached the first century of the cohort, composed of picked men. Their commander, Centurion Metellus, saluted as Cato reached him.

'Hot work, sir.'

'And about to get hotter.' Cato smiled grimly. 'We're going to cover the withdrawal through the gate. When I give the order, I want the first cohort to form a wedge. We'll move up towards the gate and hold the ground in front of it until the rest of the cohort are through.'

'I understand, sir,' Centurion Metellus replied calmly. 'My lads won't let you down.'

Cato smiled. 'I know.'

He glanced round and saw that the last of the cohort's wounded men, and the mounted troops assigned to protect them, were already trotting back through the gate as the auxiliaries withdrew towards the citadel. The time had come for the first century to move away from the buildings on their right, opening the way for the rebels to sweep round their flank. Cato nodded to Centurion Metellus. 'Give the order.'

Metellus filled his lungs and bellowed. 'First century will form a wedge!' He paused a moment and counted to three under his breath and then, 'Manoeuvre!'

At once the flanking sections folded back to form the second and third sides and then the auxiliaries faced out so that the wedge presented shields on all three faces. The rebels surged into the gaps and flowed round Metellus' century, hacking and thrusting at the shields.

'First century! Advance towards the gate!'

With Metellus calling the pace the wedge edged across the agora, surrounded by the rebels, who were shouting with excitement and triumph, like wild predators scenting an imminent kill. As Cato had hoped, the pressure eased on the other centuries and they began to retire without too much trouble through the gate, while the rebels turned their fury on the remaining unit slowly forcing its way through the mob. Looking out over the close ranks of the auxiliaries Cato could see that most of the rebels surrounding them were lightly armed. As yet, only a handful of Prince Artaxes' regular soldiers had reached the fight, but then the blast of a horn echoed across the agora and Cato glanced round to see a column of soldiers emerge on the other side of the agora. Immediately they broke into a trot, making straight for the fight in front of the citadel gates.

'We have to pick up the pace,' Cato decided. 'Metellus!'

'I see them, sir,' Metellus replied quickly and called out to his men more frequently. 'One! . . . Two!'

Cato saw that they were no more than fifty feet from the gate. Macro had retreated through the arch and Cato could see his transverse crest amongst the dense formation of legionaries formed up just inside the citadel. On the walls above, the archers had turned their attention towards the new enemy column pounding across the agora. The dark shafts of arrows rattled on to the paving, or splintered shields, with a few shots striking men down as they ran to cut off the retreat of the last of the Romans outside the citadel.

Already the pressure from the dense mass of men outside the small wedge formation was taking its toll and the auxiliaries began to slow, all the while slamming their shields and stabbing their swords into the press of enemy bodies. Suddenly, one rebel, more daring than his comrades, grabbed the top of a shield of one the men close to Cato. Before the auxiliary could cut at the man's fingers, the rebel wrenched the shield down savagely, smacking the bottom rim into the auxiliary's shins. The man gasped with pain and in that moment of hesitation, with his upper body exposed, another rebel thrust a spear at his throat. The point tore through his neck cloth and burst out from under the helmet neck guard. As the man sagged forward on to his knees the spearman leaped forward into the gap.

'No, you don't!' Cato growled, and rushed the few paces to the rebel, throwing his weight behind his shield as a spear thrust glanced off the curved surface, and then Cato smashed into the man, sending him reeling back into the mob. Cato stopped level with the auxiliaries on either side, taking the place of the fallen soldier. His heart was racing, beating like a drum in his chest. He drew a breath and cried out. 'Keep moving! If we stop, we die!'

The men at the head of the wedge pressed forward again, punching with their shields and thrusting and hacking at the enemy with their short swords. They gained perhaps another ten paces before the formation was stalled again, tantalisingly close to the gate, just as the first of the fresh rebel soldiers reached the fight and forced their way through towards the Romans. Then Cato realised, with certainty, that the first century would make no further progress towards the gate. He slammed his shield out, then slashed his sword in an arc before he risked a glimpse towards the gate, no more than a few paces away. It was still open, and already some of the rebels were turning towards it, sensing the opportunity.

'Shut the gate!' Cato roared, the cry tearing at his dry throat. 'Macro, save yourself! Shut the gate!'

A blow against his shield made Cato stagger back and then, with an icy calmness, he resolved to kill as many of his enemies as he could before he was cut down.

'Bastards!' he hissed through clenched teeth. Then his fist tightened round his sword handle and he hurled himself back into the line, hacking at the faces in front of him. He filled his lungs and roared, 'Second Illyrian! Second Illyrian!' The men around him took up the cry as they fought on. Pressed in from all sides the wedge became an oval, tightly clustered around their standard as the first of the fresh rebel soldiers reached them. The auxiliaries were more evenly matched now and began to fall in increasing numbers. The Romans fell back over the bodies of their comrades, closing ranks, breathing heavily, limbs burning with exhaustion as they blinked away splattered blood, grudgingly giving ground to the enemy.

Cato felt a blow and then a burning sensation in his shield arm and glimpsed the blade of a falcata pulling back from a thrust into his arm just below the chain mail. He gritted his teeth and gave vent to a deep groan of pain and rage, swinging slightly as he slashed his sword down on the rebel's blade, knocking it from his grasp. Then Cato reversed direction, slashing his blade up across the man's breast, ripping through his light tunic and the flesh beneath, leaving a vivid crimson streak in the wake of his blade.

There was a loud roar from the direction of the gate as Cato stepped back, his shield sagging as the last reserves of strength faded in his left arm. He glanced to the side and saw a dense column of legionaries spewing from the citadel gate. At their head was Macro, bellowing his war cry. The heavily armoured legionaries crashed through the loose throng of rebels closest to the gate and then carved a bloody path through those surrounding the small knot of the remaining auxiliaries. The ferocity of the attack momentarily stunned the rebels and Cato took his chance to call to his men.

'On me! This way!' He lowered his sword and drove his shield into the thinning enemy ranks between him and Macro. The auxiliaries let out a weary cheer and followed him, wildly hacking at the enemy as they fought their way towards their legionary comrades. Cato slammed his shield into one rebel's side, sending him sprawling, and then he saw another man's back ahead of him. His blade thrust forward, taking the rebel just below the shoulder. As his blade cut into the body, the glistening red tip of a sword burst through the man's back. Cato wrenched his blade free and the rebel toppled aside, the weight of the corpse pulling it off the other sword, and there stood Macro, wild-eyed, splattered with blood and grinning like a madman.

'So there you are! Go on, lad, get your men through to the gate. We'll take it from here.'

Cato nodded, then waved his men past as Macro's legionaries cleared space on either side and held the enemy back. The exhausted auxiliaries staggered through the gate and collapsed or bent double along the walls on either side. Cato was the last in, and stood and watched as the legionaries fell back, in good order, pressed hard by the bitterly denied rebels, now crying out with rage and frustration that the auxiliaries had escaped them. The legionaries withdrew under the arch and the clash of blades echoed sharply off the masonry.

'Get ready to close the gate!' Macro yelled over his shoulder and the party of legionaries standing behind the stout doors placed their shoulders against the solid timbers and braced their booted feet against the paving slabs. As Macro and the last of the legionaries passed into the citadel he shouted the order. 'Close the gate!'

With a grunt the legionaries heaved and the doors began to swing as the iron hinges groaned. The gap steadily narrowed until only Macro remained hacking at the closest rebels, snarling defiance and insults at them. Cato, fearing that his friend would be caught between the doors, sheathed his sword and rushed forward to grasp Macro's harness and haul him back with all his might. Sword arm flailing as he stumbled away from the enemy, Macro shouted, 'What the fuck? What are you doing?' Then the doors slammed into place with a reverberating thud and the legionaries thrust the locking bar across into its slot.

The shouts of the rebels were at once deadened and around Cato men stood chests heaving as they gasped for breath. At last he released his grip on his shield and it slipped to the ground with a loud clang. He loosened his grip on Macro's harness as Macro turned round and puffed out his cheeks.

They looked at each other for a moment and then laughed

spontaneously at the sheer surprise and delight of still being alive. Macro thrust his blade into his scabbard and jerked his thumb towards the gate.

'So, that went as well as could be expected.'

Cato smiled for a moment, before he was aware of the survivors of Metellus' century around him, battered and bloodied with barely enough strength left to stay on their feet. 'It could have been worse,' he said quietly.

'Yes.' Macro's smile faded. 'Still, we made it. Life has become just a bit more difficult for that Prince Artaxes now that we're here.' His eyes moved to Cato's arm, streaked with blood that dripped from the ends of his fingers. 'You'd better get that seen to. Before we report to the ambassador.'

'I will. Once the rest of my injured have been taken to the hospital.' Before he turned away to give the necessary orders, Cato paused and stared fixedly at Macro. 'Why did you do it?'

'Do what?'

'Come for us just then.'

Macro tried to brush the comment off. 'We're short-handed enough as it is. Last thing I can afford is to lose a century of good men, even if they are auxiliaries. That's why. Anyway, what are friends for? You'd have done the same for me.'

Cato nodded, but could not help smiling as he took a step back, grimacing at the odour clinging to his friend. 'But if you don't go and clean that filth off I might just think twice about returning the favour.'

'Ha bloody ha. Now why don't you just piss off to the hospital before I add to your injuries?'

179

CHAPTER NINETEEN

The hospital was filled with the wounded. Even the colonnade outside the rooms set aside for the injured was lined with men slumped against the wall, or lying on the bare ground. The handful of medical orderlies were overwhelmed by the number of injured men from the king's bodyguard and the relief column. The legionary surgeon who had taken charge assessed each man in turn, and those who were beyond help were carried across the courtyard to a small cell in the corner. As Cato eased one of his men on to the ground for the surgeon to examine he nodded towards the cell.

'What happens to them in there?'

The surgeon glanced at him with a warning look as he replied, 'They are helped out of their pain.'

'Oh . . . I see.' Cato looked uneasily at the wounded man. A spear thrust had found a weak spot in his mail armour and burst through his stomach. The stench of his torn intestines and bowels wafted up and made Cato want to retch. The man's eyes were clamped shut and he moaned continually as he clutched both hands over the wound. Cato turned towards the surgeon and saw the fleeting look of pity and resignation in the man's face before the surgeon spoke softly.

'Trust me, sir, they feel little pain and it is over quickly.'

Cato did not feel reassured and rose up and stepped away from the wounded man feeling helpless and shamed. The surgeon beckoned to the orderlies assigned to stretcher duty and indicated the wounded man. 'Special case,' he said evenly before leaning over the man and squeezing his shoulder gently. 'You'll be taken care of, my friend. You will rest and your pain will be gone.'

He stood up and let the orderlies shift the man on to the stretcher. Then they picked it up and carried him away. The surgeon turned to Cato and tilted his head to see the wound on his arm. 'Let me see that.'

'It's not serious,' Cato said in alarm. 'A flesh wound.'

'I'll be the judge of that. Stand still and let me see.'

The surgeon eased the mail and tunic sleeve up on to Cato's shoulder and closely examined the cut, probing gently with his spare hand. Cato gritted his teeth and stared straight ahead until the surgeon released his arm.

'The wound is clean enough. It will heal, once sutures have been applied.'

'Sutures?'

'Stitches.' The surgeon patted Cato on the back and gestured towards the room at the end of the corridor. 'In there. I have a most charming member of staff who will take care of you.'

'We've already met,' Cato muttered.

'Good. Don't be put off by the fact she's a woman. I hear that the lady has been more help than most of the orderlies put together.'

'Fair enough.' Cato nodded to the surgeon and the latter hurried away to tend to his patients. Cato set off down the corridor, not best pleased by the prospect of renewing his acquaintance with the sharp-tongued ambassador's daughter. As he entered the room, the early morning light was streaming in through the two high windows, bathing the interior with a fine golden light. Julia was carefully winding a dressing round an auxiliary's head.

'I'll deal with you in a moment,' she said wearily without looking up. 'Wait by the door.'

Cato paused, consumed with frustration over any delay to his treatment. He needed to rejoin Macro and speak to the ambassador. He was also keen to quit the company of this overbearing woman. She seemed typical of her class: loud, arrogant and steadfast in the assumption that she would be obeyed at once. It was tempting to dislike her straight away. Cato drew a deep, calming breath, entered the room, and sat on the bench beside the door. The ambassador's daughter did not look up as she reached the end of the dressing and gently tied it off.

'There!' She stepped back to address the soldier. 'You'll need to rest a day or so.'

The auxiliary laughed. 'I wish I could, my lady. But I doubt the prefect will let me. He's a hard case.'

'Hard case?' Julia smiled. 'Him?'

'Oh yes, miss! Been driving us on like slaves ever since we set off from Antioch. Looks fresh-faced enough, but underneath it he's a right bast—'

Cato cleared his throat loudly and they both looked round at him. The auxiliary was on his feet in an instant, standing stiffly at attention, staring fixedly at some spot above Cato's head. His mouth opened and closed and he bit his lip in anticipation of the tirade to come. Cato looked steadily at him for a moment, devoid of expression. Then his eyes flickered to the woman.

'Have you done with this man?'

'Yes, Prefect Cato. The question is, have you?'

'He is a soldier and he will do his duty as I see fit, my lady.'

'But only when he is fit, surely?'

Cato frowned. 'That is my decision. Soldier, you are dismissed. Return to your century.'

'Yes, sir.' The auxiliary saluted and marched from the room, and out of the sight of his commander, as quickly as he could. Once he had gone Cato waited on the bench. Julia stared at him a moment and then placed her hands on her hips impatiently.

'Well, what is it this time?'

'Sword wound.' Cato gestured to the streak of blood on his arm.

'Come over here then,' she replied tersely. 'In the light, where I can see properly. Don't keep me waiting, Prefect. There are others who need my attention.'

And they are welcome to you, Cato reflected irritably as he rose to his feet and crossed over to her. The ambassador's daughter took his elbow and eased him round into the shaft of light streaming through the window. She inspected the wound briefly. 'So, you are intent on losing this arm one piece at a time, it seems.'

Cato pursed his lips, and his frown deepened. Julia glanced up at his face and he could see that she was fighting back the urge to laugh. To mock him. He sniffed bitterly. 'A soldier expects wounds, my lady. Whether he's a common soldier, like that man, or an officer. It's in the line of duty. Not something I imagine a lady of fine breeding would be used to.'

The words had been spoken before Cato realised how rude he must seem. Julia's eyes widened for a moment, and when she replied she spoke in a cold tone.

'I know my duty, Prefect. And, in recent days, I have come to know more wounds than I care to remember. I'd be obliged if you would remember that.'

Their eyes met and Cato gave her the kind of hard stare he reserved for scaring raw recruits, until Julia gave way and turned her gaze back to his wound. 'It's a flesh wound. Looks clean enough, but I'll wash it and stitch it.'

She reached round to a bowl of water on the table and pulled out a damp rag and squeezed the excess water out. She poised it over the wound. 'Well, here we go again. You know the routine. It's going to be painful, but then a hard case like you never feels pain.'

Cato flushed angrily but refused to respond to her baiting. 'I am obliged to make my report to your father. So, my lady, I'd be grateful if you finished dressing the wound and let me get back to work.'

'Very well,' Julia muttered. She prepared a needle and twine, and set to work at once, pricking the point through Cato's skin and gradually sewing the wound shut, until there was a length of puckered purple skin and bloodstained thread. Cato stared fixedly at the door with gritted teeth despite the pain. At length Julia completed her work and tied the knot with a sharp tug. 'There you are, Prefect.'

Cato nodded his thanks and turned to stride back towards the door, grateful for the chance to get away from the woman. As he reached the door she called after him.

'Until the next wound, then.'

'Hmmphhh,' Cato managed to grumble before he quit the room and emerged into the corridor. Outside the surgeon was organising a party of men to fetch the day's water and food rations for his patients. He looked up as Cato approached, and cocked an eyebrow.

'Feeling better, sir?'

'Better?' Cato paused. 'Of course not. It's a sword wound, not a bloody cold.'

'Still,' the surgeon continued, 'a woman like that has a way of taking a man's mind off his pain.'

'Oh, yes.' Cato nodded with a bitter smile. 'I could hardly wait to get away from her.'

The surgeon looked confused. 'I didn't mean . . .'

But Cato was already marching off again, his expression fixed in a frown as he contemplated the prospect of being shut up in the citadel in the company of an irritating, haughty daughter of Rome's aristocracy. As if her superior manner was not bad enough, she had the kind of looks that could only serve as a distraction to the officers and political leaders packed into the citadel. The thought came upon him in an instant, and considering the matter a moment longer Cato was forced to concede that the ambassador's daughter was indeed attractive; beautiful even.

'Beautiful,' he muttered sourly to himself. What did it matter what she looked like? She was an irritant and a distraction at best. And at worst? He felt a sudden light surge of heat in his breast and slapped his fist against his thigh as he strode off to find the ambassador.

Lucius Sempronius looked up as the two officers entered the small chamber that had been allocated to him by the king's chamberlain. Although as an ambassador of Emperor Claudius he deserved better, the severe overcrowding of the citadel meant that there was little opportunity to observe diplomatic niceties. His small staff was crowded into the corridor outside, which served as both their office and their sleeping accommodation. Macro had smiled as he and Cato had marched past the huddle of young aristocrats forced to rough it with the ambassador's clerks and his bodyguards. It would do them good, he thought, to get a bit of hard experience before they rose through the ranks of the imperial bureaucracy. That was assuming they survived this siege, of course, he reflected, his smile fading.

They strode up towards the ambassador and halted.

'Centurion Macro and Prefect Cato reporting, sir.'

The ambassador nodded to the seats arranged before the table he was using as a desk. 'You look tired, gentlemen. And no wonder, given what you've been through in recent days, and nights.' He smiled at Cato. 'My thanks to you both. The arrival of your column has given the king and his supporters fresh hope. I was very worried that they were about to surrender before you turned up. Now they can see that Rome does not abandon her friends. However . . .' Sempronius paused and lowered his voice. 'The arrival of Prince Balthus is something of a mixed blessing.

He is not the king's favourite son. That honour lies with Prince Artaxes.'

'Artaxes?' Macro looked puzzled. 'The rebel? The one who's thrown his lot in with the Parthians?'

'The same.' Sempronius nodded. 'Vabathus doted on the young scoundrel. He was blind to the prince's faults, and even though word of his treachery had reached the chamberlain's ears some months before the revolt broke out, the king dismissed the reports and refused to act against Artaxes. Even when the rebels rose up against him the king would not believe that Artaxes was behind it. He said that Artaxes was being forced to lead the rebels against his will. Can you imagine?' Sempronius shook his head wearily. 'It appears that some fathers are utterly blind to the faults of their children. Well, that's not entirely true. Vabathus has little regard for his eldest, Amethus. Not that I can blame him. Amethus is a fool. Quite stupid, you understand, and easily persuaded. He spends his life being a passionate advocate of the last thing that anyone says to him. The king may be fond of Amethus, but he has long since given up on him as a worthy successor. Same goes for Prince Balthus. Or did, until the revolt broke out. Now that Prince Artaxes has proved to be a treacherous little snake, the king has been forced to reconsider his choice of successor.' Sempronius leaned a little closer to Macro and Cato. 'What's your impression of Prince Balthus?'

Macro stirred uneasily and resisted the impulse to glance at Cato before he replied. 'He's a damn good fighter, sir. Just the kind of man the king needs at his side at the moment.'

'Well, that's good to hear.' Sempronius eased himself back in his chair. 'I haven't met the man yet. From what I'd heard, Balthus was supposedly no more than a drunken rake. A wastrel with no sense of duty. I just hope there's more to him than a good fighter.'

'Oh, there's more to him than that, all right,' Macro responded uneasily. 'The prince has disturbing ambition, sir.'

'How do you mean?'

'He aims to be king after Vabathus. Once Rome persuades Vabathus to abdicate after the revolt is crushed.'

Sempronius chuckled bitterly. 'Taking rather a lot for granted, isn't he?'

This time Macro could not help glancing at Cato before he responded, 'Well, there's something more, sir.'

'Which is?'

'Well, sir, it seems that I made something of a deal with Prince Balthus. In exchange for helping the column make its way through to the citadel, sir.'

'A deal?'

'Yes, sir. I said as how I'd do my best to help him out when we reached here, sir. We needed his help. There was no way we could have got through without Balthus. We owe him our lives.'

'I see.' Sempronius rubbed his face wearily. 'And did it not occur to you that he was in the same predicament as you were?'

'Sir?' Macro frowned and turned to Cato with a questioning expression as the ambassador continued.

'Once the revolt started, our friend Prince Balthus might well have been desperate to join his father, to trade on the old man's vulnerability. The problem was getting through to him. And then you came along, desperate for help, and he sees his chance. He offers you a deal, and you jump at it. What exactly did you promise him, Prefect Cato?'

Cato started guiltily. During the previous exchanges his eyelids had been growing irresistibly heavy and he would have fallen asleep but for the ambassador's sudden shift in attention. Cato swallowed and hurriedly collected his thoughts.

'Sir, we had little choice in the matter, as Centurion Macro has said. Either we cut a deal with the prince or he would have left us stranded in the desert. Or at least—'

'At least that's what he'd have you believe,' Sempronius completed the sentence. 'Dear Gods! So you have pledged your word to help this man become king. Is that it?'

Macro pursed his lips briefly. 'Well, yes, sir. That's about the size of it.'

'Centurion Macro,' Sempronius replied with considerable restraint. 'You are a soldier. What the hell did you think you were doing making any kind of deal with such a man? You're supposed to stick to soldiering. That's what you are paid to do. That's your job. So please, concentrate on fighting your man from the front. Leave it to the diplomats to put the blade in from behind, all right?'

'Yes, sir.'

'And you, Prefect Cato. Did you know about this?'

'Yes, sir. I was there when the deal was made.'

186

'And you made no attempt to intervene?'

'No, sir. It seemed the best thing to do at the time. Prince Balthus was the only chance we had of finding a way through the enemy's defences.'

'You're as bad as Centurion Macro.'

'Yes, sir,' Cato conceded meekly.

Sempronius ran a hand through his thick grey-streaked hair. 'There's nothing we can do about it now. Best I take this up with the prince later on. In the meantime, you do not play at politics in Palmyra. Is that clear?'

'Yes, sir!' Macro and Cato chorused.

'Then we'd better make our way to the king's audience chamber. He's summoned what's left of his council, and us. When we get there I'd be greatly obliged if you both kept your mouths shut. Let me do the talking. That's an order.'

'Yes, sir.'

Sempronius rose abruptly from his chair. 'Come on, then. I'm keen to see exactly what kind of man we are dealing with in Prince Balthus.'

CHAPTER TWENTY

The guards closed the doors to the royal audience chamber and a dull boom echoed off the high walls. For a moment then there was a brief silence as the king's chamberlain, Thermon, rose and looked round at the small gathering of Roman officials and Palmyran nobles. King Vabathus had abandoned his earlier melancholy, Cato noticed, and now sat erect and attentive as his chamberlain opened proceedings, speaking in Greek so that all might follow his words.

'The king bids you welcome, and in particular he welcomes the brave commanders of the Roman relief column. The arrival of fresh troops has greatly strengthened the king's position and the news that a Roman army is on its way to crush the rebellion fills his heart with hope. The king is also grateful that Prince Balthus has seen fit to join His Majesty's side in the present conflict. It is hoped that he will have further opportunities to prove himself worthy of his royal lineage in the difficult times to come.'

Cato glanced at Balthus and saw that the prince was sitting quite still with a composed expression as he gently nodded his acknowledgement. To his right sat another Palmyran, in a richly decorated tunic. The man was thin with a weak chin and fine features yet there was no mistaking the family resemblance between him and Balthus. Prince Amethus, Cato realised, studying the man more closely as Thermon spoke. Amethus did not have the same controlled poise as his younger brother and his left foot tapped in a continuous light rhythm as he stared at some point on the ceiling, mouth slightly agape.

'His Majesty has summoned this council to deliberate the options that are open to us, given the current state of the siege. This morning, after the relief column had entered the citadel, we received the usual demand to surrender. Only this time, the rebels have added a warning to our Roman allies. Every Roman citizen and soldier in the citadel is to quit the city by dawn tomorrow or they will be put to death if the citadel is taken.' Thermon paused and looked towards Sempronius who was already pulling his formal toga into shape to rise up and respond, and Cato realised that this part of the meeting had already been prepared for. The ambassador looked steadily round the room until he stared at the king and began to speak in the deliberate, measured manner in which most Roman aristocrats were trained by their teachers of rhetoric.

'Your Majesty.' Sempronius bowed his head. 'It is with scorn that I respond to such a demand from our enemies. Rome is your ally, and Rome honours her obligations to her allies, whatever the cost. I speak for every Roman in the citadel in this regard.' He gestured towards Macro and Cato. 'While these fine officers and their gallant men draw breath we shall fight for King Vabathus. We shall not quit the great city of Palmyra, no matter what vile threats are made by the craven enemies of His Majesty. Together, we shall hold the citadel until the governor of Syria arrives with his army and crushes the rebels!'

Before Sempronius had sat down another figure had risen to his feet, just behind Prince Amethus. The man was broad-chested and clearly had a powerful physique beneath the folds of his fine embroidered robes. He bowed his head to the king and turned to the Roman ambassador.

'Might I ask our Roman ally how long we are to wait before the army of Cassius Longinus reaches us?'

Sempronius remained in his seat as he replied, a calculated rebuff and expression of contempt for the speaker.

'The commander of the relief column tells me that the governor will reach us within a matter of days, Krathos.'

'Days? How many days, exactly?' The man's gaze shifted to Macro and he held up his hand to silence Sempronius as the latter started to respond. 'I address my question to the centurion. Well, how many days?'

Macro shifted uncomfortably as all eyes turned towards him. He looked to Sempronius and the ambassador nodded, and muttered, 'Be honest, Centurion.'

Macro swallowed and thought hard as he calculated the likely time it would take for the governor to concentrate his forces and march across the desert to Palmyra. The baggage train would find it tough going, Macro realised. He drew a deep breath and gave his answer.

'At least another fifteen days. Perhaps as many as twenty, sir.'

'Twenty days,' Krathos repeated emphatically.

Sempronius leaned slightly closer to Macro and hissed, 'Not that honest, Macro. For pity's sake!'

'Twenty days!' Krathos spread out his arms. 'How can this citadel endure for twenty days?'

'We have held out for longer than that already,' Sempronius countered. 'We can last another twenty days.'

'On what?' Krathos shot back. 'The water supplies are close to exhausted, and the food will not last much longer. Thanks to the arrival of Prince Balthus and his friends, and our Roman allies, we now have another thousand mouths to feed, not counting the hundreds of horses they have brought with them. Far from rescuing us, these Romans have made the situation even worse! By the time the governor's army reaches us we will have died of thirst and hunger and Prince Artaxes and his rebels will be picking over our bones.'

'Very well then,' Thermon interrupted, rapping his staff on the flagstoned floor. 'What would you suggest we do, Krathos?'

'Negotiate with the rebels. Come to terms so that those who have taken shelter in the citadel are spared.'

'Even if that means His Majesty abdicates? And we break our treaty with Rome?'

'Even that.' Krathos nodded. 'Although my loyalty to His Majesty is boundless, he must accept that his continued reign would divide Palmyra. As would Prince Artaxes, should he take the citadel and proclaim himself king. As I see it, there is only one way out of this predicament. We must offer the people of Palmyra a compromise: a ruler who is beholden neither to Rome, nor to Parthia. We must offer them Prince Amethus as their new king.' He took a pace forward and laid his hand on the prince's shoulder. Amethus started and glanced round quickly. Krathos gave him a reassuring smile and Amethus nodded happily and stared off into the mid-distance again.

Krathos cleared his throat and continued, 'Let Prince Amethus preserve the balance of power between the great empires that have us caught between them. Let His Majesty step down from the throne, in favour of his eldest son and heir. And let Prince Amethus bring peace to our kingdom.'

'Peace!' Prince Balthus snorted as he stood up and faced Krathos. 'There would be no peace under my brother and you know it. Amethus is a fool. He's easily led. Particularly by you, Krathos. You have but to tug his leash and Amethus follows you like a whipped cur. Everyone knows it. Just as everyone knows that you would have us beholden to which ever empire offered you the most gold!'

Cato noticed that Amethus barely stirred during his brother's tirade. He wondered how Amethus could be oblivious of the insults. Unless his simpleness had made him immune.

For a moment Krathos' eyes widened in anger, then he forced himself to smile and wave his hand dismissively. 'The prince forgets himself. Has my family not supported King Vabathus, and all his forebears, with unimpeachable loyalty? I will take no lectures on loyalty from a man whose sole sense of duty is to his own self-indulgence.'

Balthus paced towards the nobleman, his hand instinctively reaching to his hip before he recalled that his sword had been handed to the guards at the door. No man was permitted to carry arms in the king's audience chamber except the king himself and his bodyguards. Krathos recoiled as Balthus fumed and stabbed a finger towards his face.

'Truly, you are the son of a dog.' He drew his head up. 'I am loyal to my father, and I would fight and die for him at his merest word of command. Honour is my master. Gold is yours.'

Krathos' smug expression hardened. Cato saw his hands ball into fists, and feared the consequences of any division in the beleaguered ranks of those trapped in the citadel. Before either man could strike, the king rose to his feet and bellowed, 'That is enough! Sit down, both of you! Now!'

With a last glance of mutual hate, Krathos and Balthus reluctantly resumed their seats. The king glared at them for a moment before he continued, in a lower voice. Cato, who had seen him in a tired, despairing mood the night before, was surprised by the sudden power of his presence, and the firmness in his voice that spoke of the man he had been in better days.

'There will be no negotiations with the rebels, let me make that clear for all of you. In any case, I know my son, Prince Artaxes. He would feel nothing but contempt for our offer to negotiate. He will not accept that Amethus is the rightful heir to my throne.' The king's voice wavered for a moment as he continued, 'I had hoped that Artaxes would be his brother's first minister, his general. He promised great things, once. Now? He is no more than a burden to torment an old man's memory.' The king paused and swallowed. 'Amethus will be king, when the time comes.'

'And what of me?' asked Balthus.

'You?' The king seemed surprised. 'When this siege is over, I am confident that you will be what you have always been: a drunken wastrel.'

Balthus' lips pressed together in a thin line as he gripped the arms of his chair.

'That ain't fair,' Macro muttered softly. 'He's a damn good fighter.'

'Quiet,' Sempronius hissed. 'Not another word.'

Macro nodded, but tried to register his protest to Cato as they exchanged a glance.

The king was still looking at his middle son. 'If I am wrong in my judgement of you, my son, then you must prove it.'

'I shall,' Prince Balthus replied coldly. 'Then you will eat your words.'

Much of the audience gasped at the temerity of the prince's remark, and the king stared at his son, brows knitted together in a deep frown. There was a tense silence, until Thermon cleared his throat and broke the spell.

'Your Majesty, there is still much we have to discuss.'

The king's gaze flickered away from his son, and fixed irritably on his chamberlain.

'The supply situation, Your Majesty?' Thermon prompted. 'We have to address that.'

'Yes . . . yes, we must.' The king eased himself back on to his chair. 'Continue.'

Thermon bowed his head and turned to address the others. 'As Krathos has pointed out, our supplies will be exhausted. The garrison is already on half rations. The refugees inside the walls of the citadel are surviving, barely, on even less. Now we have more mouths to feed than ever. The question is, what can we do?'

There was a pause as the king's advisers considered the question. Then Balthus spoke. 'Clear the refugees out of the citadel. Send them back into the city.'

'We can't do that,' Thermon replied. 'It is more than likely that they would be slaughtered by the rebels.'

'My brother might spare them.' Balthus shrugged. 'If not, then they die either way. At least we could save their rations for the soldiers defending the citadel, and protecting the king. Unless anyone has a better idea?' Balthus turned and looked round at his audience.

'Kill the horses.' Cato spoke out loudly.

Balthus turned towards him and cocked his head to one side. 'What?'

'Kill the horses,' Cato repeated. 'They are consuming water we could put to better use, and the meat would feed the garrison and the civilians for a while yet. Maybe not until the governor arrives. But at least it would buy us some time.'

The suggestion seemed reasonable enough to Cato, but he was suddenly aware that the Palmyran nobles were looking at him in horror. He leaned towards Sempronius. 'What have I said?'

'They tend to place rather a high value on horseflesh in this part of the world,' Sempronius explained. 'Some even seem to have more affection for their horses than for their wives.'

'Reminds me of my father,' Macro mused unhelpfully.

Cato was not dissuaded. He stood up and raised his hand to quell the angry muttering amongst the Palmyran nobles. 'If I may?'

The king's chamberlain nodded and rapped his staff on the ground to silence his countrymen. Cato waited until all was still before he continued, 'This is no time for misplaced priorities. Everything depends on the citadel's holding out for as long as possible. The horses could make the difference between survival and defeat. If we keep the horses, and they consume our supplies, then they will only hasten our defeat. They must be killed,' Cato insisted. 'After all, they are only animals.'

'Only animals?' Balthus shook his head. 'To you Romans, perhaps. After all, your horses are miserable creatures. If you must kill any beasts, then let it be your own. You shall not touch mine.'

The other nobles muttered their support for Balthus, but Cato stood his ground. 'So you would rather feed your horses than your people? Is that it?' He shook his head. 'How long do you think the people will stand for it? When their children go hungry and they feel starvation gnawing at their guts, do you think for a moment that they will share your passion for fine horses? They will tear you to pieces. Or at least

193

they would try to. And you would be forced to kill them all, for the sake of your horses. And when Prince Artaxes hears of your folly he will be sure that every man, woman and child between Syria and the Euphrates knows of it. He won't be seen as a rebel, but as a liberator.'

Cato paused to let his words sink in and glanced round the room, briefly meeting Macro's gaze as his friend winked at him and nodded his approval. Cato took a deep breath to still his rapidly beating heart and continued in a calmer tone.

'You must sacrifice the horses, or you will lose everything. But there's another reason why they must be killed. It will be a clear signal to everyone in the citadel that there will be no escape, no attempt to break out and ride to safety. We will fight on, together, until Cassius Longinus arrives, or we will die, together, defending the citadel.'

Cato eased himself back down on to his chair and crossed his arms. Macro nudged him and muttered, 'Nice job. Too nice, actually. You aren't thinking of chucking in soldiering and taking up law when we get back to Rome, I hope.'

'That was low, even for you, Macro.'

Sempronius was surveying the response around the hall to Cato's brief address, and he nodded with satisfaction before turning to the young officer. 'I think you might have won them round, Prefect. A crude appeal to reason, and fear, and rather lacking in rhetorical flourishes. But it worked well enough.' He looked closely at Cato for a moment, appraising him. 'There's more to you than I thought. If we survive this, you'll go far.'

'I sincerely hope so,' Cato muttered. 'The further from here the better.'

The king beckoned to his chamberlain and they conferred quietly for a moment and then Vabathus leaned back in his chair, grim-faced, as Thermon spread his arms to attract the nobles' gaze.

'My lords! The king commands your attention! Quiet there.'

When the chamber had settled down once more, the king drew himself up and cleared his throat. 'It is my will that every horse in the citadel is to be slaughtered at once. There are to be no exceptions in this. All of you will surrender your horses to the commander of the royal bodyguard. Even you, Balthus.'

'Really?' Balthus smiled humourlessly. 'And what of the mounts in your stable, Your Majesty?'

'They will be the first to be killed.' The king gestured towards Cato. 'The Roman officer is right. We are all in this together. There is only one fate for every person in the citadel. And if Artaxes does get to hear of it then he will know that we are resolved to defeat him, or die in the attempt. That is my command. Now, the audience is over.'

Thermon's staff thudded down. 'All rise for the king!'

A handful of chairs scraped as the nobles and the Romans stood up and bowed their heads. King Vabathus rose and made his way across the chamber to a small doorway in one corner, and disappeared from sight. Thermon waited a moment longer, and then turned to the others and gave them permission to leave. The Palmyran nobles talked in hushed, bitter tones as they filed out of the hall, until only the three Romans and the supporters of Prince Amethus remained, standing behind the prince. Krathos glared at Cato.

'We could have negotiated with the rebels. We could have saved many lives.' He smiled thinly. 'We could even have spared the horses Prince Balthus cherishes so much. But now? Now you have persuaded the king to fight and we are all doomed. I hope you are satisfied, Roman.'

Cato stood stiffly and did not respond. For a moment there was a tense silence, and then Krathos sniffed with derision and turned to Prince Amethus. 'We should leave.'

Amethus nodded vaguely and rose to his feet. Krathos gestured towards the door and the prince walked away, trailed by Krathos and the rest of his small retinue.

'Don't worry about Krathos,' Sempronius said softly. 'He has little influence over the king, or even within the court for that matter. But his power over Amethus is a different matter.'

'I'm not worried about him,' Cato replied calmly. 'It's his brother who poses the real danger to us.'

'Prince Artaxes?' Sempronius raised his eyebrows. 'Of course.'

'No, not him,' Cato continued. 'Prince Balthus. Come what may, he will never forgive me for coming between him and his father. I fear we have just made a new enemy.'

'Really?' Macro shrugged. 'Right now, what's one more or less? Besides,' he licked his lips, 'it seems that fresh meat is back on the menu.'

CHAPTER TWENTY-ONE

The slaughter of the horses began shortly afterwards, beginning with those of the royal stable, just as King Vabathus had commanded. The animals were held in place by strong men holding stout leather traces. Then the butcher from the king's kitchens cut the animals' throats, collecting the blood in wide wooden tubs to be saved as a thickening agent for the gruel that was cooked each day for the civilian refugees. The carcasses were quickly gutted and the inedible organs were carted away to be dumped over the side of the wall, downwind of the bulk of the citadel. The bodies were efficiently flayed and then the meat was cut from the bones ready to be packed into the massive brine-filled jars that had been prepared in the cellars beneath the royal quarters. Anything else that could be boiled down for stock was carried off to the pots steaming over the cooking fires in the barracks of the royal bodyguard.

Cato and Macro spent the day seeing to the accommodation of their men and drawing up duty rosters and inventories of their remaining equipment. All the time the air was thick with the whinnying of terrified horses, and the stench of cooking horsemeat filled their nostrils to such an extent that Macro had almost gone off the idea of fresh meat by the end of the day. Almost. When the duty orderly brought the two officers a tough piece of grilled horse meat and a jar of watered wine to share, Macro quickly forgot his complaints about the smell and tucked in eagerly, cutting a hunk off for Cato to eat. They shared one of the small tack rooms in the king's stables. The scent of the previous occupants still lent a sharp tang to the air. The rest of the auxiliaries and legionaries occupied the stables and courtyard and most of the men were already asleep, after being pushed to the limit in the last few days.

'Good idea of yours, this,' Macro managed to say as he chewed on the meat. 'I was getting a bit sick of hard bread and tack.'

Cato had pulled out his dagger and was busy cutting small strips off his portion. 'Maybe. But I doubt it has won me many friends amongst the nobles.'

'Bollocks to 'em. You were right. If they can't see beyond their bloody possessions to what's really important then they don't deserve them.' Macro chuckled. 'But the expression on their faces was priceless. What I wouldn't give to see that again!'

He continued chewing for a moment before he looked at Cato and spoke again. 'That was quite a performance, by the way.'

Cato shrugged. 'I said what needed saying, that's all.'

'I know, but it's the way you said it that counted. I could never have managed it,' Macro said quietly. He felt a stab of pain at the recognition of this fragment of inferiority. He did not have the same facility with language as his young friend, and never would have, he realised. Despite being a good soldier, Macro doubted that he would ever be promoted to a senior command. In his heart, like most men of the region, he harboured the ambition of one day becoming a chief centurion – the primus pilus. Very few men ever attained that rank. Most had been killed or injured and discharged long before they became eligible for the position. Even then, only those men with spotless records and a chestful of bravery awards would be considered. Macro reflected sourly on the last two years which he and Cato had spent performing special duties for Narcissus. The secret nature of the work meant that they would never be rewarded publicly for the dangers they had faced in the service of Rome. Vital though the missions had been, they would count for nothing when he and Cato returned to service in the legions.

Until then, Macro would have to make the most of his temporary command and hope that his good service would be entered on his record. That was his only path to preferment, he reflected. Cato, on the other hand, with his brains, was bound to be plucked from the ranks of the centurionate and appointed to permanent command of one of the more prestigious auxiliary cohorts. That would mean entry into the ranks of the equites, Rome's second tier of aristocracy, and Cato's heirs, if he lived long enough to have any, would be eligible for the senate. A giddy prospect indeed, Macro acknowledged as he watched Cato guardedly. It occurred to him that one day his friend would outrank him. The thought startled him, and for a moment he was pricked by resentment. Then he shook the feeling off, angry at himself for letting such an unworthy sentiment enter his head.

'Anyway,' Cato picked up a small piece of the meat and popped it in his mouth, 'it's not important now. What matters is making sure that we hold out until Longinus reaches Palmyra. If he takes longer than we expect then killing the horses won't be enough. We'll have to do what Balthus suggested.'

Macro paused a moment to recollect, then raised his eyebrows. 'Ah, you mean pitch the civilians out of the citadel.'

'Yes.'

'That's harsh, coming from you, lad.'

'What else can we do?' Cato sighed wearily. 'If we let them stay in the citadel and are starved into surrender then Palmyra will fall under the control of Parthia. The Emperor won't allow that, so there'll be a war, in which case tens of thousands will die. If we have to sacrifice the civilians here, then it may be justified in the long run.'

'Maybe,' Macro responded. 'But there's a more immediate issue you might consider.'

'Oh?'

'Let's not forget what Prince Artaxes has in store for us, if he takes the citadel.'

'I hadn't forgotten.'

Macro shrugged. 'If it comes down to a choice between the civilians and us, well, there's no choice in my book.'

Cato did not reply. He was still thinking about the threat to massacre all the Romans found inside the citadel. That would include the ambassador's daughter, Julia – though not before she was handed over to Artaxes' soldiers to use as they wished. He felt anger rise up in him at the prospect, and there it was again, that thrill of affection, like a warm ache in his heart. Cato reached for the jug and took several mouthfuls. Macro watched him in amusement.

'You drink as if you've only just discovered wine.'

Cato lowered the jug. 'I needed that. It's been a long day.'

'And then some.' Macro laughed. 'Ever the one for understatement, aren't you?'

Cato joined in the laughter and for a moment the strain of recent days lifted from his shoulders and he was glad that he would be at

Macro's side in the struggle to come. Whatever the odds, whatever the likelihood of defeat and death, somehow Macro had always managed to make Cato feel that they would come through the ordeal alive.

He rose up and stretched his shoulders with a weary grunt.

'Going somewhere?' Macro asked.

Cato nodded. 'One last walk round the sentry posts before I turn in. That's all.'

'Make sure it is. You need the rest, lad. We all do.'

'Who are you, my mother?'

'No. Just your commanding officer. And I order you to get a good night's sleep.'

Cato smiled and made an exaggerated salute. 'Yes, sir!'

He left the stables and climbed up on to the battlements. Tonight it was the turn of the Second Illyrian to provide the watch and Cato went from post to post to make sure that his men were awake and keeping a close eye on the enemy. The sentries were as tired as the rest of the men, but they well knew the penalty for sleeping on duty – death by stoning – and kept moving, steadily marching up and down the stretch of wall that had been allocated to them. When he had checked the last of his men and was happy that the duty centurion had properly prepared the passwords and changes of the watch, Cato climbed up into the beacon tower to have a last look out over the city before he made his way to his bed and a desperately needed sleep.

At the top of the stairs, he paused to catch his breath, and then emerged on to the platform and nodded in response to the salute of the auxiliary manning the pyre. Within a heavy iron frame split palm logs lay on top of a pile of dried palms that acted as kindling. Under the frame lay the ashes of the fire that had been lit the previous night to signal Macro to make his attack on the eastern gate of the city. Cato crossed to the battlements overlooking the agora and stared across to the temple precinct where the rebels had laboured through the day to make repairs to the ram and its housing. Torches flared around the structure where men had replaced the severed ropes, and now long lines of men heaved on pulleys as the ram was raised into position and support ropes hurriedly lashed to the timber frame of the housing. As he watched their progress, Cato felt a sinking sensation in his stomach as he realised that the ram would be repaired before the next day dawned. The brave attack by the Greek mercenaries had cost the enemy one day. That was all it had achieved, aside from diverting the enemy's attention away from Macro's assault on the eastern gate. A small enough gain, Cato reflected, but he had been a soldier long enough to know that one day might yet mean the difference between success and defeat.

He lifted his gaze and slowly scanned the surrounding area. Lights from fires in the streets on the other side of the city revealed the heart of the enemy's activity. Cato realised how completely outnumbered the garrison of the citadel was. And if the Parthians reached the city before Longinus did then there was no hope.

Cato heard footsteps as another person climbed into the signal tower, but he was too tired and depressed by his thoughts to bother turning to look.

'Why, it's Prefect Cato,' said Julia.

Cato looked round, straightening up to greet her with stiff formality. 'Lady Julia.'

'What are you doing here?' she asked bluntly.

Cato was frustrated by the interruption and replied tersely. 'My job. And you?'

'I've finished my work for the day, Prefect. This is where I come to be alone.'

'Alone?' Cato could not hide his surprise. 'Why would you want to be alone?'

She looked at him shrewdly. 'For the same reason as you, I imagine. To think. That is why you are up here, isn't it?'

Cato frowned, angry that she had guessed his mind and habits so easily. The extreme irritation of his expression made his face comical and she suddenly laughed: a light, pleasing sound that Cato would have liked under different circumstances, but now only made his expression harden even more. She reached out and touched his arm.

'I'm so sorry. We seem to have got off on the wrong foot.' She smiled. 'Believe me, I meant no offence. I didn't mean to make you angry.'

Her tone was sincere and the light of the small brazier glowing beside the pyre made her eyes sparkle. Much as Cato wanted to maintain his cold mood, he could not help warming to her.

He nodded. 'It wasn't the most cordial of introductions. I apologise for my behaviour. Sometimes it's hard to forget that I'm a soldier.'

'I know. My father sometimes suffers from the same complaint as a diplomat. And after all you have been through, I'm sure you have a right to be short with me.'

Cato was embarrassed by his earlier behaviour and all the more self-conscious about it now that Julia had shown him a graciousness that he had not returned in kind. He swallowed nervously and bowed his head as he took a half-step back from her. 'I'd better leave you to your thoughts then, my lady. I apologise for intruding on your privacy.'

'But it is I who have intruded. You were here first,' she reminded him. 'Would you not share the tower with me? I promise I'll be quiet and won't distract you.'

There was that faintly amused tone to her voice again and Cato felt that she was mocking him. He shook his head. 'I must rest, my lady. I bid you good night.'

Before he could turn away completely Julia blurted out, 'Please, stay and talk to me. If you're not too tired to spare me a moment.'

He was exhausted, and the thought of sleep was beyond temptation, yet the pleading look in her eyes melted his resolve. He smiled. 'It would be a pleasure, my lady.'

'You know, you could call me Julia.'

'I could. But only if you call me Cato.'

'But that's your cognomen. Might I know your familiar name?'

'In the army we only go by the cognomen. Force of habit.'

'Very well, Cato it is.' Julia moved away, towards the side of the tower that looked over the agora. She glanced back at him and smiled, and Cato went over and joined her, conscious of her closeness and yet not daring to make any kind of physical contact. He was aware of her scent for the first time, a citron tang mixed with something sweet, and he savoured it as he stood beside her and stared out across Palmyra.

'Such a beautiful thing,' Julia mused. 'A city at night. I used to sit on the roof terrace of our house in Rome when I was a child. We lived on the Janiculan Hill, with views towards the forum and the imperial palace. At night torches and braziers sparkled like diamonds, and amber, right across the city. On moonlit nights you could see the details clearly for miles, as if Rome was a toy made of blue stone. Sometimes a mist would rise from the Tiber.'

Cato smiled. 'I remember that. It was like a fine silk veil. Looked so soft that I wanted to reach out and touch it.'

She glanced at him with a surprised expression. 'You too? I thought I was the only one who saw it that way. You lived in Rome?'

'I was raised in the palace. My father was an imperial freedman.' The words were out before Cato could stop himself and he wondered if she would think worse of him for his lowly origins.

'The son of a freedman, and now a prefect of auxiliaries,' Julia mused. 'That's quite an achievement.'

'Acting prefect,' Cato confessed. 'Once a permanent commander is found I will revert to the rank of centurion. A junior one at that.'

She saw through his modesty at once. 'The fact that you were chosen for the command at all must mean someone thinks you have potential, Cato.'

'It would be nice to think so. Otherwise it'll take a long time to work up enough seniority for any further promotion in the legions.'

'And you'd like that?'

'What soldier wouldn't?'

'Forgive me, Cato, but you don't seem like a typical soldier to me.'

He looked at her. 'I don't?'

'Oh, I'm sure that you are a fine officer, and I know that you are brave, and you have quite a way with words according to my father.'

'But?'

She shrugged. 'I don't really know. You seem to have a certain sensitivity that I haven't encountered in the soldiers I've met before.'

'Blame it on the palace upbringing.'

She laughed and then stared out across the city again, and a silence grew between them, until Cato spoke. 'What about you? What happened to the young girl who spent her evenings staring out across Rome?'

Julia smiled faintly, then gently clasped her wrist by the other hand and rubbed it slowly. 'Like all girls from a good family, I was married to a man three times my age as soon as I was fourteen. It was supposed to establish a bond between two families with proud lineages. Only my husband used to beat me.'

'I'm sorry to hear that.'

She looked at him sadly. 'I know what you're thinking. All husbands beat their wives from time to time.'

'I didn't mean . . .'

'Well, maybe it's true. But Junius Porcinus used to beat me almost every day. For any fault he could find in me. I took it for a while . . . I thought that was how marriages were supposed to be. After two years of looking at a bruised face in the mirror every morning I asked my father for permission to divorce Porcinus. When he learned what had been going on he agreed. I've travelled with him on the Emperor's business ever since. I suppose I run the household for him in place of my mother. She died giving birth to me.' Julia was silent for a moment and then smiled awkwardly. 'How silly of me! Boring you to death with my family history when you need to rest.'

'No, it's quite all right,' Cato replied. 'I mean, I'm not bored. Honestly. You're very . . . open.'

'Indiscreet, you mean.'

Cato shook his head. 'Open, honest. It's just that I'm not used to it. Soldiers tend not to be too forthcoming about their feelings. So this is a refreshing change.'

'Oh, I'm not normally so candid. But now?' Julia shrugged. 'Life might be somewhat shorter than I had expected. There's no point in holding back those things I want to say. The prospect of death can be quite liberating.'

'Ah, that I can agree with.' Cato chuckled as he recalled the wild exhilaration of combat, mixed with dreadful fear. Paradoxically, he had never felt more alive than at such moments. A sad truth, he conceded to himself. There was a time when his greatest pleasure had been the pursuit of knowledge. Since becoming a soldier he had discovered a side of his nature that he had never suspected was there. But then, perhaps that was the gift of soldiering – the gaining of self-knowledge. Four years ago he had been a timid youth, filled with doubts about his worth. Everything had seemed impossible. Now he knew what he was capable of, the good as well as the bad. He had achieved feats of endurance and courage that once he would never have thought possible.

Cato realised that he had been silent for a while, and that Julia was watching him, sidelong.

'Sometimes I wish I had been born a man,' she said quietly. 'So many experiences are denied to women. So many opportunities. But since the revolt broke out, I'm not so sure. I can't think how many broken bodies I've had to deal with in the hospital. It's a brutal business being a soldier.'

'True enough,' Cato agreed. 'But it's only part of the job. We don't live to kill.'

'If you had only seen what happened here the day the revolt broke out.' Julia shuddered and closed her eyes tightly for a moment. 'The killing began and didn't stop. Soldiers killed soldiers, then women and children. Butchery, that's what it was. I've never seen anything so barbaric.'

'Perhaps.' Cato rubbed his cheek. 'The thing is, that barbarian is there in all of us. It just takes the right kind of provocation, or opportunity, before the barbarian emerges.'

She looked at him closely. 'You really think so?'

'I know it.'

'And you think you have it in you to act the barbarian?'

'It's not an act. Not for me. Not for any man. Not even for you, Julia. Given the right circumstances.'

She stared at him for a moment before easing herself away from the battlements. 'It's been nice to talk to someone about something other than their injuries. But I must let you rest. I thank you for your kindness. I shouldn't impose on you any further.'

Her tone was firm, and Cato did not feel confident enough to press the issue. Besides, he was too tired to think clearly and dared not risk saying anything foolish to this woman he keenly wanted to know better.

'We can talk again another night,' he suggested.

'That would be nice. I'd like that.'

They both stared across the agora to where the rebels were putting the finishing touches to their battering ram and its housing.

'Will they take the citadel?' Julia asked softly.

'I can't say,' Cato replied wearily.

'Can't say? Or won't say?'

'I wouldn't lie to you about our chances, Julia. I just don't know. It depends on so many factors.'

She turned to him and pressed her hand to her chest. 'Forget the details. Tell me from your heart. Do you feel we can live through this?'

Cato stared into her eyes and nodded slowly. 'We'll survive. I give you my word. I will let nothing happen to you.'

She looked back at him and nodded. 'Thank you for being honest with me.'

Cato smiled at her. Julia turned and descended into the tower. Now that she had gone Cato was aware of the coolness of the night and he shivered. Perhaps they really would talk again another night, he mused. He hoped so. But as he took a last look across the agora at the enemy clustered about the battering ram he knew that the morrow would bring a fresh assault on these walls and only a handful of tired Roman soldiers and Greek mercenaries stood between Prince Artaxes' blood-thirsty rebels and the terrified civilians sheltering inside the citadel.

CHAPTER TWENTY-TWO

The defenders had been at their posts on the walls of the citadel since first light, intently watching the approach to the gate and waiting for the rebels to begin their attack. Stocks of arrows, javelins and sling shot had been placed at regular intervals along the battlements and heavy blocks of stone had been piled on the rampart above the gates. The smell of heated oil filled the air as smoke billowed lazily from one of the large ovens close to the barracks of the Greek mercenaries.

Macro and Cato, together with the commander of the royal bodyguard, a wiry veteran named Demetrius, and Prince Balthus, stood on the battlements above the gate and stared towards the rebel soldiers forming up around the ram housing.

'It didn't take them long to repair the damage,' said Balthus.

Demetrius took a sharp breath. 'We did what we could in the short time available to us, my Prince.'

'So you say. Just a shame that it has won only one day, while it cost you over thirty men.'

Demetrius pressed his lips together in a thin line to bite off an intemperate response. Then he managed to mutter, 'A shame, as you say, my lord.'

'Well, what's done is done,' Macro intervened. 'They're coming and we'll have to make sure we send 'em packing. It's time we joined our men. Good luck.' He turned to Cato and clasped arms, and then did the same with the others. 'Stick it to 'em!'

Macro made for the staircase leading down to the courtyard behind the gate. His legionaries were waiting for him, in close formation a short distance from the studded timbers. If the rebels succeeded in breaching the gates, the task of keeping them out would fall to the best soldiers in the citadel. Behind the legionaries were small parties of men with thick mats and staffs capped with iron hooks, ready to fight any fires caused by incendiary missiles. Up on the wall, Prince Balthus and his followers were positioned to the left of the gate while the Greek mercenaries were to the right. Cato and the pick of his men had been entrusted with guarding the towers on either side of the gate and the battlements that stretched between them. The rest of the auxiliaries were stationed along the remainder of the citadel's walls under the command of Centurion Parmenion.

Cato clasped arms with Balthus and Demetrius before they turned away and joined their men. He was still tired and his wounded arm felt stiff and sore as he flexed it and then stretched his shoulders to try to loosen them. The men had already been fed and as he walked round his command Cato was pleased to see that they were alert and determined-looking. Their kit, which had become dusty and grimy on the march from Antioch, was clean again and helmets and shield bosses were polished and gleaming in the rays of the early morning sun.

'No need to worry, lads.' Cato smiled as he passed amongst them. 'This time there's a bloody great wall between you and those gutless archers. If the moment comes, then they'll not be so cocky when they face Roman iron.'

Some of the men grumbled their assent as they recalled the showers of arrows they had endured during the skirmish in the desert. This time they had the advantage, and the rebels were going to pay dearly.

'It is up to us,' Cato continued firmly, 'to see to it that the gate is held. Keep a cool head, keep your shield up and make the enemy die hard! Second Illyrian!' Cato drew his sword and thrust it into the air. 'Second Illyrian!'

His men raised their weapons and repeated his cry, the name of the cohort echoing back off the buildings inside the citadel. The chant was taken up by the rest of the cohort posted round the wall. Then a new cry rose up inside as Macro's men bellowed out the name of their legion and used the flats of their swords to beat a furious rhythm against the metal trim of their shields.

'That's the spirit.' Cato grinned to himself. The men's blood was up, and he almost felt sorry for the first of the enemy who came within reach of a Roman sword.

'They're on the move!' a voice cried out from the left tower, and the

207

cheering quickly faded away as Cato forced himself to walk and not run to the steps leading up to the top of the tower. His men were crowded along the battlements overlooking the agora.

'Clear the way there!' he snapped at them. 'Quickly, damn you!'

They parted as he approached and Cato looked down towards the temple precinct just as a blaring of horns and the boom of drums echoed across the agora. Hundreds of men were crowded into the ram housing and had taken their places behind the wooden spars that had been slotted into place across the frame, passing under the long shaft of the ram. As the drums beat a steady pace the men heaved against the spars and the heavy structure began to rumble across the flagstones towards the citadel. Armoured men walking alongside pulled down the leather flaps while small boys ran up and down with jars of water, soaking the leather before it came in range of any fire arrows shot from the walls of the citadel. The rebels were preparing their own incendiaries, Cato noted, as his gaze turned to some activity on the edges of the streets that led from the agora. Columns of men pulling on ropes spilled out into the open. Behind them carts emerged, each one bearing a bolt-thrower or a catapult, light artillery pieces to be sure, but more than capable of shooting their missiles over the citadel's walls. Then came men carrying glowing embers in heavy iron braziers above which the air shimmered.

Last of all emerged a number of men carrying large stout shelters. With them trotted the archers, clutching spare bundles of arrows under their arms. The shelters were hurriedly set up as the artillery crews sighted their weapons and began to crank back the torsion cords. There was a shouted command to Cato's left and the first of Balthus' archers began to loose their arrows. Dark shafts darted down towards the rebels, clattering off the flagstones, occasionally thudding into the shelters that had been set up. The rebels paid them due respect and took cover as they arranged their arrows and lit the first of them, ready to shoot up at the battlements.

'Watch out!' Cato shouted. 'Incoming fire arrows!'

The auxiliaries crouched down behind the rims of their shields or ducked behind the hard cover of the stone battlements. A moment later a glittering arrow whipped over the wall, trailing a fine line of smoke, before it reached the top of its trajectory and curved down towards the palatial buildings of the royal accommodation. The arrow shattered as it struck a roof tile and the flaming fragments exploded in all directions. More arrows followed. Most struck the roof or walls, or fell harmlessly to the ground, but a handful lodged in the timber of doorways or window frames and the fire parties pounced on them immediately to beat the flames out.

'Sir?'

Cato turned and saw Centurion Aquila coming towards him, crouching low. Now that his horses were gone, Aquila and his men fought as infantry and Cato had chosen Aquila to act as his second-in-command in the defence of the gate.

'What is it?'

'Shall I give the order for our slingers to shoot back? And the bolt-throwers on the towers?'

Cato shook his head. 'No sense in exposing our men just yet. Let the rebels waste their ammunition; they're not doing us any harm. We'll hold back until the ram is within range. Then the slingers can target those archers.'

'Yes, sir.' A look of disappointment flickered across Aquila's face. 'Very good.'

'Don't worry, Aquila. The men will get their chance to carve 'em up soon enough.'

'I can hardly wait,' Aquila muttered grimly as he risked a quick glimpse over the wall. 'Time to pay them back for the horses.'

'The horses?' Cato wondered, and then shook his head. His cavalry commander was clearly one of those men who cared deeply for his mounts. Still, if he blamed the rebels for the mass slaughter of the previous day, so much the better.

'Centurion Aquila, when this is all over, I promise to let you have the pick of the enemy's horses.'

'Yes, sir. Thank you.' Aquila grinned.

There was a dull whack from below in the agora and a moment later a flaming bundle of rags tied tightly round a rock blazed over the battlement. The missile dropped down towards the part of the citadel being used for the hospital and crashed through the tiles and vanished from sight. Cato felt his throat tighten with anxiety for Julia's safety, but he was powerless to do anything to protect her, or even find out if she was safe, while the enemy attack was under way. He tried to push all thought of her from his mind as he took a breath and rose up to check on the progress of the battering ram.

The rebels had got it a third of the way across the agora. Prince Balthus and his archers were keeping up a steady barrage of fire arrows, which formed a sparse stubble across the leather roof of the ram housing. The arrows smouldered in the damp leather but before they could catch the boys would dart forward and hurl fresh water over the roof. The groan from the axles of the large wheels carried up to the battlements even above the din of the iron rims grinding across the flagstones. The drums continued to beat a steady rhythm to the men straining inside the housing as they pressed forward.

'Man the bolt-throwers!' Cato commanded. 'Load incendiaries!'

The crew of the ballista in the left tower jumped up on to the firing platform and began to crank the arms back. Another man held the tip of a three-foot-long heavy bolt in the flames of the brazier at the rear of the platform. The oil-soaked rags wrapped round the shaft just behind the iron head quickly caught alight and the auxiliary hurriedly carried it across to the bolt-thrower. He carefully placed the bolt in the channel as the optio in command of the artillery section took aim on the ram housing. Already the rebel archers had spotted the crew clustered round the weapon and were loosing shots up at the tower. There was a crack as an arrow shaft trembled briefly in the frame of the bolt-thrower. Smoke trailed up from the oiled rags.

'Get some water on that!' shouted the optio and then turned his attention back to the weapon. As soon as he was satisfied with the laying he straightened up and reached for the release lever.

'Stand clear!'

The crew stepped away and an instant later the arms snapped forward and smacked against the padded restraints. The flaming bolt shot out of the weapon in an almost flat trajectory, lancing across the agora. It struck the leather covers of the ram housing, burst through and disappeared inside. The crewmen punched their fists into the air, but the optio turned on them angrily.

'What in Hades are you doing? You're not paid by the day. Reload the weapon, and you, put that fucking fire out!'

Cato had watched the fall of the shot and nodded with satisfaction.

'Keep it up, Optio. Fast as you can shoot. Won't take the rebels long to move the ram so close to the wall that we can't depress the bolt-throwers enough.'

'Yes, sir,' the optio replied. 'We'll do the best we can.'

Just then, the man who had been standing at the front of the platform extinguishing the burning arrow with his canteen let out an explosive gasp. He dropped the canteen and staggered backwards, arms scrabbling for the shaft sticking out of his back, just below the shoulder blade.

'Watch it!' Cato shouted. 'Stop him!'

But it was too late. The auxiliary's calves struck the rim of the battlement and he tumbled backwards, arms flailing, then was gone. His scream was mercifully short, but they all heard the heavy thud as he landed at the foot of the tower. The optio gritted his teeth, strode to the front of the bolt-thrower, plucked the burning arrow out and threw it back towards the enemy before striding back to the rear of the weapon and snarling at his men, 'Next cunt who lets that happen to him is on a charge. Remember, keep your bloody heads down!'

There was a distant crack and Cato turned to see that the other bolt-thrower was also targeting the ram. As the rebels slowly angled in towards the gate several more shots struck the housing, passing straight through the leather and tearing into the packed ranks of the men inside, or lodging in the stout timbers of the framework, burning there until one of the rebel water-carriers managed to extinguish it. Behind the ram housing a wake of blood smears and the bodies of dead and injured told of the destruction being wrought by the citadel's thrower.

The one-sided barrage from the towers could not last for ever, and just as the ram housing reached the point at which the auxiliary crews could not depress their weapons any further, one of the enemy bolt-throwers mounted in the carts down in the agora scored a lucky hit. The heavy iron tip of the bolt smashed into the throwing arm of the weapon on the left tower. With a splintering crack the torsion arm snapped and under the immense strain of the thick cord of the bowstring the arm slashed round in an arc, crushing the head of the nearest man and shattering the arm of the next as splinters exploded in all directions, showering the soldiers closest to the weapon. Three more men were

211

injured, one of them screaming in agony as he raised a hand to pluck a long sliver of wood from his eye.

'Get the wounded away!' Cato yelled. 'Down to the hospital. Optio!'

'Yes, sir?' The optio was wincing as he removed a large splinter from his forearm.

'Pull the weapon back and get that throwing arm repaired.'

'Repaired, sir?' The optio glanced at the bolt-thrower. The splintered stump of the throwing arm protruded a short distance from the torsion coils. 'It's fucked.'

'I don't care. Get it out of sight of the enemy and get it fixed. We'll need it.'

The optio stiffened up and nodded. 'Yes, sir. Right, lads! You heard the prefect. Let's get to it.'

Cato stepped away as the surviving members of the crew clambered round the broken weapon and heaved it away from the battlements. Around him some of the auxiliaries were helping the wounded men over to the stairs and down into the courtyard. Cato raised his shield and went forward again to check on the progress of the ram. The rebels had managed to heave it close enough to the wall to take it out of the line of fire of the citadel's bolt-throwers, and yet not so close as to be vulnerable to falling rocks or flammables. All the time the archers and the bolt-throwers down in the agora kept up a steady barrage of missiles aimed at the battlements, while catapults continued to lob the occasional blazing bundle in a high arc over the wall to crash down on the buildings and people inside the citadel.

Even though the ram was safe from the defenders for the moment, the rebels would have to run it up to the gate soon and there it would be directly exposed to the men immediately above. Prince Artaxes had anticipated the danger and already many of the archers and bolt-throwers were being repositioned to cover the ram. Cato ran down the stairs to the wide walkway directly above the gate. He leaned over and called down into the courtyard.

'Get the heated oil up here! Now!'

Cato turned to the men with pitchforks standing beside the braziers a short distance from the bound bundles of kindling and rags soaked in pitch, then gave the order to stoke the flames up and be ready to set fire to the faggots. While some of his men thrust their pitchforks into the

212

bundles and heaved them over towards the battlement, others used bellows to heat the braziers to a brilliant golden glow and sent sparks whirling into the air.

'Light 'em up!' Cato shouted, and an optio grabbed a torch, held it in the fire until it was well alight and then ran across to the faggots and touched it to each one until the flames caught and smoke swirled round the battlements as the kindling crackled. 'Over the wall!'

At the prefect's order the men with the pitchforks heaved them up and over and shook them out to dislodge their blazing burdens. One by one the bundles roared down from the battlements. Below, the water boys glanced up in terror and turned to run for their lives as the faggots crashed on to the roof of the ram housing and burst apart, showering the surrounding area with burning debris.

'Keep them coming!' Cato ordered.

As the faggots tumbled down from the gate tower most hit the ram housing, but some missed and burst on the flagstones of the agora. Cato glanced down just as one knocked a water boy to the ground. He rolled to one side, covered in flaming material. A shrill scream pierced the air, and went on and on as the boy writhed on the ground. His comrades who had run from the bombardment were now beaten back towards the ram housing by soldiers with whips. They darted round the leather-covered structure dashing water on to the flames and fleeing whenever they saw a burning faggot plummeting towards them, only to be forced back by the whips. And through it all the men, invisible beneath the roof of the housing, strained as they heaved the ram on towards the gate.

The last of the faggots went over the wall and Cato ran to see what had become of the heated oil. The carriers were still struggling up the last flight of stairs to the top of the gate tower: four men gripping two long wooden staves that passed through iron rings on each side of the cauldron.

'Hurry it up! Move yourselves!'

As they reached the platform, a tremor ran through the tower as the first blow of the ram thudded into the gate.

'Cato!' Macro's voice called up, and Cato leaned over the wall, 'Sir?'

'Get that oil on to the ram, and the rocks, whatever you can!'

'Yes, sir.'

Cato turned to the auxiliaries in the tower and drew a breath as he pointed to the pile of odd-sized chunks of masonry piled behind the battlements. 'Get the rocks over the wall.'

The men piled their pitchforks to one side of the tower and joined Cato as he grunted under the weight of a large stone and staggered to the battlements. With a strained grunt he heaved it up on to the wall and risked a glance directly down at the ram housing. The long leather mantle stretched out from the gate, and as a drum beat the time there was a crash below and again the impact was felt through the gate tower. Cato could see that the only serious damage caused by the faggots was a small scorch-fringed hole close to the head of the ram housing. The glistening torsos of the rebels swinging the ram could just be glimpsed. Cato waited a moment until some more of his men stood either side of him, ready to shove their crude missiles over the parapet.

'Now!'

With a scraping of stone on stone the Romans pushed and the lumps of masonry tumbled off the wall and plummeted towards the roof of the ram housing. The rocks crashed straight through, tearing gaping holes in the leather padding and the wooden planks beneath. Those rebels directly below were crushed by the impact.

'Keep it up!' Cato ordered, and then turned to the men with the cauldron of oil. Smoke and steam wisped up from the blackened iron sides of the vessel and the air was filled with the thick odour. 'Bring it over here!'

As the auxiliaries at the parapet continued to rain stones down on the ram housing, Cato helped the others manoeuvre the cauldron towards the battlements, directly above the ram. Once it was in place Cato called more men to brace themselves under the far stave and slowly the cauldron began to tilt towards the enemy. A plume of steam rose up as the liquid began to stream down, splashing over the shattered roof above the ram and through the gaps on to the men beneath. At once their agonised screams cut through the air and they abandoned their positions and scrambled away, stumbling from the rear of the ram housing. Balthus' men turned their attention on the fleeing rebels and arrows arced across at an angle, cutting down several of them as they ran for the safety of their own archers' shelters. Their comrades did their best to force Balthus' men to keep their heads down as a furious exchange of arrows ensued.

While the enemy's attention was drawn from the gates' defences Cato took the chance to examine the damage below and saw that the heated oil had done its work. The ram was on fire and the flames were quickly spreading along the damaged wooden framework. The enemy's water-carriers were fleeing along with the warriors and no one remained to fight the blaze. A hard smile of satisfaction flickered over his lips before he felt the first wash of heat strike his face. Then Cato felt his guts clench in a moment of anxiety at the memory of the fortified gate of a German village he had defended alongside Macro years before. He hurried across the tower and shouted down to the legionaries below.

'Sir! The ram's on fire!'

Macro's face split into a wide smile as he stared up at Cato. 'Good!'

Cato shook his head desperately. 'It's directly under the gate.'

Macro's smile faded. 'Oh, shit. Shit! What's the situation to your front?'

'Enemy's pulled back, sir. For now!'

'Right then. Only one thing for it.' Macro filled his lungs. 'Open the gates!'

The leading century trotted forward to raise the locking bar and take up the heavy lengths of chain that drew the doors inwards. With a grating rumble from the hinges the great slabs of studded timber slowly swung apart. Smoke billowed through the opening and Macro glimpsed the flames licking across the wooden frame of the ram housing. The leather hides had already burned away leaving the skeleton of the structure beneath, and the iron-tipped ram itself, still suspended even though the support ropes were alight.

Macro sheathed his sword and strode forward through the smoke, blinking as his eyes began to smart. 'Follow me!'

The fire had engulfed the siege weapon and the heat struck Macro like a blow. He raised his shield and pressed it up against one of the stout corner posts and nodded to the men of the first century. 'Like this! Use your shields and push. We must get this pile of shit away from the gates!'

His men, wincing at the heat of the flames, pressed forward, slammed their shields up against the ram housing and heaved with all their strength. With painful slowness the siege weapon moved away from the gates, and as more men piled in, adding their weight, the huge wheels ground backward across the flagstones.

'That's it, lads!' Macro called out, and his lungs filled with smoke that made him cough painfully as if his chest was filled with broken glass. As the fire consumed the ram the heat swelled in intensity and there was a sudden sharp smell as the crest of his helmet smouldered and began to burn. Every instinct told Macro to draw back, away from the flames that were searing his face, but he could see that the ram was not yet far enough from the gates to be certain that the flames would not spread to them. 'Keep going!' he rasped. 'Heave, you bastards!'

Something clattered on the ground close to his feet and glancing down Macro saw an arrow shaft. Then another skittered over the flagstones. He looked round the side of his shield with narrowed eyes and saw that the enemy archers had turned their attention away from Balthus and his men and were now shooting at the Romans struggling to get the ram clear of the citadel's gates. Beyond the archers a large body of rebel soldiers had formed up and begun to quick-march across the agora. Macro looked over his shoulder and saw that they had pushed the flaming structure back perhaps twenty feet from the gates.

'Just a bit further,' he muttered through clenched teeth.

There was a dull thud that Macro felt almost as much as he heard as the ropes supporting the end of the ram gave way and the huge shaft of timber hit the ground. The siege weapon lurched to a halt.

'That's it then!' Macro called to his men. 'Get back! Back inside the citadel!'

They broke away from the ram and retreated, keeping their shields to the enemy as more arrows flitted over and through the flames now licking high into the air. As soon as the rebels realised that the legionaries were pulling back, their commander bellowed an order and they charged towards the gate with a full-throated roar. The moment the rain of arrows began to slacken Macro turned round and shouted, 'Run!'

The legionaries pounded through the gate, the harsh thud of their nailed boots echoing off the curved stonework of the gateway. Macro was the last through, and he turned, drawing his sword as he faced the enemy.

'Close the gates!' he bellowed. 'Smartly does it!'

The first of the enemy soldiers were racing up alongside the burning ram, desperate to reach the gates before the Romans could get them closed. Once more the iron hinges groaned as the doors were pushed forward. The gap between them narrowed and Macro grinned when he saw that the rebels would not reach them in time.

'Hah! Too late, you bastards!'

The doors came together with a boom and immediately the legionaries dropped the locking bar into place. Almost at once there was a muffled cry of anger from the far side, and a dull thud as one of the rebels struck the outside of the gate in frustration.

Macro sheathed his sword and turned away. 'Well done, lads!'

The men of the first century acknowledged his praise with nervous smiles as they stood breathing heavily. A handful had been injured by arrows that had struck their unprotected arms and legs, and strained to stop themselves from crying out in pain. Macro gestured to the nearest section of the next century.

'You there! Help these men to the hospital.'

'Are you all right, sir?'

Macro looked up as Cato came hurrying down the last flight of steps towards him. 'I'm fine.'

Cato looked him over and shook his head. 'You look pretty cooked to me. Especially the helmet crest.' He grinned.

Macro lowered his shield and untied his chin straps. Lifting the helmet from his head he saw that the fine red crest had been burned black and the ends crumbled as he ran his fingers over them.

'Bloody thing cost me a fortune back in Antioch,' he growled. 'Fine piece of kit, that. Or it was. Those bastards out there are going to suffer for it.'

'Sir.' Cato pointed to Macro's arms, and for the first time Macro was aware of blisters and livid red patches of red where his skin had scorched, and then the raw stinging sensation hit home. Cato nodded towards the wounded men being helped towards the hospital. 'Better go and get those burns seen to.'

'In a moment. Just tell me, is the ram far enough from the gates?'

'Yes, sir. There's no danger of its spreading. And it'll make a nice obstacle to get round if they make another attempt.'

'And the rest of them?'

'They've pulled back. Archers, infantry and artillery.' Cato indicated the parties putting out the last of the fires started by the rebels' incendiaries. 'Damage is light and we've not suffered many casualties. We've beaten them, this time.'

'This time.' Macro nodded. 'But they have the luxury of another attempt. We get beaten once, and it's all over. One thing is certain: they'll try again, just as soon they can.'

CHAPTER TWENTY-THREE

'Ah, the other Roman officer.' Julia shook her head as Macro eased himself down on to a stool beside her table. 'Tell me, are you two accident prone, or is it just that you happen to be in the thick of the fighting all the time?'

Macro shrugged. 'Goes with the rank, miss. Don't suppose we get injured more than any other officers.' He paused and thought about that for a moment, then shook his head. 'No. That's not true. The lad and I seem to have found ourselves in quite a few scrapes since we ran into each other.'

Julia bent her head over his outstretched arms, examining the burns. 'Oh? How long ago was that, then?'

'Four years. I was serving with the Second Legion on the Rhine when Cato joined up.' Macro smiled as he recalled the rainswept winter's evening when the convoy of fresh recruits trundled in through the fortress gate. 'He was just a skinny streak of piss in those days.' Macro looked up. 'Pardon my language, miss, but that's how he was. You should have seen him. Huddled in a cloak, clutching a small bundle of belong-ings under one arm and his writing set and a few scrolls under the other. The most dangerous thing he'd had in his hands up until then was a stylus. I thought he'd be dead before the year was out,' Macro mused. 'Well, he surprised us all, did Cato. Turned out to be one of the finest officers in the army.'

'You can lower your arms,' Julia said as she straightened up and reached for a pot of fat on the table. 'The burns will need to be protected for a few days. Those arms are going to smart for a while, but I dare say you will pretend not to notice it.'

Macro laughed. 'It seems you have the measure of me.'

'No. Not you, just soldiers in general. Most of you seem to think you're as hard as the Spartans.'

'Spartans?' Macro snorted his derision. 'Bunch of tunic-lifters, that lot. Wouldn't last quarter of an hour up against the legions.'

'If you say so.' Julia dipped her hand in the pot and cupped a dollop of the fat in her palm. 'Hold still.'

Macro clamped his lips together as she applied the unguent and started to smooth it out across the raw red burns on his arms. It hurt, as she had said it would, but Macro was damned if he would show it. He forced himself to speak in a relaxed conversational tone. 'So, how long have you been a surgeon?'

Julia chuckled. 'Hardly a surgeon. But one of my father's slaves in Rome was. He taught me some basics, and the rest I have learned in the last month, on the job as it were.'

'You seem to know what you're doing,' Macro conceded, a little grudgingly. 'For a woman, that is. Not that a woman should have to do this in the first place. Especially not a senator's daughter.'

'Nonsense. There's no reason why a senator's daughter should not be allowed to serve the Empire in any way that she can. Some would say it was my duty to help. In any case, I want to.'

Macro smiled slyly. 'Do you always get what you want, miss?'

She looked up and caught his expression and smiled back. 'Always.'

'Your father must find you something of a handful.'

'I wouldn't say that. I'm a loyal daughter and I would never shame him. But I know my own mind, and he respects that well enough.'

'Not sure that I would let any daughter of mine be so headstrong.'

'Good thing I'm not your daughter then.' She leaned back towards the pot for some more ointment. 'Other arm, please.'

She was silent for a moment as she began to gently apply the grease. 'Your friend, Cato, seems to be rather an unlikely warrior.'

'You're telling me, miss. But, for all his quirks, he's a damn fine soldier. Fights like a fury and can march almost any man into the ground. Except me, of course. And he's got a good head on his shoulders. His only fault is that he thinks too much at times.'

'Yes, he does seem rather a sensitive type.'

'Sensitive?' Macro repeated the word with distaste as if it was an insult, which in his view it certainly was. If any man ever had the balls to call Macro sensitive to his face, he resolved, he would knock seven shades out of him. Of course, he'd try to feel bad about it afterwards. Maybe. He looked up at Julia. 'Don't know about sensitive, but he has a heart as well as a head, if that's what you mean.'

'Yes, that's what I meant,' Julia replied diplomatically. 'I imagine being an officer doesn't leave much room in your lives for family.'

'No, it doesn't. Especially if you're not on garrison duty. Since Cato turned up I've been on campaign in Britain, served in the fleet, and been sent out here.'

'No wife then,' Julia concluded. 'And how about your friend Cato? Is he married?'

Macro shook his head.

'And no woman waiting for him back in Antioch, Rome, or wherever?'

'Hardly. We've not been anywhere long enough, or we've simply been too busy to find time for such things, beyond the odd tart or two.'

'Oh.'

Macro looked at her shrewdly. 'So he's available, if anyone's interested, miss.'

Julia blushed as she finished applying the fat in a rush, rubbing it on firmly enough to make even Macro wince at the pain it caused. She stepped away and reached for a rag to wipe her hands on. 'There you are. Try not to disturb that – it'll protect the burns for a short time. I'll have a pot sent to your quarters. Apply it at the start and end of each day.'

Macro nodded. 'Thank you, miss.'

'Off you go then,' she responded tersely. 'There are other men who need my attention.'

I bet, Macro thought as he rose to leave the room. Now that he looked at her she was something of a beauty, but her aristocratic air killed any appeal she might have had for Macro. Too well brought up, too clever and too independent for his taste. Still, for the right man, she would be a fine catch.

There were no further attempts to attack the citadel and the sentries patrolled the walls and watched over the city as the sun beat down. A handful of rebels kept an eye on the defenders from the edge of the agora and from small lookout posts outside the city with a view of the citadel where it stood on top of the rise in the ground. Otherwise a semblance of normal life continued in and around the city. A handful of traders and merchants still entered the gates of Palmyra to sell their wares and an unladen caravan of camels began its return journey to the distant banks of the Euphrates. The only sign of the struggle for power was the steady procession of bodies out towards the funeral plain to the south of the city. There, scores of pyres had been built to receive the bodies of the fallen and one by one they were set alight and greasy black smoke billowed into the air as the corpses were consumed by the flames. Later the ashes were scooped into small pottery urns, which were sealed and then carried to the strange funeral towers that rose up from the plain, where the remains were reverentially placed with those of their forebears.

Inside the citadel there was little room for such rituals and the bodies were burned on a common pyre in the royal garden, before the remains were scooped into urns and placed somewhere where they could be stored until the siege was over and they could be interred properly.

Macro and Cato made a tour of the defences to ensure that adequate supplies of arrows, sling shot and other missiles were ready and to hand in case of further attacks. Towards the end of their reconnaissance, as they stood on top of the signal tower and stared out across the city's roofs, Cato scratched his jaw and muttered, 'What do you think they will do next?'

'It depends. They could sit on their arses and try to starve us out, or wait until the Parthians arrive, complete with siege experts and maybe some equipment. Or they could build a better ram and try again.'

'What would you do in their place?'

'Me?' Macro considered the matter for a moment. 'I'd assume that a Roman column, however small, that had been sent to aid Vabathus was a sign of Roman commitment. I'd expect a much larger force to follow. That would mean that I had a limited time in which to reduce the citadel.' He turned to Cato. 'I'd attack again as soon as I had the chance.'

Cato nodded. 'So would I.' He glanced quickly over his shoulder, but the only other men on the tower were on the far side, absorbed in a game of dice. 'And I'd take further comfort from the fact that there's a fair amount of dissent amongst the defenders.'

'How can Artaxes know that?'

'Because he's family. He knows how deeply divided his brothers are, and how little faith his father has in either of them. Artaxes will also know that Balthus is no great admirer of Rome and is likely to resent our presence here. There's one other thing. If any of the nobles or refugees begin to lose confidence that the king will hold out against Artaxes, they might well come to believe they have more to gain by throwing their lot in with the prince, and betray us. The prospect of some kind of reward might be an added inducement to treachery.' Cato smiled bleakly. 'Not the best situation we have ever been in.'

'And not the worst, either.'

'Perhaps not.'

Macro gave his friend an appraising look.

'What?' Cato frowned. 'What is it?'

'I'm just glad you and your devious mind are on my side. It's as I told that woman: you're a thinking man, a thinking soldier.'

'Which woman?'

'The one in the hospital. She saw to my wounds. The ambassador's daughter, Julia Sempronia.'

Cato felt a tremor of nerves in his gut. 'You were discussing me?'

'Sort of. She was asking questions.'

'About me?'

'Yes. What of it? I didn't tell her anything you wouldn't have told her yourself.'

Cato wasn't sure about that at all. He thought he knew Macro well enough to fear that some indiscretion, large or small, would eventually be teased out of him by Julia. 'What did she want to know?'

'What I thought of you. Whether you were married, or had a woman of some kind.'

'And what did you say to her?'

'That there was no one at the moment, and that you were available.'

Cato swallowed nervously. 'You told her that?'

'Of course!' Macro slapped him on the shoulder. 'She's a lovely-looking girl. Bit too classy for my liking, though. More your type.'

Cato shut his eyes and rubbed his forehead. 'Please, please tell me that you didn't suggest that she might like to . . . attach her affections to me.'

'Oh, very well put!' Macro swore softly. 'Very romantic. Anyway, what kind of idiot do you take me for? I just hinted that you were free of any commitments and you'd be a fine catch. Cato, this isn't a children's party. There is every chance that we may not hold out against Artaxes for much longer. If that's the case, what has she got to lose? For that matter what have you got to lose? I think she's taken a shine to you. If you are interested in her then make your move, while there's time.'

'And if we all survive this? What then?' Cato could imagine the awkwardness of a relationship forged in the shadow of annihilation, only for the participants to emerge unscathed back into the same old world of hazardless routine. That was assuming that Julia did not rebuff him in the first place.

Macro yawned. 'You could always make an honest woman of her.'

They stared at each other for a moment, before Macro burst out laughing. 'Just joking!'

'Funny bastard,' Cato muttered sourly. Nevertheless, the merest suggestion of marriage to Julia briefly filled his mind and made his heart feel light. Then he cursed himself for such foolish speculation. What could a highborn Roman woman ever see in the son of a freedman? It was unthinkable, and yet . . .

Cato pushed himself away from the parapet and composed his expression. 'Sir, I think we're done here. I still have to do an inventory of my cohort's weapons.'

'An inventory of kit?' Macro tried not to smile at his friend's obvious attempt to avoid further discussion of the matter. Instead he mimicked Cato's officious tone. 'Very well then, Prefect Cato. Carry on.'

They exchanged a formal salute and then, as Cato turned and strode stiffly away, Macro shook his head and muttered, 'She's got right under that boy's skin . . .'

Shortly after noon a messenger from King Vabathus arrived at the makeshift quarters Macro was sharing with Cato. The latter had finally completed his inspection and reluctantly joined Macro in the cool interior of the citadel to sit out the heat and glare of the midday sun.

'His Majesty requests your company at a small feast he is giving this evening in your honour,' the royal servant explained. 'At sunset. Formal dress code.'

'Formal dress?' Macro's expression darkened. He gestured at his worn and dirty tunic and dusty boots. 'This is all we have. When we set off from Antioch we were marching to war, not a bloody dinner party.'

The servant bowed his head and responded, 'His Majesty's chamberlain suggests that you procure some spare clothes from the Roman ambassador. His excellency Lucius Sempronius has already said he would be happy to provide you with tunics, togas and sandals.'

'Oh, very well,' Macro grumbled. 'We'll be there. You may go.'

The servant made a deep bow and backed out of the room, quietly closing the door behind him. Macro lay back down on his mattress, folded his arms behind his head and stared up at the rafters. 'Here we are, surrounded by bloodthirsty enemies and we're off to a fancy dinner. Still, at least it'll make a nice change from horsemeat.'

'I suppose so,' Cato replied. 'But I hardly think it's going to do much for the morale of the people in the citadel to know that the king and his circle are feasting while they're on limited rations.'

As the sun dipped towards the horizon and bathed the city in an orange glow Macro and Cato entered the royal quarters. At the rear of the citadel, tucked between the main building and the wall, was a small roof garden with a colonnade that stretched along each of the open sides. Occasional pergolas provided shade and small trees and shrubs grew in large tubs and raised flower beds. A slave was watering the plants as Macro and Cato entered and Cato could not help wondering about the king's sense of priorities. On the far side, overlooking the city wall and the lush oasis beyond, a number of couches had been arranged around low tables. An awning had been rigged above the couches and in the light breeze blowing in off the desert it gently shimmered and billowed. Most of the guests were already present. Cato recognised some of the nobles, alongside Thermon, Balthus, Amethus, Sempronius and his daughter.

Cato felt a quickening of his pulse at the sight of her, but when she looked his way his gaze shifted to examine the other guests. He saw Balthus approach Julia and with a gracious bow begin to engage her in conversation.

Sempronius smiled as he caught sight of the two officers and came over to greet them.

'Centurion Macro, I see that my tunic is a bit tight around the shoulders.'

Macro swung his arms loosely. 'It's comfortable enough, sir. I'll manage. And thank you for helping us out.'

'My pleasure.' Sempronius turned to Cato. 'You on the other hand seem made to fit my clothes. They look even better on you than on me.'

Cato shifted self-consciously and Sempronius smiled.

'Don't grow too used to them. I'll want them back later on. Anyway, let me show you to your places.' He put a hand on each man's shoulder and steered them towards the couches. 'The king will be seated at the head of the centre table, when he joins us. Thermon and the princes will sit to his left and you two have been given the place of honour at his right. I and my daughter will be on the other side. Normally the locals don't approve of women feasting alongside the men, but they have made an exception for Julia.'

'Very accommodating of them,' said Macro.

'I suppose so, but I imagine it's mainly because Balthus has his eye on her.'

'Really?' Macro looked at Cato and raised an eyebrow. 'That's understandable enough, sir. She's a lovely-looking young woman. Any man in his right senses would be proud to have her as his wife.'

Cato glared furiously at his friend, while Sempronius frowned and said with evident sadness, 'I just wish her former husband had shared your sentiments. Anyway, the prince seems to like her well enough, which is useful.'

'Useful?' Cato was surprised by the odd choice of word.

'Of course. Right now I value any influence that I can get over Balthus, or any of these people. So please, think like diplomats tonight, and not like . . .'

'Soldiers?' Macro suggested.

Sempronius nodded. 'If you wouldn't mind. For the sake of the Empire.'

'In that case,' Macro assumed a thoughtful expression, 'I suppose I might try to avoid any behaviour that could cause a scandal, although I can't speak for my friend Cato. He's the one you should keep an eye on.'

'Really?' Sempronius looked at Cato with raised eyebrows.

'Ignore him,' Cato muttered. 'Just ignore him.'

226

Thermon rapped his staff on the ground and the conversation died abruptly as the Palmyran nobles turned towards the entrance to the roof garden and bowed their heads. Sempronius gestured to his companions to do the same. After a moment's stillness, King Vabathus came striding through the doorway. He swept through the small crowd of guests and eased himself down on to the royal couch. Thermon waited for his master to settle and then rapped his staff again.

'All may be seated!'

The guests hurriedly took up their places and a low hubbub of conversation slowly swelled to a more comfortable volume. Macro and Cato, lying on their couches to the right of the king, kept quiet, waiting to be addressed by him. Vabathus regarded them for a moment and then cleared his throat.

'We owe you our gratitude, Romans, for the fine defence of the citadel gates this morning.'

Macro bowed his head. 'Thank you, sir, but we were just doing our duty.'

The king gestured towards Macro's arms. 'You are wounded?'

Macro shook his head. 'Just a few burns, sir. They'll heal in a few days.'

'I see.' The king glanced past Macro to address Cato. 'And you?'

'Your Majesty?'

'Are you wounded?'

'No, Your Majesty. Not today.'

'Ah.' The king nodded and turned away with a dull expression to stare out over the wall, towards the oasis. The molten glow of the sun barely rimmed the horizon and long shadows spilled across the sand and the dark green fronds of the palm trees. Macro waited a little longer, in case there was any further remark from the king, and then he turned to Cato with a subtle shake of his head. But Cato was already looking the other way. Julia was lying beside her father and Cato was pleased that she was temporarily parted from Prince Balthus.

'So tell me, Prefect.' Sempronius spoke just loudly enough in Greek for the other guests to hear. 'How much of a fight did the rebels put up?'

Cato could not help a small smile as he considered the staged question and he made sure that his reply was equally audible. 'The majority of them are little more than a rabble, an armed mob. We have nothing to fear from them. Apart from that, I'm sure we can deal with Prince Artaxes' regular soldiers if they have the stomach for another fight. But I doubt they'll trouble us for a few days yet.'

Sempronius nodded sagely. 'And by then, I imagine General Longinus will be approaching the city with his legions.'

'I should think so, sir.'

'Good. Then we're saved.' Sempronius turned to face the king's chamberlain, who was standing a short distance in front of his master's table, his post for the night as he oversaw the timing and announcement of each course. The two men exchanged a slight nod and Thermon rapped his staff and called out towards a small side door on to the garden. At once a steady stream of slaves spilled out carrying platters of food. The king was served with a large selection first and he began to pick at some meat dainties. Then the rest of the guests were presented with a somewhat less generous range of dishes. Macro propped himself up on his elbows and looked over the offerings before him.

'Horsemeat sausage, horse steaks, horse cutlets in honey . . .' He forced a smile and raised his voice. 'Best rations I've had in months.' He paused as he saw a small bowl of what looked like a curious white fibrous fruit. He turned to Sempronius. 'Sir, excuse me. Do you know what those are?'

'Those?' The ambassador glanced at the bowl and smiled slightly. 'Why of course I do. That's a local delicacy, Centurion. You should really give them a try. And remember, always use the right hand,' he added as Macro leaned forward.

'Delicacy, eh?' Macro grinned. 'My favourite kind of food.'

He reached over and plucked one out of the bowl. As he withdrew his hand and examined the object in his fingers his expression froze. 'It looks like an eye.'

'It is. A sheep's eye to be precise.'

'Sheep's eye? Good Gods! What kind of delicacy is that?'

'One that you must try,' Sempronius insisted. 'And you too, Prefect, if you don't want to mortally offend our hosts.'

'What?' Cato looked horrified. But there was an earnest expression of compulsion from the ambassador. Even so, Cato shook his head. 'I can't.'

Despite his reservations of a moment earlier, Macro was amused by his friend's squeamishness. He leaned forward again and picked out another eye. 'Here, this one looks nice and juicy.' He held it out to Cato, who tried not to shrink away too obviously. Then Cato became aware that the other guests were looking at him expectantly, and reluctantly accepted the offering. Macro watched him with amusement for a moment and then winked.

'Bottoms up!' With one swift movement Macro popped the eye he still held into his mouth and made a brief chewing motion before he swallowed and smacked his lips. 'Delicious.'

Cato felt sick, but dared not refuse for fear of causing offence. He swallowed nervously, and with a last quick battle against his stomach's inclination to retch raised the eye to his lips and pressed it into his mouth. The tough muscle tissue surrounding the eyeball was slimy and tasted vaguely of vinegar. He tested the texture with his teeth and it was as unyielding and chewy as he had feared. Summoning up all his courage, he forced the eye to the back of his mouth and swallowed.

The guests cheered and grinned at him, some holding up eyes for him to see, as if they were making a toast, before they ate them. Cato snatched at the goblet of wine that had been poured for him and took a big mouthful, swilling it round his teeth and gums to eradicate any hint of flavour left behind.

'Well done.'

Cato turned and saw Julia nodding at him. He forced a smile in return and replied in Latin, 'Not so bad once you've tried it.'

'If you say so. Now try some of the sweetmeats. They'll help take your mind off it.'

As the guests settled down to eating their banquet, while continuing to talk in an animated fashion, Cato turned his attention briefly away from Julia to glance at the two princes sitting side by side, but not speaking, nor even willing to meet each other's gaze. It had been a mistake to seat them next to each other, Cato decided. The king's chamberlain had obviously hoped for a display of solidarity before the guests, but it was clear for all to see – the two brothers positively despised each other.

Macro had followed his friend's gaze and guessed his thoughts precisely. 'So much for unity,' he said softly. 'I fear we're going to be fighting on two fronts before too long.'

'Let's hope not.' Cato turned away and quickly helped himself to some chunks of spiced horsemeat in a rich sauce before Macro could offer him another eye.

The king stirred and shifted himself to face his Roman guests. 'You're a lucky man, ambassador.'

'How so, Your Majesty?'

'You have a fine daughter. A loyal daughter no doubt.'

'I like to think so.' Sempronius smiled and patted Julia on the arm.

'Quite,' the king continued. 'Sometimes I wish that I had had daughters, and not two younger sons who fight like wolves in a pit. They always have. And when they have not been fighting each other, they have been defying me. As for Amethus – well, at least he has a good heart, even if he has no brains.'

Cato was astonished that the old man had spoken so openly before his sons. Behind Vabathus' back Cato saw Balthus staring rigidly ahead as he ate with a leaden lack of enthusiasm. On hearing the king's words Amethus had turned to stare at his father. Gradually his blank expression turned into an angry frown.

Vabathus continued in a weary tone. 'Such has been my burden, and the burden of my people. For who shall inherit the throne after I am gone? The most able and cherished of the three has proved to be a traitor, the oldest changes his mind more often than the wind changes direction, and Balthus pursues his pleasures to the exclusion of all else. What chance of survival has my kingdom if I choose one of them to succeed me?'

Prince Balthus set his cup down with a sharp rap. 'Enough! You do me wrong, Father! All I have ever tried to do is please you.'

Although the guests stirred and the conversation died at once, King Vabathus' tired expression did not flicker, as if he had not heard a thing, or had simply heard it too often.

'If you find fault in us,' Balthus continued, 'then I say it is your fault that you have not settled the matter of succession. Even though I am not your firstborn, I am the natural choice as your heir. If you had only confirmed me as your successor from the outset none of this would have happened. But no, you had to put it off. Year after year, and this is the result. Why do you think Artaxes is out there with his rebels? You dangled the prospect of the throne in front of his eyes for too long. You tempted him until his patience snapped. If you had only chosen me then Artaxes would have known his place, and he would not be out there with an army and we would not be caught in this trap . . .' Balthus shut his eyes and clenched his fists, trying to control his anger.

Vabathus sighed. 'Have you finished, my son?' When there was no reply, the king gestured towards Sempronius. 'You see? What hope is there for Palmyra?'

'There is always hope, Your Majesty,' Sempronius replied smoothly. 'I am certain that whoever succeeds you will be able to count on the friendship and support of Rome. Rome never abandons her allies.'

Prince Balthus laughed at that, and turned to face the ambassador. 'It's funny how today's ally so often turns out to be tomorrow's imperial province. If this fool does succeed the king, then we might as well hand Palmyra over to Roman tax farmers and the Roman legions right now.'

Amethus scrambled off his couch and glared down at his father. 'No brains . . . That's what you said. No brains. No mind of my own. Well, let me tell you . . . I've had enough of it. I'm not an idiot. I may not have the intell . . .' He paused and his brow twisted in concentration. 'Intelli . . .'

'Intellect?' Balthus suggested. 'Intelligence?'

Amethus nodded vigorously. 'Yes! That's the word.'

'Which one?'

'Both. Either. Anyway, the point is I still have a good heart. I know right from wrong and I would be a good king. That's what Krathos says. So I've had enough of being called a fool!'

Amethus turned and strode across the roof garden and disappeared through the formal doorway, leaving the other guests shocked by the openness of the rift between him, his father and Prince Balthus.

Vabathus shook his head sadly. 'You see what I have to put up with. You see my dilemma? I could weep for my people.'

Cato and Macro had been startled by the previous outbursts and an embarrassed silence hung over those seated around the banquet tables. At length Sempronius cleared his throat and spoke in as reasonable a tone as he could manage. 'It has been a long day, Your Majesty. I expect everyone is exhausted.'

'Yes.' The king smiled. 'Too tired to tame their tongues.'

'Then perhaps we should all retire for the evening. I am sure that Centurion Macro and Prefect Cato are most grateful for the honour you have shown them tonight and would not object to an early end to the banquet, to allow tempers to cool.'

'You are right,' the king conceded. 'It would be for the best.'

The guests began to rise from their couches to take their leave of the king. Balthus went with them. Macro glanced round and then pulled a bread basket towards him and started loading it with the food spread out on the other platters. 'Here, Cato, lend a hand.'

Cato frowned. 'I'm not sure if this is the time or place for foraging.'

'Well, if it isn't, when is? Suit yourself.' Macro cleared a few more platters and then grasped the handles of the basket and turned towards the king.

'Er, thanks once again, your majesty.'

Vabathus acknowledged the remark with a lift of his fingers and continued chewing slowly. The Romans were almost the last to leave, and as they reached the entrance to the roof garden Cato looked back and saw the lonely figure of the king sitting at the abandoned banquet, with only his chamberlain still standing before him to keep him company. Night had fallen and the velvet heavens were sprinkled with stars. Low on the horizon a nearly full moon was rising over the desert, bathing it in a faint ethereal blue glow.

Cato fell in alongside the others. 'Even if we do hold out until Longinus arrives, what will become of Palmyra?'

Sempronius shook his head. 'I don't know. Unless Vabathus chooses an heir we can work with, Rome will have to intervene.'

'Intervene?'

Sempronius glanced round hurriedly and lowered his voice. 'Annex the kingdom, turn it into a province. What else could we do?'

Macro nodded. 'With those two sons of his, there is nothing else.'

As they headed down the corridor to leave the royal quarters Cato found himself walking alongside Julia. Her scent came to him again and as a warm rush of longing swept through his body he felt his heart beating against his chest. More than anything in the world he wanted to ask her to come to the signal tower again and gaze out over the city and the surrounding landscape. This time he would not be

232

surprised by her presence, and it would go far better. He had sensed some kindred feeling in her and the desperation to know if he was right gnawed at him.

They reached the end of the corridor, and the arch that gave out on to the paved area between the buildings and the gate. The ambassador's quarters were one way, and Macro and Cato's the other.

Sempronius paused and clasped each officer's arm in turn. 'Fine work this morning. When I get back to Rome I will be sure to inform the Emperor.'

'Thank you, sir,' Macro replied.

Cato nodded.

'Well, then, good night. Come on, my dear.' The ambassador and his daughter took a step away.

'Julia,' Cato blurted out. They paused.

'Yes?'

'I wondered . . . I wonder if you would do me the honour of walking with me.' Cato winced at the awkwardness of his words.

'Walking with you?' Julia arched one of her fine eyebrows. 'Where?'

'Ah! The, er, same place as last night, I was thinking.'

Sempronius turned to her and smiled as he patted her cheek. 'There, I told you the prefect was interested in you. Go, my child. Walk, talk, but nothing else, mind. Cato, I trust you are an honourable man.'

'Yes, sir.'

Sempronius stared at him for a moment, and a flicker of anxiety crossed his face before he smiled. 'Good night to you all, then.'

He turned away and made off through the moonlight towards his quarters. Macro shifted awkwardly. 'Me too, then. I'll see you later, Cato. You too, miss. Tomorrow I mean.' Macro turned away, took a few steps and then paused. 'Want me to save you any of the food?'

'No, thank you. I'm fine.'

'Well then. Be good.' Macro nodded and trudged off into the darkness. Cato and Julia listened to his footsteps fading away, and then turned to each other with shy expressions. Julia's lips parted in a smile.

'Now that the parents have gone . . .'

They both laughed, and then Cato took her arm in his and tugged gently. 'Let's go, then.'

The anxiety of a moment ago had disappeared and in its place he felt a pure joy at being with her, even here in the besieged citadel, sensing the warmth and softness of her arm against his in the cool night air. They walked in silence for a moment before Julia spoke.

'I feel so sorry for him.'

'Hmm?'

'King Vabathus. He looks so weary, so heartbroken.'

'Yes,' Cato said vaguely. The comment had jolted him back from his little reverie and now the prospect of the troubled days to come settled on him like a dead weight. 'It can't be easy for him, but he has to be strong for all our sakes. If he lets the situation in the citadel overwhelm him, then Artaxes has won, and we . . .' He could not complete the sentence as a vision of Julia lying amongst the slaughtered Romans flitted through his head. 'Anyway, let's not think about it. It's early, and there's so much I want to say.'

'Like what?'

Cato laughed. 'I don't know. Nothing . . . Everything. I don't care.'

'Oh dear.' Julia knitted her brows. 'That doesn't sound very specific. But I'm sure we will manage.' She gave his arm a little squeeze as they reached the base of the signal tower and stepped into the dark entrance to the staircase.

'Careful,' Cato warned. 'It's pitch black in there.'

Julia lightly stepped ahead of him. 'Coward. There's nothing to be—'

She gave a sharp cry and pitched forward.

'Julia!' Cato leaned forward and felt for her arm. As he found it, his fingers closed and he lifted her back to her feet and out of the darkened entrance. She looked shaken and Cato saw that there was a dark smear down the front of her stola.

'There's someone in there.' Her voice trembled. 'I tripped over him.'

'Stay there. I'll look.'

Cato crouched low and eased himself into the entrance, feeling across the stone floor. His fingers brushed against cloth, and he probed further until he discovered a limb, a leg encased in a soft boot. Taking hold of the ankle he dragged the body out into the moonlight and stood up. The man's dark outer robe was pulled up over his head.

'Who is it?' Julia asked. 'Is he . . . dead?'

'Only one way to find out,' Cato muttered as he leaned over and pulled the loose fold of material down to reveal the face. The dark wavy hair and handsome features of a nobleman emerged into the dim light. As Cato continued to draw the robe back they saw the ragged slash that cut right across his throat. The garments on his upper body were drenched in blood and glistened in the moonlight.

Julia touched her hands to her mouth. 'Oh, no . . . Prince Amethus.'

CHAPTER TWENTY-FOUR

The corpse lay on a low table in the guard room close to the gate. Cato had run to find Macro and between them they had carried the body here. Julia had arrived a moment later with her father.

'Then it's true.' The ambassador nodded as he drew back the robe and made out the dead man's features, streaked with blood. 'Prince Amethus.'

Julia glanced at the face and quickly looked away. 'Poor man.'

Sempronius flicked the robe back so that it covered the jagged tear in Amethus' throat, but left his face exposed. 'This has complicated the situation somewhat.'

'Really?' Macro folded his arms. 'I'd have thought it made things simpler. With one son his father's enemy and another dead, that clears the path to the throne for Prince Balthus. Which makes him the most likely suspect, don't you think?'

'Quite.'

Cato thought back to the end of the banquet and shook his head. 'No. Balthus was one of the last to leave. Just before us, and he left with some of the nobles. He couldn't have done it. He wouldn't have had the time.'

'Maybe so,' Macro conceded. 'But then it's obvious. He was setting up an alibi while someone else did the deed on his orders. Balthus is our man all right. He certainly had a strong motive. You remember what he said to us on the way here, Cato? All for taking the throne and disposing of his brother, with our blessing. It looks as if he's not prepared to wait any longer.'

Cato nodded slowly as he thought it over. 'It certainly appears that way.'

'Appears?' Macro frowned. 'Who else do you think could be behind this?'

'I don't know.'

'Have you sent anyone to notify the king?' asked Sempronius.

'No,' Cato replied. 'We thought it best to tell you first, sir. So you could be prepared.'

'Prepared?' Sempronius raised his eyebrows. 'Prepared for what? Surely you don't think I had anything to do with this?'

'We assumed that you didn't, sir. But it's always best to have time to think a situation through before you have to act on it.'

'There is that. Anyway, we'd better let the king know. Prefect, I want you to find Thermon. Tell him what has happened and tell him to inform the king at once. Then I want you to post one of your best men outside Prince Balthus' quarters. They're not to be obtrusive. I want him watched for any suspicious activity, understand?'

'Yes, sir.'

'Then go.'

'Julia.' Sempronius undid the folds of his toga and tossed it to one side. 'Help me clean the body up. I don't think the king should have to see him this way.'

'Yes, Father.' Julia turned to meet Cato's eyes just before the latter turned towards the door. She shook her head in regret at their lost opportunity and Cato nodded in understanding. Then he turned away and hurried from the guard room.

Thermon was still fully dressed when he came to the door of his quarters in response to Cato's sharp rapping.

'Prefect? What is it?'

Cato nodded towards the guard who had escorted him from the entrance of the royal quarters. 'In private.'

Thermon sent the guard away and, when they were alone, tilted his head to one side. 'Well, what is it?'

'Prince Amethus is dead. Murdered.'

'Murdered?' Thermon clasped his hands together. 'What happened?'

'Someone cut his throat. I found the body.' Cato paused to clarify the detail to avoid any suspicion. 'The ambassador's daughter and I found Amethus. At the bottom of the signal tower. Someone must have followed him when he left the banquet, knocked him cold and dragged him there before killing him.'

'How could you know that?'

'Amethus had no reason to be there, and his blood was pooled around him. There were no drag marks on the ground.'

Thermon nodded at the explanation. 'Has anyone told the king yet?'

'No. That's why I'm here. Sempronius thought it would be better coming from you.'

'He's probably right. I'll do it at once. Where is the body?'

'The guard house beside the gates.'

'Who's with the body at the moment?'

'Centurion Macro, the ambassador and his daughter.'

'Then find the commander of the Royal Guard, and Prince Balthus. Have them join us there.'

Prince Balthus was the last to arrive. He had changed into a simple nightshirt and was attended by his slave, Carpex. Cato had not told him the reason for his summons, only that the king's chamberlain had required him to attend. Balthus swaggered into the guardhouse with an irritated expression.

'Someone mind telling me what in Hades is going on?'

A small group stood round the table and as they turned towards the new arrival Balthus could see the body, and his father leaning over it, staring at the face of his dead son. Balthus hurried across the room and then slowed down as he recognised his brother.

'Amethus? Dead?'

Thermon nodded. 'Yes, Prince.'

Balthus stared at the body for a moment. 'When did this happen?'

'Shortly after the end of the banquet.'

Cato coughed. 'We don't know that yet. Prince Amethus left before the banquet was over. His killer could have been waiting for him outside, or it might have been one of the guests who left shortly afterwards.'

'I see.' Balthus turned his gaze towards his father. Vabathus was sitting on a stool beside the body, staring at the still face. Dull unblinking eyes stared back at him. The old king lifted his hand and gently stroked the hair of his dead son, teasing it away from the forehead. One of the locks slid back into place the moment his father's hand passed over it. King Vabathus smiled fondly. 'He always did have unruly hair, even as a small boy . . . My son, My little boy.'

He leaned, forward and kissed his son's forehead, then pressed his cheek against Amethus' head as the first tears trickled down his creased and weathered face.

No one else spoke. They stood quite still and watched as Vabathus grieved for his son. At length, Balthus knelt down opposite his father and hesitantly reached over the table to put his hand on his father's shoulder.

'Father. I'm so sorry.'

Vabathus continued weeping, his chest heaving convulsively, quite oblivious of those standing around him. Even as august a figure as a king was reduced to a mere man, and a father, before the body of his son. Cato wanted to offer some comfort, some help, but knew that even now, in this most intimate of situations, there were boundaries of rank that he must not cross. He felt someone's hand slip into his and glanced round as Julia looked up at him, and he saw that she shared his feelings, and sense of powerlessness.

Eventually, Thermon cleared his throat and spoke softly. 'Your Majesty . . . Is there something I can do?'

When there was no response, Thermon leaned closer to his king and spoke again. 'Would you like us to leave you alone for the present?'

Vabathus blinked away the tears and sat up. Prince Balthus leaned back and rose to his feet. The king frowned and looked round at the others, as if they were complete strangers, until his eyes fixed on Thermon.

'Who did this?'

'We do not know, Your Majesty. We only just discovered the body.'

'Who found him?'

Cato swallowed nervously. 'I did.'

'And I,' Julia added at once. 'Just inside the signal tower, Your Majesty.'

Vabathus looked from one to the other. 'Was he still alive when you found him?'

Cato shook his head solemnly. 'He was already dead. We could not have saved him.'

Vabathus glanced down at the body and then looked at Thermon. 'I want the killer found. I don't care how you do it. I don't care how many suspects you have to torture. Find the killer.'

'Yes, Your Majesty. I'll see to it.'

'You had better. Someone will suffer for this!' Vabathus spat out. 'They'll die for it. If you can't find the killer, then you'll be put to death in their place.'

'Sir?' The chamberlain was startled, and drew back nervously before his master's vehemence.

Sempronius shook his head. 'That isn't right, Your Majesty. This man is blameless. I must protest that you should threaten him so.'

'Protest all you like, Roman,' Vabathus responded. 'This is my kingdom. My will is law here. Thermon will do as he is told, or pay the price. Just as my son has paid the price.' Vabathus' voice faltered as he glanced down again. 'I never said farewell to him. We parted on such bad terms, and he will never know that I loved him. How can a father endure that? I have lost him. Lost him for ever.' Vabathus lowered his head and his chest shook as more tears came.

Balthus drew a deep breath and spoke. 'Father, you still have me. I am still here, at your side.'

Vabathus looked up sharply. 'You? You are worthless to me. The one son who is incapable of responsibly ruling my kingdom is all that is left to me.'

Balthus froze, his lips pressing together in a thin line as his expression hardened into bitter hatred. 'I am responsible, Father. I had to fight my way here to your side. Have I not proved myself worthy of some respect, some affection?'

Vabathus stared at him for a moment and then shook his head sourly. 'You just want my throne when I am gone. Amethus would have been king, until . . . this.' He gestured at the body, wincing as he saw the torn flesh of his son's throat. 'Now he's gone. I imagine that you are gratified by this state of affairs, Balthus. You can't wait to have my crown. I can see it in your eyes.'

'Father, you have lost a son, and I have lost a brother. Can you not at least let me share your grief?' Prince Balthus warily extended his arms towards the king. 'Father?'

For a moment Vabathus gazed at his son with a pained expression. Then his eyes narrowed and he slapped Balthus' embrace aside and shrank back. 'Viper, how dare you? For all I know you are the one behind this. You and these Roman friends of yours.'

'Roman friends?' Balthus shook his head. 'Father, do you accuse me

240

of this murder? My own brother? Flesh of my flesh? How could I?'

'I know you. I know your ambition. You desire nothing more than my throne.' The king's gaze flickered towards the ambassador and the other Romans in the room and Cato saw the fear in his eyes as he continued, 'Enemies. I'm surrounded by enemies.'

Sempronius shook his head. 'Your Majesty, I assure you that we are your loyal allies. We had nothing to do with the death of your son.'

Vabathus stared at him, unmoving, and Sempronius gestured towards Macro and Cato. 'Is not the presence of these two officers and their men proof of our good faith towards your kingdom? We are not your enemies. On the life of my daughter, whom I love above all things, I swear it.'

King Vabathus was still for a moment and then his shoulders sagged as he looked down at the body again. 'Leave me. All of you, leave me alone.'

Sempronius made to speak again but Thermon caught his eye and shook his head firmly, gesturing towards the door. The ambassador hesitated a moment, glancing towards the king, before he backed away slowly and quietly opened the door, ushering the two officers and his daughter outside. Thermon waited a moment before he whispered to Balthus.

'My prince?'

Balthus turned to him quickly and stepped in between the chamberlain and the king. 'You heard my father. Get out.'

'But . . .' Thermon tried to step round the prince but Balthus blocked him.

'Out!'

The king stirred and looked up. He drew a deep breath and shouted, 'Go! Both of you! Get out of my sight!'

Balthus turned round, mouth open to protest, but his father stabbed his finger towards the door. 'Go!'

Thermon hurried out, and then a moment later Balthus followed him, taking one last glance at his father before he closed the door.

Outside in the large open courtyard by the main gate the others waited and there was an awkward silence before Balthus spat with contempt. 'I know what you're thinking. You think I had Amethus killed.'

'Well, did you?' asked Cato.

'Does it matter what I say? You already know what you believe.'

Cato shook his head. 'Not yet. I want to hear it from your own lips. Did you kill him?'

'No,' Balthus replied immediately. 'There. Satisfied?'

Macro snorted with derision. 'Well, that proves nothing, friend. If you, or one of your retinue, didn't kill him, then who did?'

'Why not a Roman?' Balthus smiled faintly. 'You, perhaps.'

Macro slapped a hand to his chest. 'Me?'

'If the king has no heirs then Rome will find it easier to annex Palmyra when my father dies. That's motive enough. Of course, that means that you will have to make sure that I am killed as well.'

'And you have nothing to gain from your brother's death, I suppose,' Macro countered. 'Other than the fact that he was your only rival for the crown.'

'That's enough, Centurion Macro!' Sempronius cut in harshly. 'Keep quiet. You're not helping.' He turned towards Balthus and moderated his tone with some difficulty. 'Prince, let's accept, for the moment, that neither party had a hand in your brother's death. We can't afford to let ourselves become divided on this matter. Not while an enemy army surrounds us. You might think you have good reason to suspect us, just as we have good reason to suspect you. And, for now, it seems that the king suspects everyone. We have to put the matter aside until the siege is over.'

'Put the matter aside?' Balthus mused. He turned to Thermon. 'What do you say, old man? You've been my father's adviser as long as I can remember. Do you think he will put the murder of his son aside?'

Thermon paused a moment before he replied. 'His Majesty's mind will be filled with grief for some days. Then, when Prince Amethus has had his funeral, I believe the king will not rest until he has discovered the identity of the killer and avenged his son.'

'Very well,' said Sempronius. 'We have a few days' grace then. Let there be no more exchange of suspicions. After the funeral we'll all co-operate with the king to find the killer. Agreed?'

Balthus nodded. 'Now, if you don't mind, I would like to return to my quarters so that I might grieve in private.'

'Of course.'

Balthus nodded curt farewells to Cato and Macro before he turned to Julia. 'My lady, I trust that when this is all over we may come to know each other better.'

Julia forced a smile. 'I hope so, Prince Balthus.'

He took her hand, raised it and then bowed his head to kiss it, lingering as his lips grazed her flesh. Julia remained motionless until he released her hand and then she drew back a step.

'I bid you all good night then,' Balthus said quietly, then turned away and strode back towards his quarters.

They watched him for a moment before Cato gently took Julia's hand and muttered, 'Are you all right?'

She trembled. 'That man makes my flesh creep.'

'You did well, daughter,' Sempronius said with quiet pride. 'He would never have guessed your feelings.'

'I wouldn't be worried if he had.'

Macro puffed his cheeks out and scratched the back of his head. 'Well? Do you think he did it? Did he kill his brother?'

Sempronius thought for a moment before he replied, 'No question about it. It has to be Balthus.'

Cato nodded. 'In which case, we're in trouble. Deep trouble. We have an enemy at the gate, a killer inside and an ally who suspects us of killing his son. Long odds.'

Macro chuckled grimly. 'Since when did you take up gambling, my lad?'

Cato was silent for a moment before he shrugged. 'Since I met you, sir.'

CHAPTER TWENTY-FIVE

'What do you suppose they are up to?' asked Macro as he squinted, trying to make out the activity down in the merchants' yards on the other side of the agora. Cato was standing beside him on the gatehouse, shielding his eyes from the sun's glare as he stared in the same direction. A hundred paces away the rebels were busy, and from beyond the wall of the merchants' yards came the sounds of sawing and hammering.

'Another ram, perhaps,' Cato suggested. 'They've had enough time to gather more materials.'

Eight days had passed since the previous attempt to batter down the gates, and the death of Amethus. The king had spent the time grieving for his son. Rather longer than was wise, since the corpse had quickly putrefied in the heat, even though it had been moved to one of the coolest underground storage chambers beneath the citadel. Vabathus had finally allowed the priests of the Temple of Bel to anoint and dress the body for the funeral and a pyre had been prepared in the courtyard outside the royal quarters. Shortage of wood had forced the palace servants to break up some furniture and doors in order to build a pyre worthy of a prince. As the sun set at the end of the day Amethus would be placed on the pyre and it would be lit, allowing the flames to purify his body and send his spirit whirling into the night sky.

Rumours about the prince's death had swept through the hungry ranks of the soldiers and civilians in the citadel and the various camps regarded each other with mutual suspicion and wariness. Cato had experienced it at first hand when he went to visit Archelaus in the hospital two days after the murder. The Greek mercenary was sitting on a bedroll in the colonnade overlooking the courtyard when Cato found him. His shoulder was heavily bandaged and his eyes looked sunken as

244

they flickered towards the Roman officer. Cato smiled and raised the small jug of wine he had brought with him.

'Medicine.'

Archelaus smiled briefly. 'Just what I needed.'

Cato eased himself down on to the ground beside the tetrarch and leaned back against the wall with a weary sigh, offering the jar to the other man.

'How goes it?' asked Archelaus. 'Haven't heard any more action from the walls.'

'No. The rebels have been quiet enough. But then, maybe they can afford to be. We're running very short of water and food, and they're waiting for a Parthian army to join them. Our only chance is that Longinus gets here before the Parthians.'

'Is that likely?' Archelaus pulled the stopper and took a long swig of wine.

'I don't know,' Cato admitted. 'Anyway, how is the shoulder?'

'Painful, Roman. My arm's useless. I don't think I'll be back in the fight. Not for a while.'

'That's a damn pity. We need every man who can hold a sword or a spear. Mind you, the way things are, people in the citadel are as likely to use them on each other as on the rebels.'

There was an uncomfortable silence between them before Archelaus took another quick swig and continued, 'Word has it that the prince was killed by his brother.'

Cato shifted so that he could look straight at the Greek. 'Is that right? Is that what they're saying?' He shrugged. 'Balthus might have done it. He has plenty to gain from ridding himself of a rival to the throne. But he was with others when the murder happened.'

'Then look to that slave of his. Carpex.'

Cato thought about it and nodded. 'It might be worth having a little talk with Carpex. Just to see if he knows anything.'

'You might also like to know that other people are accusing a Roman of killing the prince. One of the king's advisers, Krathos, is spreading that story. He's saying that now that Amethus is dead, you'll kill Balthus, and then the king himself, and claim Palmyra for Rome.'

Cato laughed at this, then stopped as he saw that Archelaus was watching him, stony-faced. 'Surely you're not falling for that story?'

245

Archelaus pursed his lips. 'I'm just telling you what I've heard. Doesn't mean much to me, or most of the other mercenaries in the king's guard. As long as we get paid. Trouble is, if the rumour is true, then we're out of a job. So be careful, Prefect, when you're around the king or the prince. Their guards will be watching for any sign of treachery. They'll strike first and ask questions later.'

'Just what we need,' Cato muttered. 'Men jumping at shadows.'

'Well, someone killed the prince. And they had their reasons.'

Cato shook his head. 'This is starting to get out of hand. Anyway, I have to go. Keep the wine.' He stood up and stretched his back before nodding to Archelaus. 'Look after yourself.'

'You too, Roman. And watch your back.'

'I will.' Cato turned away and after a moment's hesitation made for the room at the end of the colonnade. Julia was washing some dressings in a bronze basin beneath the window as Cato entered.

'Don't you ever take a break?' he called to her.

Julia stopped and glanced over her shoulder with a tired smile. 'No. Do you?'

As Cato crossed the room she quickly wiped her hands on her long tunic. Standing in the shaft of light angling through the window she looked radiant in a way that Cato had never seen before and he felt his heart quicken as he approached. Then something wholly unexpected happened. Without thinking, Cato took her hands, dipped his face towards hers and kissed her on the lips. He sensed Julia freeze, but only for a moment before she responded, pressing her lips gently against his, and releasing his hands so that she could circle her slender arms behind his back and draw Cato into a tight embrace. Cato felt a rush of light-headedness and a thrill of passion coursed through every vein in his body. He closed his arms round her, holding her close to him, tightly.

She suddenly drew her mouth away from his. 'Ouch! Do you mind?'

'What? What's the matter?'

Julia nodded down towards the pommel of his sword. 'That was poking into me. I think.'

Cato blushed. 'I'm sorry. I didn't mean to . . . I got carried away.'

'You certainly did!' Julia kissed him again, quickly. 'At last. I was wondering when you would kiss me. At least, I was hoping you would.'

Cato cupped her cheek in his hand and gazed into her eyes. 'Then you feel the same?'

'Of course I do, you silly fool.' She kissed his hand. 'Honestly, Cato, most men can't keep their hands off women. I was beginning to despair of you. But then, I imagine you are not like most men. That's what I like about you.'

'We've only known each other for a few days. Am I that transparent?' Cato smiled ruefully.

'Only in the way that matters to me.' She reached up to his shoulder and pulled his face down towards hers and kissed him again, much more fully and for longer this time, until there was an embarrassed cough and a knock at the door frame. Julia pulled herself away from Cato and glanced towards the surgeon. 'Yes, what is it?'

'Found some more dressings, my lady. They'll need washing.'

'Fine. Then bring them here.'

'Er,' Cato mumbled. 'I'd, er, better get back to the men. I'll see you again, then?'

'Of course.' Julia looked surprised. 'You don't get away from me that easily.'

Cato smiled at the memory of that encounter, and some of the more intimate encounters that had taken place since.

'What are you grinning at?' asked Macro.

'What?' Cato stirred guiltily, shaking off the memory of Julia's slender figure as they had sat in the moonlight the night before, watching silver clouds drift across the stars. 'I'm sorry, I wasn't concentrating.'

Macro stared at him for a moment and then shook his head. 'Just what I need, a love-struck puppy for my second-in-command. Come on, Cato. Keep your mind on the job, and off her arse. We've got problems enough as it is. Look there.'

Cato followed the direction Macro indicated and saw a stout timber frame rising up behind the wall of the merchants' yards. Then he recognised what he was seeing.

'An onager.'

'Yes. And there will be more of them. The rebels have gone and built themselves an artillery platform behind that wall. Very clever. There's no way we can assault them and they're well in range of the gates and the

247

buildings beyond.' Macro scratched the bristles on his chin. 'Better tell Balthus to get his archers up here. And have the ballista crews do what they can to disrupt the rebels. See to it.'

By the time the defenders began to loose a steady barrage of missiles on the enemy the rebels had brought up eight large catapults, only the tops of which could be seen protruding above the wall of the merchants' yards. They continued their preparations unhindered, and as evening approached the first wisps of smoke curled into the air above the rebel position.

'Great,' Macro muttered. 'They're going to hit us with incendiaries again.'

Cato nodded and hurried over to the far side of the gatehouse to call down to Centurion Metellus, who had taken charge of the fire parties. 'Incoming incendiaries. Have your men ready.'

'Yes, sir.' Metellus saluted and turned away to call his motley collection of wounded soldiers and civilians to form up. They rose wearily from whatever shade they had found and hurried to their positions by the tubs of water spread out along the inside of the wall. Some carried buckets, others rolls of matting to smother the flames. Around them the civilian refugees snatched up their possessions and gathered up their children before making for the nearest shelter, packing into the doorways and entrances of the main building. Despite the danger to his subjects, King Vabathus had forbidden them entry to the royal quarters. After the murder of his son he had doubled the guard surrounding him and rarely emerged from his suite of rooms, such was his fear of assassination. Since all the other buildings had been allocated to the nobles and Roman officials, and the stables served as the barracks for the defending soldiers, the civilians had been forced to stay out in the open. Keeping to the shadows by day and shivering in family huddles at night, they eked out the siege on the meagre rations of water, horsemeat and grain distributed each day by the king's guards.

Cato could see over the wall of the royal courtyard and saw that the small funeral procession was emerging from the king's private quarters. Behind the priests, tearing their clothes and crying out their grief, came several more bearing the bier on which lay the body of Amethus, bound in scented cloth. The king, in a plain black robe, followed solemnly behind.

'Not the best of timing,' Cato muttered to himself.

But for the recent atmosphere of distrust and dislike, Prince Balthus would have walked behind his father. Glancing towards the tower to his right Cato saw Balthus directing his archers, seemingly unaware that the ceremony had begun. Or was it that the prince could not face witnessing the funeral of the brother whose death he had caused, Cato wondered briefly. Then he dismissed the thought. Balthus did not strike Cato as the kind of man who might be consumed by remorse. Cato turned away and returned to Macro's side. Macro was adjusting his chin straps to make sure that his helmet was on as securely as possible. Seeing Cato, he smiled wearily.

'It's about to get hot around here.'

Just then both men's attention was drawn to the rebel position by a dull thwack. Cato saw that the throwing arm of one of the onagers was pressed against the cross bar. A flaming bundle was arcing up into the late afternoon sky, trailing an oily black plume. The defenders on the wall could hear the roar of the flames clearly as it passed over their heads and then plummeted down into the heart of the citadel. Before it landed, more thwacks sounded from the rebel position and several more incendiary missiles rose into the sky, briefly scoring the air with smoke that marked their passage, before dissipating. The tightly bound, pitch-soaked bundles blazed down and burst as they struck roof tiles and paving stones, or rebounded off walls in a sudden intense flare caused by the impact. The bombardment continued, and soon the uneven rate at which the crews worked their weapons meant that there was an almost continuous rain of flaming missiles.

Macro and Cato moved to the rear of the gatehouse and looked down on the citadel to gauge the effect of the incendiary barrage. Several fires had already taken and the fire teams were crowding round the flames, beating at them frantically and dowsing them with water. But even as one fire was controlled, and then extinguished, another missile would land and start a new blaze somewhere else. One of the onagers, with greater torsion power than the rest, was shooting its incendiaries further into the citadel and as the two Roman officers watched one shot fell over the wall of the royal courtyard and scored a direct hit on the funeral pyre. The priests who were in the middle of raising the bier up on to the top of the pyre nearly dropped their burden in their surprise and fright. Just in time they steadied themselves and hurriedly placed the body in position as the flames from the incendiary bundle spread through the pyre. Then they scurried back to their place behind the king.

'Saved someone a job,' said Macro. 'At least that's one fire no one will need to put out.'

'Just as well. Metellus and his men are going to be hard pressed.'

Macro glanced over the interior of the citadel, weighing up the situation. 'He's not going to cope. I want you down there now. Organise your cohort into fire-fighting teams and put those fires out. We can't afford to let any of them get out of control or the rebels will burn us out of here.'

'But sir, what if they attack? My men are needed on the wall.'

'I can manage with my cohort, and Balthus and his boys,' Macro decided. 'Now go!'

Cato ran along the rampart tower left of the gate and waved to Centurion Parmenion. 'Tell the men to down shields and spears and get down off the wall. We're to get those fires out. Pass the word to the other centurions!'

'Yes, sir.'

Cato called on the nearest auxiliaries to follow him and hurried down the steps from the wall. As soon as they reached the paved area behind the gates he led them to the nearest water butt and the pile of mats and buckets beside it. 'Pick 'em up! Get water in buckets and form up over there!'

As soon as the men were ready Cato ordered them to work in sections, one to each incendiary as it landed. They were to return to the butt the moment the fire was extinguished and wait for the next strike. Not that they would be waiting long, Cato mused. The rebels were working their weapons with furious determination and it seemed that the fresh fires were breaking out all the time. Even so, Macro's decision to send Cato's men to join the fire parties meant that the defenders were able to keep on top of any blazes, and put them out before they had a chance to spread. Around them the afternoon gave way to evening as the bombardment continued. Only a handful of fires posed any serious threat, where the incendiary had managed to strike places that could not easily be reached by the fire-fighting teams.

Then, as dusk closed round the city, the onager with the greatest torsion power shifted its aim slightly and its shot began to land on the courtyard being used for the hospital. Cato noticed the change and as soon as he realised where the incendiaries were falling his heart was seized by fear for Julia. He thought about making a quick run to the hospital to ensure she was unharmed, but realised that he could not abandon his men, and his duty, for however short a time. As the incendiaries continued to fall on the hospital he saw a wavering orange glow from that direction, and then the first lick of flames rising into the darkness. Cato knew that there were no fire parties allocated to any position so deep inside the citadel and the fire would spread quickly if unchecked. He beckoned to Metellus' optio and shouted orders as the man ran up to him.

'You're in command here! I'm taking two sections to the hospital.' Cato indicated the flames already leaping up from that direction. 'Carry on!'

'Yes, sir!'

Cato rushed to the pile of mats and snatched one up. It was damp and smelled mouldy – perfect for smothering flames he thought, smiling grimly. Then he turned to the nearest parties of men from his cohort. 'That section, and that one. Follow me!'

They ran along the side of the main building of the citadel until they reached a corner and turned towards the courtyard serving as the hospital. Cato glanced back over his shoulder. 'Keep up! There's no time to lose, damn you!'

The men pounded across the paving stones and through the arch that led into the courtyard, illuminated by the glare of the blaze. As Cato drew up just inside he saw that one side of the courtyard was consumed by flames – the side where Julia treated her patients. He felt an icy fist clench round his heart, then shook off his fears as he realised he must give his men orders. The surgeon and his assistants were desperately clearing men out of the rooms closest to the heart of the fire as it spread like a wild raging animal.

'Help them!' Cato shouted. 'Get the wounded men out of here first! Take 'em out of the courtyard.'

The fire-fighting parties dumped their mats and buckets and ran across to pick up the patients still lying on mattresses along the endangered side of the courtyard. Cato saw Archelaus supporting a comrade with his unwounded arm.

'Can you manage?'

Archelaus nodded.

'Where's Lady Julia?'

'Back there.' Archelaus nodded towards the fire. Smoke was billowing from a doorway just beyond the flames. 'There are still some men in that room.'

Cato rushed forward, dodging round the men escaping from the flames and the choking smoke. When he reached the door Archelaus had indicated he took a deep breath and plunged in. There was a withering heat in the confined space and great tongues of flame leaped across the rafters of the ceiling as burning and smouldering fragments drifted down through the smoke. Cato ducked as low as he could, where the smoke was less dense, and looked round. Nearly all the bedrolls were empty, save for two in the far corner. Julia was on her hands and knees dragging the nearest man across the floor and Cato scrambled across to her.

'Here, let me take him.'

She looked round, eyes streaming from the smoke as she coughed and spluttered 'Cato. Thank the Gods. You take him. I'll go for the other.'

'No,' Cato spluttered, but she had already turned away and was crawling back to the last man, laying motionless on his bedroll.

'Shit,' Cato hissed, then grasped the man she had left under the shoulders and began to haul him towards the door. The wounded man had a splint on either side of one leg and he howled with agony as Cato dragged him across the door frame and into the colonnade. Cato saw some of his men running towards him. 'Get him out of here.'

Then he plunged back inside. The heat was more intense than ever and Cato winced as it struck his exposed flesh like a stinging blow. The smoke was thick and he dropped on to his hands and scurried towards the far corner. He saw Julia lying beside the man, covering her face with folded arms as she gasped. Cato siezed her elbow.

'Get out of here! Now!'

Julia squinted at him through watering eyes. 'Not without him. I'm not leaving him.'

Cato clambered over her and grabbed the man's tunic and pulled.

The man's limbs rolled lifelessly and his mouth hung open. Cato released his grip and turned to Julia.

'He's gone! Dead. Let's go.'

She resisted a moment, then nodded, taking his hand as she began to choke on the smoke. Cato made for the door, pulling her behind him. There was a sudden crack and flaming debris from the roof cascaded around them.

'Get out!' Cato cried. 'Run!'

They scrambled in the direction of the door, the heat and smoke forcing Cato to shut his eyes. Then his outstretched hand slammed painfully into the wall. He groped along it, found the door frame and pulled Julia out of the room just as the ceiling began to collapse behind them in a roar of falling timber, tiles and plaster. A wave of heat burst through the door frame and singed Cato's legs as he thrust Julia ahead of him down the colonnade. They ran several paces, out into the courtyard, before collapsing on the ground, coughing in fits as they tried to clear their stinging eyes.

As soon as he recovered his breath Cato leaned over her. 'Julia . . . Are you all right?'

She was still coughing too much to speak and nodded quickly.

'What the bloody hell were you doing back there?' he said furiously. 'Trying to get yourself killed?' He stared at her for a moment, then his anger faded and he gently brushed the loose hair back from her face, revealing her smudged forehead. He kissed her and took her into his arms. 'Don't you ever do that again. Ever. Do you understand?'

She blinked and stared back at him, and then smiled, before spluttering again as a coughing fit seized her.

'Julia?' Cato said anxiously as he felt her slight frame shudder in his arms. But, at length, the coughing died away and she gulped down several deep breaths and folded her arms round his neck, holding him close.

'Why did you come back for me?' she whispered hoarsely into his ear.

'Why?' He kissed her neck. 'Because I love you.'

The words had come spontaneously, before he could think about them, and now he felt partly scared that he had said too much, and partly liberated. It was the truth. He did love her, and he realised that he was glad he had said it.

She drew her head back from his neck and looked into his eyes intently. 'Cato . . . My Cato. My love.'

They kissed quickly, then Cato stood up and hauled Julia to her feet. He called one of his men over.

'Take the ambassador's daughter to her quarters. Then find someone to treat her burns.'

'Yes, sir.' The auxiliary was a burly man and he swept her off her feet and into his arms before Julia could protest. As the auxiliary strode towards the entrance of the courtyard Julia looked over his shoulder at Cato and mouthed the words he so wanted to hear again. Then she was gone, and Cato looked round the courtyard to assess the situation. The side that had been used for the sick and wounded was an inferno and the bright red and orange glare of the flames lit up a broad swathe of the surrounding citadel and its walls. But the wounded had been pulled clear and were already being carried out of the courtyard by the medical orderlies and Cato's auxiliaries. He stood for a moment, wondering about the danger of the fire's spreading. But a moment's examination showed that the arch would act as a natural fire break on one side, while the mass of the citadel wall would contain it in the other direction.

He was still standing there when an auxiliary from one of the other centuries came running into the courtyard. As soon as he saw Cato he sprinted across the open ground to make his report.

'Sir! You must come at once!'

Cato drew himself up and growled, 'Stand to attention when you speak to your commanding officer!'

'Yes, sir.' The auxiliary snapped his heels together and stared straight ahead, across Cato's shoulder. 'Beg to report, Centurion Parmenion sends his respects and says that he needs every available man to join him, sir.'

'What's happened?'

'They've hit the sheds containing the grain supply, sir. Several shots close together. The whole bloody lot is going up.'

CHAPTER TWENTY-SIX

Next morning the air was heavy with the acrid smell of burning. Macro poked one of the blackened and still smouldering baskets of grain with the toe of his boot. Ash and brittle chunks of charred material crumbled away. Much of the grain had fused into a solid black mass. He looked up and surveyed the smoking remains of the store sheds stretching out opposite the stables. Even though the rebels had run out of ammunition halfway through the night and the defenders had been fighting scores of fires through the remaining hours of darkness until first light. Now, a blaze was still consuming one corner of the royal quarters where a chance shot had passed through a high window and set light to the tapestries that lined the chamber. The king had been forced to flee while the fire was dealt with and retired to his audience chamber, surrounded by picked men from the Greek mercenaries of his bodyguard.

A pall of smoke hung over the citadel like a shroud in the pale light of the dawn. Billowing clouds from the remaining fires added to the gloom, while even the fires that had burned out still gave off myriad wisps of smoke.

'How much of the grain did we save?' Macro asked quietly.

Cato consulted his waxed slates. 'Thirty baskets. Most of what remained of the horse meat. I have men going through the fire-damaged grain vats to see what they can salvage, but it won't amount to much.'

'So I can see.' Macro gestured to the smoking ruin at his feet. He drew a deep breath. 'So how many days' rations does that leave us?'

'At the current level of distribution . . . two days.'

'Two days,' Macro repeated bitterly. 'The men are already on half rations.'

'We could cut the rations by half again. Any more than that and soon they'd be too weak to resist another assault.' Cato glanced up from his notes. 'There's more bad news, I'm afraid.'

'Really? Now there's a surprise.' Macro sighed. 'Go on.'

'We had to use a lot of water to fight the fires. The remaining supply in the cistern is less than six inches. Looks as if we're going to run dry about the same time as the food gives out. Of course, if we have another night like last night then we're as good as cooked.'

'Shit,' Macro muttered. 'Do you have any good news for me?'

'Some.' Cato tapped his stylus on the waxed slate. 'Casualties were light enough. Eight dead, five of those civilians. Twenty injured, three from falling masonry and the rest with burns.' Cato closed his waxed notebook and stared at the ruins of the storehouses. 'What I don't understand is why they didn't make another effort to get through the gates or scale the ramparts. They must have known we'd have to strip the walls of men to tackle the fires.'

'That's obvious enough. Why lose men when they know they can burn us out, or starve us into surrender?'

'Makes sense.' Cato yawned and stretched his shoulders. 'What are your orders, sir?'

'Hmm?' Macro rubbed his weary eyes a moment before he responded. 'The men who stayed on the wall can take the first watch of the day; the rest can stand down. They've earned a rest. And they need one.'

'Don't we all?'

'We'll get ours later. First things first.' Macro turned to his friend. 'We have to decide what we are going to do about the food and water supply, or lack of it. Better send word to Thermon to arrange a meeting. The king, his advisers, the ambassador, Balthus, and us.'

'Yes, sir. At what hour?'

Macro thought a moment. 'Soon as possible. Better make it the third hour. In the king's audience chamber.'

'Yes, sir.'

Cato was turning to leave when Macro touched his arm. 'That girl of yours, Julia. Is she all right?'

'Some burns. That's all. She sent me a message,' Cato explained quickly. 'I didn't have time to see for myself.'

Macro smiled. 'You don't have to justify yourself to me, lad. I'm just glad to know that she's still with us. If we get out of this scrape, do you have any plans?'

Cato shrugged. 'I don't know. It's too early to say. I mean, I'd like to have plans, but she's the daughter of a senator, and I'm just a common soldier.'

'No, you're not,' Macro replied. 'You're an uncommon soldier. I've no idea how far you might rise one day, Cato, but your potential is there for all to see. Including the ambassador. I should think he would be proud to welcome you into his family. If not, then he's a bloody fool, and Sempronius doesn't strike me as much of a fool.'

'No,' Cato replied uneasily. 'I don't suppose he'll be in the dark about my relationship with Julia for much longer. If he hasn't guessed already.'

'Relationship?' Macro looked at Cato shrewdly. 'How much of a relationship are we talking about?'

'What do you mean?' Cato asked defensively.

'I mean have you two had it off yet?'

Cato winced at the expression and Macro chuckled. 'Well, if you want me to dress it up, have you two formed a basis of physical intimacy yet?'

Now it was Cato's turn to laugh. 'Where did you get that from?'

'Oh, some book. Load of romantic bollocks, but I was running short of things to read at the time. Still, answer my question. Have you done the deed?'

Cato nodded and Macro let out a sigh.

'Oh, that's nice going, Cato. Just when I thought Sempronius was going to approve of you. If she's up the gut, and he finds out before you have a chance to make an honest woman of her, then there's going to be a bit of a stink. You know how precious those aristocrats can be.'

'Well, what was I supposed to do? I love her, and there's every chance we'll be dead before we ever discover if she's expecting. What did we have to gain by denying ourselves?'

'Seize the day, eh?' Macro chuckled bitterly. 'Well, if I'm honest, I'd probably have done the same in your place.'

'Bollocks,' Cato responded. 'You'd have been in there quicker than Cicero up a triumvir's arse.'

'Ah, you're not wrong there!' Macro laughed. 'Now away with you! See to that meeting at once.'

257

'Yes, sir.' Cato saluted with a broad smile, and hurried away.

Macro watched him pick his way through the party of auxiliaries searching through the least burned baskets of grain. In spite of his friend's foolhardiness, he was happy for Cato, and fervently hoped that there would be a future for him and Julia.

He muttered to himself, 'In any case, the Gods know, that lad needs a good shag.'

King Vabathus sat stiffly on his temporary throne, surrounded by four of his guardsmen. In front of him chairs had been set out in a curve, and once Prince Balthus had finally completed the gathering the king nodded to Thermon.

The chamberlain cleared his throat. 'Centurion Macro, His Majesty requires to know the reason for this meeting that you have insisted upon calling at such short notice.'

Macro rose to his feet and bowed his head briefly towards the king. 'Very well then.' He looked round the room before he spoke, to make sure that he had everyone's attention. Most of those in the hall were as tired as he was, and had been engaged in fighting the fires or, like Balthus, defending the walls. Macro cleared his throat and began. 'Gentlemen, we are facing some tough decisions. Decisions we need to make and act on immediately.'

'Why?' Krathos interrupted. 'What's happened?'

'I'm coming to that,' Macro replied testily. 'If you would do me the courtesy of listening . . .'

Krathos frowned and sat back in his chair, crossed his arms and nodded his assent.

'Thank you. As some of you already know, the enemy's incendiaries burned down the grain store last night. We've salvaged what we can, but with the limited supplies of water that remain my second-in-command, Prefect Cato, has calculated that on current ration levels we will be out of supplies within two days. Less if the rebels hit us with another barrage of incendiaries tonight. All the remaining water will need to be used to fight the fires. Even then, we will run dry before the fires are extinguished. Of course, we can cut the grain and water issue even further, but that will give us a few days' grace at best, and our men will be in a much weakened state if they are called on to defend the citadel.'

Macro paused to let his words sink in, and then Thermon asked, 'What are our options, Centurion?'

'They're fairly straightforward.' Macro counted them off on his fingers. 'One: we negotiate a surrender. Two: we cut the rations and continue to resist for as long as we can, and then surrender, or go down fighting.'

'We cannot surrender,' said Balthus. 'Artaxes and his followers would kill the king, me, and most of us here. We must fight on.'

'Wait.' Krathos raised his hand. 'The Roman said we could negotiate a surrender. We could try to get good terms. Prince Artaxes knows that it will cost him a great many men to take the citadel by force. If we were to surrender, and leave the kingdom to him to dispose of as he wills, then surely he would be prepared to let us leave here alive. Some of us, at least.'

'You, perhaps?' Balthus did not try to hide his scorn. 'I think you know what fate my dear brother has in mind for me. I don't think I will surrender, thank you.'

'What then?' Krathos countered. 'We stay in here and starve to death?'

'No.' Balthus shook his head and turned back to Macro. 'There is a third choice, Roman.'

'I know that,' Macro replied. 'I just wanted to see what people made of the first two.'

'Third choice?' the king said slowly. 'What's that? Speak, Roman.'

'Your Majesty, we could send the civilians out of the citadel and use the extra rations to try to hold out until General Longinus arrives. But if the supplies run out before then, we're back to the first two choices.'

There was a brief silence as the others digested this, and then Krathos shook his head. 'They would be massacred, surely?'

'It's possible,' Macro conceded. 'But they'll die anyway if they remain in the citadel. Starvation will get them if the enemy doesn't storm the place first, in which case they'll be slaughtered along with the rest of us. So, they die in here with us, or take their chances out there in the city. At least their sacrifice can buy us a few extra days.'

Krathos pursed his lips briefly. 'I see. Perhaps it is for the best.'

'Easy for you to say,' Balthus responded coldly, and then there was a glint in his eye. 'Of course, it would be necessary to rid ourselves of all the civilians, so that the food goes as far as possible amongst the remaining soldiers. Isn't that right, Centurion?'

Macro nodded.

'In which case we would have to dispense with all non-essential people, like the king's slaves, the Roman ambassador and his retinue, and nobles like you, Krathos.'

'Me?' Krathos pressed his hand against his heart. 'Preposterous! I am one of His Majesty's most loyal subjects. My place is at his side.'

'Oh, and what good are you there? Can you shoot a bow? Can you wield a spear or sword as well as a soldier? Well?'

'That is not the issue,' Krathos blustered. 'His Majesty needs good advisers. When this is all over, the kingdom will need good men to help rebuild law and order and revive trade and business.'

Balthus shook his head. 'What the king needs now is fighters, not fat merchants like you.'

'How dare you?' Krathos stood up indignantly.

'Enough!' The king slammed his fist down on the arm of his throne and his voice echoed back off the high walls of the chamber. The others instantly fell silent. Vabathus drew a calming breath and continued steadily. 'There is no question of ejecting any of my nobles from the citadel. Nor any of the Romans. If we did that then the full fury of Rome would be visited on us the moment they got to hear of the act. We have no choice but to accept the third option offered to us by the centurion. It is the best chance I have of defending my throne. The people must be sacrificed.'

Thermon turned towards the king with a pained expression.

'What is the matter?' asked Vabathus.

'Your Majesty, we all know the probable outcome of throwing the people on the mercy of the rebels, but many of them are the families of our soldiers. What will they say when they are told?' Thermon gestured to the four men guarding the king. All eyes turned on the guardsmen who, true to their profession and training, did not show any reaction.

Balthus broke the awkward silence. 'Then we must proceed carefully. The men with families must be confined to barracks while the civilians are rounded up and escorted out of the citadel.'

'What if they don't want to leave?' asked Cato. 'What if they refuse?'

'We will have to use force,' Balthus replied. 'Desperate times require desperate actions, Roman.'

'I know that.' Cato thought quickly. 'But we must try to negotiate terms with Artaxes for their safe passage. They deserve nothing less from us.'

'Fine sentiments, Roman, but why would Artaxes negotiate? He has nothing to gain from us.'

'There is one thing we can offer him that he will find difficult to resist.' The other men in the chamber stared at him expectantly and Cato swallowed nervously as he explained his thinking.

At noon the gates of the citadel opened and Cato stepped outside into the agora. He carried no weapons, and neither did the two men who accompanied him. One auxiliary carried a bucina and blew a steady series of notes as they advanced; the other man carried a large red banner that could easily be seen from the rebel lines. The small party marched thirty paces and halted in full view of both the defenders and the rebels curiously watching them from the wall of the merchants' yards. He swallowed nervously and wondered briefly about the wisdom of his action. There was still time to turn and run back to safety. But then there was a dull thud as the gates swung back into place, leaving Cato and his men no choice but to carry on.

They marched another thirty paces and halted, the bucina's shrill notes echoing back off the citadel walls. The man carrying the standard slowly swirled it in the air so that it was clearly visible. They moved forward again, stopping just short of the wall of the merchants' yards. A figure appeared above them, one of Artaxes' officers, Cato decided, judging from the fine scale armour and accoutrements.

'No closer, Roman!' the man called out in Greek. 'What do you want?'

'I wish to speak to Prince Artaxes.'

'Why?'

Cato smiled at the man's directness. 'I will not speak to his minion. Only to the prince himself.'

The rebel officer scowled for a moment and then pointed at Cato. 'Stay there, Roman. Move from that spot and my archers will shoot you down like dogs!'

'Very well.'

The rebel officer ducked out of sight and Cato and his companions were left staring at the enemy soldiers lining the wall and talking in excited tones as they tried to guess what the Roman emissary wanted with their prince. The man with the standard was still waving it from side to side.

'That's no longer necessary.' Cato said to him. 'We have their attention.'

'Very well, sir.' The auxiliaries stood at ease and waited behind their commander in the bright sunshine. Time dragged past and Cato undid his neck scarf and dabbed at the sweat trickling down his face from under his helmet. He was tempted to undo the chin ties and remove it for a moment to escape the stifling burden as he stood under the midday sun. Then he fought the temptation off. It would only look like weakness in front of the enemy. A small weakness, and a justifiable one, he reflected, but he was damned if he was going to show them any sign of discomfort. Far better to let them see how hardy Roman soldiers could be. He casually retied the cloth round his neck and stood at ease, staring directly at the wall before him and not shifting his gaze as he tried to create the look of a wholly imperturbable man.

After what seemed an age in the still, baking heat, Cato sensed movement to one side and turned to see a small party of men turn the corner of the wall of the merchants' yards. At their head was a young, slender man in fine yellow robes whose folds shimmered as he strode towards the Romans. He wore a sword belt from which hung a bejewelled scabbard that glinted as the sun caught the polished gold trimming and jewels set into the design. His beard was neatly trimmed and his hair glistened in the bright sunlight from the scented oil that had been combed into it. Behind him marched a bodyguard composed of six large spearmen, well muscled beneath their scale armour.

Cato turned towards them and raised his hand in salute. 'Do I have the honour of addressing Prince Artaxes?'

'You do,' the prince replied curtly. 'What do you want?'

Cato had memorised the statement he wished to make and spoke carefully to ensure that there was no misunderstanding.

'The king wishes to inform you that this is a struggle between you and him. Between your followers and his. The ordinary people of his kingdom are harmless bystanders and should be treated as such. Accordingly, His Majesty has sent me to ask you to offer a safe passage for the civilians presently sheltering inside the citadel. They were misguided in thinking that they had anything to fear at your hands and only want to return to their homes and businesses that they might continue with their lives, under whichever king your God chooses as ruler of Palmyra.'

Artaxes nodded slightly, and glanced round at his bodyguards. 'Stay there.' He cautiously paced up to Cato until they were well within dagger thrust of each other, and then lowered his voice so that only the two of them would hear his words.

'At the risk of being impious, it is my men, and my Parthian allies, who will decide the fate of Palmyra. We both know that, Roman, so let's leave the Gods out of this, eh?'

'As you wish, Prince.' Cato nodded. 'But General Longinus may reach Palmyra before your Parthian friends, in which case it would serve you and your followers well to let the civilians leave the citadel. One act of mercy might be rewarded with another.'

Artaxes shook his head mockingly. 'Roman, the Parthian army is less than fifty miles from the city. Where is your general? If what I hear is true, your Roman army marches like a snail. It cannot possibly reach Palmyra before the Parthians. Your time is short. Why should I show any mercy to my enemies?'

'Because they are not your enemies. If you are right, then in a matter of days they will be your subjects. Show them mercy and they will respect you.'

'Ah, but if I show them none, then the rest of my subjects will fear me.' Artaxes smiled. 'You tell me, Roman, which quality a king should value most, respect or fear?'

'I cannot answer for a king, but I would say respect.'

'Then, truly, you are a fool. We stand here right now because my father was not feared. Nor was he respected at the end. When he lost respect he could not rely on fear to save him. I will not make the same mistake. I will make men fear me utterly, and they will do my bidding with no thought of dissent. And the slaughter of the civilians who are presently cowering behind the walls of the citadel will be useful proof of my intentions. They are dead the moment you throw them out.'

'Who said we would throw them out?'

Artaxes feigned surprise. 'Surely that is why you are here, pleading for their lives? I am not a fool, Roman. You cannot feed them; that is why my father wants them out. That means you are short of supplies, and that I am close to victory.' He stared at Cato for a moment. 'Is that not so, Roman?'

Cato did not reply at once. As he had feared, Artaxes had seen through the ploy in an instant. Cato could deny that they were short of supplies but he saw that Artaxes would not believe him. Now there was only one final bargaining counter to bring into play. He nodded his assent to Artaxes.

'You are right, Prince. However, I have a proposal for you. If you let the civilians leave, and do no harm to them, then in five days' time the two Roman cohorts will leave the citadel and surrender to you. You can dispose of us as you will.'

Artaxes stared at him briefly before replying. 'Have you not heard of the fate I have promised to any Romans that I take alive?'

'I have heard.'

'Then why make such a foolish offer?'

'As you said, we cannot hold out for much longer. We are dead men either way. At least this would give some purpose to our deaths.'

'I see. And if you are dead either way, why should I agree to this?'

'You know the quality of Rome's soldiers. If you have to destroy us in battle then how many of your men do you think we will take with us?' It was a bluff, since by that time the men would be too weak to put up much resistance, but Cato needed Artaxes to believe it, and he stood with an unflinching expression as he waited for the rebel leader to reply.

'You would give your lives for the people of Palmyra?'

'Yes.'

'Why?'

Cato drew himself up as he replied. 'It takes the Empire several months to create and train a cohort. It has taken the Roman army a hundred years to build a reputation. We are not going to be remembered for throwing defenceless people to jackals like you.'

Artaxes' eyes widened for an instant and his hand clasped the handle of his sword. Then he forced a smile and relaxed his hand. 'Why should I believe that you would give yourselves up freely?'

'For the same reason we will believe that you have spared the civilians. Trust. If you give your word that they will not be harmed, then I give you my word that we will surrender to you, if we have not been relieved within five days. If either of us breaks his word the penalty is the same: infamy across the whole region.'

Artaxes considered this for a moment and Cato prayed that the prince's desire to visit destruction on the men of Rome outweighed his reason. Artaxes shut his eyes for a moment and stroked his neatly trimmed beard. Then he shook his head.

'No. I will not make a deal with you. If we are to destroy your cohorts then we will do it in battle and prove to the world that the soldiers of Palmyra are more than a match for your legionaries and auxiliaries. As for the civilians? You will have to force them out of the citadel, and see what happens to them.'

The cold malice in his tone was clear to Cato and he felt the icy grip of fear clutch at the base of his neck. It was clear that Artaxes had the makings of a tyrant. Inspiring fear came as naturally to him as striking at prey came to a snake.

'Is that your final word?' asked Cato.

'Yes . . . No.' Artaxes smiled again. 'Just one more thing. Tell my father, and my brothers, assuming they still live, that when the citadel is taken, I will have them flayed alive and their bodies will be cast into the desert for the jackals to feed on.' His dark lips curled back in a grin as he raised a hand and pointed a finger at Cato. 'And you can join them, Roman. Then we'll see how long your superior attitude lasts.'

Cato swallowed, and tried to keep his face composed as he turned towards the two men who had accompanied him. 'Back to the citadel. Quick march.'

As they tramped back across the agora Cato sensed the cold stare of Artaxes boring into his back and could not resist one glance over his shoulder. Artaxes saw him and smiled with satisfaction before turning to stride towards the far corner of the merchants' yards, followed by his bodyguards. Before he reached it a man came running round the end of the wall, sprinted towards Artaxes and dropped down on one knee as he began to speak. Cato was too far away to hear the words and continued towards the gates at a slower pace while he watched. He saw Artaxes ball his hand into a fist and turn to glare at Cato, his expression twisted into a mask of rage.

Artaxes' voice cut through the air as he turned and ran for shelter. Above him, along the wall, his men were hurriedly stringing their bows. Cato turned to his companions.

'Run!'

The three men sprinted towards the citadel. Cato heard Macro's voice bellowing down to the men behind the gates and a moment later the hinges groaned in protest as they began to swing open. An arrow whirred overhead, then another clattered off the ground to one side. Cato hunched his head down and ran as fast as he could, weighed down by his armour. He saw the gap between the gates slowly widen ahead of him as the arrows continued to fly past. Then there was a sharp cry from his right. He glanced round and saw that the man carrying the standard had been struck in the back of the thigh, just above the knee.

'Oh, shit!' the auxiliary cried out, as he staggered another few paces and stopped.

Cato turned to the other man. 'Help me!' He grabbed the injured man's arm and threw it across his shoulder as the other auxiliary threw his bucina aside and took the other arm.

'Let's go!' Cato growled through gritted teeth. 'Go!'

They hurried on, half carrying, half dragging the wounded man, who groaned with the agony of using his wounded leg. They were close to the gate, but the rebels were shooting more arrows at them than ever and Cato felt a hammer blow to the back of his shoulder as they stumbled under the gatehouse and through the gap, and then dropped to the ground as the legionaries on either side heaved the gates back into place and slid the locking bar across. Cato, gulping for breath, gestured towards the wounded man. 'Get him to the surgeon.'

While a pair of legionaries hauled the man up and carried him away towards the royal garden courtyard which now served as the hospital, Cato stood up and felt round towards his back, wincing at a sudden stab of pain. But there was no shaft of an arrow; the chain-mail vest had done its job well. If the impact hadn't cracked a rib then he would only suffer bruising. Macro emerged from the gatehouse staircase.

'I take it he wasn't interested in our offer?'

'You could put it that way.'

Macro tilted his head to one side. 'Can't say I'm sorry that we're going to go down fighting, rather than be butchered in cold blood. All the same,' he turned and looked towards a family huddled together in the shadow of the royal quarters, 'I pity those poor bastards. They haven't got a chance now.'

CHAPTER TWENTY-SEVEN

'The decision has been made,' Balthus said firmly. 'We must sacrifice the civilians, and it must be done now, before they consume any more supplies.'

There was a mumble of assent around the handful of senior officers and officials who had gathered in the audience chamber that night, but Cato refused to give in and spoke again.

'I'm telling you, something's happened. A messenger approached Artaxes just after the parley finished. Whatever he told him must have been bad news.'

'Why?' asked Balthus. 'Did you hear what he said?'

'No,' Cato admitted. 'But there was no mistaking the look on his face.'

'So you say. But it could have been almost anything.'

'I don't think so. What bad news could he be expecting? The Parthians are on the way to join him. We've almost run out of supplies, and all Artaxes has to do is bide his time and the citadel will fall into his hands.' Cato paused to let his words sink in before continuing. 'The only bad news he could be expecting is the approach of Longinus and his army.'

Macro cleared his throat and Cato glanced round as his friend shook his head. 'Cato.' Macro spoke gently. 'It's possible that you're right. Just possible. It's probable that you're wrong.'

'I'm not wrong. I know it.'

'You know only what you saw. What you thought you saw in a glance back at Artaxes. That's not enough. We can't take the risk that Longinus is coming. We must go through with the plan. The civilians have to be sacrificed.'

'And what if I'm right?' Cato stared round at the others. 'The blood of hundreds of people will be on our hands.'

There was a tense pause before Thermon rose to his feet. 'That is the price we must accept, Roman. What if we let them stay? The remaining water and food would be exhausted in another day or two at the most. All we would have achieved then is a short delay in their deaths. At the cost of the lives of everyone in the citadel.'

'But if Longinus is close to the city then we can all be saved.'

'And if he isn't? If he arrives just a day after we have been starved into submission? Then it would all have been for nothing. So let the sacrifice be made, and let us hope that it achieves something. It would be far better that the people died in order to save their kingdom than to wait a few more days and die in vain. Surely you can see that?'

Cato's lips pressed into a thin line as he held in his anger and frustration, and Macro gently drew him back on to his chair. 'Lad, he's right. We can't take the risk. You're the one who thinks things through. If it had been me who had gone to speak to Artaxes, and I came back with some story, what would you think? What would you do?'

Cato looked at his friend. 'I would trust your judgement, that's what I'd do.'

Before Macro could respond, Thermon brought the meeting to an end. He spoke in a sombre tone. 'As I see it, there is no good reason to change our plan. Before I report to the king, does anyone else wish to speak in support of Prefect Cato's position? . . . No? Then the matter is decided. I bid you good evening, gentlemen. Get some rest. Tomorrow is likely to be a very trying day.'

The round-up of civilians began before dawn. Those soldiers with family in the citadel were assembled in one of the storerooms and placed under guard with no explanation. They were provided with some bread and wine from the king's kitchens, and once they were safely contained the legionaries began the task of rousing the civilians from their makeshift shelters in the courtyards. It was a distressing task for the men, but Macro had volunteered the legionaries for the job. They were hard-bitten professionals with a higher proportion of veterans than Cato's cohort, men who could be relied on to carry out their orders without sentiment. Cato's auxiliaries, together with the Greek mercenaries and the followers of Balthus, had been posted on the walls with strict instructions not to leave their posts until relieved.

Flickering torches in hand, the legionaries gathered up the men, women and children and drove them towards the open area behind the gates. Two centuries created a cordon blocking any attempt at escape with their broad shields and lowered javelins. The civilians were not given time to collect any belongings and any food or drink that was found on them was taken away. Soon the cold dawn air was filled with their cries of anger and despair. Women clutched their children in their arms while the men confronted the Romans and shouted their rage, shook their fists, but kept just out of reach of the deadly points of the javelins. When all the obvious places had been searched Macro led one of his centuries out to scour the citadel for any remaining civilians who had tried to conceal themselves, and a steady trickle of individuals and families were added to the wailing crowd packed in behind the gate.

Having searched the area close to the burned-out grain stores Macro was about to move on to the ruins of the courtyard which had served as the hospital when he heard a thin cry. He paused and turned, listening, as his eyes scanned the blackened debris around him. Nothing moved and all was quiet. He relaxed his attention as one of his legionaries came tramping up and saluted.

'Sir, beg to report we've swept this area. The optio wishes to know if you have any further orders.'

Just then Macro heard the sound again, a faint yowl, like a hungry cat. He raised his finger to his lips. 'Quiet.'

Both men stood still, ears pricked as they slowly looked round. There was another cry, more pronounced this time, and Macro knew that it was no cat.

'Came from that way, sir.' The legionary pointed towards a blackened heap of burned grain baskets close to the remains of a wall. 'I'm sure of it.'

Macro nodded, beckoned to the man to follow him and then began to pick his way across the ruins towards the heap. The crying became continuous as they closed in and now Macro could hear a voice muttering anxiously. He stepped round the pile of burned baskets and saw that there was a narrow gap between it and the wall. A dark robe covered part of the gap and he saw it move slightly as the muttering grew in intensity.

'There!' said the legionary, and started to draw his sword.

'Leave it,' Macro ordered. 'There's no need.'

He brushed past the legionary and crunched over the charred remains of baskets that littered the ground around the pile. When he reached the robe Macro bent down, grasped a corner and pulled it away in one swift movement. There was a gasp as a young girl, no more than thirteen or fourteen, looked up from the crying infant cradled against her breast. Her mouth remained open, as if to scream, but she just swallowed and shook her head.

'Please! Please don't take us away.' She spoke in Greek and Macro noticed that her blue stola and her cloak were cut from good-quality material. Her dark hair was neatly braided and she wore a gold pendant round her neck. The baby had been hurriedly wrapped in a shawl and its tiny sickly face wrinkled as it bawled, and little clenched fists trembled in the cool air.

'He's hungry,' she explained. 'Starving. We both are. Please help us.'

Macro took the girl gently under the arms and lifted her on to her feet. 'Any more of you hiding round here?'

'No, I don't think so.' She clutched Macro's arm with her spare hand. 'Please let us stay.'

'Sorry, young lady. We have our orders.'

'I know, but you look like a good man.' She glanced at the legionary. 'Both of you do. Spare us. Let us stay.'

Macro shook his head. 'We're not going to harm you. Now just come with us.'

'If you mean no harm, then where are you taking everybody?'

Macro looked at her and replied flatly, 'To the main gate.'

'The gate? Why?'

Macro felt pity for the girl and decided he would not deceive her. 'The king has ordered that all civilians are to leave the citadel.'

She stared at him as the implication of his words rushed into her mind. 'No . . . But that's murder. Plain murder.'

'Those are my orders, young lady. Now, come with us.' He took her arm firmly. 'Don't give us any trouble, eh?'

She tried to pull away but there was no resisting Macro's powerful grip. She bit her lip and then tried another tack, the words tumbling from her thin lips. 'I can cook for you. Look after your kit . . . Keep you

271

warm at night. Just spare me and my brother. I swear you won't regret it.'

Macro felt a stab of guilt at her suggestion and a sense of world-weariness at the lengths that despair drove people to. The legionary had been listening to the exchange and glanced at Macro.

'What about it, sir? Can I have her before she has to go with the others?'

'What?' Macro frowned as he turned to the man.

'She's a nice piece of cunny, sir. Be a shame to let it go to waste. She'll be dead soon.'

'Shut your mouth,' Macro growled. 'Get out of my fucking sight and search the next courtyard.'

'Yes, sir.' The legionary snapped to attention, saluted and then turned and trotted away. Macro glared after him, knowing full well that the man would assume that his commander had decided to save the girl for himself. Another officer might have taken advantage of the situation, Macro realised, but he felt heartily sickened by his orders, even though he had no choice in the matter. The civilians would die to permit the king and his followers to hold the citadel for a little longer. It was hard, but it made sense, Macro told himself. He looked at the girl and the infant again and suddenly he was not so sure.

'What's your name?'

'Jesmiah,' she replied quickly, sensing a change in his mood. 'My brother's name is Ayshel.'

'Where is your family, Jesmiah?'

'I don't know, sir. We got separated from them when everyone was trying to reach the citadel. Ayshel and I were some of the last to make it inside before the gates were shut.'

'How have you managed to survive since then?'

'We had rations like the others. I gave most of mine to Ayshel, but he's still hungry.'

Macro looked at her and noticed how thin her face was and he guessed that beneath the folds of her stola she was skin and bones. 'Maybe you'll find your family in the city.'

She looked at him in alarm. 'But you can't throw me out. They will kill me. They'll kill little Ayshel.'

Macro hardened his heart. 'Come on, young lady, let's go.'

He steered her by the arm out of the ruins of the grain store and towards the gate. Jesmiah began to cry and begged him to let her stay behind. In her desperation she promised every kind of sexual favour that her young mind could imagine but Macro continued striding towards the gate with stony resolve. At the sound of the gathered crowd, Jesmiah fell silent. When they turned the corner and saw the civilians packed together behind a screen of heavily armed legionaries, Jesmiah's legs collapsed and she fell, clutching her brother to her chest.

'I won't go! I won't! I don't want to die. I won't go!'

'Yes you will,' Macro said firmly. 'Get up. Now!'

'No . . . please. I beg you.'

'On your feet!' Macro pulled her up and held her still.

The girl's eyes darted towards her little brother, and then back at Macro. 'If I have to go, at least take my brother and see that he lives.'

'I can't.'

'Please!'

'No. How could I look after a baby? He is your brother. He must stay with you. Let's go.'

Macro swept her off the ground and into his arms and strode towards the gates. Jesmiah fell silent, closed her eyes and began muttering what sounded like a prayer. Macro glanced at her once and then kept his gaze fixed straight ahead. He shouldered his way through the line of legionaries and set her down roughly, then took a quick step away from her and pointed at the crowd. 'There you are. Go and join your people.'

She took one last look at him, eyes filled with withering contempt, and then, cradling her brother's small head against her shoulder, she walked slowly through the wailing crowd until she stood directly in front of the closed gates. To be the first one cast out. The first one to be butchered by the rebels. She turned and stared accusingly at Macro. He watched as one of the legionaries on the gate approached her, reached out and wrenched the gold pendant from her neck, and tucked it into his purse before resuming his post. For a moment Macro thought about reprimanding the man, but then what was the point? If the legionary didn't take the pendant it would only be seized from her body by a rebel. The same rebel who might take it from the corpse of the legionary in a few more days' time. Macro shook his head wearily and stood aside as the last of the search parties bundled their discoveries through the line of soldiers.

When the last of the fugitives had joined the crowd Macro took a deep breath.

'Open the gates!'

The men assigned to the gates drew back the locking bar and hauled on the chains. The gates rumbled open and the rosy light of dawn flooded into the citadel. The crowd turned to the light and for an instant their cries faded away as they contemplated their immediate fate.

'Let's move them out!' Macro bellowed. 'Present javelins!'

His men lowered the points of their weapons and the nearest civilians recoiled in fright. The cries of panic and fear rose up once again so that Macro had to cup both hands to his mouth and bellow at the top of his voice for his orders to be heard.

'At the slow step . . . advance!'

The line of Roman soldiers rippled forward, closing in on the crowd. At first none moved, and then the pressure from those closest to the javelin tips inevitably forced them to flow towards the gate and they began to spill out on to the agora. Macro strode across to the gatehouse stairs and climbed up on to the rampart. Cato was looking out over the agora towards the rebels' artillery platform.

'Not our finest hour,' Macro said quietly as he joined his friend.

Cato glanced at him distractedly, then grasped what Macro had said. 'No, I suppose not. Couldn't be helped.'

'That's small compensation for those poor bastards, and not much better for those of us who had to deal with it.'

Cato had turned his attention back towards the enemy lines and Macro sighed with frustration. 'What's eating you?'

'It's gone very quiet over there,' Cato replied. 'Hardly seen any movement.'

Macro shielded his eyes and stared towards the merchants' yards, then along towards the temple precinct. Two figures, boys he guessed, were busy picking over the equipment outside the temple. 'I see what you mean.'

'So what are they up to?'

Macro shrugged. 'Buggered if I know. But they're out there. They have to be. We'll know soon enough, once they see that lot.'

He nodded down to the civilians streaming out across the agora. Most went a short distance and stopped, staring warily at the buildings and the street openings opposite the citadel. A handful of others, bolder than the rest, sprinted for the nearest cover in a bid to escape before the rebels could respond. Macro's gaze scanned over the fringe of the crowd until he saw the thin figure of a young girl in blue holding a baby in her arms. Jesmiah strode boldly towards the nearest street and disappeared from sight. Macro's heart felt leaden as he contemplated his betrayal of the young girl and her brother.

The rampart trembled beneath their boots as the gates were closed. Still there was no sign of the enemy and Cato's fingers drummed nervously against his scabbard.

'What the hell are they waiting for?' he muttered.

Down in the agora the civilians had become aware of the silence from the rebels and began to move swiftly from the open area into the streets leading away from the marketplace. Soon the paved expanse was empty and silent, and no distant cries of panic nor sounds of slaughter drifted up from the city.

'Something's happened,' said Cato. 'We have to find out.'

'It could be a trap.'

'Perhaps. But we have to know.'

'All right then.' Macro nodded. He turned away and crossed over to the other side of the gatehouse and called down to the legionaries below. 'Centurion Braccus!'

'Yes sir?'

'Send out two sections. Check the temple precinct and the merchants' yards. Have your men report back to me as soon as possible.'

'Yes, sir.' Braccus turned to the nearest men and gave his orders. Moments later one of the gates was opened far enough to permit the legionaries to pass through in single file. From the ramparts Macro and Cato watched them separate, one party jingling obliquely across the agora towards the temple while the other made straight for the position the rebels had fortified to protect their artillery battery. They trotted round the corner and out of sight. A short while later Macro and Cato saw some of the men moving along the wall. There was no sign of the enemy. It was the same over by the temple. Then the section leaders came running back towards the citadel.

Macro cupped his hand and shouted down to them. 'What did you find?'

'Nothing, sir. They've gone. They've abandoned everything. The catapults are still there. So's the makings of another ram. But the rebels seem to have disappeared, sir.'

Macro turned to Cato. 'What's going on? Why would they abandon the siege? Anyway, where the hell have they gone?'

'I don't like it. It could still be a trap.'

Macro smiled thinly. 'Look on the bright side. No sign of a wooden horse.'

Cato flashed an irritated look at his friend.

'All right. Sorry. Now isn't the time.'

'No.'

Macro undid the straps of his helmet and took it off. His sweat-drenched hair was plastered to his skull and he rubbed his hand over the dark curls. Then he thumped his fist on the stone parapet in front of him. 'What the fuck are they playing at? If they're not there then they must have left the city during the night. Why the hell would they do that?'

Then Cato recalled the parley he had held with Prince Artaxes, and the man who had rushed to the prince to bring him a message. He turned to Macro, eyes bright with excitement. 'It's Longinus! Their patrols must have seen him approaching. The rebels have fled.'

'Longinus?'

'Yes. It has to be!' Cato clapped his friend on the shoulder. 'We're saved!'

'Easy there,' Macro cautioned him. 'If it's Longinus, then where is he? Besides, he'd have had to march like the wind to reach Palmyra so soon.'

Cato ran across to the nearest tower and climbed the steps two at a time. At the top, heart beating wildly, he ran to the rampart and scanned the horizon beyond the sprawl of the city. At first he could see nothing. Then, away to the east, he saw a thin haze of dust beyond a low ridge. That had to be Artaxes, fleeing towards his Parthian allies. Cato's gaze swept to the north and then west, and then he saw it, another smudge in the sky. He thrust his arm out towards it.

'Over there! Macro, over there!'

Below, Macro followed the direction indicated by his friend, squinted

276

for a moment, and then let out a loud whoop and punched his fist into the morning sky. 'We're saved!' He turned to the other men on the ramparts. 'It's Longinus! General Longinus!'

The cry was taken up along the wall and down below by the gate and the air swelled with the wild cheers of the defenders. All the weariness and hunger of the previous days was forgotten as they cheered and laughed and slapped each other on the back. Cato came running down from the tower and grasped Macro's arm.

'We did it! We held out!' He tried to summon up a little composure. 'Congratulations, sir.'

Macro waved the praise aside. 'That was close. A few more days . . .'

'It doesn't matter,' Cato cut in. 'We're saved!'

'Saved?' Macro nodded. He looked out over the agora, towards the street down which Jesmiah had marched to meet her fate. 'Yes, we're saved. All of us.'

CHAPTER TWENTY-EIGHT

'You've done an outstanding job, gentlemen,' said General Longinus. 'In the best tradition of the service. You can be assured that I will mention your achievement when I report to Rome.'

'Thank you, sir,' Macro responded.

They stood in the king's audience chamber of the citadel. King Vabathus and his advisers had returned with the Greek mercenaries to the far more comfortable accommodation of the royal palace at the other end of the city. His Majesty had first offered his profuse thanks to General Longinus and then thrown the city open to his army, partly out of a desire to cement his friendship with Rome, but mostly to have his revenge of those inhabitants of the city who had supported Artaxes, or at least had done nothing to resist him. Longinus had thanked him for the offer but declined, as he could not afford to let his army be compromised by drunkenness and looting. As soon as his meeting with the king was over, Longinus had arranged to meet the two officers commanding the advance column. Together with Sempronius and his staff he had formerly offered his congratulations, and now it was time to return to business.

'According to your report, Prince Artaxes quit the city yesterday evening. He will have a fifteen or twenty-mile head start on us. It's my intention to set out after him as soon as my column is resupplied with water and food. I took the risk of leaving most of the baggage train behind at Chalcis so that we could reach Palmyra as swiftly as possible. We'll march on with whatever we can carry. When we catch up with the rebels we will wipe them out. We should be more than a match for Prince Artaxes and his ragtag army.'

Cato had little doubt about that. Longinus had brought two legions with him, the Tenth and the Third, as well as several cohorts of auxiliaries. The Sixth had been left behind to defend the province. Only one thing concerned Cato about the composition of Longinus' army, and he cleared his throat.

'Sir?'

'Yes, Prefect?'

'Prince Artaxes said that a Parthian army was within two or three days' march of Palmyra. That was yesterday. If he was telling the truth then we run the risk of catching up with him after he has joined forces with the Parthians.'

Longinus nodded. 'So much the better. My spies tell me that the Parthians cannot field a large army for some months yet. We will crush the rebels and teach the Parthians a lesson at the same time. After they are defeated they won't dare to meddle in the affairs of Palmyra for many years to come.'

'I'm sure you are right, sir. If we defeat them.'

'If?' Longinus smiled. 'Do you doubt that we will defeat the Parthians?'

'No, sir. Of course not, provided we take the appropriate precautions.'

'Precautions? What precautions are you referring to, Prefect?'

Cato paused a moment to consider the best way to present his worries. General Longinus shifted his weight from one foot to the other impatiently. 'Well? Out with it, man.'

'Sir, you may well have two legions, but what's needed most of all is cavalry. If the army does run into the Parthians then it is vital that you can match them horseman for horseman.'

'Ah.' Longinus nodded. 'You must think me a fool not to be familiar with the, er, legendary Parthian horse-archer. Prefect, let me reassure you. The legions of Rome are more than a match for any horsemen or archers that have ever lived. The fact that our Parthian friends have seen fit to combine the two roles makes little difference.'

'You wouldn't say that if you'd been with us in the desert when we took on a small force of horse-archers, sir. If it hadn't been for Prince Balthus and his men . . .'

'Then it's as well that the prince and his followers are joining our force. They are finding fresh mounts even now.'

'Balthus is coming with us?' Macro interrupted. 'Why?'

'His father made the offer of his son's services, and I'm happy enough to add a few levies to my strength. They might be useful in a scouting role and save our men the job. We should have enough mounted men to counter any threat of horse-archers. Does that set your mind at rest?'

'Frankly, sir, no,' said Cato.

General Longinus frowned. 'Why is that?'

'The desert is cavalry country for the most part, sir. You cannot protect your flanks. You cannot prevent the enemy from circling round behind you. I would not offer battle unless you can choose your ground, somewhere the terrain permits a large infantry force to confront the enemy with secure flanks, or use high ground to slow down their mounts. If the Parthians catch our column in the open desert they can strike from any direction, loose off their arrows and retreat before our cavalry can close on them.'

'No more than a nuisance, Prefect. It won't stop us advancing on their main force.'

'But their cavalry is their main force, sir. That's the point. At first it will seem like just a series of harassing attacks. They will lure us on, deeper into the desert, all the time whittling down our numbers and making our men fear living under the threat of a sudden shower of arrows.'

'Then what would you have me do, Prefect?' There was an exasperated edge to the general's voice. 'Call off the advance and let Artaxes and his rebels escape?'

'With respect, yes, sir. That's precisely what I would do.'

'Why?'

'We have Palmyra. There is nothing of any strategic value between here and the Euphrates. If the Parthians want war, then let them attack us here, on our terms. They will only wear themselves out attacking the walls of the city. As for Prince Artaxes? The best he can hope for is exile in Parthia. His rebels will have to join him there, or drift back to Palmyra and seek a pardon from the king. Artaxes is a spent force, sir. We can ignore him.'

'I will not ignore him. I will not hand the initiative to the enemy. I will find them and defeat them. They cannot be allowed to defy Rome.'

'I'm sure that's what General Crassus thought, sir.'

Longinus waved his hand dismissively. 'Crassus was a fool. He ventured too far into enemy territory. I am simply going after a band of rebels. Of course, if there is a Parthian force out there, they will have to stand and fight with their Palmyran allies, or abandon them. If that happens, then we will have Prince Artaxes in the bag, and we will have proved the worthlessness of any alliance with Parthia. We have the advantage now.' General Longinus smiled reassuringly. 'I understand what you and Centurion Macro have endured these past days, and you and your men could well do with a rest and a chance to recover. It might be best if you remained here, if you are not fit and ready to join the campaign.'

Cato shook his head. 'We don't need a rest. We're ready to fight, sir.'

'Good. I will need every man I can get to track down and crush the rebels. So, if you have nothing further to add, Prefect?'

Longinus paused and fixed Cato with a hard stare, daring him to continue to stand in his way. Sempronius stepped forward.

'General, if I may say something?'

Longinus' gaze flicked to the ambassador. 'Well? What is it?'

'These officers have proved their courage, and their ability, time and again, not only in defence of the citadel, but in fighting their way across the desert and into the city in the first place. I have no doubts about their mettle, nor their understanding of the enemy and his tactics. You would do well to heed their advice.'

'Would I?' Longinus turned to his small coterie of staff officers, mainly young tribunes on their first military posting. They smiled knowingly. Cato felt his blood burn in his veins. What did they understand of desert fighting? What could they know, fresh from their fine houses in Rome? The only action they could have seen since arriving in the east was in the whorehouses of Antioch and the other fleshpots of the cities garrisoned by the legions in Syria. He suddenly felt the full weight of his weariness and knew that there was nothing he could do to persuade Longinus to change his plans. He glanced at Macro and bowed his head in resignation.

Longinus noted the gesture and clasped his hands together behind his back as he continued. 'There. The discussion is over, gentlemen. I want our men ready to begin the pursuit the moment they are reprovisioned. See to it that the orders are given at once. Sempronius, I'd like a word with these two officers alone, if you wouldn't mind?'

Sempronius stared at the general for a moment before he nodded. 'As you wish. I'll be in my quarters, Cato. Please do me the kindness of calling in before you leave the city.'

'Yes, sir.'

The staff officers saluted and filed out of the chamber, together with the ambassador. Longinus waited until the last of them had closed the door behind him, and then he rounded on Cato.

'What do you think you were doing, questioning my authority like that?'

'I have a duty to express my professional opinion, sir.'

'Damn your professional opinion! You are a subordinate officer, and merely an acting prefect at that. Why do you think I chose to send you and Macro out here in the first place? Because you were the best men for the job? Wake up, Cato. I chose you because you were expendable. Because I wanted you out of the way. Permanently. You two are little more than Narcissus' pet spies. You're not real soldiers at all. It's a miracle you ever made it through to the garrison. The pair of you have the most damnable luck. Maybe it's as well that you will join my army. Your good fortune may rub off on us.' Longinus paused, and for the first time Cato sensed that he had some doubts about his decision to pursue Artaxes.

'Have you finished with us, sir?' Macro asked gruffly.

Longinus stared at him fixedly for a moment and then nodded. 'Have your men ready to march. You can fall in at the rear of my column, where you belong. Now get out of my sight.'

Sempronius leaned back in his chair and shook his head. 'There's nothing I can do about it, Cato. I'm only an ambassador. I was sent here to conclude a treaty with King Vabathus and that's all. Longinus has a far greater authority than mine in this situation. If he's determined to press ahead with his campaign then he will.'

'But it's foolhardy,' Cato responded. 'He's going after Artaxes with a few days' supply of food and water. If there's no immediate contact then he'll be forced to retreat. If he leaves that too late then who knows how many men he's going to lose on the way back.'

'He must know that,' Sempronius replied. 'He's no fool, Cato. I know the man well enough. He's just ambitious.'

'Ambitious?' Macro laughed bitterly. 'Oh, he's more ambitious than you can ever know.'

Sempronius stared at Macro for a moment. 'What do you mean by that?'

'Nothing.' Macro waved a hand dismissively. 'Just tiredness speaking. I didn't mean anything by it. Well, just that he's a glory-hunter, like most of his kind.'

'I see,' Sempronius replied evenly. He turned to his daughter, who was sitting next to Cato. 'My dear, would you mind finding us a jar of wine?'

'Wine?' Julia looked surprised. 'Now?'

'Of course. These men are about to march off to war. They deserve a drink. Find some of the good stuff. I believe the steward has a few jars left.'

Julia frowned. 'Why don't you send someone else to fetch it, Father?'

'I'd like you to go, my dear. Right now.'

For a moment Julia did not move and her father looked at her intently. With a frustrated sigh, she rose from her seat and strode towards the door, shutting it loudly behind her.

'Was that necessary?' Cato asked.

'She is my daughter. I will do all that I can to protect her. Which means there are certain things she must not know, for her own safety. Like this business with Longinus. You are not being straight with me, either of you. What is going on?'

Cato smiled. 'As you said, sir, there are certain things it is dangerous to know.'

'This is bollocks,' Macro said in a sudden burst of frustration. 'I've had enough of this, Cato. I'm a bloody soldier, not a spy.'

'Macro!' Cato warned him. 'Don't.'

Macro shook his head. 'I'll have my say, damn it. If that bastard Longinus is going to lead us into disaster then I want someone to know why. Someone who can go back to Rome and tell the truth.'

'What truth would that be?' Sempronius asked.

'Longinus has a taste for the purple,' said Macro. 'That's how ambitious he is.'

'Is it true?' Sempronius asked Cato.

Cato glanced angrily at Macro and then took a deep breath and resigned himself to explaining the situation. 'We think so. We don't have enough evidence to prove it. He's been good at covering his tracks.

That's what I think all this is about. He wants a victory. To build his reputation and prove what a good servant he is of Rome, and the Emperor. It's also why he sent me and Macro out here ahead of the main column. We weren't supposed to succeed. It seems we were supposed to die. Just another incriminating detail disposed of.'

Sempronius looked at them both before he spoke. 'If that's the case, he's going to rather a lot of trouble to get rid of you.'

'He has good reason to want us dead.'

'You're not just ordinary line officers, are you?'

Cato did not reply and shot a warning glance at Macro, who just shrugged and looked out of the window.

Sempronius let the awkward silence drag out for a while and then cleared his throat. 'I'll have you know that I am a loyal servant of Emperor Claudius. I can be trusted. But there's something else. I'm well aware that there is more than a passing friendship between you and my daughter, Cato. Julia has told me everything. Everything, you understand? Now, I assume that means that you wish to take her as your wife?'

Cato's mind raced to grapple with the unexpected direction the conversation was taking. His intense feeling for Julia was thrown into conflict with the need to keep secret the true purpose of his and Macro's being sent to the eastern Empire. Sempronius sensed his dilemma and continued.

'Like Longinus, I am no fool, Cato. I can sense the hand of Narcissus behind all this. I am Julia's father. Before I can consent to her marrying you, I need to know that she will be safe. That she will not be in danger if she binds herself to you. I'm well aware of the risks of being a soldier. I'm also aware of the far greater risks a man runs in serving Narcissus. All that I ask is that you are honest with me. Are you an imperial agent?'

Cato felt trapped. There was no easy way out of this. No glib answer that would save him from revealing the truth. Besides, Sempronius had obviously guessed almost as much as Cato could have told him. He already knew that the two officers were working for the imperial secretary.

'We were sent east by Narcissus to report on Longinus,' Cato admitted wearily. Ever since Narcissus had pressed them into his service Cato and Macro had been thrown into situations as perilous as any they had faced in the ranks of the Second Legion. Cato wanted, more than ever, to return to a military career free of the secret plots and political infighting that made up the world of the imperial secretary. He drew a deep breath and continued. 'Narcissus suspected that the general was preparing to use the eastern legions in a bid for the imperial throne. Macro and I managed to upset his plans, and now he's covering his tracks. If anything happens to us, you should tell Narcissus that he was right, but we had too little evidence to prove it. We're not imperial agents, sir. Macro and I are soldiers. Somehow we just got caught up with Narcissus.'

Sempronius smiled sadly. 'You wouldn't be the first men that had happened to. That's how Narcissus operates. Some men he recruits directly. Some he bribes. Others are threatened into working for him. Men like you are just slowly sucked into his world of plots and conspiracies. My advice to you is to get as far from him as you can, if you live through this campaign. Whatever rewards he offers you, go back to soldiering, and nothing else.'

'That'll be the day,' Macro grumbled.

'Nothing would please us more,' said Cato. He leaned forward and crossed his arms on the table. 'And Julia?'

'Julia?'

'Do I have your permission to marry her, sir?'

Sempronius looked at the young officer for a moment. 'No. Not yet.'

The answer struck Cato's heart like a hammer blow and he bit back on the wave of bitterness and despair that threatened to engulf him. 'Why?'

'By your own admission, you are facing great danger in the coming days. However, if you live, if you return to Palmyra unharmed, if you can complete your work here in the eastern Empire, then I would give my consent. But only then.'

Cato felt the relief wash through him, but it was tempered by the knowledge of the odds stacked against him, and he nodded sombrely. 'I will live.'

The door opened and Julia entered the room with a plain wooden tray bearing a small stoppered amphora, and four silver goblets.

'The last of my Falernian?' Sempronius frowned as he recognised the amphora.

'You said the good stuff, Father.'

'Yes. Yes, I did. Well then, let's have our toast.'

Sempronius reached for the amphora and pulled out the stopper. The musty fruit scent of the wine wafted into the air. He carefully poured them each a full goblet and put the stopper firmly back in place.

In the distance the flat blast of a bucina rang out.

'They're sounding assembly,' Macro explained to Sempronius and his daughter. He turned to Cato. 'Better drink up quickly. We have to go.'

'Wait,' said Sempronius. He glanced at Julia and then raised his goblet. 'We shall always be grateful to both of you for what you did here in Palmyra. I doubt that there are two finer men in the Roman army. Rome needs you. To that end, I propose this toast. Come back alive.'

Macro laughed. 'I'll drink to that!'

He raised his goblet and drained it in one gulp and set his cup down with a sharp rap on the table. He smacked his lips. 'Nice drop of wine.'

Sempronius, who had sipped his, winced slightly as he glanced at the empty goblet. 'If there was time, I'd offer you some more.'

'Ah, thank you, sir. You're most kind.' Macro picked up the amphora and tucked it under his arm. 'For the road, then. Come on, Cato, we have to go.'

Julia reached her spare hand across the table and clasped Cato's. She stared into his eyes pleadingly. 'Come back alive.'

Cato felt the warm pressure of her fingers and caressed the soft skin on the back of her hand with his thumb. 'I will come back. I swear it, by all that's sacred.'

CHAPTER TWENTY-NINE

The army set off along the trade route that Artaxes had retreated down the previous night. General Longinus had sent his two cavalry cohorts and legionary scouts ahead to skirmish with the enemy's rearguard in an attempt to slow the rebels down. The rest of the army trudged along in a haze of dust that choked the lungs and made them squint and blink as it found its way into their eyes. Some tried to pull their scarves over their mouths to filter the dust even though it was awkward and made them feel the heat still more.

Naturally, the worst place to be in the line of march was at the rear, where Macro and his men marched behind the rest of the Tenth Legion, with Cato and the Second Illyrian following. On their flanks rode Prince Balthus and his small contingent of horse-archers, now remounted from the few horses left behind by the rebels. Cato and Macro were marching together beside their men when Balthus trotted over to them and dismounted, leading his horse by the reins as he closed up with the two Romans.

'So here we are again, my friends,' he said cheerfully. 'This time the tables are turned and my brother is on the run. Ha, when we catch up with him, I pray to Bel that it is my arrow, or blade, that takes his life.'

Macro shook his head. 'Growing up must have been fun in your family.'

'Family?' Balthus thought for a moment. 'A royal palace is not like a home, Centurion. And the people who live there are not like a family. From childhood one knows that one's brothers are rivals. Deadly rivals. Once the king has chosen a successor, then his brothers are unnecessary distractions at best, and ruthless competitors at worst. It has always been so. Did you know that my father was the oldest of five brothers? How many of the others are alive today, do you think?'

Macro shrugged. 'How should I know?'

'One.'

'One?' Cato mused. 'Where is he then?'

'Did you not realise?' Balthus looked amused. 'He is Thermon. My father's youngest brother. And he only lives because my father ordered him to be castrated so that there would be no family rivals for my brothers and me.'

Macro frowned. 'By the Gods, this is a truly fucked-up little kingdom.'

'You think so?' Balthus raised his eyebrows. 'Is it so different in Rome? What happened to your previous emperor? Gaius Caligula? Was he not butchered by his own bodyguards? I am not an ignorant provincial, Centurion. I have read many books. Many histories. Yours most of all. Truly you have a uniquely violent past.'

'What do you mean?'

'Before Caesar Augustus, how many of your people died fighting each other? Your generals and great statesmen were tearing at each other like wolves in a pit. Raising vast armies against their rivals. It's a wonder there are enough of you left to rule your empire.'

Macro stopped abruptly and turned towards the prince. 'Did you ride over here just to have a go at me and my empire?'

'No, of course not.' Balthus smiled. 'I meant no offence. I merely wished to say it is good to have the chance to fight at your side again. After the bad atmosphere back in the citadel.'

'There was a reason for that. I don't take kindly to being accused of murder.'

'And nor do I.'

'Ah, but who benefits from Amethus' death? That's the question.'

Cato glanced at his friend. 'You've been reading Cicero?'

'I was bored. What else was there to do when you were off every spare moment with that aristocratic bit?'

'Her name is Julia,' Cato said tersely.

'So I gathered. Anyway, Prince, I'd say that you had rather more to gain than Rome did from his death. That's logic.'

'Logic? You make it sound like an accusation.'

'If you like.'

'I'm telling you. I did not kill my brother.'

'So you say.'

288

The tension between the two men was getting on Cato's nerves and he glanced round at the prince's retinue, now reduced to little more than forty men. 'Where is that slave of yours, Carpex?'

Balthus frowned. 'I don't know. He disappeared this morning when I was looking for horses for my men.'

'Disappeared? What happened?'

'I don't know. I sent him to my father's palace to bring me a spare bow and arrows from my quarters. He never returned. I had to take one from one of my men and then we left. As far as I know he's still in Palmyra. No idea where he got to. Strange.'

'Yes,' Cato reflected. Carpex had never been far from his master's side during the siege.

'If he's decided to run away, he'll pay dearly for it when he's found.'

'But why would he run away?' Macro asked. 'He has it as good as any slave, and better than most freedmen.'

Cato smiled. 'I doubt he saw it that way when we were picking our way through the sewers. That's probably why he's run off. Sick of being in the shit.'

'Well, in that case he's done the smart thing,' said Macro. 'I get the feeling we're about to be in the very deepest of shit.'

By mid-afternoon the army had crossed the low foothills to the east and Palmyra and its oasis were left behind. General Longinus did not permit his men to take more than the briefest of rests as they strove to close the distance between them and the forces of Artaxes. As the sun sank towards the horizon the army passed over some broken ground, deep gullies stretching out on either side for a distance of some miles. Then the trade route emerged on to a great flat plain that spread before the Romans, desolate and lifeless in the still shimmering heat. Miles ahead the dust raised by the rearguard of the rebel force was clearly visible and in its wake were the tiny dots of stragglers. Small clusters of mounted men tracked across the wasteland, mostly keeping a wary distance from each other, and sometimes charging forward in a brief flurry of action before they broke off and resumed their positions.

When the sun set the air cooled to a more comfortable temperature and the army looked forward to halting to make camp for the night. But no command to halt was given and the Roman soldiers trudged wearily on, like a great river gliding steadily across the desert. A crescent moon and starlight provided enough light to see by and cast faint shadows across the gloomy sand. Close to midnight, as far as Cato could estimate it, the column halted and staff officers rode down the lines calling all the unit commanders forward to General Longinus.

'Surely he's not thinking of making a night attack?' Cato muttered as he and Macro jogged to the front of the column. The men of the two legions and the auxiliary cohorts had been given permission to down packs and fall out. They sat or lay on the sand, spread out each side of the track. The low hubbub of conversation filled the air and Cato could not help being aware of the generally disgruntled tone of the exchanges.

'Who knows?' Macro responded, panting from his exertions. 'Seems like the general's not going to let us rest until we catch those rebels.'

'I hope that's not the plan, or the men will be dead on their feet by the time any fighting starts.'

Macro grunted. 'They'll be dead, right enough.'

A gathering of horses and men to one side of the head of the column revealed the general's location and Macro and Cato made their way through the loose throng of orderlies and scouts and the screen of the general's bodyguards.

Macro made out the figure of Longinus standing before his assembled officers and cleared his throat. 'Centurion Macro and Prefect Cato, sir.'

'Finally. Then we can begin.' The general paused a moment until everyone had fallen silent and had focused their attention on him. He drew a breath and began. 'The scouts report that Artaxes is camped just beyond that slight rise two miles or so ahead of us. They could see the loom of the campfires above the crest. Our scouts have drawn back, so I doubt he knows how close we are to him. It is my intention to close up on the ridge, form the army into line, legions to the centre, auxiliaries on the flanks, and then cross the rise and attack his camp. With surprise on our side we should cut them to pieces before they can organise any defence. The cavalry and mounted scouts can conduct a pursuit at daybreak and run down any who escape.' He paused. 'Gentlemen, in a few short hours we will have defeated the enemy, crushed the rebels and won the campaign. Once the Parthians know that Palmyra is in our hands and that Artaxes has been defeated they will have no choice but to withdraw.'

Macro leaned towards Cato. 'A night attack. Seems that you are right, and that he is a fool.'

Cato was not so sure. 'It could work. As long as we hit them before they can form up. And we will outnumber them.'

'Still, I don't like it,' Macro muttered. 'No soldier ever does. There's too much that can go wrong.'

'That's true,' Cato responded with feeling. 'I still don't think Longinus has grasped what kind of enemy he is up against.'

'Shhh!' one of the centurions standing nearby hissed. 'Do you mind? Can't hear a bloody word the general's saying.'

Macro took a step towards the man, and Cato caught his arm. 'Leave it.'

For a moment Macro stared at Cato and then he nodded reluctantly. 'All right then.'

The general had wound up the traditional eve of battle address to his officers and now dismissed them back to their units. As the small crowd of officers broke up Macro shook his head. 'That was hardly worth it. What the fuck was the point of dragging us to the front of the column for a pep talk?'

'Posterity,' Cato replied. 'Longinus thinks he's making history and he wants us all to remember the moment.'

'I'll not forget how tired he has made me, that's for sure.'

Led by staff officers, each unit was directed into position. Despite the dim loom of the moon and stars the column rippled forward slowly as each cohort peeled off the head of the column and moved across the desert at a right angle, warily picking its way over the stone-strewn ground. The Third Legion formed to the right of the track, the Tenth to the left. Macro's cohort was on the legion's flank, and the Second Illyrian took up position just beyond. Another cohort, the Sixth Macedonian, marched a short distance behind, as a reserve. Behind Cato, Prince Balthus formed his horse-archers. The two cohorts of cavalry and the mounted scouts from the legions were stationed at the rear, waiting for daylight to play their part.

At length the army had formed into line of battle. Fifteen thousand infantry and nearly a thousand cavalry stood in silence, waiting for the order to advance. There would be no strident blast from the bucinas as that would alert the enemy. Instead, the general's staff officers were spread out a short distance in front of the line, each man holding one of the small flags the engineers used to mark out the boundaries of marching camps.

Ahead of the army a small force of cavalry scouts screened the line of advance. Only a handful of enemy horsemen, and a few Romans, stood between the army and Artaxes and his rebels on the other side of the rise.

It seemed to Cato that the army stood waiting for an age. His feet ached terribly from the long day's march and his mind felt so numb with exhaustion that he feared he would fall asleep on his feet. He made himself walk up and down the front of his formation, having a quiet word every so often with the commanders of each century, and any soldier who looked like dropping off. He returned to his position beside the standard and turned to Parmenion.

'Tell me, have you ever taken part in a night attack before?'

'I've been in some night actions, yes, sir.'

'But have you ever seen an entire army make an attack under cover of night?'

'No, sir.'

Cato was silent for a moment. 'Me neither.'

'We'll be all right, sir.'

'Really?' Cato grinned. 'Care to take a bet on that?'

'Of course, sir,' Parmenion replied at once, playing along with the well-worn exchange. 'And where should I send the money if you win?'

They both chuckled quietly, then Cato stopped suddenly. 'Heads up!'

Fifty paces in front of them the staff officer had raised his flag and started to wave it slowly from side to side, as had the other staff officers all along the line. Cato turned to Parmenion. 'Pass the word. Prepare to advance.'

'Yes, sir.' Parmenion saluted and trotted along the front of the Second Illyrian calling out softly as he passed. The whole line of the army stirred as men made a final check on their equipment and lifted their shields. The staff officer suddenly swept his flag down and began to run back towards the centre of the line. Cato's officers had been watching for the signal and immediately gave the order to advance, and the Second Illyrian crept forward over the open ground. Cato quickened his pace until he had drawn a short distance ahead and could see down the length of the army towards the right flank. It was an impressive sight, even in the dim light cast by the moon and stars, and he felt his confidence grow slightly. If they could achieve surprise, then victory was surely theirs for the taking. There was no shouting of orders, no strident notes from bucinas, no rapping of the flat of the sword against the metal trim of the shield, none of the usual cacophony of a Roman army marching to battle. Just the rumbling crunch of thousands of nailed boots crossing the desert and the chink and clatter of loose equipment. The overall effect was eerie, Cato reflected.

The dense ranks of soldiers crossed the desert plain and at last began to climb the slight rise in front of the enemy camp. Cato saw a dark mass on the ground ahead of him and as he approached it he made out the body of a Palmyran soldier, one of the enemy's pickets, he realised. A short distance ahead he saw the crest of the rise haloed by the dull loom of the enemy's campfires and the doubts about Longinus' plan that had burdened him suddenly rushed to the front of his mind and he felt a cold chill of anxiety seize the base of his spine. There was far more light than he had expected from the fires of a force of the size that Artaxes commanded. Cato quickened his step, and heard the thud of boots as Parmenion closed up on him.

'I don't like the look of it,' Parmenion said softly.

'Me neither.'

The ground began to even out and as Cato reached the crest he strode forward and stopped as he saw the vista of fires spread across the desert before him. Parmenion came up beside him and whispered, 'Bloody hell. What is that?'

'That,' Cato responded steadily, 'is the army of Artaxes, and his Parthian allies. They reached him before we did. Seems like the general's spies lied to him.'

'What in Hades happens now?'

'We continue the attack.' Cato started forward again. 'We have to. That's the only chance we have. Catch them all by surprise before they have a chance to react.'

The rest of the Roman line had crested the ridge and advanced far enough to see the enemy camp spread out before them, just over half a mile ahead. The general had been right, Cato conceded. Against the odds he had succeeded in catching the enemy unawares. He had misjudged Longinus.

A horn blasted a short series of notes across the top of the hill. More joined in and repeated the signal. Parmenion stopped and stared at Cato. 'What is he doing? What is the bloody fool doing?'

Cato shook his head, stunned. All along the line the Roman soldiers drew up in response to the signal to halt. Cato felt sick.

'The general's lost his nerve,' Parmenion reasoned. 'When he saw that lot down there.' He was silent for a moment before he continued. 'The gods help us.'

'You'd better pray that they do,' Cato muttered. 'Because we've just lost the initiative. Look.'

Down below the first shrill cries of alarm began to sound. A moment later the beat of a drum carried up the slope and by the light of the campfires Cato could see thousands and thousands of men rising up from their sleep and scrambling for their weapons and their horses.

CHAPTER THIRTY

The Roman army stood and watched as the enemy began to mass. Artaxes and his rebels, most of whom were infantry, were forming a thin line in front of the camp. But they were an insignificant danger. Far more worrying to Cato were the groups of Parthian horse-archers and cataphracts already beginning to edge forward towards the rising ground on which the Roman waited.

'What is he doing?' Centurion Parmenion pounded his fist against his thigh as he stared to his right, towards the centre of the line where General Longinus and his staff were positioned. 'Why doesn't he give the order to attack before it's too bloody late?'

Cato cleared his throat and stepped towards his subordinate. 'Centurion Parmenion.'

'Sir?'

'I'd be obliged if you kept your mouth shut. Think about the men. As far as they are concerned this is part of the plan. Understand? Now show them some reserve. You're a veteran, man. So act like one.'

'Yes, sir.'

Cato watched him for a moment, until he was sure that Parmenion understood, then he nodded. 'Carry on, Parmenion.'

'Yes, sir.'

Over towards the eastern horizon a thin strip of lighter sky heralded the coming dawn and moment by moment Cato could see more detail in the surrounding landscape. Still there was no order to advance. Then, at last, a staff officer, one of the junior equestrian tribunes, came riding along the line, pausing to give orders to each commander in turn. Cato strode up to meet him as the officer reached the Second Illyrian. The tribune saluted.

'General's compliments, sir,' he said breathlessly. 'He says we will await the enemy attack here on the high ground. He will give the order to advance the moment we have broken them up. In the meantime, you are to guard the flank. If there's any attempt to cut behind our line it will be up to you and the Palmyran prince to hold them off.'

'Very well.' Cato nodded. 'We'll do our duty.'

'Yes, sir.'

They exchanged a salute and the tribune wheeled his mount round and galloped back towards the general. Cato turned to Parmenion.

'You heard that?'

'Yes, sir.'

'Then we know what to expect. We need to guard the flank,' Cato decided. 'Pull the men in and form a line away from the crest at the end of Macro's cohort. Send a man to Balthus. His men are to form up behind us and be ready to shoot up any Parthians that attack the left of the line.'

'Yes, sir.'

'Then let's get moving! We're not being paid by the day.'

Once the Second Illyrian had taken up their new formation Cato's command position was only a short distance from Macro's and he strode across to speak to his friend. As Cato approached, Macro shook his head with a weary expression. 'Longinus has screwed it up beautifully.' He motioned to the new crest adorning his helmet. 'Paid some bastard in the second cohort five denarii for this. A fine waste of money now that we're about to provide the Parthians with some target practice.'

'Looks that way,' Cato agreed. 'And the general seems to have it in his head that they're going to charge us.'

'He'll know the score soon enough.'

'And then?' Cato lowered his voice so that only Macro would hear him. 'What do you think he'll do?'

'What can he do? We've got bugger all cavalry to pin the enemy in place while the legions close on them. My guess is that Longinus will order a retreat the moment our men start hitting the ground.'

'I agree. It'll be difficult to pull off without heavy losses.'

Macro sighed. 'Well, he wanted his battle. Now he's got it. The trick of it will be living to tell the tale.'

'Yes.' Cato glanced up at the sky. 'It's getting lighter. I'd better get back to my men. Good luck, sir.'

'And you, Cato.' They clasped arms and Cato turned and strode back towards the standard of the Second Illyrian.

As the light strengthened the Parthians began their attack. There was no wild charge of the kind the legions had faced before on other battlefields. Small groups of Parthian horse-archers trotted their mounts up the slope and began to loose arrows at the dense ranks of Roman soldiers. The power of their compound bows was such that some could shoot almost straight at their targets, while others aimed high so that their arrows arced into the sky before plummeting down. Receiving missiles from two different directions immediately upset and confused the solid ranks of infantry. As the first men were struck down the centurions hurriedly ordered the front two ranks to raise a shield wall while the rear ranks raised their shields overhead. While it offered a solution to the enemy's method of attack it was tiring work and could not be continued for long by the men in the rear ranks.

As soon as the Parthians realised that their arrows had ceased having much effect on the front of the Roman line they began to shift their effort to the flanks.

'Here they come!' an auxiliary near the crest shouted.

'Down!' Cato ordered. 'Behind your shields!'

The men dropped to one knee and lowered their helmets until they could just see over the rims of their shields. Cato turned to Balthus and his men and cupped a hand to his mouth.

'Get ready to shoot!'

Balthus nodded and bellowed an order to his small force and they rapidly strung their bows and fitted arrows as the sound of drumming hooves swelled in volume. Then Cato saw them, perhaps fifty of the enemy, riding over the crest a short distance from the Roman flank. The foremost riders tried to rein back as they caught sight of Cato's flank guard, but those behind pressed on, trying to weave a path through their comrades and causing a moment's confusion and loss of impetus. Balthus seized the chance to hit the tightly packed and immobile target and shouted the order to his men. The arrows arced high over the Roman lines and fell, like a fine veil, amongst the Parthians. The effect was impressive, Cato noted. Unlike the Roman soldiers, the horse-archers had no armour and no shields, and the arrows tore through their robes and punched through skin, muscle and bone. Several men pitched from their saddles, and wounded horses reared up with shrill whinnying cries of agony. A second flight of arrows added to the confusion and carnage as more men and horses tumbled into the churning clouds of dust. Then, as more arrows fell amongst them, the Parthians turned and fled, galloping back over the brow of the hill as fast as their mounts would carry them.

At once the men of Cato's cohort and the nearest century of Macro's legionaries let out a loud chorus of jeers. Parmenion stood up, ready to silence them, but Cato caught his eye and shook his head. 'Let them enjoy themselves for a moment. They'll need plenty of good spirits for what's to come.'

'Very well, sir.'

Cato stood up and stared at the ground in front of the Second Illyrian. Perhaps as many as twenty of the enemy had been shot by Balthus and his men. A few lay still, sprawled on the slope. Others moved feebly, crying out for help. One man, his shoulder pierced through, was staggering back towards the crest of the hill. Cato heard Balthus shout an order, then one of his men slung his bow over his shoulder and spurred his horse into a gallop. The rider swung round the end of Cato's line and headed after the fleeing man. A curved blade flickered in the rider's right hand as he leaned out to the side while he rapidly gained on the Parthian. The latter glanced back, then turned and ran for his life. As he drew abreast of the Parthian, the rider slashed down and a sheet of crimson flicked into the air and the body crashed to the ground. The jeers died in the men's throats for an instant, before Parmenion punched his fist into the air and roared with triumph. 'Stick the bastards! Kill 'em all!'

Balthus' man duly obliged, riding back amongst the enemy wounded, finishing them off one by one until nothing moved, save the wounded horses that bucked on the ground, or just lay on their sides, nostrils flaring in pain and terror as their chests heaved like bellows. The rider wiped his blade on the robes of one of the Parthians, then calmly sheathed it and trotted back round the flank and rejoined his comrades, to fresh cheers from the auxiliaries.

As the sun rose over the crest of the low hill the staff officer came down the line again.

'Sir, the general has ordered a withdrawal,' the tribune explained quickly. 'The Third Legion will form the vanguard, then the main body of the auxiliary cohorts. The Tenth Legion will follow, then the Sixth Macedonian. Centurion Macro's cohort, the Second Illyrian and the Palmyran contingent will form the afterguard.'

Cato smiled bitterly at the officer.

'Sir?' The tribune looked at Cato with a puzzled expression.

'It's nothing. Nothing I'm not getting used to.' Cato pointed along the line. 'Give the general a message from me. You tell him that Prefect Cato feels another miracle coming on. Got that?'

'Yes, sir. But I don't understand.'

'Just tell him what I said.'

'Yes, sir.' The tribune snapped a brief salute. 'Good luck, sir.'

Cato nodded. 'That's something we'll all need today.'

As the sun rose slowly into a clear sky, promising another day of blistering heat beneath its harsh glare, the Roman army began to pull back from the crest of the slope. One cohort at a time, from the centre of the army, they formed into column and moved off along the track towards Palmyra. All the time the Parthians kept up a steady shower of arrows, loosing all their shafts before riding back towards the strings of camels to refill their quivers from the large baskets of fresh arrows slung over the beasts' backs. Along the crest the shields of the Romans bore the splintered scars of arrow impacts and some still carried arrows that had become lodged in place. Shafts lay scattered on the ground, or stood up at an angle, so thickly that they looked like the stalks of a torched field of wheat. Already hundreds of men had been killed or injured. Most were walking wounded and fell back to join the units already on the track. Those who were too badly injured to walk were placed on the backs of the few supply mules that had been brought along with the army.

As each unit moved out of line, the Roman front shrank as the remaining cohorts closed ranks. By mid-morning the last elements of the Tenth Legion began to move down the slope, leaving Macro's and Cato's cohorts to cover the end of the column.

'We'll form a box,' Macro decided. 'Shields out as we march. It'll be slower going, but we'll lose fewer men. Any wounded can go to the

299

centre. We'll carry as many as we can, but the triage cases will have to be dealt with. I'll not leave them to the enemy.'

Cato muttered his agreement.

'And what orders have you for me?' asked Balthus.

'I'll need your men as a flying column. Do what you can to disrupt their attacks, but keep your distance as far as you can, or they'll cut you to pieces.'

Balthus nodded. The two men looked at each for a moment, weighing the odds of their survival. Despite his previous suspicion of the Palmyran prince's motives Macro knew that Balthus was in his element on the battlefield and the Roman felt a grudging respect in his breast as he nodded to the prince. 'Last one back in Palmyra buys the drinks. Let's get moving.'

The army retraced its route at a slow pace under the beating sun: a long column of armoured men tramping through the dust, anxiously hunched behind their shields as they waited for the next flight of arrows to whirl down through the haze. The Parthians, many thousands of them, clung to the flanks of General Longinus' army, riding along its length and almost casually loosing their arrows before breaking off to fetch some more. Their only hindrance was the occasional charges of the auxiliary cavalry, who managed to drive them off for a short distance before having to return to their positions, and then after a little while the horse-archers would ride back in and continue their barrage of arrows. Prince Balthus and his men had only a small reserve of arrows and used them sparingly whenever a Parthian ventured too close to the rearguard.

Macro's men, being the best armoured, formed the very tail of the column and the broad legionary shields absorbed a steady crack and thud of missiles as the cohort marched slowly over the parched desert. Every so often a shaft found a way through or over the shields and struck one of the men inside the elongated box. The impact of the arrows made the victims stagger, with an explosive gasp or cry of pain. Sometimes it was a flesh wound, passing straight through without touching bone or any vital organ, and the shaft could be cut free and the wound hurriedly dressed by one of the hard-pressed orderlies. The more severely wounded were unceremoniously thrown over a comrade's shoulder and carried to the centre of the box where the surgeon hurriedly assessed the wound. If there was a good chance of recovery the man was dumped into one of the small mule carts, or over the back of a mule, where the jolting of the carts and the plodding of the mules made the wounds hurt even more. And all the time the sun blazed down. Some of the men, less self-controlled than the others, had already drained their canteens and their lips dried out and the thirst began to burn in their throats.

For those with little or no chance of recovery, the surgeon discreetly drew out a razor-sharp blade from his kit and deftly opened an artery so that the critically wounded bled to death before they even realised what had happened. Their bodies were left with those men who had died outright; and soon the route of the Roman retreat was marked by a grim wake of scattered corpses and equipment.

An hour or so into the march, Cato's men began to pass the long lines of packs that had been set down the night before when the army had formed its line of attack. There was little of any value to pick over as the two cohorts stepped round the scattered packs. The units that had crossed the ground before them had collected up the spare canteens and food, and only clothes, mess kits and personal keepsakes remained, spread over the sand. In amongst the detritus lay the occasional body of a soldier who had fallen further up the column.

'Leave that!' Cato bellowed at one of his men who had bent down to search through a bundle of silk cloth. 'What bloody use is that to you now? Optio! Take that man's name! Next man who picks anything up will be beaten!'

'Sir!' Parmenion ran to Cato's side and pointed ahead of them. 'Look there!'

There was an interval of more than a hundred paces between the Second Illyrian and the next unit ahead of them in the line of march. The Sixth Macedonian was an under-strength infantry cohort attached to the Tenth Legion and, as Cato watched, a strong force of Parthians closed in on them and loosed their arrows at point-blank range. But they were only a screen for the real threat. Behind them came a solid mass of cataphracts, lancers in scale armour mounted on large chargers, each protected by a padded mantlet. They reined in and waited as their companions concentrated their rain of arrows on one point of the auxiliaries' line. Inevitably a number of men were struck down, and others gave way, and a gap opened. At once the horse-archers wheeled their mounts aside and the cataphracts burst through the Roman ranks.

'Oh, no . . .' Parmenion watched, ashen-faced, as the Sixth Macedonian disintegrated. The men scattered in all directions, some throwing down their spears and shields as they fled. The enemy, cataphracts and horse-archers, galloped amongst them, cutting the infantry down with lance thrusts, sword cuts and arrows from those who still used their bows. The nearest survivors ran towards the Second Illyrian and some of Cato's men began to move aside to let them through. The moment they were safely inside the rearguard Cato filled his lungs and bellowed, 'Close up there! Do you want to share their fate! Close up!'

The Parthians reined in as the auxiliaries lowered their spears and presented a bristling line of vicious points towards the horsemen. Then the nearest of the cataphracts lurched as his horse was struck in the rump by an arrow and bucked the rider from his saddle. More arrows whirred through the air as Balthus and his men rode up and shot into the Parthians. Caught between the spears of the advancing cohort and the arrow barrage the Parthians quickly gave way and galloped off in the opposite direction. Behind them lay a scattered carpet of bodies and equipment belonging to the Sixth Macedonian. Only the standard-bearer and a handful of men clustered about him still stood. As Cato's cohort reached them they fell in with his lead century, chests heaving, spattered with blood and wide-eyed with terror and battle fury.

As soon as he saw that the enemy had galloped off Balthus turned to look for Cato and waved his hand. Cato responded and with the glint of a wide smile the Palmyran prince led his men back to their position on the flank of the rearguard.

Cato turned back to his men and called out to them as they continued marching over the remains of the Sixth Macedonian.

'Take a good long look, lads! That's the fate that awaits any man who gives ground to those Parthian bastards!'

The march continued through the afternoon and only as the sun dipped towards the horizon did the enemy at last break off their attack and fall back towards the camel train and the column of Artaxes and his men following a few miles behind. The Third Legion, no longer forced to maintain close ranks, formed a loose perimeter as the rest of the army crept into the site chosen for the night's camp. Macro's and Cato's men were the last to pass through the picket lines and the legionaries and auxiliaries broke ranks and collapsed in exhausted heaps the moment the staff officer had led them to their sleeping lines. But there was no rest for Macro and Cato.

'The general wants to see all unit commanders in his tent at once, sir,' the tribune explained to Macro.

'His tent?'

'Yes, sir. The general had some men retrieve his personal baggage train during the retreat.'

'Very wise of him,' Macro replied evenly. 'Can't have a general going without his creature comforts, can we?'

'Er, no, sir. If you say so.'

'Very well, you can go.'

As the tribune marched away into the darkness Macro turned to Cato. 'Glad to see that our brilliant commander has managed to snatch his kit from the jaws of defeat. Wonder if that was part of his plan?'

They picked their way through the sleeping lines, where the sombre mood of the men was evident in the muted and grim tones of their conversation. Every so often the cry or groan of a casualty carried across the sprawl of exhausted soldiers. Despite the hardships of the day, the rigorous training of the Roman army had ensured that clear lanes had been well marked and there, at the heart of the camp, was the general's tent. A small brazier burned by the entrance and in its wavering glow Longinus' bodyguards stood sentry. Inside there was more light, and as Macro and Cato were waved inside they saw that the tent was filled with the other cohort commanders and the legates of the two legions, seated on stools around their general.

Longinus sat behind his campaign desk, listening to Legate Amatius.

'It's at least another full day's march to Palmyra, sir. Most of the men are out of water, they've had nothing to eat for a day and they're exhausted. I've lost over four hundred of my men and another three hundred wounded. It's the same story for the auxiliary cohorts attached to the legion. And that's not counting the Sixth Macedonian.'

'I see,' Longinus looked up as he caught sight of the latest arrivals. 'What's the condition of your cohorts, gentlemen?'

Macro took the waxed slate out of his sling and flipped it open. 'Fifty-two dead, thirty-one wounded from my cohort. Thirty dead and twenty-seven wounded from the Second Illyrian, sir.'

Longinus briefly noted the figures down. 'You made a good job of the rearguard, Macro.'

Macro shrugged and conceded, 'We got this far at least.'

'True. The question is, how much further can we go, gentlemen? We've lost perhaps a fifth of our strength. We're likely to lose far more than that tomorrow, if the enemy hit us as hard as they did today.'

'We have to go on as long as we can, sir,' Amatius replied. 'That's all we can do.'

'It is one option,' Longinus countered. 'We could save the cavalry at least and send them back to Palmyra tonight. The infantry would have to make its own way.'

Macro leaned towards Cato and whispered, 'And I wonder which officer, and his tent, would accompany the cavalry?'

'What are the other options, sir?' Amatius asked.

Longinus shifted himself and settled back in his chair as he looked round at the faces of his assembled commanders. 'The enemy surprised us, gentlemen. The Parthians joined with Artaxes sooner than I anticipated. We had to pull back; I had no choice in the matter. We have been worsted. There's no shame in that. There were far more Parthians than I was led to believe. It was a gallant attempt, and the people back in Rome will recognise that in due course.'

'No, sir,' Amatius interrupted. 'They will see this balls-up for what it is.'

Longinus stared at him and then a smiled flickered across his face. 'It seems that Legate Amatius disagrees with my version of events.'

'I do, sir. We should have attacked.'

'Attacked? Against that host?'

'It was our best chance of defeating them, sir.' Amatius shrugged. 'And now? We'll be lucky to get out of this alive. Even then, it will have cost us thousands of good men, not to mention dealing a serious blow to our prestige right across the region. Parthia will come to be seen as the major power in the east.'

'That's enough!' Longinus slapped his hand down on the table. 'You are overplaying this, Amatius. Once I get back to Syria I will raise another army. I will use all three legions next time, and come back here and destroy the Parthians.'

'Really? And do you think there is a man here who would follow you?'

There was a fraught silence as the two men glared at each other. Then Longinus opened his hands in a gesture of resignation. 'That's an issue for another time. We are where we are, gentlemen, and we need to move on, to coin a phrase. I need solutions to our predicament. Not complaints.'

Amatius sagged back into his chair with a sigh, and the general looked round the tent. 'Well? Has anyone got anything to suggest?'

Cato bit his lip, cleared his throat and stood up. Macro glanced round at his friend and then lowered his head into his hands and stared helplessly at the ground between his boots as he muttered to himself, 'Bollocks, here we go again.'

'Prefect Cato, speak.'

All heads turned to look at him and Cato had to make an effort to keep calm and control the thoughts rushing through his mind as he considered the landscape on the road ahead of them and what might be achieved in the remaining hours of the night.

'There is a way we might turn the tables on the Parthians, sir. It will be risky, but no more of a risk than continuing to retreat as we are. The trick of it is finding a way to contain their horsemen. What we need is the right ground to do it on, and a few items from stores.'

Cato paused, suddenly aware that he was surrounded by older and, in most cases, vastly more experienced officers than himself. They might well ridicule his plan, but he knew with certainty that it was the best chance to save the army. If it didn't work it would cost his life and those of many more. Men who might well die along the route in any case. His eyes met the general's and Longinus nodded. 'Well, Prefect, you'd better tell us what's on your mind.'

CHAPTER THIRTY-ONE

'Not much longer until first light,' Centurion Parmenion muttered. He stretched up and took a last look round their position. The broken ground with its deep gullies spread out on either side. Towards the north they became steadily more shallow until they gave out on to the flat desert. A mile or so beyond that the ground crumbled again, forming a similar set of rough channels and jumbles of rocks. Behind Cato the men of the Second Illyrian and another two cohorts of auxiliaries lay concealed at the bottom of the gully that wound roughly north across the landscape. On the other side of the open ground, Macro lay hidden with his cohort, Balthus and his men, and another auxiliary cohort. The rest of the army was retreating along the trade route, steadily marching towards Palmyra, a dark mass crawling across the loom of the sand. Cato watched it for a moment, with a growing sense of unease. It was vital that Longinus did not march the men too swiftly so that they cleared the chokepoint before the Parthians caught up with them and forced the battle. He stared back into the open desert behind the army. By now the Parthian scouts must have seen the abandoned camp and picked up the trail of Longinus and his army. They would have raced back to their commander and told him that the Romans were trying to steal a march. If, as Cato hoped, the Parthian leader was as much of a glory-hunter as Longinus, then he would break camp at once and come after the retreating Romans. Even now, his advance troops must be close at hand, probing forward as they searched for the exhausted legions.

'Better keep your head down then,' Cato responded. 'Don't want to risk giving the position away.'

Parmenion nodded and lowered himself until his eyes were just level with the lip of the gully. Both officers had removed their helmets with the familiar, and conspicuous transverse horsehair crests. It had been a cold night and with the coming of dawn Cato was sitting hugging his knees against his chest as his teeth chattered and his muscles trembled from time to time. Parmenion looked at him with sympathy. The veteran was more generously covered with flesh, and long years of service in far colder climates had gone some way to inuring him to the present discomfort. He reached into his sling and pulled out a strip of dried mutton, and tore a strip off.

'Sir, have some of this.'

Cato stirred from his thoughts and looked at the dark fibrous meat and shook his head. His stomach was knotted with anxiety over the details of his plan and he felt more sick than hungry.

'Be a good idea,' Parmenion persisted. 'It will take your mind off the cold and you'll need food in your belly for when the fighting starts.'

Cato hesitated for a moment and realised that this was an opportunity to make himself look calm and unconcerned in the face of battle. He took the offering. 'Thanks.'

The dried meat had the consistency of wood until it had been gnawed at and chewed for a while, when it gradually became as pliable, and about as desirable, as boot leather. Still, Cato mused as his jaws worked, the smoked flavour became fairly pleasant to a man with an empty stomach. And, as Parmenion had said, the vigorous effort expended in eating the dried mutton made him forget the cold for a moment.

'It's good,' he mumbled between mouthfuls.

Parmenion nodded. 'I have it done to a recipe I got from an old Alexandrian merchant I knew once. The trick to the flavouring is to marinade it in garum before it's hung to dry.'

'Garum?' Cato was not a heavy consumer of the sauce made from rotten fish guts, though Macro tended to dash it over everything whenever he got hold of a flask. 'Well, it works well enough. Tasty.'

Parmenion smiled, pleased to have given his superior some small comfort as they waited for the enemy to appear. They ate for a little longer in silence, watching as the first faint hues of dawn spread across the eastern horizon.

'If we get out of this in one piece,' Parmenion transferred a wad of chewed meat to his cheek as he spoke, 'what do you think will happen to the general?'

Cato thought for a moment before he responded bitterly, 'Nothing. If this goes as well as I hope then you can be sure he will claim the credit and be revered back in Rome as the man who beat the Parthians. Yesterday's little fuck-up will be quickly forgotten. I imagine some lickspittle in the Senate will stand up and recommend Longinus for an ovation.'

'Not a triumph?'

Cato turned to him in surprise before he reflected that Parmenion was not Roman by birth, and probably had never been to Rome, so had no reason to be conversant with the ritual celebrations that Rome conferred on her successful generals. When a triumph, or the lesser ovation, was awarded, the Sacred Way, the ancient street that passed through the heart of the great city, would be packed with jubilant citizens, freedmen and even slaves, cheering their hearts out as their heroes paraded in full military regalia at the head of the soldiers who carried aloft the spoils of their conquests.

'Triumphs are reserved for members of the imperial family these days. Wouldn't do for a senator like Longinus to have one. Might just turn his head and encourage just a little bit more ambition than is good for the Empire. So he'll have to settle for an ovation instead, and our reward will be that he gets given a different command as far from Syria as possible.'

Parmenion laughed. 'The lads will be glad to see the back of that one all right! Can't say that I've been very impressed with many of the generals or legates that I've served under. Most have just used their appointments to mark their cards on the course of honour. Bunch of amateurs really.'

'Some of them know their stuff,' Cato reflected. 'Macro and I had a good commander in Britain. Vespasian. You heard of him?'

'Vespasian? No, can't say that I have.'

'Well, you will one day, if I'm any judge of character.'

Parmenion suddenly stiffened and stared intently over the lip of the gully. 'They're coming.'

Cato swallowed the ball of pulped meat in his mouth and tucked the rest of the strip into his sling as he gazed to the east. The rearguard of the army, now under the command of another of Legate Amatius' officers, was just passing into the open ground between the tangles of gully and jumbled rocks. Just over a mile behind them, on the very fringe of the slowly settling haze kicked up by the Roman boots, small clusters of horsemen were trotting forward. As the light grew, Cato could see more and more of them, spread out across the desert as they moved forward to subject the legionaries and auxiliaries to another day of torment. Towards the rear of their host marched a long column of men: Prince Artaxes and his rebels. Cato concentrated his attention on them for a moment. The trap would be sprung the moment Artaxes stepped into it.

Cato lowered his head. 'Right then, pass the word. Enemy in sight. None of our men is to move a muscle. Last thing we want is some curious squaddie putting his head up for a quick look and having the sun glint off his equipment.'

'They understand well enough, sir.'

'Tell them again, anyway.'

'Yes, sir.' Parmenion saluted and then crept slowly down the side of the gully, taking care not to disturb too much of the sand and dust that could give them away just as easily as a reflection.

Cato watched him trot along the bed of the gully towards the silent ranks of men squatting a hundred paces away. Cato knew that they would be tired. This was their second night without sleep, and they had marched an entire day under frequent barrages of arrows. If all went well, however, they would soon have a chance to wreak their revenge on the enemy, and Cato knew that at that moment they would discover a fearsome reserve of strength in themselves that would carry them through the fight. He had often seen it before, even in himself, and it always surprised him just how much a man could endure when the need arose. As it did now.

The men of the rearguard must have seen the enemy as well, through the dust haze in their wake, and began to pick up their pace. Cato frowned. They had strict orders not to speed up. But then again, he realised, it was only human nature to step out that little bit faster when enemies like the Parthians were breathing down your neck. Besides, it would look natural enough to the enemy, and enhance the deception.

With a sudden increase in their own pace, the nearest groups of Parthians urged their mounts forward and closed in on the rearguard, shooting arrows into the air that looked like tiny splinters from this distance, although the distant figures of their victims tumbling to the sand were all too real. Cato turned his attention to the front of the Roman column. As yet it was still heading west and Cato had a moment's anxiety as it occurred to him that Longinus might change his mind once again, abandon the plan and make directly for Palmyra leaving Cato, Macro and the others to their fate. Then, a moment later, Cato breathed with relief as he saw the column halt and begin to deploy across the line of march. Unlike the day before their flanks would be covered by the broken ground on either side and the Parthians would only be able to attack them from the front. The rearguard would take the brunt of the enemy's early attacks, and they would endure heavy casualties. Cato hardened his heart to their plight. They would be buying their comrades time to set the trap and if it worked they would not have suffered in vain.

As soon as the line was complete the remaining Roman units on the track stepped out and hurried through the gap left for them. Dense masses of horsemen harried the flanks and rear of the end of the column, being drawn steadily further and further into the strip of open ground between the gullies and rocks on either side. At last, the camel train carrying the spare arrows and Artaxes' rebel column marched past Cato's position and he turned towards Parmenion and swept his hand round in a low horizontal swoop towards the enemy, the signal they had agreed earlier. Parmenion turned to the first century of the Second Illyrian and ordered them up on to their feet. The auxiliaries were keyed up for action and snatched up spears, the light javelins they had been issued for the coming fight, and shields, then stood ready to move. Further down the line were the men carrying the baskets loaded with four-pronged iron spikes drawn from the army's stoves. Speed was vital, since Cato had realised that they were bound to kick up enough dust for the enemy to spot the danger even before they emerged from the gullies on either side.

He carefully clambered down to the floor of the gully, put on his helmet and tied the straps securely as Parmenion led the cohort forward. Cato snatched up his shield and fell in alongside the standard as the auxiliaries reached him.

'Second Illyrian! At the double . . . advance!'

They trotted along the floor of the gully, following its course towards the open ground, nearly a mile away, far enough for the enemy to have missed their presence as they pursued Longinus. Somewhere on the other side of the open ground Macro would be leading his force forward, converging with Cato's. If speed was one vital component of the plan, then timing was the other, and Cato trusted that his friend would have started his advance at roughly the same moment.

Cato ran on, forcing his tired legs forward as his heart pounded and his breathing came in ragged gasps. He tried to keep to an even pace which he knew he could maintain for long enough to get the cohort in position. The rumbling crunch of the auxiliaries' boots sounded unnaturally loud in the confined space. But at least the rising sun's rays had not yet appeared over the lip of the gully to add glare and heat to their discomfort.

The ground began to slope up gently and the sides of the gully began to fall away as they reached the open ground. Cato glanced to his left. The rear of the rebel column was just visible through a dust haze half a mile away. Beyond that, the Parthian horse was packed into a flat space between the two expanses of broken ground. They stood their ground, releasing a torrent of arrows on Longinus' battle line: damage the front rank of legionaries would have to soak up until Cato and Macro were in position. Then Longinus would give the order to advance and the Parthians would turn their mounts to retire to a safe distance to resume shooting their bows. Then they would see the new danger and realise the trap they had been lured into. Cato smiled as he anticipated their surprise. It would not endure, of course. They would see the thin line and know that they could charge through it without too much difficulty. Except that they would not reckon with one other aspect of Cato's plan.

'There's Balthus!' Parmenion called out and Cato turned to look ahead. The small band of horse-archers had emerged from the gully and were galloping towards Cato, ready to take up position behind the infantry line. Behind them came Macro, distinguishable by his transverse scarlet crest. The column of legionaries with their curved oblong shields came after him, spilling out on to the open ground. So intent were the enemy on destroying the army in front of them that they did not react until the two arms of the trap had linked up to their rear. Then Cato saw faces in the rebel column turn to look back, then wave their arms to attract the attention of their comrades.

'Not much time before they hit us,' Cato gasped to Parmenion. 'Form the line.'

Parmenion nodded, drew a deep breath and bellowed, 'Halt! . . . Left face!'

The Second Illyrian stood in a long line, two deep, with a pace between files. The men's chests heaved with the exertion of their run to get into position. The other auxiliary cohorts formed up on their left, covering the ground back to the gully. To Cato's right he heard Macro shouting orders for his men to complete the line. Cato felt a moment's elation that they had managed to close the trap without interruption. There was one final detail.

'Caltrops!' Cato called down the line and the other officers relayed the order.

The men carrying the baskets moved through the line, advanced thirty paces and quickly began to scatter a belt of caltrops across the front of the formation. The iron spikes had been designed so that they could be thrown to the ground and always land resting on three of the spikes while the fourth stood proud, ready to impale the foot, or hoof, of any unwary enemy charging over them.

'Well, didn't take them long to wise up.' Parmenion pointed and Cato saw that the Parthian horses had wheeled round and were moving towards them at an easy gallop. He cupped a hand to his mouth and shouted, 'Get busy with those caltrops, before those bastards are on us!'

The men with the baskets glanced up quickly and then hurried along, casting out the contents like farmers sowing seeds. As soon as they had emptied their baskets they dropped them and ran back towards the Roman line and snatched up their weapons.

'Slingers!' Cato shouted. 'Prepare!'

Those who had been issued with slings lowered their spears and shields and stepped ahead of the line as they took the leather cords and pouches from round their shoulders and reached into their haversacks for a lead shot to fit to the weapon.

All the time Cato's men had been hurrying their preparations to receive the enemy attack, the Parthians had been closing on them. Now they were so close that Cato could see the nearest of them fitting arrows to their bows.

'Shoot at will!'

The first whirring sounds filled the air as the auxiliaries swung the cords overhead, took aim and then released their missiles. The deadly lead shot zipped out in a low trajectory towards the oncoming horsemen. A moment later one of the Parthian mounts was struck square on the head and it tumbled forward, pitching its rider into the dust. More hits were scored and several of the enemy were knocked down, or were thrown by their crippled horses. But all the time more and more of them were riding up and even though that made the target even easier for the slingers Cato knew that the balance was about to shift in the Parthians' favour.

'Slingers! Withdraw!'

The last of the sling shots whipped out towards the dense mass of the enemy and the auxiliaries looped the cords over their shoulders and hurried back to join the main line.

'Prepare to receive arrows! Take cover!'

All along the line the order was repeated and the Roman soldiers knelt down behind their grounded shields and angled them slightly back to make the most of the sparse shelter they offered. In the distance, beyond the pounding hooves of the Parthian mounts, Cato could hear the strident blasts of bucinas as the main Roman line charged forward.

'Not long now, boys!' Cato called out. 'We just have to hold them until Longinus takes them in the rear.'

'Bloody general always was a toga-lifter!' a voice called out and the men roared with laughter until Parmenion screamed, 'Who said that? Which insubordinate fuck said that? You! Calpurnius! It was you . . . When this is over you can have a drink on me!'

The men cheered and Cato smiled at Parmenion's little act of spirit-raising. It was just what the men needed. The kind of thing that Macro would say, and that Cato felt too self-conscious to attempt.

'Arrows!' a voice cried out and the cheers died in men's throats as they hunched down. The dark shafts whistled through the air an instant before they cracked into shields and shicked into the desert sand. Cato

313

kept his head down and tried to tighten his slim frame as far as possible into the shelter of his shield. Twisting his head to each side he saw that none of his men was injured yet. The open spacing of the line and the angled shields were serving their purpose well – well enough for the Parthians to become impatient with their lack of success, especially with the main body of the Roman army quickly closing in on their rear. There was a lull in the arrow barrage and Cato risked a glimpse round the shield rim and saw that the Parthians were urging their mounts on so that they could close the range and shoot the Romans down far more accurately, before charging home and shattering the line.

Cato watched fixedly as they galloped closer, faces wild and exultant as they anticipated an easy kill. Then the foremost riders hit the belt of caltrops. Cato knew that there was bound to be a handful of Parthians fortunate enough to negotiate the caltrops without spiking a hoof. But many, perhaps most, would not be so lucky and those behind them would be wary about crossing the belt of spikes. They would make fine targets for Balthus and his men.

The pounding of hooves was suddenly pierced by the shrill whinnies of injured horses and the surprised cries of their riders. In front of him Cato saw several horses go down. One man made it through and hearing the chaos behind him he reined in and turned to look. Cato pointed him out to the auxiliary squatting nearest to him. 'That man, take him down!'

The auxiliary nodded, snatching up his light javelin. He rose, drawing his throwing arm back, sighted the Parthian and threw the javelin with an explosive grunt. It was well aimed, and the target was not moving, and the point caught the horse-archer in the back, piercing his heart. The impact made the man arch his back and throw his arms out before he fell from his saddle, dead before he hit the ground.

'Fine throw!' Cato grinned at the auxiliary. 'Get down!'

Along the line a number of other riders had made it through the caltrops, but they were isolated and caught by surprise and quickly finished off by auxiliaries using javelins or slings. On the other side of the caltrops the Parthians were densely packed and struggling to find enough space to draw their bows and pick a target. Cato turned and called out over his shoulder.

'Balthus! Now!'

This was the moment the prince and his men had been waiting for and they urged their mounts forward as they notched the first arrows to their bows. As soon as they were within range of the Parthians they reined in and loosed their arrows as swiftly as they could. Almost every one told as it struck man or horse and the enemy's confusion deepened so that only a handful of them still managed to shoot at the Roman line.

'Slings and javelins!' Cato shouted out, his voice straining above the din from the other side of the caltrops. 'Slings and javelins!'

With a throaty roar the auxiliaries rose up and the air between the two sides was filled with the whirr and zip of sling shot and the dark streaks of the javelins. More men and horses crashed down and already a line of bodies, some writhing, some inert, was heaping up along the edge of the belt of caltrops. Beyond, Cato could see that the Parthians were wavering and the less brave spirits were already falling back. He turned to his men.

'They're breaking! They're breaking! Pour it on!'

Cato bent down, snatched up a small rock and hurled it towards the enemy. Some of his men, their javelins spent, followed his example, for what little added effect it was worth. The frantic barrage of arrows, sling shot, javelins and rocks proved too much for the Parthians and suddenly they were recoiling all along the line, desperately struggling to turn their horses round and escape. A pall of dust hung in the air, kicked up by thousands of horses, and it billowed all along the front as the fleeing Parthians disappeared into the gloom and the rumbling thunder of hooves slowly receded.

But there was no escape for them, Cato knew. Behind them lay Longinus and the solid ranks of his legions. To the rear of the Roman line rode the cavalry, waiting for the moment when the enemy was utterly broken and they would be unleashed to begin the pursuit. Cato dropped the rock he was holding and waved his arm overhead to attract his men's attention.

'Cease shooting! Back into line!'

The slingers put the cords back round their necks and retrieved their shields and spears. In a few moments the men were back in position and the line was ready to react to any new threat. The sound of hooves continued to fade and the cries and groans of the enemy wounded called out of the gradually dispersing haze. Cato stepped back from the line and glanced to either side. Several Roman soldiers lay sprawled on the ground amid the angled shafts of arrows, and a handful of others had been injured and had been helped to the rear where they were being tended to by medical orderlies.

A new sound carried through the dust, the thunderous clatter of thousands of swords on the sides of shields as the Roman army bore down on the Parthians. Then the sound dissolved into the general din of battle. The clang of weapons, the war cries of men, the rise and fall of cheering from entire units and the blasts of bucinas, clash of Parthian cymbals and deep beat of their large drums all blended together in a dreadful cacophony.

Macro's voice carried down the line from Cato's right. 'Heads up! Enemy infantry to the front!'

Cato strained his eyes but could see nothing clearly through the dust as yet. A fluke waft of air must have provided Macro with a better view.

'Second Illyrian! Close ranks! Form battle line on me!'

The long line quickly contracted as the men shuffled together and alternate sections dropped back and to the side to form up in centuries four lines deep. Then they turned and doubled up towards Cato and the cohort's standard. Looking to his right Cato saw that Macro was doing the same with his legionaries and a gap opened between the two units. When both cohorts were still Cato heard the faint shuffling rumble of the approaching enemy and realised it must be Artaxes and his rebels, making an attempt to break out of the trap. The sounds came from Cato's right as the enemy column made for Macro's legionaries. Then he saw them emerge from the dust, picking their way through the bodies of the Parthians carpeting the desert floor. Artaxes had placed some of his regular soldiers at the head of the column and their armour gleamed in the muted sunlight. They stopped as soon as they saw the belt of caltrops and an officer immediately shouted orders to the nearest men, who bent down and began to clear a path. It would be the work of a few moments to clear a gap wide enough for the column to pass through and then Macro's four hundred would have to hold off thousands.

Cato looked at the dust haze in front of his men and made an instant decision.

'Parmenion!'

'Sir?'

'Send word to the other auxiliary cohorts to hold the line.'

As Parmenion summoned an orderly, Cato turned to the nearest section of auxiliaries. 'You! With me!'

He ran forward to the caltrops and began to pick them up and fling them to one side. 'Clear a path! Hurry!'

The men followed his lead, working systematically through the belt, until they had created a gap ten paces across. Cato snatched up a Parthian quiver and laid the arrows out in two lines to mark the channel.

'Second Illyrian! Form column and follow me!'

As the cohort marched through the gap and over the bodies on the far side, Cato looked towards Macro as the enemy surged through the gap they had made a hundred paces further along. With a thud of shields and scraping clatter of blades the two sides crashed together. Cato ran through the channel and took up position at the head of his men, counting his steps as he went. There were bodies everywhere, most still moving, and the enemy wounded eyed him with fear as they marched. There were horses too, riderless and pawing the ground. Once he had counted off enough distance to clear the caltrops by a safe margin Cato halted the cohort.

'Right face!'

He called to the nearest optio. 'Pass the word. When I give the order to charge I want the loudest war cry I've ever heard. We're going to teach them, and Macro's precious legionaries, a lesson they'll never forget!'

As the message went down the line Cato and the standard-bearer took up position at the head of the third century, in the centre of the formation. He waited until the last repeat of his orders died away. Ahead, to the right, he heard the bitter struggle between Macro's men and the rebels. Cato drew his sword, took a deep breath and called out, 'Second Illyrian . . . advance!'

The line tramped forward, unevenly picking its way across the Parthian dead and wounded. Cato knew that they must arrive as a single mass and bellowed to the officers to keep dressing the ranks as they moved forward. Then, Cato's eyes detected the forms of men through the dust, and a few paces further on he saw the flank of the rebel column. The regular soldiers were at the front of the column and the rest was made up of levies, little more than an armed rabble, whose eyes widened in terror as the auxiliaries emerged from the haze.

There was no time for parade ground protocol and Cato roared the order. 'Charge!'

His shout was drowned out by the rest of his men as they hurled themselves on the flank of the rebel column. The rebels did not have a chance to brace themselves for the impact. Some turned quickly towards the new threat, legs braced, shields out and swords raised. Others turned away and fled, hurling down their weapons as they ran for their lives. Most simply froze, staring at the auxiliaries bearing down on them as they roared out their battle cries. An instant later the Second Illyrian crashed into the rebels' flank. Cato's wild, meaningless roar was cut off as he gritted his teeth, raised his shield and braced himself for the impact as he threw himself into the press of rebel bodies in front of him. He struck the nearest man with the full weight of his armoured body and the breath was driven from the rebel in an explosive gasp. Cato paused an instant to balance himself, and then stepped forward, thrusting his sword to the right, into the side of a man about to slash down with his falcata at the auxiliary beside Cato. Instead he collapsed as his sword dropped from his fingers. Cato tugged his blade free and swept it round at the man he had crashed into with his shield. The blade glanced off the edge of the rebel's buckler and thudded into his padded skullcap. He staggered away from Cato and vomited down his ragged tunic before he collapsed.

'Second Illyrian! Second Illyrian!' the auxiliaries shouted over and over again as they laid into the enemy in a frenzied and ferocious assault of slamming shields and slashing swords. Cato punched his shield forward, stepped in behind it, and punched again, striking home with a solid thud. This time he swung his shield aside and threw his sword forward. There was an instant when Cato saw the look of wide-eyed terror in a man twice his age, before the point crunched through his eye socket into his skull and Cato felt a warm spray of blood spatter his face as he snatched the sword back.

'Keep going, Second Illyrian!' Cato bellowed. 'Forward!'

The mêlée was spreading out as more and more of the rebels fell back and ran. Cato, crouching and poised on the balls of his feet, glanced round quickly. His men had already fought their way right through the enemy column and were turning on the pockets of rebels who still stood their ground. To his right, near the head of the column, Cato saw a serpent standard in the middle of a ring of men in scale armour and purple robes. The personal bodyguard of Prince Artaxes, Cato decided. He pointed his bloodied blade towards the standard and called out, as loudly as he could, 'Second Illyrian! Make for the enemy standard!'

He caught the eye of one of the optios and pointed towards the ring of bodyguards. With a nod, the man turned and bellowed the order, and it was swiftly passed along the line. At once, there was a perceptible movement towards the standard as the auxiliaries made for Artaxes and his bodyguards. Now Cato could see a man positioned a short distance from the standard, urging his men on. As Cato cut his way through he recognised the features of the man and nodded grimly to himself.

'Artaxes . . .'

The auxiliaries closed in round the prince and his bodyguard and Cato could see beyond them to where the legionaries of Macro's cohort had made a path through the caltrops and were hacking their way into the head of the column. The rebels were finished, Cato realised. All that remained for Artaxes was the choice between fleeing, or fighting to the end. The Palmyran prince must have become aware of the situation at almost the same moment, for he drew a deep breath and shouted an order to his men, and they closed ranks with overlapping shields and raised their spears overhead, ready to thrust at any Romans who came within reach of the long iron heads of their spears. Cato glanced behind him and saw that the rest of the cohort were completing the destruction of the rebel column. The desert was littered with bodies and splashes of blood and the men still fighting had to be wary of their footing as they mercilessly cut down the rebels who were still mad or brave enough to continue the fight.

There were perhaps as many as a hundred men with Cato as the Romans closed in on Artaxes and his bodyguards. As the auxiliaries sized up their enemies there was a tense pause and the air was filled with the sound of laboured breathing as the men of both sides stared at each other, waiting for the spell to be shattered.

Cato drew himself up to his full height and raised his sword to attract the attention of his men.

'Second Illyrian! Hold your ground!'

The men glanced at him, some with surprised expressions, but they stopped where they were and waited on their commander's next order. Cato turned towards the rebels.

'Prince Artaxes! You are beaten. The Parthians have scattered. Your rebellion is over.' Cato let his words sink in for a brief moment before continuing. 'There is no point to further resistance. Save your men's lives and surrender.'

There was no response at first. Artaxes just glared at Cato and bit his lip. Then one of his men glanced back at him and began to lower his spear.

'No!' Artaxes screamed out. 'No surrender! Kill them!'

He grabbed the spear from the nearest of his men and hurled it towards Cato. His aim was wild, but so was the force behind the throw and before the auxiliary standing next to Cato could react, the head of the spear pierced his stomach and burst out of his back in a welter of blood and exploded flesh. The man's arms spasmed and his shield and sword flew from his hands to clatter on the ground. He fell back, kicked once and died with a frothy gurgling sound as blood spurted and bubbled from his throat.

'Kill the bastards!' one of Cato's men yelled, his voice shrill with rage. 'Kill 'em!'

With an angry roar the auxiliaries swept forward before Cato could stop them. Spears cracked off the auxiliaries' shields. Those rebels with a more powerful thrust sent the tips of their weapons splintering through the shields, one gouging a slough of skin and muscle from the arm of an auxiliary. Then the legionaries slammed into the prince's bodyguards, using their bigger shields and greater numbers to push the enemy back. The spears continued to stab over the rims of the auxiliaries' shields, clattering off helmets, glancing off those who had scale armour. Meanwhile the Romans tried to keep their shields up and their heads down as they pressed forward into the enemy. Close in, they had the advantage with short swords, and whenever a gap appeared between the enemy shields they thrust home at any exposed limbs. Some hacked at the shafts of the spears as they darted overhead, and split the wood, or even knocked them from the grasp of the rebels.

The grunts of the men on both sides, the snarled cries of triumph and the gasps and groans of the wounded sounded so close that Cato was sure he was breathing in the dying gasps of other men, and felt a momentary chill of superstitious dread at the thought. He pushed his way through his men, aiming for the enemy standard and Prince Artaxes. He could still see the prince, shouting defiantly as he drew his sword and punched it into the air, urging his men on. But one by one they were cut down and crushed as the auxiliaries trampled over them in iron-nailed boots. Before Cato reached Artaxes, one of the auxiliaries killed the man to his front and thrust his way through the gap in the tight knot of the surviving rebels. Artaxes was in front of him and before the prince could react the Roman soldier flew at him, knocking the standard-bearer aside with his shield. The standard toppled to the ground as the auxiliary hacked at Artaxes, driving him back and then down when there was no further room to retreat. Artaxes threw up his sword to block a blow to his head, and at the last instant the auxiliary shifted his aim and the edge of his blade cut through the prince's arm just above the wrist, smashing bones and severing tendons. Artaxes cried out and his sword dropped from his useless fingers. The auxiliary stepped forward to make the kill.

'No!' Cato bellowed, charging through behind the auxiliary. His shield caught the soldier in the side and knocked him away from Artaxes so that the sword blade bit harmlessly into the sand. 'Leave him!'

He turned and shouted in Greek, 'Surrender! The prince is down! Surrender!'

The last of the bodyguards wheeled towards Cato and, after hesitating a moment, one of them threw down his sword. Then the others followed suit, but not before one of them fell to the weapon of an auxiliary still overwhelmed by the frenzy of battle.

'Second Illyrian!' Cato shouted. 'Stand fast! Hold back there!'

His men stepped back a few paces and lowered their swords. Only then did the surviving bodyguards warily lay down their shields and stand waiting to be taken captive, the fear and despair of defeat etched into their expressions. Cato let down his guard and allowed his shield to rest on the ground. At his feet Artaxes clutched his ruined arm to his chest with his other hand and moaned in agony through gritted teeth. Cato's chest heaved as he breathed deeply and he was aware of an unbearable tiredness and how much his body ached from the exertions he had demanded of it. But now it was all over. The attack on the rebel column, the battle against the Parthian army, the rebellion. Everything. He looked down at Artaxes and nodded wearily to himself at the thought. Then his eye was drawn to the bright red serpent banner and he stirred himself and bent to pick it up. Looking for the auxiliary who had cut Artaxes down, he beckoned to the man and held the standard out to him.

'Yours . . . You've earned it, soldier.'

The man smiled faintly and took the shaft of the standard. 'Yes, sir. Thank you, sir.'

'Cato! Cato! Where are you, lad?'

He turned towards the sound of Macro's voice and saw that the legionaries had driven off the front of the column and now approached the battered and bloodied men of the Second Illyrian, clustered round the enemy standard. The bodies of rebel and Roman alike lay sprawled and heaped about them, and to one side the handful of prisoners stood together and stared at the scene in dejection.

'By the Gods,' Macro muttered as he picked his way over the bodies towards Cato. 'What a bloodbath. Are you all right, Cato?'

Cato saw the concerned expression on his friend's face and took a moment to realise that his face and helmet must be spattered and streaked with blood. 'I'm fine, sir. I'm fine.'

'Good.' Macro patted his arm. 'Fine job. Is this our man Artaxes?'

'That's him. I'd better get his arm seen to.'

'If you think it's worth it.' Macro shrugged. 'I don't see the point. I doubt he'll survive the reunion with his doting father.'

'I suppose not,' Cato conceded. 'But that's their affair. Just as long as we deliver him to the king alive, we'll gain some favour with Vabathus. And with the Parthian threat removed . .' Cato turned and looked over the battlefield. Now that the fighting was over and the dust had begun to settle he could begin to see the scale of the enemy's defeat. The Parthian army had been broken entirely, and was being ruthlessly pursued and run down by General Longinus and his men. Most of the Parthians were fleeing into the gullies of the broken ground, desperately trying to put some distance between them and the victorious Roman soldiers.

Macro chuckled as he saw his friend survey the battlefield. 'I guess the plan worked then.'

Cato turned to him then, and after a brief hesitation he laughed. 'So it seems.' Around them the legionaries of Macro's cohort crowded round Cato and his men surveying the auxiliaries' handiwork with open admiration. Then, from the ranks, a voice called out, 'A cheer for the Second Illyrian, lads!'

At once the legionaries let out a throaty roar of approval and after a moment's surprise the faces of the auxiliaries looked on in delighted smiles and triumphant grins as they mixed ranks with the legionaries.

There was a drumming of hooves and they both looked round to see Balthus and his men approaching them. The prince was smiling broadly and his eyes widened in delight as he saw the standard. Slewing his mount to a halt he slid from the saddle and clambered across the bodies towards the two Roman officers.

'My friends, it is a great victory. Parthia has been humbled. Humbled, I tell you! Have you seen my brother? Has his body been found?'

Macro stepped out of the way and gestured towards Artaxes. 'There. Alive but perhaps not so well.'

Balthus' smile faded and he stood and stared at his brother lying on the ground, nursing his nearly severed hand. 'You . . . Still alive.'

Artaxes opened his eyes and sneered when he saw his brother. 'Very much alive, brother, and when the king sees me, I shall be remorseful. I shall weep as I confess to the ambitious spirit that deceived me. And you know what? He will forgive me.'

Macro laughed out loud. 'I don't think so, sunshine! Not after what you've done.'

'Really?' Artaxes smiled and then winced as another wave of pain momentarily seized him. A cold sweat broke out on his brow as he continued. 'You don't know my father. Like most fathers, he has a weakness. A compulsion to indulge his favourite son, whatever I may have done.'

There was a moment's silence as the others considered his words. Then Balthus nodded and said quietly, 'He's right. It will be a difficult situation . . .' He turned to the nearest of his men and barked an order.

Before Macro and Cato realised what was happening, several bows were raised and arrows whipped through the air, thudding into Artaxes where he lay on the ground. He gasped, looking at his brother with a shocked expression. Then his eyes glazed over and he slumped back and stared into the sky, mouth open and slack.

Balthus looked at him for a moment and tipped his head slightly to one side.

'But not any more.'

CHAPTER THIRTY-TWO

The day after the battle the legions' priests performed the funeral rites for the men who had been killed. The pyres flared up into the night sky and by dawn their blackened remains dotted the desert as the army began its march back to Palmyra. The suffering of the enemy injured was ended with merciful thrusts to their throats, while the Roman wounded were carried from the battlefield and treated as well as they could be before being loaded on to carts, the backs of mules and horses, or makeshift stretchers carried by their comrades. Other parties of soldiers scoured the battlefield to retrieve any usable weapons that lay scattered over the ground.

The enemy dead were left where they lay, sprawled in heaps across the sand. Many hundreds more were dotted about the surrounding landscape where they had been cut down by the pursuing Roman cavalry. The Parthian army had been effectively destroyed. The survivors were scattered and leaderless and most had abandoned their weapons and armour. There was nothing left for them now but a long retreat back across the desert to the Euphrates and the lands of Parthia beyond. Without water few would make it home, and those who did would have a sorry tale to tell. It would be many years before Parthia dared to challenge Rome again.

Two days later, as the army constructed a marching camp close to the walls of Palmyra, General Longinus led a procession of officers and Prince Balthus, picked soldiers and captives through the gates of the city and along the main thoroughfare towards the royal palace. As soon as the king had received a message from Longinus announcing the outcome of the battle Vabathus had declared a public holiday to celebrate the end of the rebellion and the defeat of Parthia. Yet there was little sign of rejoicing as the Romans tramped along the paved road behind their standards. Macro and Cato marched just ahead of the standards with the other officers and they could see by the rigid set of the general's head that Cassius Longinus was not best pleased by his muted reception.

'What's going on?' Macro asked quietly. 'You'd think they'd be happy the rebellion is over.'

Cato glanced round. Only a handful of the city's inhabitants stood along the route, and they watched in wary silence as the soldiers passed by.

'You can hardly blame them. They've seen more than enough fighting this last month. They'll be grateful once they accept that peace has returned.'

Macro considered his friend's explanation for a moment and then shrugged. 'Maybe, but I'd like my gratitude now. I didn't march all the way across a bloody baking desert, and sit out a siege, then fight a battle just so that I could be made to feel as welcome as a fart in a testudo.'

'Please yourself, but I'm grateful just to get back to Palmyra.'

Macro glanced at him and grinned. 'I'm sure you are. Of course that has nothing to do with that daughter of Sempronius, right?'

Cato felt a flush of irritation but managed to make himself smile back. 'It has everything to do with her. With Julia.' He felt his heart warm even at the mention of her name. 'Her father gave me his word that I could marry her when I got back.'

'*If* you got back, is what he said.'

'If, when, what's the difference?'

Macro smiled sadly. 'Everything, when you don't expect a man to survive long enough to make you honour your word.'

Cato's eyes narrowed. 'What do you mean?'

'Oh, come on, lad! You're not thick. Sempronius is an aristocrat. You're the son of a freedman. Hardly the best match for his precious daughter. He was humouring you.'

Cato thought it over for a moment and shook his head. 'No. It doesn't make sense. If Sempronius had no intention of letting me marry Julia, then why promise her to me if there was any chance that I would return? I think you've got it wrong, Macro. Very wrong.'

'Well . . . All I can say is that I hope so, lad. I really do.'

They marched on in silence, through the almost deserted avenue that ran through the city towards the palace complex. As they drew near the entrance, a lofty arch that spanned the paved road, a small crowd of ragged woman and children on either side began to cheer half-heartedly at their approach. Once General Longinus drew level with the crowd they began to throw brilliant white petals in his path.

'A nice thought,' Macro remarked quietly. 'But hardly reeking of sincerity. This lot must be the dregs of the street, hired to greet us.'

'You wanted a welcome fit for a hero,' Cato responded. 'Well, here it is. At least the general is making the most of it.'

Macro glanced ahead and saw that Longinus was bowing his head gravely to each side and holding his hand up in an aloof gesture of acknowledgement. The centurion sniffed. 'From the way he's carrying on you'd think he had already been awarded his ovation and was marching down the Sacred Way in Rome with a vast crowd on either side and a personal escort of vestal virgins.'

'Perhaps he's treating this as a dress rehearsal for the real thing,' Cato added wryly.

'Do you really think Longinus deserves a prize for what he's done? Those Parthian boys nearly had us cold.'

'You know how it is, Macro. Doesn't matter how many men you lose, nor how many mistakes you make along the way. As long as you get the right result. And any victory over the Parthians is bound to go down well in Rome. So there'll be a celebration. Anything to keep the plebs happy.'

'Great . . .'

Cato looked round at the other officers and then lowered his voice still further. 'And it has the added benefit of separating him from his legions for a while. Given his ambitions, that's no bad thing.'

Macro nodded. Despite having frustrated Longinus' plans to build up an army capable of overthrowing the Emperor, they had still not uncovered enough evidence to prove his treachery. Narcissus was not going to be satisfied with their efforts, Macro thought with a sinking feeling. The Emperor's secretary was not noted for his patience with those who failed to deliver what he required of them. Macro and Cato had been sent to the eastern provinces to expose Longinus as a traitor. Whatever else they had achieved, Longinus had not incriminated himself enough to justify removing him from office and destroying him. It had been different in the days of Caligula, when any Roman could be executed on a whim. His successor was determined that such extrajudicial excesses would no longer be encouraged. Macro smiled to himself as he reflected that Narcissus probably pined for the brutal simplicity of the previous regime.

Just then he caught sight of a familiar face on the edge of the crowd and he paused a moment and stepped out of line. Cato turned with a quizzical expression and joined his friend. 'What's the matter?'

'You go on. I'll catch you up.'

'Why? What is it?'

'Someone I have to speak to. You go on,' Macro said firmly.

Cato shrugged, then rejoined the column. Glancing back he saw Macro walk slowly towards the small crowd of ragged people lining the street and stop in front of a girl.

Then the procession passed through the arch and into the large courtyard in front of the royal palace. A guard of honour, formed from the surviving Greek mercenaries, lined the steps leading up to the palace entrance, where Thermon waited in front of the two columns that supported the portico. General Longinus rode across to the base of the stairs and reined his horse in before slipping gracefully down from the saddle. He gestured to his officers and Balthus to follow him and climbed the steps towards the entrance. The commander of the royal bodyguard snapped an order and the mercenaries turned smartly inward, stiffened to attention and presented their spears. Thermon bowed deeply as Longinus approached him.

'My lord Cassius Longinus, it is a great pleasure to welcome you back to the city. The news of your victory has been the cause of great joy and celebration in Palmyra.'

'So I noticed,' Longinus replied acidly as he nodded towards the avenue leading back through the city. 'It seems that your people must still be sleeping it off.'

Thermon paused a moment as he understood the tone of the Roman's remark and then he smiled at Balthus. 'My prince, the king is delighted by your success and looks forward to embracing his conquering son.'

'I'm sure,' Balthus replied.

'If we might get a move on,' Longinus interrupted. 'I must report to the king and then I must return to my army and see to the men's needs.'

'Of course, my lord. If you would be kind enough to follow me.' Thermon bowed again and backed away through the entrance before turning to lead the party down a long wide hall whose walls were richly decorated with bright paintings celebrating the exploits of past kings of Palmyra. At the end of the hall were two large brass-plated doors which were swung open by palace guards to reveal the king's audience chamber. Vabathus sat on his throne, raised above the heads of those around him by a round dais approached by a small flight of steps. A throng of Palmyran nobles and the richest men of the city stood before him in their best robes. They parted before Longinus and his party and retreated on each side. There were more guards inside the chamber and these now took up position to create an avenue of spears and shields leading towards the dais and King Vabathus.

Behind the general, Cato's eyes darted round the chamber. He saw Sempronius standing close to the king, then looked over the crowd until he saw Julia, standing slightly apart from the rest beside one of the gilded pillars. He gave a brief nod towards her and smiled quickly. She half raised her hand in acknowledgement, her face illuminated by a mixture of relief and joy at the sight of him.

Thermon led Longinus up to the foot of the steps and then stood respectfully to one side as he announced them formally.

'Your Majesty, I present Cassius Longinus, governor of the Roman province of Syria, his officers and Prince Balthus.'

The king nodded at his guests and there was a short pause before he drew himself up on his throne and spoke.

'General Longinus, we welcome you to our palace. There are no words adequate to express my thanks to you and your fine soldiers. You have delivered us from the hands of Parthia and those traitors amongst my people who would have sold their city into slavery to the Parthian kingdom.' There was a slight tremor in his voice as he continued. 'I understand that Artaxes died on the battlefield, by the hand of Prince Balthus. That is, perhaps, fitting. But while I grieve for the loss of yet another son, even one who betrayed me, I accept that I am for ever in Rome's debt.'

Cato noticed Balthus stir at these words. The prince frowned and his lips compressed into a thin line as his father continued.

'Such is my gratitude that I have today signed a treaty with the ambassador of Emperor Claudius. Henceforth, Palmyra and its domain will be accorded the status of a client kingdom of the Roman Empire.' The king paused and looked straight at his surviving son. For a moment there was pity in his eyes and then sad resignation. 'I understand, full well, that this treaty will not be to the liking of some of my people. But the choice that faces us is between being an ally of Rome or a conquest of Parthia.'

'No!' Prince Balthus shook his head, then pointed at his father. 'You know what client status means, Father. Once you are gone, Palmyra will become a Roman province. We will lose our independence. We will lose our king and fall under the heel of Rome.'

'Yes,' Vabathus said loudly. 'But that is the price that I must pay, and that you must accept.'

'I shall not accept it,' Balthus replied hotly. 'It is the king's duty to preserve his kingdom. Anything less would be a betrayal of the people of Palmyra.'

'You speak to me of betrayal,' Vabathus said icily. 'You dare to speak to me of betrayal? You who betrayed your own flesh and blood and ordered the death of your brother Amethus?'

Balthus shook his head. 'I did no such thing! You have no proof.'

'No?' Vabathus turned to the side and barked out an order. 'Bring him out here, where all can see.'

There was a soft grunt and moan of pain and some sounds of shuffling footsteps from behind the dais, and then two of the king's bodyguards emerged carrying a dirty bundle of rags and scabbed and bruised flesh between them. They dragged their burden round to the front of the throne and threw it down.

'What is this?' General Longinus stepped back with a look of disgust. 'This . . . this man?'

The king ignored the Roman and fixed his attention on his son. 'Balthus, surely you recognise the most loyal of your slaves?'

Prince Balthus stared down at the man huddled on the ground, battered and bloodied all over, and yet still clinging on to life as the bones of his ribcage rose and fell in a fluttering rhythm. Slowly a look of horror filtered on to Balthus' face as he grasped the truth. 'Carpex,' he muttered. 'Carpex, what have you done to me?'

The slave suddenly seemed to become acutely aware of his

surroundings and recoiled from the voice as if he had been struck a hard blow.

'Master.' The slave's voice was little more than a hoarse whisper. 'O master, I beg for your pardon. I—'

'Silence, you slave dog!' Vabathus roared out. 'How dare you speak in the presence of your king?' He glared at Carpex as the slave shrank back with a look of terror. Vabathus nodded and gave a small sneer of satisfaction as he turned back to his son and continued. 'Balthus, this worthless scum provided us with all the answers we needed, once enough torture had been applied. This slave confirmed what I already suspected, that it was you who gave the order to kill Amethus. And that it was Carpex who carried it out.'

'Lies!' Baltus blustered. 'Lies, I tell you.' He took a step forward and kicked Carpex. 'This slave is deceiving you, Father. I had nothing to do with it. I swear by almighty Bel.'

'Quiet!' Vabathus glared at his son. 'Would you debase yourself even further by lying under oath to the city's God? Have you no honour at all?' He rose up and stabbed his finger towards the prince. 'You are no son of mine. I renounce you. A common killer and traitor is what you are, and there can only be one punishment for such crimes. Guards, seize him!'

As the mercenaries closed in on him Balthus gritted his teeth and looked round like a cornered animal. His hand dropped to the handle of his sword and he swiftly drew the blade with a quick rasp and pointed it towards the nearest of the bodyguards.

'Another step towards me and I'll gut you.'

'Put that sword down!' Vabathus ordered. 'You cannot escape.'

For a moment Balthus stared defiantly at his father, and then took a deep breath and lowered his head. The tension eased for an instant and the guards paused a moment before continuing their approach towards the prince. At that moment Balthus sprang towards Carpex and his blade glittered through the air. Even as the slave let out a terrified cry the sword cut through the bony hand he had flung up to protect himself. The finely honed edge sliced through the arm and continued on through the slave's throat and buried itself in his spine, silencing the cry. Blood spurted across the floor of the audience chamber as Carpex fell back, his head almost severed. Balthus watched with a look of contempt as the body trembled a moment and then lay still. Then he threw his sword down and made no effort to resist as the bodyguards seized him and pinned his arms behind his back.

'Get him out of here,' Thermon ordered, then turned to some more men and pointed to the slave's body. 'And remove that.'

Balthus was dragged from the chamber under the eyes of the Roman officers and the Palmyran nobles. Once he had gone, Vabathus' shoulders drooped wearily and he stepped down from the dais.

'Thermon, I am returning to my quarters. See to it that I am not disturbed.'

The chamberlain glanced awkwardly at Longinus and the Roman officers. 'But, Your Majesty, the celebrations . . . the banquet tonight.'

'Celebrations?' Vabathus shook his head. 'What have I to celebrate?'

He was still for a moment, then continued. 'But you are right. The celebrations must go ahead. They will not be spoiled by the absence of a grieving man. See to it, Thermon.'

He turned and made his way to the small rear entrance to the audience chamber. The nobles bowed their heads as he passed, but Vabathus ignored them, staring down at the floor as he walked through them, disappeared through the small doorway and left them standing in silence.

Long shadows were stretching across the palace courtyard as Macro stood stiffly to attention in front of General Longinus and the Roman ambassador. The two senators were sitting at a small table drinking lemon-scented water. Behind them a slave wafted air over them with a large fan made from woven palm leaves.

Longinus lowered his cup and cleared his throat. 'So then, Centurion Macro, what is it that you want to say to us?'

'Sir, it isn't right. This business with Balthus. The man saved my neck, and those of every man in the relief column. He fought alongside us in the citadel, and that battle with the Parthians. He's a brave man,' Macro concluded with a firm nod. 'It'd be wrong to let him be killed like a dog. It ain't right, sir.'

General Longinus pursed his lips for a moment, as if in thought. 'I see. And I agree, we owe him a debt of gratitude. Under any other circumstances there would be no question of letting him go to his death like this.'

Macro felt a leaden fatalism settle on his heart at the general's words. 'What do you mean, sir? Under any other circumstances?'

Sempronius leaned forward. 'If I might explain the situation to our friend here?'

Longinus waved a hand dismissively. 'Be my guest.'

The ambassador looked at Macro and smiled sadly. 'I've no doubt that what you say about the prince is true.'

'Then why must he die?' Macro cut in stubbornly.

'Political necessity, that's why. Rome needs to make Palmyra a client kingdom. We must have that treaty, and so must Vabathus. There is no place in the new arrangement for Balthus. He cannot become the ruler of Palmyra. Balthus knows that and would scheme against his father just as Artaxes did before him, just as surely as summer follows spring. Why else would he have had his other brother killed? He was clearing his way to the throne.' Sempronius waited a moment to let his words sink in. 'I'm sorry, Centurion. There's nothing we can do about it. Prince Balthus may well have fought at your side. He may well be a brave man. But he is also ruthless and ambitious and if he was allowed to live, then there would be no peace in Palmyra. So, tomorrow morning, Prince Balthus will be executed.'

Macro felt a wave of bitterness welling up inside him and it took a great deal of self-control to bite back on his anger. He looked at the two men with contempt. 'Political necessity, you say. That's a fine euphemism, sir. From where I'm standing, it just looks like murder.'

Longinus set his cup down violently. 'Now just a minute, Centurion! I've had enough of your impertinence. I've a good mind to—'

'Macro's right,' Sempronius interrupted. 'Strip away the weasel words and it's murder, plain and simple. There's no hiding that. But it changes nothing, Centurion. For the good of all, Balthus must be disposed of . . .' The ambassador smiled self-deprecatingly. 'He must be killed. There is no alternative. Do you understand?'

'Yes.'

'Good. Then there's one last thing.' Sempronius reached inside the bag that rested on the ground beside his stool and pulled out a folded document bearing the imperial seal. 'The imperial courier brought this with the other dispatches yesterday. It's addressed to you and Cato.'

Macro took the letter and glanced at the words under the seal. 'From Narcissus, Imperial Secretary. Bound to be bad news.'

Sempronius chuckled and after a moment Macro joined in. 'Well, I'd better read it through and find Cato.'

'Yes.' Sempronius nodded, and then smiled at some private amusement. 'I imagine you will find that remarkable young man in the king's gardens.'

'Cato! Cato! Where are you?'

Macro strode through the garden courtyards, looking round the potted shrubs and trees that were arranged around ornate colonnades and peristyles. A short distance behind him hurried Jesmiah, still in the tattered remains of her stola and cloak. Around them the cooling dusk air brought out the scent of jasmine and other herbs. The final preparations were being made for the night's banquet and many of the king's courtiers and servants were either sitting down enjoying the evening while they could or passing through the gardens on some errand or other. They stopped conversing and glanced irritably towards the bellowing Roman officer.

'Cato, where are you, damn it?'

A figure rose up from a stone bench and waved to attract Macro's attention in the failing light. 'Over here.'

'Ah! At bloody last!' Macro strode towards his friend, and drew the opened letter from Narcissus from inside his harness. 'News from Rome! Great news.'

As Macro approached the bench he saw another person sitting just beyond Cato and drew up awkwardly as he realised who it was. 'Miss Julia, sorry. I didn't mean to interrupt anything.'

'Oh, that's all right.' She beamed at him. 'We've said what needed saying. Don't mind me.'

'Fair enough.' Macro turned to Cato and thrust the letter at him. 'Read that.'

'Can't it wait?' Cato replied, then cocked his head slightly to one side as he caught sight of the girl behind his friend. 'Who is this?'

Macro glanced back, and waved her forward. Jesmiah stepped up to join the others shyly. Macro placed his hand on her shoulder as he explained. 'This is Jesmiah. She and her baby brother were with us in the citadel.'

The full implication of his words was not lost on Cato, who shifted uneasily as he recalled the harsh manner in which the civilians had been forced out of the citadel.

Macro continued. 'Her family died in the revolt, and her brother followed them yesterday. He was no more than an infant and very ill during the siege. Now Jesmiah has no one to look out for her. So, I was wondering . . .' Macro fixed his gaze on Julia. 'A young Roman lady is always in need of good servants and companions, from what I've heard.'

'Oh really?' Julia arched an eyebrow. 'I can't imagine where *you* heard that.'

Macro shrugged. 'Well, anyway, I was hoping you might find a position for Jesmiah. She has nothing here in Palmyra. No family, no friends. Her house was burned to the ground and she's been living on the streets since the siege ended.' He cleared his throat. 'I can't look after her. I was hoping you could, my lady.'

Julia looked at him in amusement, and then quickly ran her gaze over the bedraggled girl. 'Very well then, I'll see to it.'

Macro's expression brightened at once. 'Thank you. I mean, I, er . . . thank you on the girl's behalf . . . Anyway.' He turned his attention to the letter in Cato's hands. 'You have to read that. Now.'

Cato glanced at the broken seal. 'Why don't you spare me the trouble and just tell me what it says?'

'Very well then, you idle sod!' Macro grinned as he slapped Cato on the shoulder. 'Narcissus has read our report and recalled us to Rome. Job's done and we're out of here. Best of all, he says we are to be given a new posting to a legion. We're to quit the army in Syria the moment it returns to Antioch and then head to the coast to take the first available ship to Ostia, and – oh, read the bloody thing for yourself.'

'That's great news.' Cato smiled back and tapped the letter with his finger. 'I doubt there's much to add to what you've just told me.'

'Just read it.'

'In a moment. First I have some good news for you too.'

'You have?' Macro frowned. 'Well, don't be so bloody coy, lad. Spit it out.'

'Very well.' Cato tucked his hand under Julia's arm and eased her up so that she stood at his side. 'It seems I am to marry Julia after all.'

'Marry?' Macro's eyebrows climbed up his forehead. 'Sempronius gave his permission?'

'He did, and very graciously too. Although I must admit I had feared that he was saving Julia for Balthus at one point. But as things have turned out . . .'

Macro's expression hardened for a moment. 'Yes, quite. Hardly a fair death.'

'Anyway.' Cato put his arm round Julia's shoulder and kissed her forehead. 'As soon as we reach Rome we'll make the arrangements.'

'Well, I'm buggered,' Macro said in astonishment, and then recovered his manners. 'I mean, my heartiest congratulations to you. To both of you, that is.'

Julia laughed. 'Why, thank you, Centurion Macro.'

'Yes, thank you,' Cato echoed. 'I have to confess, Sempronius' permission came as something of a shock to me as well.'

'Well, it shouldn't have,' Julia said firmly. 'I had made up my mind to marry you. And it'd be a brave father who tried to stop someone like me.'

Macro stared at her for a moment and then raised the back of his hand to his mouth and spoke in a stage whisper. 'Cato, my lad, you'd better watch yourself with this Amazon.'

Julia swatted his arm, and then before Macro could react she slipped it under his so that she had a man in her grasp on either side. 'Well then, that's that. Now let's go and join the other celebrations and find something to drink.' She paused a moment and smiled at Jesmiah. 'You too. I imagine you could use some good food.'

Jesmiah nodded vigorously, causing the others to laugh. Julia turned to Macro and squeezed his arm. 'We could all use a good drink. What's that expression? Wetting the baby's head, yes, that's the one.'

Macro looked quickly at his friend. 'She's not up the—'

'No,' Cato cut in.

Julia laughed at their embarrassment. 'As I said, just an expression . . . for now. Come, let's go.'

AUTHOR'S NOTE

The ruins of Palmyra still stand in the eastern desert of Syria and are well worth a visit. Much of what remains provides evidence of the main developments of the city across the centuries since its founding. The high water mark of Palmyra's history comes some two hundred years after this tale when the warrior queen, Zenobia, briefly threatened to overrun the eastern half of the Roman Empire. That is an epic tale in itself (and one I might well turn to at a later date!). I have taken a few liberties with the layout of the city as it would have been in the mid-first century. A vast temple was built over where the citadel of this book would have been, and I have largely followed the lines of the later walls.

The kingdom of Palmyra occupied a critical position between two powerful empires who were separated by desert. Rome and Parthia had long been engaged in a protracted cold war that had, on occasion, flared up into open warfare. Rarely had these conflicts been resolved in Rome's favour. General Crassus, at the head of a mighty army, had been annihilated at Carrhae in the first century BC, and Mark Antony failed in a disastrous campaign a few years before he was crushed by his political rival Octavian (the future Augustus).

Ultimately Palmyra was annexed and brought into the Roman province of Syria around the time this novel is set. The typical means by which this was achieved was through a treaty conferring client kingdom status on the small kingdoms that surrounded the Roman Empire. In exchange for Roman protection, the autonomy of the kings who signed these treaties was gradually eroded until their lands were absorbed into the Empire.

The key difficulty faced by Roman armies was the highly mobile nature of the Parthian army, which was made up of mounted missile troops and a small force of heavy shock cavalry. The Romans had great difficulty in finding a way to pin the enemy down long enough for the legions to close on them. An early case of asymmetrical warfare, one might argue. The only way to force the Parthians into a full-on battle would have been to choose a confined ground over which the armies must clash. The trick of it would be to lure the Parthians in, since they would be very wary of closing with the Romans unless the prospect of victory was imminent. In other words, something very much along the lines of the plan conceived by the acting prefect of the Second Illyrian.